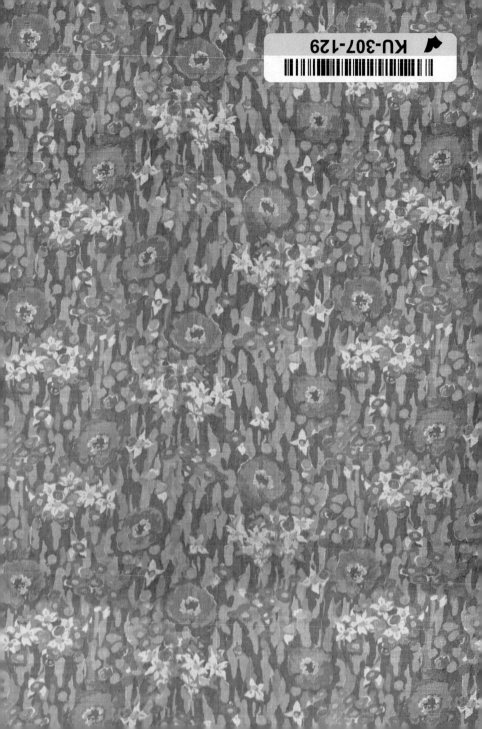

THE CROWDED STREET

Persephone Book N° 76
Published by Persephone Books Ltd 2008
Reprinted 2011, 2015, 2020 and 2022

First published 1924 by John Lane
Reprinted 1950 by John Lane and 1981 by Virago

Endpapers taken from a printed silk dress fabric
designed by George Sheringham for Seftons, Belfast in 1920,
reproduced by courtesy of the
Victoria & Albert Museum, London

Typeset in ITC Baskerville by Keystroke,
Wolverhampton

Colour by Banbury Litho

Printed and bound in Germany by
GGP Media GmbH, Poessneck

ISBN 978 1 903155 660

Persephone Books Ltd
8 Edgar Buildings
Bath BA1 2EE
01225 425050

www.persephonebooks.co.uk

THE CROWDED STREET

by

WINIFRED HOLTBY

✳✳✳✳✳✳✳

with a new preface by

MARION SHAW

PERSEPHONE BOOKS

BATH

PREFACE

****

'"The thing that matters,"' Delia tells Muriel towards the end of *The Crowded Street*, '"is to take your life into your own hands and live it, accepting responsibility for failure or success. The really fatal thing to do is to let other people make your choices for you, and then to blame them if your schemes should fail and they despise you for the failure"' (p.261). The novel has worked towards this resolution, showing how Muriel, who has laboured dutifully to please others and to conform to social expectations, finally achieves a measure of freedom from these constraints.

In many ways *The Crowded Street*, which was published in 1924 when its author was 26, is a *roman à clef*: Winifred Holtby, like Muriel, had a strong-willed mother who considered her Yorkshire world to be the centre of the universe, and she had a sister who made very different choices. But, unlike Muriel, Winifred left home after her schooldays to go to Somerville College, Oxford. After a year there she served (in the WAACs) in the First World War, and then returned to Oxford where she met Vera Brittain. These events had a significant effect on her and led to a conflict between her duty to her family and her wish to be of service to a larger community. When Muriel says in *The Crowded Street* that '"my head was full of dreams about love and service. I wanted to be wise and unselfish . . . I thought that Mother needed me,"' (p.301) she is expressing some of the conflicts felt by Winifred herself. These were to be enduring themes in Winifred's writing. Each one of her novels, and in particular her best-known book, *South Riding* (1936), explores issues such as a woman's right to freedom, her responsibility to herself and to society and the need to withstand the tyranny of '"sex success. Turn and twist how you will, it comes to that in the end"' (p.94).

The Crowded Street was Winifred Holtby's second novel, following *Anderby Wold* (1923), which drew on her own child-hood experiences of a farming family having to face up to agricultural unrest in the early years of the century. The original title of *The Crowded Street* was *The World is So Full*, and in 1922, writing to her friend Jean McWilliam, to whom the book is dedicated, Winifred gave a rough idea of its plot. It is, she wrote, about a girl who thinks life is full of interesting things but then finds it is not, because she has nothing to do, until another girl takes her away 'and gives her people to look after and things to do, and she has no time to consider whether the world is empty or not, and so she finds it full.'[1]

A year later the idea had been refined to a story 'about a girl who never found romance . . . no knight, no kisses, nothing but respectable spinsterhood.' The friend who takes

---

[1] Winifred Holtby, *Letters to a Friend*, edited by Alice Holtby and Jean McWilliam (London: Collins, 1937), p.113.

****

her away is by now called Delia, and Muriel's jealousy over Delia's love affair with the now-dead Martin is mentioned: 'For Delia at least had her memories, and romance had never failed her.'[2] John Lane advertised the finished novel as 'a mercilessly clever study of a girl's life in a Yorkshire town.' Winifred disagreed with this: 'My Muriel is myself – part of me only – the stupid, frightened part. [All the characters] are too near me . . . I could not have been merciless to them.'[3]

Yet the book does have merciless qualities, particularly towards the society of Marshington, based on the large village of Cottingham, a suburb of Hull, to which her parents had retired in 1919 whilst Winifred was still in the WAACs and about to return to Somerville College to finish her degree. Winifred would never fully live again with her parents, although she visited frequently and was always available to support her mother at times of family trouble. The decisive break from an expected pattern whereby an unmarried daughter would return home to look after her parents had been made, and became the autobiographical event that propels the novel. The decision was helped by Winifred's dislike of Cottingham, which she considered complacent and snobbish. In *The Crowded Street*, the routine of tennis and bridge parties, the emphasis on 'sex success', the gossip and the class-ridden jostling for position, reduce Muriel to a state of 'frigid and self-conscious terror'. By the end of the novel she has rejected Marshington and all it represents:

[2] Ibid. p.152.
[3] Ibid. p.288.

'"I loathed it with all my heart and all my soul and all my spirit"' (p.281).

Earlier in the novel Muriel has wondered what her life has to offer after her sister's death: '"What on earth shall I do when I get home? Read? All books are the same – about beautiful girls who get married or married women who fall in love with their husbands . . . Why doesn't somebody write a book about someone to whom nothing ever happens – like me?"' (p.245). *The Crowded Street* is an answer to Muriel's request and also a reflection on both the literary market place and the lives of women in the early part of the twentieth century. Partly it is a response to popular romantic novels such as Ethel M Dell's *The Way of an Eagle* (1912), where the heroine, also called Muriel, experiences love and adventure on the North-west frontier, or Ethel M Hull's *The Sheik* (1919) in which the heroine falls in love with her (rapist) husband. This wish-fulfilment fiction spoke powerfully to women, particularly unmarried women, who were in excess of men by 1.7 million by the time of the 1921 census. By the late 1920s, forty-three of every thousand persons were spinsters or widows.

Yet Muriel is not quite right in saying that nobody wrote about someone to whom 'nothing ever happens'. That kind of novel, usually featuring spinsters, had been popular from Elizabeth Gaskell's *Cranford* (1853) through George Gissing's *The Odd Women* (1893) to contemporary examples such as F M Mayor's *The Rector's Daughter* (1924). And waiting in the wings, of course, is that most formidable of post-war spinsters, Agatha Christie's Miss Marple, who will first appear in *The Murder at the Vicarage* in 1930.

The Crowded Street thus joins these and other similar novels in making the life of the woman who does not marry of interest; sad, amusing, daunting or mystical, these spinsters are made significant to the reading public. Initially at least, Muriel is among the most 'cowardly' of these girls doomed to spinsterhood ('"I think you are probably right,"' she tells Delia. '"I was a coward, I've always been afraid. Desperately afraid . . . of hurting other people"' p.260) and it is no small achievement on Winifred's part that Muriel's trifling satisfactions and disappointments are yet so vividly depicted. The book is a provincial *bildungsroman*, which triumphs as a story about how to learn to live with dignity and courage as a spinster, a figure in the popular imagination of the time as pathetic and despised as Muriel's aunt Beatrice. In *South Riding* Winifred's most redoubtable spinster, Sarah Burton, says '"I was born to be a spinster, and by God, I'm going to spin."' As Virginia Nicholson comments in *Singled Out* (2007), her book about 'surplus' women in the years after the First World War, 'funny, intelligent and courageous, Winifred Holtby was herself a powerful embodiment of her own creation Sarah Burton's compressed philosophy.' And she adds that in her own writing Winifred

> made the point that . . . the unmarried had liberty to make progress in many fields – education, medicine, politics, art and exploration. Provided they're prepared to make the break from their families, and turn their backs on the expectation that they would live unmarried under the parental roof as unpaid – and often

unthanked – carers, the 1920s and 30s were full of openings for talented ambitious women.

In Muriel we see the beginning of the spinning that Sarah Burton announces. Although she does not have the fear-some personality of Sarah, nor her possession of a fulfilling career, neither does she have ambition or (she feels) talent, in her modest way she eventually realises she can make choices instead of them being made for her. ' "I've got an idea – I don't know how to express it – that I think I've always had in my head somewhere. An idea of service – not just vague and senti-mental, but translated into quite practical things" ' (p.305).

One of the other strong themes in *The Crowded Street*, as in many inter-war women's novels, is the relationships between women: mothers and daughters, sisters, friends, rivals, women in the community. Winifred signals their importance early in the novel and also the disapproval often accorded them. The head mistress at Muriel's school warns against passionate friendship between girls as 'usually silly and frequently disas-trous. If carried too far, it even wrecked all hope of matrimony without offering any satisfaction in return' (p.39). The novel will prove the last part of this opinion wrong in the eventual relationship between Muriel and Delia but in portraying it Winifred was all too conscious of the possible charge of lesbianism. Novels of the period depicting love between women were harshly judged, finding publication difficult and reviews hostile. Radclyffe Hall's *The Unlit Lamp* was repeatedly denied publication before finally appearing in 1924, and, more notoriously, *The Well of Loneliness* (1928) was successfully prosecuted as an obscene libel. The head mistress is reacting to Muriel's infatuation with Clare Duquesne and it is notable that this is the most sustained erotic experience that Muriel has. Although she thinks she is in love with Godfrey Neale, it is the idea of him that appeals to her; with Clare it is her physical presence: 'To sleep in the same room with her, to see her bath-salts and her powder . . . to touch her underclothing, embroidered in a Belgian convent – was to live perpetually on the threshold of a marvellous world, removed by millions of miles from school or Marshington' (p.30).

The head mistress continues her advice by saying that Muriel's destiny after she leaves school will be to be 'a fine womanly woman' serving her husband and children. But the men who are, or are likely to become, husbands are scarce and largely unsatisfactory, and are in any case sketchily drawn figures. Although viewed as objects of female desire, they are little more than the stock characters of the handsome squire, the coarse industrialist, the absent-minded Socialist and the uncouth farmer. Men exist to give purpose to women's lives, as fathers, husbands and sons, but it is as ciphers rather than rounded characters that they fulfil this function, and in any case the novel will show that even this need not be the case. Women can live alone or companionably with other women, providing they have financial security. Muriel's freedom is purchased by her father's money. It will not be until *South Riding* that Winifred will show a completely independent woman, earning her own living as a head mistress.

To some extent, the women in the novels, other than Muriel, are also types. The glamorous socialite Clare Duquesne, the flighty, impetuous sister Connie, the socially ambitious mother, the country women at High Farm, and the reformer Delia are common figures in 1920s and 1930s writing (and many of them would be satirised in Stella Gibbons's *Cold Comfort Farm*, published in 1932). Winifred's 'types' drew on figures from her life: Clare was based on two school friends, Connie on Winifred's sister Grace, and Mrs Hammond on Winifred's mother Alice Holtby. There are differences, of course; Grace did marry the 'little Scottish doctor' who does not come up to scratch in the novel, and she died some four years after it was published. Mrs Holtby was socially ambitious but more for recognition as a powerful figure in the community and in local politics than for prestigious marriages for her daughters. Her courage, dominance and organising abilities find their way into Mrs Hammond, the formidable mother who would tailor her daughters' lives to suit her ideas of superiority. What happens to those daughters is a kind of retribution; she is left with no daughters whom she can exhibit as socially successful.

The women in Muriel's life offer versions of female behaviour and experience in contrast to Muriel herself, which is why she responds so feelingly to them. All of them are sexually attractive and also sexually active. Even Mrs Hammond reacts glowingly to her husband's coarse virility. Muriel cannot compete on these terms, indeed, she is so dominated by the ideal of respectability that her sexuality is repressed and inhibited, and she cannot respond even when a sexual opportunity is offered. The contrast is most marked in the figure of Delia, the political idealist as well as the woman who

****

has passionately loved a man and been loved by him. She is based on Vera Brittain, and in the death of Delia's lover, Martin, the novel draws on Vera's loss of her fiancé in the First World War. Delia is physically like Vera – small, dark, highly-strung – and as a feminist and socialist she represents the new woman citizen of the war and post-war years whose life will be devoted to the reform of an outmoded and unequal social system. Explaining why she left Marshington she challenges Muriel's sense of duty towards it: '"I happened to think that service of humanity was sometimes more important than respectability. I valued truth more highly than the conventional courtesies of a provincial town"' (p.93). Though Winifred was by no means the pathetic figure she portrays in Muriel, it was true, as Winifred herself acknowledged, that Vera not only introduced her to a world of political activism but also encouraged her to live a modern woman's life in London. The flat in the Maple Street of the novel, with its blue curtains, hand-painted lampshades and blue and yellow pottery, owes much to the top-floor flat at (first 52 and then 58) Doughty Street in Bloomsbury shared by Winifred and Vera.

It is, however, slightly ironic that Muriel's life with Delia in some ways resembles her life in Marshington. She does a little charity book-keeping in the mornings for the Twentieth Century Reform League, rather like the work she did for the Nursing Club in Marshington. In the afternoons she keeps house for Delia, cooking unappreciated meals and knitting jumpers for her. She is also bullied by Delia, much as her mother had bullied her. When Muriel says she wishes she could do something to help, an exhausted Delia replies irritably:

'"Do. Do? Oh, you never do anything except the things I tell you. You're always ringing your hands and looking sorry, but I always have to think of the things to *do*"' (p.273). Nevertheless Muriel does change; although we don't see the process of transformation, it is registered in her behaviour during her summer visit to Marshington: 'She was more sure of herself. She expressed her opinions with an assurance that amazed her mother. And people seemed to be interested in her' (p.293).

The marriage between Muriel's sister Connie and the 'tall, shambling' Ben Todd, is an example of Marshington respectability in its most harsh and tyrannical form in that if a girl becomes pregnant, she must marry someone, it hardly matters whom. Winifred's sister Grace did not in the least disgrace the family but Winifred always believed, perhaps unfairly, that there was an element of desperation in Grace's search for a husband, which, in someone more rash and boisterous, could lead to desperate actions. Grace was Winifred's antithesis and she seems to have roused contempt in Winifred for the stay-at-home woman, which also carried an element of fear. Without the Delia/Vera intervention, Winifred might have become like her sister, or more like the Connie of the novel. The verdict on Connie, and by implication on the might-have-been Winifred, is given by Muriel: '"In every woman there must be so much nature – of her womanhood. Take from her all other outlet for vitality; strip her of her other interests, and in some cases the instinct, reinforced by social influence, breaks down her control. I had to stand by helpless and watch – somebody else – come to complete ruin"' (p.303).

****

The North Yorkshire episode, when Muriel goes to visit
Connie, verges on melodrama and fits oddly with the rest of
the novel, which is remarkable for its depiction of uneventful
lives. The bizarre Todd household, with the religious fana-
ticism of William Todd and the witch-like presence of old
Mrs Todd, Muriel's frantic search for the suicidal Connie,
followed by Connie's death, seem to belong to a different
tradition of novel writing, one populated by writers like
Thomas Hardy, D H Lawrence or Mary Webb. It is tempting
to see this breaking out from the mould of the rest of the
novel as a form of protest against the restrictive lifestyle that
middle-class suburban girls were forced to lead. Only a violent
episode can appropriately express the violence done to the
nature of women in such an environment as Marshington.
This section of the book seems to subvert the *Cranford* ideal,
in which the frustrations of women are, on the whole, met with
resignation and cheerfulness.

The other site of violence is the war. Its impact on
Marshington is negligible; it came to Marshington 'with the
bewildering irrelevance of all great catastrophes' (p.119),
raising the price of butter, creating new rivalries about who
could show themselves the most patriotic and upsetting Mrs
Hammond's plans for her daughters:

> Of course the War must be over soon, and things would
> settle down to their normal condition, but meanwhile
> it was hard to see Mrs Marshall Gurney becoming
> President of the Belgian Refugee Committee, while
> Phyllis, who had nothing like Muriel's ability for

handling figures, was made treasurer of the Junior Red Cross Association, and went daily into Kingsport in her becoming uniform (p.123).

Only the old woman in the village shop, whose sons had died in the Boer War, registers the enormity of the event: '"War's bloody hell," she remarked mildly. "Ah'm telling you God's truth. Two o' my lads went i' South Africa. Bloody hell. That's what it is"' (p.122).

But the violence of war is registered outside Marshington, in Scarborough, where Muriel and her mother experience the German bombardment from the sea that had happened to Winifred in 1914 when she was at Queen Margaret's school. Winifred's enthusiastic, humorous account of the incident at the time becomes in the novel a complex and disturbing working through of Muriel's reactions. When she thinks Godfrey Neale may die in the war, 'then the thought came to her that she loved him. Here at last she had found all that she had been seeking. The fullness of life was hers, here on the threshold of death' (pp.135-6). But death does not come, the German invasion does not happen, and a kind of paralysis of the spirit prevents Muriel from responding to Godfrey's embrace: 'She lay there, limply, unreasoningly, thinking of nothing but that the bitterness of parting had passed over her long ago.' At that moment her mother calls her. 'She responded to the claim that she had always known . . . and ran upstairs' (p.138).

It is this that Delia rescues her from: '"If it hadn't been for Delia, I should have died"' (p.304). This poignantly foreshadows Winifred's deathbed comment to Vera: 'I am intensely grateful to you – you are the person who's made me.'[4] It is, however, a weakness in the novel that the final, extremely interesting and thought-provoking sections about Delia and Muriel living together in London are not given much weight and the turn of events that leads to Muriel's salvation is only thinly outlined.

So, at the end, the novel comes to rest in Marshington. Here Muriel finally realises that '"I've actually got tastes and inclinations and a personality"' (p.305). To this reader, the scenes of Marshington life, visualised through Muriel's developing consciousness, are among the most memorable. Perhaps this is because these scenes touch our own lives: who has not suffered from a safety pin that will not stay in place, or been without a partner at a dance, or had a crush on a school friend who left one bereft, or generally felt that one was not popular or successful? The details of these humiliations change from generation to generation but the experience of them remains a human constant, perhaps, particularly, in the lives of girls and women. In the end, of course, Muriel survives and triumphs but only by leaving the Marshington community can she do so and begin to develop into the woman she has the potential to be.

Marion Shaw,
Loughborough, 2008

[4] Alan Bishop (ed.), *Chronicle of Friendship, Vera Brittain's Diary of the Thirties, 1932-1939* (London: Gollancz, 1986), p. 210.n

CONTENTS

PROLOGUE

December, 1900

" Beware !
You met two travellers in the town
Who promised you that they would take you down
The valley far away
To some strange carnival this summer's day.
   Take care,
Lest in the crowded street
They hurry past you with forgetting feet,
And leave you standing there."

VERA BRITTAIN

PROLOGUE

FROM the crowded doorway to the piano at the other end of the room the surface of the floor stretched, golden, empty, alluring. Ladies in white trailing gowns, the mothers and aunts of other little girls at the party, drifted across it like swans on a lake. Their reflections floated after them, silver-white along the gold. When Muriel rubbed her foot against the floor she could feel with joy its polished slipperiness, broken only at rare intervals by velvet-brown knots in the wood.

Mrs. Marshall Gurney was talking to Mrs. Hammond, so Muriel could wait in the shelter of the doorway. Soon she too would have to cross that shining space and join the other children on the chairs near the wall. She was grateful for the interval of waiting. It was fun to stand there, peering round her mother's skirts at the straight rows of cracks running together up the floor till they met somewhere under the piano. It was fun to watch the black jackets of small boys approaching small girls in stiff muslin dresses who grew like paper flowers round the walls. It was fun to tell herself over and over again that this was the Party, the Party, the Party—and even while saying it to know that the Party lay in none of these things ; neither in the palms nor the piano, the pink sashes nor the programmes, even though these had pencils dangling seductively from scarlet cords ; nor in the glimpse of jellies and piled-up trifles seen through the half-open door of the supper-room as she walked along red carpets to shake the terrifying splendour of Mrs. Marshall Gurney's white-gloved hand. No,

3

the Party lay in some illusive, indefinable essence of delight, awaiting Muriel beyond the golden threshold of the hall.

"Muriel has been looking forward so much to your party," Mrs. Hammond was saying. "She has never been to one at the Assembly Rooms before."

Mrs. Hammond was small and soft and dove-like. She cooed gently when she talked, and visitors spoke of her to Muriel as "Your Dear Mother." For the Party she wore a new lilac satin gown and amethysts round her pretty throat. Muriel knew that she was more beautiful than anyone in the world.

Mrs. Marshall Gurney replied in the deep throaty voice that belonged to her because she was Mrs. Marshall Gurney. Muriel could not hear what she said, but Mrs. Hammond answered with her gentle little laugh, "Oh, yes, she's only eleven and rather shy." So Muriel knew that they were talking about her.

Grown-ups, of course, always did talk about children as though they were not there. Muriel wished that it wouldn't make her feel hot inside as though she had been naughty, or had begun to cry in front of strangers. Connie, she thought enviously, rather liked it.

What did it matter? What did anything matter? She was at the Party. Her new dress had been made by her mother's dressmaker. It had cost her hours of breathless standing, trying to keep still while that dignified lady crept round her on her knees, with pins in her mouth, for all the world as though she were only nine and a half like Connie, and were playing at bears. There had been a lengthy ceremony of dressing before the nursery fire, with Connie dancing around irrepressibly, wanting to try on Muriel's sandals and silk mittens, and to touch the soft folds of her sash. All the way to Kingsport, dangling her legs from the box-seat of the brougham—she always rode outside with Turner, because to sit inside made her sick—Muriel had watched the thin slip of a moon ride with her above the dark rim of the wolds, and she had sung softly to herself and to the moon and to Victoria, the old carriage horse, " I'm going to the Party, the Party, the Party."

And here she was.

The ecstasy caught and held her spellbound.

Most of the chairs round the wall were full now. Mrs. Marshall Gurney had been seized upon by Mrs. Cartwright.

"It's nearly time to begin dancing," said Muriel's mother. "We must get your programme filled. There are a lot of little boys here whom you know. Look, there's Freddy Mason. You remember him, dear, don't you ? "

Muriel remembered Freddy. Once, when they had all gone to tea at his father's farm, Freddy had taken Connie and her to play on the stacks. They had climbed a ladder—dizzy work this at the best of times, paralysing when Freddy followed close on one's heels, recounting grisly details of recent accidents. Half-way up, Muriel had felt her hands slip under the weight of a great sack of corn, and the earth sprang up to meet her before the grinding thud of her shoulder on the ground, when she fell as those poor men had fallen. She had scrambled fearfully across the slippery barley straw, shuddering from the pain of a fall that she had felt, although she still miraculously crouched on the top of the stack, instead of lying broken in the yard. She had sat with her legs hanging over space at the top of Freddy's lovely slide, clutching at the treacherous straw with desperate fingers, watching the hens, small as flies, pecking in the yard below, while fear tickled the soles of her feet, and fear breathed on her paling cheeks. Then, as merciful release or culminating agony, she was not sure which, Freddy had pushed her over, and she had dropped limply down, down, down, with a blinding rush, till she lay half buried in straw below the stack, past hope, past fear, past speech, past agony.

That had been a long time ago. But she did not now want to dance with Freddy.

"I don't think——" she began in her prim little voice. She was about to add—"that I want to dance with Freddy," when Mrs. Hammond finished her sentence for her.

"Of course he'll want to dance with you, dear." Mrs. Hammond claimed that she knew what went on in Muriel's mind—her own child's mind. She often finished Muriel's hesitating sentences for her. "You mustn't be so shy, dear,"

she reproved gently. " Well, Freddy, how is your mother ?
I hope her cold is better. You know my little Muriel, don't
you ? Of course. You were so kind showing her round your
nice farm that summer. Dear me, what a big boy you've
grown since then ! She did enjoy it, didn't you, dear ? "

The edge of Muriel's chair had become a shelf of yielding
straw, slipping, slipping beneath her. Miles away below,
hens, small as flies, pecked on the polished floor.

" Where's your programme, dear ? " asked Mrs. Hammond.

Muriel produced it, but hope died in her heart as the scarlet
pencil moved in Freddy's stubby fingers.

Polka, barn-dance, waltz. . . .

Her eye ran down the list of dances. Freddy's name alone
marred the virgin whiteness of the opposite page. At the
thought of the second polka she shivered. Still, he had only
asked for one dance. That could not spoil the Party.

A gentleman with a red flower in his buttonhole crossed
the room and sat down by the piano. From the way that he
walked, Muriel knew that he was going to be one of the funny
ones. She could always tell.

The gentleman ran his fingers along the piano like playing
a scale, only prettier. In a minute the black coats and muslin
dresses would twirl together in a solemn polka. Muriel did
not want to dance. She wanted to sit and watch the
moving figures weaving strange patterns of shadow across the
gleaming floor. She wanted to hear the music, and to
tap her foot against the side of her chair to the beat of its
" *One*, two, three, four."

The rows round the wall dissolved. Already Nancy Cartwright—a forward child, Mrs. Hammond said—had lured her
blushing partner towards the centre of the room. A second
couple followed, and a third.

" Haven't you got a partner for this ? " asked Mrs.
Hammond.

" Not just for this, Mother," Muriel murmured, vaguely
aware of duty unfulfilled.

" Oh, dear, well, let me see," said Mrs. Hammond.

She rose and began to search the room. Muriel wanted to

run, to call, to stop her; but she dared not venture into that
revolving traffic of dancers. She sat very still, while the
circling skirts brushed against her knees.

If only she could be quiet, and watch and listen, somehow
during her vigil the Party would come upon her.

From the ceiling swung dark festoons of gleaming laurel and
holly, and vivid flags, and lanterns of orange and vermilion.
A child's laugh rang out, challenging the echoes of the skipping
tune. Oh, be still, be still, said Muriel's dancing heart, and
somehow here shall be delight.

The drooping leaves of a palm tickled the back of the
pianist's neck. His left hand stopped banging out the bass
chords and swooped as though to kill a fly. It missed the leaf,
and flung itself back on to the keyboard to do justice to the
Fortissima of the Coda. Back swung the leaf over the edge of
his collar. Up went the hand, clutching and waving. There
followed a battle royal between the palm and the polka.
Muriel's chuckles now rose to her throat, but, being a polite
child, she sought to stifle them. This would be something
to tell Connie. Connie might be trying sometimes, but her
sense of humour was superb.

With a savage tug the gentleman at the piano had wrenched
a leaf from the palm and flung it aside. At the expense of the
polka he had striven for peace. With a sudden burst of rapture,
Muriel saw that it was the wrong leaf. Her laughter broke
out, delicious, uncontrollable.

Of such delights was the Party made.

Mrs. Hammond stood by Muriel's side.

"Muriel, dear, here is Godfrey Neale. He arrived late and
has not got a partner for this dance."

Muriel rose politely to do her duty. Mrs. Hammond was
so obviously pleased that Godfrey had not found a partner.
And, after all, the thing to do at parties was to dance.

Muriel did not dance well. Madame Bartlett, whose
classes she attended every Wednesday, said that she was a
stick. Music was beautiful, especially the sort that made clean
patterns of sound, interlacing like bare branches against a
clear sky. But while Muriel's mind responded to its move-

ment her body did not. She hopped round Godfrey with disconsolate politeness. Only her feathery slenderness made his progress endurable.

He was taller than she, and much, much older. Quite fourteen, she thought with awe. Godfrey Neale, Godfrey Neale ; vaguely she was aware of him as something splendid and remote, of a lovely house behind tall iron gates on the road to Wearminster.

They bumped into another couple.

Muriel became suddenly and devastatingly aware of her own shortcomings. She tried to remedy these by moving her feet with conscientious accuracy.

" *One*, two, three, hop ! *One*, two, three, hop ! "

" I beg your pardon," murmured Godfrey.

Only then did she realize that she had been counting aloud.

The next hop brought her down with unexpected violence on to Godfrey's shining dancing pump.

" Sorry ! "

" Oh, that's nothing. A fellow kicked me at f—footer last week and made no end of a bump."

" Did he really ? How awful ! Did it hurt ? "

" Oh, nothing to speak of. I say ! That was a near shave ! "

In her concern, Muriel started suddenly to the right and nearly accomplished the downfall of the offending palm. She had just been summoning her courage to lay before this dazzling creature her greatest conversational gift, the story of the tickling episode. But their latest peril put her tale to flight. Still, she felt that some further effort was required of her.

" Do you often go to parties ? " She whispered so softly that he had to ask her to repeat her question.

Repetition emphasized its inanity. She blushed, gulping and trying to control her quavering voice.

" Do you often go to parties ? "

" Not very often. These things are a bit slow. I like footer, and riding. I'm going to Winchester next autumn."

" Oh ! "

Muriel wondered what mysterious connexion bound Winchester to parties. Winchester, county town of Hampshire. Was that right? Hampshire—Winchester-on-the-Itchen. Muriel had been considered rather good at geography. Places could come real to you. Winchester. Parties. She saw the city, rich with swinging lanterns, while down the lighted streets from every window the tunes of polkas beat and sang.

"*One*, two, three, four! *One*, two, three, four!"

The music stopped. In the fairy streets of Winchester, and in the Assembly Rooms of Kingsport there was silence.

Godfrey dropped Muriel's hand and clapped vigorously. He faced life with a genial determination to find every one as pleasant as they so obviously found him. Though he had not exactly enjoyed his dance with Muriel, he smiled down at her kindly. She was a queer little thing, but not bad, though she couldn't dance for nuts.

She smiled back at him gratefully, as though she said, "Thank you for not telling me how badly I dance."

He enjoyed the comfortable feeling of having conferred a favour on her. Muriel's smiles were like that.

The polka was not repeated. The pianist turned to concentrate his attention upon the palm. Godfrey led Muriel back to her mother.

"Did he ask you for any more dances, dear?"

"No, mother."

That was the first dance. A second and third followed while Mrs. Hammond talked to Nancy Cartwright's mother, and no one took any notice of Muriel. She sat quietly, enjoying the Party. There seemed to be no better thing than to watch and listen.

Mrs. Hammond turned.

"Let me see your programme, dear."

On the empty page Freddy's name sprawled, conspicuous in its isolation.

"Dear me," observed Nancy Cartwright's mother, "doesn't Muriel know the children here? I must get Nancy to introduce her to some little boys. Nancy's getting such a little flirt. So popular . . ."

"Muriel is very shy." Mrs. Hammond's voice was, for her, quite stiff. "She really knows almost every one. But of course I like a child to be a child; and she hasn't been going about in the way these Kingsport children do."

But in spite of her implied contempt for the more sophisticated Kingsport children, Mrs. Hammond rose at the end of the dance and found another partner for her daughter. He was a small, pink person in a very short Eton jacket. He danced even worse than Muriel, and in their progress they managed to do a considerable amount of damage to the other couples. After two turns round the room he deserted her with relief. She stood by the door, a little dazed and intimidated, while far away she could see the haven of her mother's chair separated from her by a whirlpool of frothing muslin dresses.

Near the door sat poor Rosie Harpur. Everybody called her "poor Rosie" in a general conspiracy of pity. She had not yet danced one dance. Her plump hands grasped an empty programme. Her round head nodded above the frill of her white frock like a melon on a plate. She had straight, yellow hair and staring blue eyes, and reminded Muriel of her doll, Agatha, whom three years ago she had discarded without regret.

Funnily enough, Mrs. Marshall Gurney was talking about poor Rosie at that moment. Muriel could hear quite well.

"Poor Rosie, I really don't know what to do with that child. I wish that they wouldn't bring her to parties. One has to ask her of course, for the parents' sake, but it's hopeless to try to find her partners."

Muriel's orderly mind registered a new item of information. The unforgivable sin at a party was to have no partners. To sit quietly in the drawing-room at home was a virtue. The same conduct in the Kingsport Assembly Rooms was an undesirable combination of naughtiness and misfortune. In order to realize the Party in its full magnificence, one must have a full programme. All else was failure. Enjoyment of the music, the people, the prettiness—all this counted for nothing. It was not the Party.

Shame fell upon her. Taking advantage of the general confusion when the dance ended, she tried to steal unobserved from the room. Mrs. Marshall Gurney, however, saw her.

" Well, Muriel, quarrelled with your partner ? How are you getting on ? "

" Very well, thank you."

" Plenty of partners ? "

Plenty ? Oh, yes, plenty. Three was more than enough. Muriel tried to reconcile her conscience to the lie.

" Yes, thank you," she said.

The great lady nodded.

" That's right, then."

Muriel ran away.

She hadn't told a story. She hadn't. All the same, she felt as though she had.

Under the stairs she found a twilight alcove that would serve to hide her confusion. She was about to enter it when the murmur of voices told her that it was already occupied. Back to the cloak-room she ran, growing now a little desperate in her longing for solitude. A motherly old lady in black silk and bugles looked up from her seat by the fire.

" Well, dearie, have you lost something ? "

Not daring to risk a second prevarication, Muriel fled.

The door of the supper-room stood open. Inside she saw a glitter of glass and silver, of quivering crimson jellies and high-piled creams, of jugs brimming with orange cup and lemonade. There were no questioning grown-ups to drive her from that sanctuary. She slipped inside and curled up on a chair near the door. From far away came sounds of music, of laughter, of occasional faint echoes of applause.

She drew her programme from its hiding-place in her sash and, with her head cocked on one side and the tip of her tongue between her lips, began to write.

" First polka . . . Godfrey.

" First Schottische . . . Billie.

" First waltz . . . Frank."

And so on, to the end of the list. When the programme

was full she surveyed it with pride. Now, if anybody asked her, it could be exhibited without shame.

How pretty the tables looked! In every tumbler a Japanese serviette of coloured paper had been folded. One was like a lily, one a crown. Kneeling up on her chair she hung ecstatically over one arranged like a purple fan. A silver dish, filled with pink sweets and chocolates in silver paper, stood at her elbow. How perfectly enchanting it all was!

Nobody could mind if Muriel took one sweet. They belonged to the Party, and she was at the Party. They were there for her. And as she did not dance. . . . She used so little of the Party.

She stretched out tentative fingers and took a sweet, the smallest sweet, for she was not a greedy child. Daintily biting it, crumb by crumb with her firm little teeth, she ate every morsel with fastidious delight.

This was the Party. At last it had come to her, almost. Shielded safely from the alarming and incomprehensible regulations of the world, she could find the glorious thing that had kept her wakeful through nights of anticipation.

She did not notice when the music ceased.

Suddenly there came a sound of voices from the corridor. An invisible hand flung wide the door, and they were upon her.

The room was full of people, and they were looking at her, mothers with disapproving faces, little girls and boys with smug and round-eyed wonder, her own mother horrified, almost in tears, Mrs. Marshall Gurney, tactful and insufferable.

"Of course your little Muriel is welcome to the sweets. I dare say that she felt hungry. Children so love these almond fondants—from Fuller's."

"Oh, Muriel, how *could* you be so naughty?"

It was dreadful to see her mother look like that.

"Muriel Hammond's been stealing all the sweets! I say, do you think she's left us any supper?"

That was Freddy Mason. He was laughing. They were all laughing. Laughing or scolding, or looking the other way and pretending not to notice.

It was more terrible than the worst of nightmares.

But the hour that followed was more terrible still. Her mother wanted to take her straight home, but Mrs. Marshall Gurney would not allow that. There she had to sit on that chair by the door all through supper. She had to try to eat the patties and cakes and jellies. She simply could not swallow.

" She's full up already," said Nancy Cartwright ruthlessly.

How could Muriel explain that it had only been one little pink sweet, the smallest of the sweets, not even the fat round one with an almond on it ?

They made their escape as soon as possible, Muriel and her shamed, unhappy mother.

The drive home was almost the worst of all.

" Muriel, how could you be so naughty, dear ?   How could you disappoint me so ? "

Fat tears ran down Muriel's cheeks, and dripped on to the collar of her scarlet cloak.

Because her mother had forgotten that she had to ride outside, half-way home, Muriel began to feel sick. But she dared say nothing, for all that she could say must be used as evidence against her.

" I never thought that my little Muriel could be so naughty and so greedy.   Didn't you *know* that people at parties don't go and eat up all the supper ?   I don't know what Mrs. Marshall Gurney will think."

It was dreadful.

But how could she explain that it had only been the smallest sweet ?

When they reached home, Connie was bobbing up and down on her bed in the firelit nursery.

" Was it lovely ? " she demanded.   " Was it lovely, Muriel ? "

Mrs. Hammond spared Muriel the pain of a reply.

" Muriel has been a very naughty girl, Connie.   And you must lie down and go to sleep and not talk to her."

To be told no more ?   Muriel naughty ?   Good Muriel ? Muriel who had always been held up as a model to naughty Connie ?   Here indeed was a nine days' wonder.

Connie snuggled down with expectant submission in her

blankets; but even after Mrs. Hammond had kissed Muriel "Good night" with grave displeasure the culprit would say nothing. She lay gazing at the flickering fire-light with wide, tear-filled eyes, and saying over and over to herself, "The Party was spoilt, The Party was spoilt."

For, in her unhappiness, this was the most poignant anguish, that by some mysterious cruelty of events Muriel had never found the Party.

BOOK I

CLARE

June, 1903—April, 1907

I

ON the evening of June 23rd, 1852, Old Dick Hammond, then still known as Young Dick, locked the door of the little oil-shop, dropped the key in his pocket, and turned westward up Middle Street in Marshington. Beyond the village, black against the sunset, a broken windmill crowned the swelling hill, even as the hill crowned Marshington.

"One day," he vowed to himself, "my son shall marry a lady and build a house on Miller's Rise."

It was typical of Dick that he made his vow before the first sack had been sold from the factory that eventually brought to him his moderate fortune. Yet more typical was the promptitude with which he forestalled his son and began himself to build the house at Miller's Rise. When Young Arthur Hammond rode to Market Burton to court Rachel Bennet, a house stood already prepared and waiting for his lady. Whatever other objections the Bennet family might have raised against Rachel's lover, at least they could not deny that he was offering her the finest home in Marshington.

Fifteen years after Arthur's wedding, the house was more than a mere dwelling place. Wind and rain had dimmed the aggressive yellow of the brick walls, half covered now by ivy and the spreading fans of ampelopsis. The tender olive and faint silver-green of lichens had crept across the slates roofing the shallow gables. The smooth lawn sloping to the laurel hedge along the road, the kitchen garden overstocked until it suffered from perennial indigestion, the stiff borders by the drive, wherein begonias, lobelia and geraniums were yearly planted out, regardless of expense; all these testified that the vows of Old Dick Hammond had been fulfilled in no grudging spirit.

"Eleven bedrooms, three real good sitting-rooms, and no making up for lost space on the kitchens," Dick had declared. "When you go in for bricks and mortar, go handsome. It's a good investment. Houses *is* summat."

17

The house had been something more than the symbol of Old Dick's fulfilment. It had been the fortress from which Rachel Hammond had advanced with patient fortitude to recapture the social ground that she had forfeited by marrying Dick Hammond's son. Old Dick had mercifully died. When his continued existence became the sole obstacle to the fulfilment of his vow, nature performed her last service to him and removed it.

The death of her father-in-law had made it a little easier for Rachel Hammond to live down the origin of his son, but even by 1903 she still spoke with deference to Mrs. Marshall Gurney, and never passed the new store on the site of the old oil-shop without a shudder. She kept her difficulties to herself, and no one but her sister Beatrice knew how great at times had been the travail of her soul. Beatrice alone stood by her when she ignored the early callers from the Avenue and the Terrace. No small amount of courage had enabled a young bride to refuse the proffered friendship of auctioneers' wives and the Nonconformist section of the village, when refusal might have meant perpetual isolation. Old Dick Hammond had been a mighty witness before the Lord among the Primitives ; but for a whole year of nerve-racking anxiety his daughter-in-law sat in the new house that he had built, awaiting the calls of that Upper Marshington to whom Church was a symbol of social salvation, and Chapel of more than ecclesiastical Nonconformity.

Beatrice alone supported Mrs. Hammond when she carried the war into the enemies' camp by inviting a formidable series of Bennet relatives, Market Burton acquaintances, and Barlow cousins to purify the social atmosphere of Miller's Rise. Sunday after Sunday these invincible reserves appeared in the Hammond pew. The success of that campaign had been slow but solid, and Mrs. Hammond, sitting in her elm-shadowed garden on this summer afternoon bowed in gracious but satisfactory acknowledgment to the hand that waved from Mrs. Waring's carriage, rolling handsomely along the road.

She put down her sewing and gazed dreamily beyond the garden. The air was heavy with sweet summer sounds and scents, melting together into a murmurous fragrance ; the breath of the wind on new-mown grass, the cooing of doves, the sleepy orchestra of bees. On the upper stretch of lawn the two little girls, Muriel and Connie, were making a restless pretence at lessons with the governess, Miss Dyson.

Mrs. Hammond paused in her work, a faint frown on her smooth forehead. Then she spoke, to herself rather than to her sister :

" Mrs. Cartwright said yesterday that Mrs. Waring is sending Adelaide to school."

" School ? " echoed Beatrice. Having been offered no clue yet, she knew not whether to approve or to decry. Seventeen years spent as the one unmarried daughter of a large family had taught Beatrice Bennet that she existed only upon other people's sufferance. Since her parents had died, she passed her time in a continual succession of visits from one brother or sister to another, paying for their hospitality by lending her approval, such as it was, to register or to confirm their own opinions.

Mrs. Hammond had not hitherto expressed her opinion on the subject of schools. Beatrice could therefore only wait and listen.

" To school ? " she repeated, as her sister kept silence. " Did she say to which school ? "

" She was uncertain." Mrs. Hammond resumed her sewing. Her plump, white hands with round, beautifully-polished nails, conveyed in repose a deceptive impression of gentle ineffectiveness. Directly she began to hem, inserting and withdrawing her needle with sharp, decisive movements, the flashing diamonds on her finger cut through the idle softness of that first impression. Her hands never fluttered uncertainly above her work. She moved directly to the achievement of her aim, or she kept still. Just now she sewed, with rapid ease, a petticoat for Connie.

" Connie's hard on her things," she observed. " You'd hardly believe how fast she grows, and then she tears them like a great tom-boy." She sighed, clipping off a thread with her sharp scissors. " Mrs. Waring seems to be thinking of York for Adelaide."

"There are good schools in York," suggested Beatrice.

"Well, there's the Red Manor School. Miss Burdass is a lady. Daisy and Marjorie are going there, and now perhaps Adelaide. But I'm not sure."

"Mrs. Marshall Gurney's little girl still has a governess, hasn't she?" suggested Beatrice with a helpful air.

Mrs. Hammond's eyes turned for one instant to the drooping figure of Miss Dyson, now trailing wearily towards the house.

"Mrs. Marshall Gurney found a treasure in Miss Evans," she remarked dryly. "I have already tried five for the children. You know that; but they seem to be either feeble sorts of creatures like this Miss Dyson or pert young minxes like that Porter girl. Mrs. Marshall Gurney hasn't got to deal with Arthur."

Mrs. Hammond never alluded directly to those other troubles of her married life unconnected with her husband's social position; but Beatrice nodded now in perfect comprehension. With a spinster's licence, she always believed the worst of husbands.

"Besides," her sister continued, "it's not only governesses. I was talking it over last night with Mr. Hammond." She called her husband Mr. Hammond sometimes from habit, because her subconscious mind recognized that conversation with Beatrice was conversation with an inferior, and prompted her accordingly. "He agreed with me that the girls must go somewhere where they'll make nice friends. After all, there are really very few nice people round Kingsport."

Beatrice followed her sister's glance beyond the flat meadows to where Kingsport lay veiled in a light haze from the river Leame. The city rose so slightly from the fields and gardens that its silver houses gleamed like a pool of mercury poured on stretched green cloth, leaving little drops and flattened balls before it had rolled together Marshington, Danes, Kepplethorpe, and Swanfield over on the pale horizon.

"I have to think of the future," Mrs. Hammond remarked. Her sister nodded.

"Have you decided, then?"

"I did mention Heathcroft to Arthur. Mrs. Hancock's

school is not very large, but the dear Bishop recommends it, and I understand that even the Setons of Edenthorpe thought of sending their little girls there."

" The Setons. Now, let me see, aren't they some connection of the Neales ? "

" Mrs. Neale was a Miss Henessey, and the Henesseys are cousins to the West Riding Setons."

All Bennets had the gift of tracing genealogies by faith rather than by sight. A naive confidence in the magic of Birth dignified a curiosity that arose not from snobbishness alone.

A shadow fell across the lawn, darkening the upturned daisy-faces at their feet.

" Well, well, well ! Gossiping your heads off as usual, you two women ? " boomed Mr. Hammond's hearty voice.

They turned and looked up to where his figure dominated them, ponderous, aggressive, radiating heat and energy. Arthur Hammond had driven from the mill, but his great legs were encased from the knees downwards in leather gaiters, and from the knees upwards in vast checked breeches. His face was crimson, and his thick, darkly red hair damp with perspiration. He wiped his head and whiskers with a blue silk handkerchief, smoothing carefully into shape the heavy moustache of which he was inordinately proud. He beamed contentedly upon his women.

" Well, Mrs. H., how's tricks ? "

His wife flushed slightly at the vulgarity of his phrase, even while she felt, faintly across a gulf of disenchantment, the fascination of his great virility.

" We have been discussing a school for the children, Arthur," she said, her pretty voice as usual reacting with increased gentility in his presence. " Beatrice agrees with me that Hardrascliffe has many advantages."

" Bee knows a thing or two, what ? Well, Mrs. H., I leave it to you. I make the cash, Bee, but I let my wife do the spending."

It was true. His faith in her perspicacity was absolute. His offences against her womanhood had never dimmed his appreciation of her wisdom.

" You really think that it would be the best thing, Arthur ? "
Mrs. Hammond asked, with an assumption of deference only
permitted when she had already made up her mind.

" Ay, ay. Do what ye will with the lasses If they'd 'a been
lads, I might ha' had sommat to say."

He lowered his great bulk slowly into the third garden chair.

The little girls came running across the daisied lawn, Connie
dancing ahead, Muriel following more sedately. Though she
was fourteen, Muriel still looked a child in her short holland
dress and round straw hat.

" Father, Father," shrilled Connie. " When did you come
home ? Have you been to Kingsport ? How did the new
bay mare go ? "

They were singularly alike, Arthur Hammond and his
younger daughter. He smiled down at her with fond
assurance.

" She went like old Miss Deale goes when she sees the curate
coming round t' corner."

" What do you mean, father ? How does she go ? "

" Arthur, I wish that you wouldn't say such things before
the children," reproved his wife's sweet voice.

He laughed enormously, putting his hand out and drawing
Connie closer to him, and thinking what a jolly thing it was to
be sitting in his pleasant garden with the day's work done, and
an evening of uninterrupted domesticity before him.

" Ay, Connie," he asked, " how would you like to go to
school, eh ? At Hardrascliffe with old Mrs. Hancock, who'd
beat you like anything if you're a bad girl ? "

" Oh, Father ! " Connie glowed rapturously, understanding
exactly how far his threats were serious.

Muriel stood quietly before them, her slim hands clasped,
her grave eyes contemplative. She saw the sun lighting the
pale brown of her mother's hair to the soft shadow of gold.
She saw the deep blue of her aunt's flowing skirt against the
speckled green and white of the unmown stretch of lawn.
She saw her father and sister, their two red heads together,
plotting some game of boisterous childishness that was
peculiarly theirs. She saw the wind among the lime trees

tumbling their leaves to delicate patterns of green light and shade.

Her wide eyes narrowed with the intensity of her secret thought.

" Mother," she asked unexpectedly, " do you suppose that there are many families in Marshington as happy as we are ? "

A faint shadow crossed her mother's face, like a wind-blown cloud across a flower. Then she answered with the gentleness that she reserved especially for her children.

" Well, dear, I hope that many families are happy."

But Mr. Hammond, thrusting Connie aside, clapped his hand against his thigh and guffawed loudly. " Well, if that doesn't beat everything. That's a real good 'un, that is, A happy family, well, well, well. Which puts me in mind, Bee, did you ever hear tell of Bob Hickson and *his* happy family ? "

Beatrice, part of whose profession it was to have heard no tale before, gathered her scattered wits to give attention. Connie, bored by the prospect of a tale that she had heard before, danced off among the grass and buttercups ; but Muriel, who had put her question seriously, stood patiently watching, a little puzzled, a little rebuffed, a little sad.

II

SO Muriel was sent to cultivate suitable friendships under the guidance of Mrs. Hancock. Because she believed that school was a place where one learnt things, she had been pleased to go. She wanted to draw, to paint, to play the piano as no one before had played it. Most of all, she wanted to learn about Higher Mathematics and the Stars. Muriel felt rather vague about the exact meaning of Higher Mathematics. But she knew that she found in figures a sober and unfailing delight. They slid through her mind like water, separating easily into their factors, uniting quickly for multiples and additions, revealing their possibilities at a glance as a clear pool reveals the pebbles below its water. Then in figures lay a comforting assurance of absolute truth. In a world where Muriel was beginning to suspect that most conclusions were at best a compromise, she found triumphant satisfaction in the unquestionable certainty that, in all places and at all times, two and two made four.

At Marshington, Muriel's odd tastes had been discouraged. At school, she felt assured that she would reach her heart's desire. She would make wonderful friendships, win all the prizes, filling her beautiful mother's heart with pride, and Heathcroft with the glory of her triumphs.

Before a week had passed, she began to make discoveries. First, with a dull ache of disappointment, she found that school was not so different from Marshington after all ; indeed, in a queer way the new place seemed to be more familiar than her home, as the type may be more familiar than the individual. At home, for instance, her mother said, " Muriel, I wish that you would keep the school-room cupboard a little tidier." At school untidiness became a crime, to be punished by order marks, to the disgrace of the whole form or bedroom. The accidental regulations of Marshington life were shaken out of their environment and transformed into infallible rules.

For Mrs. Hancock had been a wise woman when she founded her private school for girls at Hardrascliffe. Opening in business an eye to the main chance that she would have closed in private life, she realized that a head mistress has to make a choice. Generations are like divinities, and he who is not for them is against them. A school must be run either for the parents or for the children. As a business woman, Mrs. Hancock knew that the parents who pay the bills are the indispensable factor of success. She also knew that, for most of her parents, the unacknowledged aim of education was to teach their children to be a comfort to them. And how could a child be a comfort to parents whom she makes uncomfortable ? Mrs. Hancock determined that no education received in her school should be responsible for this disaster.

Possibly these considerations influenced her when, during her first term, Muriel unexpectedly asked for an interview.

In response to her " Come in, my dear," a small shy person
stood before her, whose slight figure was tense with a tremendous effort of courage.

" Well, Muriel ? " Mrs. Hancock smiled, with that famous
motherly manner so much praised among her parents.

" Mrs. Hancock——" hesitated Muriel. Her temerity
was born of deep desire. " You said that those of us who
wanted to learn special subjects and things—extras—might
come and ask you."

" Well, dear, I don't remember, though, that your mother
said—— Now, let me see, where is her letter ? " Mrs.
Hancock searched among the orderly papers on her desk.
" I don't remember that she asked for you to learn any extras,
except dressmaking, perhaps, if it fitted in to your time-table."

" It wasn't Mother. It's me." Muriel groped her way to
an untutored request. " I want—please, may I have lessons
on Astronomy ? "

" Astronomy ? " Mrs. Hancock gasped. " My dear child,
what are you talking about ? "

Muriel, whose opinion of the wisdom of all grown-ups was
sublimely high, did not take it upon herself to explain. She
only protested fervently that she wanted to, always had
wanted to, know more about the stars, and to do calculations
and things. It must be confessed that it all sounded rather
silly. The triumphant thing, the towering audacity of her
desire, collapsed into the futility of ruined hopes. She felt
that the tears were coming. Her unique adventure beyond
habitual self-effacement was going to fail. She gazed appeal-
ingly at the head mistress.

Then, with a kindliness that Muriel found consoling even
though it sounded the death knell to her hopes, Mrs. Hancock
explained how there were some things that it was not suitable
for girls to learn. Astronomy, the science of the stars, was a
very instructive pursuit for astronomers, and professors (these
latter being evidently a race apart), but it was not one of those
things necessary for a girl to learn. " How will it help you,
dear, when you, in your future life, have, as I hope, a house to
look after ? If you really want to take up an extra, I will

write to your mother about the dressmaking. You are quite
clever with your fingers, I think, and though it is usual to
begin a little later, perhaps——"

"But, but——" Muriel began. She knew now quite
certainly that she had resolved to become a great mathematician. She was not quite sure what this involved, nor could
she trace her resolution to the day when she first read *The
Life of Mary Somerville* in the *Lives of Fine Women* Series.
She was certain that fate held for her something more exciting
than dressmaking lessons, and yet her initial failure sapped her
courage. She resigned herself to the wisdom of Mrs. Hancock.

Whatever doubts Muriel might have felt about that wisdom,
Mrs. Hancock had none. Acceptance of the conclusions
reached by experienced and older people, Muriel was told,
was one of the first lessons to be learnt by rash, unthinking
youth. One day Muriel would laugh at her childish fancies.
She did not want to be considered different from other girls,
did she ? Mrs. Hancock had noticed with regret a tendency
to hold herself aloof, to be a little odd. That should not be.
Muriel must learn to conform to the standards of other,
wiser people. One day she would be grateful to Mrs. Hancock.

Muriel, of course, was grateful. She failed to explain to
her head mistress that her aloofness was not of her own making ;
but she had learnt her lesson. She never again asked Mrs.
Hancock for anything until she said good-bye to her on her
last day at school.

And yet that interview affected her life more deeply than
she might have guessed. For at the dressmaking classes,
Muriel met Clare.

III

IT happened during Muriel's second term. She sat in
the big school-room, opposite to the door that led up
three steps into the hall. The dressmaking class was half
over, and Muriel, while her fingers carefully tacked gathered
nun's veiling, allowed her thoughts to dance away as usual

into a delightful day-dream. Always at this time Muriel
used her leisure moments to compose the next instalment of a
secret serial history of which she was the heroine. In her
dreams, her failures and timidities slipped from her. She
became fascinating and audacious. Mistress of life, surrounded
by adoring friends, she stood triumphant, poised on the
threshold of some great adventure.

At the moment, having rescued the head girl, Rosalie Crook,
from a terrible death by drowning, Muriel, still pale and
dripping, was received upon the storm-swept sea-shore into
the magic circle of " Them," the great ones. " They " were
the élite, the prefects and the games captains, the popular
and famous, surrounded by the ineffable prestige of tradition-
making youth. Yet Rosalie, with tear-filled eyes, bent forward
to her companions. " Did you know," she cried, " that
Muriel has often been lonely and neglected ? Do you know
that she has lived in hourly dread of croc-walks, for fear lest
she should not have a partner ; that she has shrunk in terror
from Speech Day, in case no one should ask her to sit next
them ? That she has been at school two terms, but nobody
has asked her to be their friend ? Who will be her friend
now ? I, for one, would have liked that honour, girls, that
honour." Her voice quivered with emotion as They, with
one accord, rose to claim the friendship of Muriel Hammond.
The raging wind swept their ringing voices out to sea, as . . .
the door opened and Mrs. Hancock entered, followed by Clare
Duquesne.

Muriel rose obediently with the rest of the class, according
to the Heathcroft rule of courtesy, but afterwards the action
appeared as the natural result of instinctive allegiance to the
triumphant personality, not of the head mistress, but of Clare.

Clare stood at the top of the three steps, smiling down at
the class, not shyly, not stupidly, but with an assured and
indestructible friendliness. She was as much mistress of the
situation as a famous actress who has entered amid deafening
applause to take her call. Not beautiful, but with the confidence of beauty, not tall, but with a radiant suggestion of
height, Clare was utterly unlike anything that Muriel had seen

before. From the surprising bow upon her sleek brown hair, to the shining buckles on her trim brown shoes, from her odd short dress of pleated tartan to the frill of muslin round her firm young neck, she defied all Marshington and Hardrascliffe conventions of the proper attire for young girls of fifteen. Wholesome as an apple, tranquil as a September morning, and unmysterious as a glass of water, she yet held for Muriel all mystery and all enchantment. From that moment, without calculation or condition, Muriel gave her heart to Clare Duquesne.

"Now, girls," announced Mrs. Hancock. She never called her pupils "young ladies," having informed their parents that this savoured of middle-class gentility. They, anxious to fling off the least suspicion of resemblance to the class to which they almost all belonged, had approved with emphasis. "Now, girls, I want you to make room in your class for Clare Duquesne. She has come unexpectedly in the middle of the term because her mother has been called to the South of France on account of her father's health. I want you therefore to be specially kind to her, and to give her a pleasant welcome, as I know that you will."

Having made her speech, Mrs. Hancock prepared to withdraw, but this surprising Clare forestalled her.

"Thank you immensely," she said in her clipped, precise voice, speaking as though English were a well-known yet foreign language to her. "It is very kind of you to take so much trouble over me. But," she bubbled with laughter, the dimples quivering in her rounded cheek, "I have no talent with my needle. Félix bet me five francs that I would never learn even to sew on a button."

Mrs. Hancock, slightly surprised, but still benevolently gracious, smiled kindly. "And who is Félix, Clare ? "

"Félix ? Didn't you know ? He's my father." She turned to the class with an engaging air of frankness. "You know, Mamma and I always call him Félix, because she hates to hear me say Mamma or Papa. It makes her feel her age, she says, and when you are on the stage it is a crime to feel your age—on account of the dear public, is it not so ? "

Clare's voice deepened to the rich intonation of Sophie O'Hallaghan, the charming Irish-American actress who had married the half-brother of Lord Powell of Eppleford, and who was, incidentٖly, Clare's mother.

Mrs. Hancock had not intended to divulge the profession of Clare's mother. It was, she considered, the approval of the dear Bishop always in her mind, a delicate subject upon which one might have expected Clare to preserve a little reticence. Especially since Félix Duquesne had been considerate enough to write his distinguished but embarrassing French prose in —French, and was, through his family connections, of unprecedented value as a parent. But Clare knew no more of reticence than a lark on a spring morning or a kettle on the boil. She saw no reason for Mrs. Hancock's sudden stiffness, and continued to smile at her with complete urbanity.

"Well, Clare," replied the head mistress, "I think that perhaps while you are at school you had better refer to your father by his proper title. Is there an empty place, Miss Reeve, for Clare? Now girls, go on with your work. There is no reason for you to let Clare's arrival interrupt it. You can continue just the same."

She swept from the room, masking a faint uneasiness behind her gracious majesty of deportment, but for the first time questioning her wisdom in admitting this new pupil.

In the school-room, however, Providence for once had favoured Muriel. The empty chair to which Clare was conducted by Miss Reeve was next to hers, and when Clare turned towards her with that dazzling smile Muriel knew, for all Mrs. Hancock might say, that things would never be quite the same for her again.

IV

THE term after Clare's arrival Muriel lay in bed staring at the faint blur against the wall where Clare lay asleep. The room was dark and still, but near the pale translucent panels of the window the curtains stirred as though moved by the breathing of the seven girls.

The miracle that had led Clare to her on that first day still endured. Clare and Muriel slept in the same room. Of course that did not mean that they were friends. Clare had immediately marched with her cheerful serenity right into the most exclusive circle of the elect, of " Them." But to see Clare was an education ; to speak with her a high adventure. To sleep in the same room with her, to see her bath-salts and her powder, only permitted at Heathcroft because she was her father's daughter, to touch her underclothing, embroidered in a Belgian convent—this was to live perpetually on the threshold of a marvellous world, removed by millions of miles from school or Marshington.

She was wonderful, this Clare Duquesne. At night Muriel would raise her head above the bed-clothes and try to tell herself that this was really true, that the world was large enough to hold people so different as Clare and Muriel. Muriel, for all her brave dreams, knew herself to be of those whose eager, clutching hands let slip prizes, friendships and achievement, as quickly as they grasp them. But Clare, lazy, careless, happy Clare, laughed when she made mistakes, was amused by her arithmetic, hopelessly confused by premature acquaintance with the metric system, cared nothing for her erratic spelling, and swung up her average of weekly marks by her staggering proficiency in languages. Her supremacy at singing and dancing cost her no more effort than the wearing of fine raiment cost the lilies of the field. Her French and German were more fluent than her clipped, accentuated English. She could swear in Spanish, order a dinner in Dutch, and write a love-letter in Italian. Impish as a street-urchin, sophisticated as a cocktail, fearless of life, loved by it and its lover, judging no man as no man judged her, she dazzled Heathcroft as a glorious, golden creature not wrought from common clay.

Muriel's heart went out to her in a great wave of adoration. Passionate emotion, stronger than any she had known, even on the hushed silver morning of her First Communion, filled her small body like a mighty wind.

"Oh, I would die for her," she breathed ecstatically. "O God, if you've planned anything awful to happen to Clare, let it happen to me instead. I could bear anything for her, even if she never knew how I cared. But do let me know her. Let me get to be her friend!"

Forlorn hope, thought Muriel next day, preparing reluctantly for the school walk. As usual the time was trapping her, and she had no partner. Life at Heathcroft being organized upon the partner system, this was Muriel's daily and hourly terror—to have no one to walk with, to be driven as an enforced intruder to walk with the last couple in the crocodile, to feel the checked resentment of the juniors upon whom she was thus imposed.

She stood in front of the small glass, pushing the elastic of her sailor hat beneath her long, brown plait, and thinking, "Well, there's one thing about Connie coming here next term. I'll never have to walk alone again." Which just showed how little at this time she knew her Connie.

Then she heard Clare's voice.

"Will you not walk with me, Muriel?"

Muriel gasped. She could not believe that Clare had spoken. But there was no other Muriel in the school, and no other voice like Clare's. Yet, Clare, who could walk with "Them," surely she would never ask Muriel? They never walked with those who were not of the elect. They would not so imperil their dignity. But, of course, Clare never bothered about her dignity. Years afterwards, when Muriel referred to "Them," Clare asked with interest, "Who were 'They'?" But when Muriel said, "Oh, you, and Rosalie and Cathie and Patricia. All the people who counted." Then Clare laughed. "Oh, was I one? How perfectly thrilling! And I never knew. What things we miss!" But now Muriel only blushed and asked: "I beg your pardon?"

"I haven't got a partner," Clare said. "Will you walk with me?"

Muriel, blushing and palpitating, answered, "If you like." Always, when she was profoundly moved, she became a little stiffer and more prim, not gauche, but prim, like a Victorian teapot, or a bit of sprigged muslin.

Clare never noticed. She was arranging her blue serge coat with the air of a mannequin trying on a Paris model.

"Would you mind holding my collar straight ?" she asked.

They took their place in the crocodile.

All the way along the Esplanade Clare chattered. Muriel at the time was too much bewildered by her strange good fortune to remember everything that Clare was saying, but she retained a glowing impression of Clare skating outside a gay hotel in Switzerland, of Clare in a box at the Comédie Française, listening to one of her father's plays, of Clare crossing the Irish Channel in a ship, and being sea-sick all the way. It was perhaps the most unquestionable proof of Clare's attraction that even her sea-sickness became distinguished.

Before Muriel had said three words, the girls had reached the cliffs beyond the Esplanade. Beyond the asphalt and clipped box hedges of the Promenade, the cliffs sprawled untidily. They were not even real cliffs, but ragged slopes, overgrown with coarse grass and tamarisk, sprinkled with yarrow, and patched with stunted bushes of rusty gorse. Far below the tide crept up in circles, flat as paper, and washed back, dragging with white sickles at the shelving sand. The place had a deserted look, and Clare was bored.

"What shall we do now ?" she asked obligingly, when Miss Reeve gave the order to break rank.

She waited for Muriel to entertain her.

"Oh, I'll do anything *you* like," said Muriel fatally.

They strolled along the winding path. Abruptly to their right rose a steep rock, witness of the time before the landslide, when the cliffs had been cliffs. For fifteen feet it frowned above the way to the sands. Clare stood still, gazing at it in contemplative silence. Then she had an idea.

"Muriel," she suggested, " do let's see if we can climb that rock. No one can see us now. Miss Reeve's miles away. I'll go first. Come on, do."

Clare was like that. She never noticed natural things

Clare 33

except as a potential background to her own action. But,
having decided to act, she was prompt. She tore off her
gloves and faced the rock. Muriel stood, suddenly smitten
dumb by an agony of apprehension. But without looking
back, Clare began to climb. Agile as a cat, she scrambled
with firm hand-grips and burrowing toes, clutching at the
sheer side of the rock and chuckling to herself.

"Clare! You can't. You'll fall. You'll be killed."

Muriel meant to cry out all these things, but somehow she
said nothing. She only stood at the bottom of the rock while
a sick numbness robbed her of her strength.

Then Clare was up. She swung herself easily on to the
summit of the rock. Her figure was outlined against a windy
sky. Her laughing face looked down at Muriel.

"It's glorious up here," she called. "But what a wind!
I say, do come on, Muriel!"

Before she had thought what she was doing, Muriel began
to climb.

"Whatever I do, I mustn't funk in front of Clare," she
thought.

Her fingers tore at the sharp ledges of the rock. Her toes
slipped on the uneven surface. She grasped at a brittle root
of broom. It came away in her hand. She almost fell.
Unused to climbing, blind with fear, she hardly saw the
places for her hands to hold.

Clare, completely oblivious of her distress, stared calmly
out to sea.

"Oh, Muriel, there's such a big steamer on the horizon.
Do hurry up and tell me where it's going."

But Muriel could not hurry. She was beyond hope, beyond
sight, almost beyond fear. For she had just remembered
Freddy Mason's stories of the Ladder, and how the men
carrying sacks up it had overbalanced and fallen to their doom,
far in the yard below.

Her grasp loosened. Rock and sky swung round her. Her
feet slipped on the narrow ledge.

She must not fail Clare; here was the time to test her
courage.

2 *

Fear swooped upon her, tore her fingers from the rock, poured drops of perspiration on her forehead.

"Clare!" shrieked a voice that was not surely hers. "Clare, I'm slipping!"

Clare's round face appeared between the edge of the rock and the reeling sky. Clare's voice remarked imperturbably: "Oh, well, if you do fall you haven't far to go, so it won't hurt. But hold on a bit and I'll give you a hand."

She came over the edge again. Her solid, shapely ankles were on a level with Muriel's hat, her eyes. A firm hand reached down for Muriel's clutching, sticky one.

"That's all right. Come along. You've got a great dab of mud on your nose, Muriel."

She never faltered. Somehow they both scrambled over the edge. Muriel flung herself down on the short turf, too sick and humiliated to notice even Clare.

She had disgraced herself. She had failed. Her cowardice was flagrant. Far from conducting herself heroically, she had risked Clare's own safety because she was afraid. Far more than her nerve had failed then. Her confidence in her whole personality was shaken. Black with the unlit blackness of youth, the future stretched before her.

"Muriel"—when Clare pronounced her name it sounded warm and golden—"do you not think that the girls here are like children?"

Muriel opened her eyes and stared as if to discover some connection between this remark and her own disgraceful exhibition of childishness. But there was none. Clare, astounding, incalculable Clare, had not even noticed the tragedy of Muriel. She had taken it for granted that if you couldn't climb, you couldn't, and that was your affair. She continued meditatively:

"You must know what I mean, for you are different." Oh, glorious triumph! Mrs. Hancock forgotten, Muriel glowed at the delightful thought that she was different. "Have you not observed? How many of them have had *affaires de cœur*? But very few!"

"*Affaires de cœur?*" It is hard to grope with a meagre

Clare

35

French vocabulary when one has just emerged from one physical and two spiritual crises. Affaires! Muriel's knowledge of Marshington phraseology assisted her. De Cœur—of the heart. Of course.

"Why, Clare, you can't mean being in love!"

"And why not?" asked Clare serenely. "I have had five affairs. There was the student at the Sorbonne, and the man who played with Mamma in New York, and my cousin Michael at Eppleford, and, and——"

"But were you in *love* with them?"

"My dear child, no! Why should I be?"

"Then, how?"

"Dear me, *chérie*, have you never observed that I am very attractive?"

Her laugh rang out, merry and spontaneous.

"What a solemn face! Muriel, do you ever smile? No, no, I shan't fall in love for years. Perhaps never. But crowds and crowds of men will fall in love with me. That's why Félix decided that I had better come to school. 'They're beginning too soon,' he said. 'You mustn't cut out your mother yet, child.' And he sighed. He's terribly sentimental, my Félix. I'm sure I didn't mind. On the whole it bores me. Men in love are so terribly alike, I think, don't you?"

Fascinating, incredible conversation!

"Of course, really, I'm rather grateful to Félix," Clare continued sagely. "It's no use getting it all over too soon. And of course one day one might go too far, and really I don't want to marry yet, however rich he was. What do you think?"

"But, Clare, do—do men fall in love with *all* women if we let them?"

"Why, of course. Else why be a woman?" Clare responded with tranquillity. "Of course there are some, poor dears, like Miss Reeve, I suppose, and most schoolmistresses, and missionaries, and things, but they are hardly *women*, are they?"

"I—I don't know. I——"

Somehow, it must be confessed, Muriel had always thought

of these unfortunates as women. That merely showed her terrible simplicity. With a sigh, she pondered over her ignorance of Life.

"Oh, Muriel, do look at Miss Reeve coming up the path!" Clare darted forward and peered over the edge of the rock. The young lady from the Swiss hotel, the sophisticated philosopher on Life, had vanished. The Irish urchin, impish, grinning, disreputable, took her place. "Do just watch her hat bobbing along the path! It's as round as a soup plate. Why do people wear such hats? It should be forbidden by law. Here, hand me one of those little stones. Quick!"

Unthinking and hypnotized, Muriel obeyed.

Plop! went the stone, right into the middle of Miss Reeve's round hat. Clare was back behind the rock.

"Oh, Clare, she'll see you," agonized Muriel.

Clare chuckled. "She won't. I never get found out."

But for once she was wrong. Her crimson scarf, blown by the wind, waved a bright pennon from the rock. Nobody else at Heathcroft wore such a scarf.

"Clare Duquesne, Clare Duquesne!" Miss Reeve's shrill voice was ripped to ribbons of sound by the wind.

Clare leant down, smiling benignly upon the furious lady on the path. "You called?" She inquired politely.

"What are you doing there? Come down! How dare you?"-

"How dare I come down? Well, it does look rather steep. I'm not sure that we can *this* way," pondered Clare, her head on one side.

"Don't deliberately misunderstand me. Who threw that stone?"

"The stone?" Clare's innocent voice repeated, but Muriel knew that the situation was growing serious. With the ardent heroism of a martyr, she flung herself into the breach—in other words, her head appeared over the rock by the side of Clare. Desire to serve her beloved had vanquished fear, hesitation and conscientiousness.

"It wasn't Clare's fault, Miss Reeve," she called. "We were trying to get to the other path, and—and I slipped, and

that set some stones rattling down, and Clare came to stop
me falling, and I do hope that nobody's hurt."

Relieved to find that this was not a situation requiring to
be dealt with by a major punishment, an embarrassing ordeal
at the best of times, devastating when the culprit was Clare
Duquesne, Miss Reeve contented herself with a haughty
stare.

" I do not think that you two have been behaving very
nicely. It is not ladylike to climb these high rocks, and I am
sure that it is dangerous. Please come down at once, both of
you."

It was impossible to scold two heads detached from bodies,
appearing from the sky like cherubs from a Christmas card
cloud. Muriel and Clare withdrew.

Safely back behind the rock, Clare chuckled delightedly.

" I didn't know you had it in you, Muriel ; that was quite
magnificent."

But Muriel, to her own surprise as much as Clare's, suddenly
began to cry, aloud and helplessly, like a little child.

" But, Muriel, *chérie*, what is the matter ? "

" I don't know. I'm so sorry to be so stupid. I think—
I—you know, I didn't mean to tell a lie. It just came out."

" You ? What ? Is that all ? But you didn't. We
were going to the lower path—sometime. And that stone
was loosened with your foot. And you did slip. That
wasn't a lie. It was a stroke of genius."

Then, with a sudden access of delighted interest, Clare
turned upon Muriel.

" My dear, is it possible that you have a temperament ?
And I never guessed it. But how very odd. I should not
have thought it somehow. It just shows that you never can
tell. And I *have* been so bored with these suet dumplings
of girls." *Them !* The elect and sacred " Them " suet
dumplings ! Muriel forgot her tears. " Although I, thank
heaven, I have no temperament myself. That is why Félix
says that I shall never be a singer."

She flashed her dazzling smile upon the embarrassment of
Muriel, who, resolutely determined to acquire a temperament

whatever this might be—immediately, was returning thanks to a benevolent providence who sends success to people in spite of their own failures.

V

FRIENDSHIPS at Heathcroft should usually be registered, like births, deaths, and marriages, with all due publicity and certitude. It was just like Muriel that, right up to the moment of leaving school, she should never know whether she could really call herself Clare's friend.

She stood on the platform, waiting for the arrival of the York train that was to carry Clare off to London, Leipzig, singing lessons and Fame. Clare, radiant, blossoming already into a young lady in a hat sent by her mamma from Paris, smiled serenely from the carriage window down at Muriel.

"Au revoir," she laughed. Her rich voice lightly dropped the words for Muriel to take up or to leave as she would. Clare did not care.

"Good-bye, Clare," Muriel replied solemnly. She made no fuss about it, for that would have been cheek, as though she had some right to mind saying good-bye. "I hope that you will have a good time in Germany. I expect that when I see you again you will be a famous singer. But don't forget that if ever you *should* want to stay in Yorkshire we should love to have you at Miller's Rise."

"Oh, thank you, *chérie*, I shall not forget."

She smiled and waved her hand, tossing back to Muriel, like a fallen flower, the invitation that had cost such terrific courage to propose. But Muriel rushed away to her own carriage on the local line to Kingsport with a sense of desolation that ached sullenly beneath the excitement of being grown-up at last.

Because Muriel did not much care for babies, they pursued her in railway trains and buses with relentless faithfulness.

The carriage into which she hurled herself after Connie's vanishing figure was hot and overcrowded, and directly opposite to Muriel sat a baby, wriggling on its mother's knee, its mouth smeared with chocolate and crumbs of biscuits.

"Disgusting," thought Muriel. "How like Connie to choose a carriage full of babies." For Connie was at this time indiscriminately friendly, always scraping acquaintance with babies, all crumbs and chocolate, or puppies, all smells and fleas. And now, because of her lack of sensitiveness, Muriel at this crisis in her life had to endure a slow train, where at every station people with baskets crowded in upon her, even more hurriedly than her own overwhelming emotions. Connie would come by this train, because it arrived at Marshington half an hour before the express, and Muriel always tried to be unselfish. She might have guessed what it would be like, for circumstances never had much reverence for her feelings. Perhaps that was why she had come to think that they did not much matter herself.

The world was all right. It was she who was wrong, caring for all the wrong things. She could not, however hard she tried, stop herself from loving Clare, though passionate friendships between girls had been firmly discouraged by the sensible Mrs. Hancock. Their intimacy, she considered, was usually silly and frequently disastrous. If carried too far, it even wrecked all hope of matrimony without offering any satisfaction in return. Love was a useful emotion ordained by God and regulated by society for the propagation of the species; or else it inspired sometimes the devotion of a daughter to a mother, or a parent to a child. It could even be extended to a relative, such as a cousin or an aunt. Or in a somewhat diluted form it might embrace Humanity, engendering a vague Joan-of-Arc-Florence-Nightingale-Mrs.-Beecher-Stowish philanthropy, to which Muriel aspired faintly, but without much hope of realization. But Love between two girls was silly sentiment. By loving Clare, Muriel knew that she had been guilty of extreme foolishness. And she wanted so much to be good.

The words of Mrs. Hancock's farewell interview returned
to her through the smoke-laden atmosphere of the train.

"My dear, to-morrow you are going to take your place in
the world outside your school, and there are one or two things
that I want you to remember. I believe that sometimes you
girls laugh at those words of Kingsley's, 'Be good, sweet
maid, and let who will be clever,' but they contain a great
truth, Muriel. Character, my dear, to be a fine womanly
woman, that matters so much more than intellectual achievement. To serve first your parents, then, I hope, your husband
and your children, to be pure, unselfish and devoted, that is
my prayer for each one of my girls." Mrs. Hancock coughed.
She had repeated this little homily so often that she did not
hesitate for words, and yet now and then, unguessed by her
hearers, would come a moment of wistful doubting whether
this message contained the final expression of her wisdom.
Below her worldly wisdom, Mrs. Hancock, like Muriel, wanted
to be good. "I want you to remember the school motto,
dear, '_Læta sorte mea_,' Happy in my lot. God will, I hope,
give you happiness, but if He chooses to send you disappointment and sorrow you will, I hope, resign yourself to His dear
will."

Forget? How could Muriel forget? It had been so
sweetly solemn. A vast desire seized upon her then to serve,
to be devoted, to be faithful. Sometimes at the early service
she had knelt in the dim chancel, and thought the fluttering
candle flames above the altar to be stirred by the soft breathing
of the Holy Ghost. Then, too, she had prayed with passionate
ardour for self-abnegation and for service. But last night the
desire had swept upon her with rushing, mighty wings, and
she had stood gazing into Mrs. Hancock's face with eloquent
eyes, and murmuring, "I will try. I will try."

Connie's strident voice swung Muriel back from the dream
of life to its business :

"Did you say that his name was Tommie? That's a nice
name, isn't it? Tommie, Tom! No, my sister isn't fond of
babies."

"Oh, I am," protested Muriel, always ready to sacrifice her

tastes to other people's feelings. " Sometimes," she added,
respectful to the truth. Her appealing eyes sought those of
the baby's mother, who nodded understandingly.

" Lor, bless you ! I know. A bit scared of 'em, eh ?
You wait till you've had eight on 'em like me. Then a bairn's
neither here nor there as the saying goes. Ah've got six an'
buried two, dearie me, but Ivy's in service now, so I'm not
complaining. The Lord's will be done, as I says to Mrs.
Dalton, who's had fourteen. The Lord's will be done so
long as He don't overdo it."

" Of course," smiled Muriel shyly, feeling somehow that
the answer was inadequate.

Was that really the end of it all ? Six alive and two buried,
and the Lord's will being done, while one's face grew florid
and coarse, with a network of purplish veins across the cheek,
and days and nights passed in an endless race to keep abreast
with small domestic duties ?

Life's not like that. Life's not like that, vowed Muriel.
Fiercely she fought this sense of inexorable doom for the
salvation of her dreams. Surely God made the world most
beautiful, and set within it to delight man's heart music, and
lingering scents, and the clear light of dawn through leafless
trees. To teach man the holiness of law, He set the stars to
ride their courses ; for patience, He showed the slow fertility
of earth ; for wisdom, He granted an eternal hunger that
would snatch its secret from the lightning, and their riddle
from the tombs of ancient men. He gave man beauty of
body, and delight in swift, free, movement. He gave him
friendship, and the joy of service. And, lest these things
should be too sweet, and cloy with sweetness, He gave him
danger, that man might know the glory of adventure. And,
lest man should grow weary in his wandering, God gave the
last and deepest mercy, Death.

Not quite in definite words, Muriel thought this, but
somehow her heart told her that Life was this joyous, regal
journey. She was grown up. The whole world lay before
her. The great adventure, which just must end right, was
about to begin.

She raised her hand to feel the long plait falling between her narrow shoulders. Soon there would be a cold feeling at the back of her neck. Her hair would be twisted up below her hat. Did being grown up really make such a difference ?

The train jerked on. Beyond the window the flat, dun country slid past wearily. Hot July fields, ripening into dusty yellow for the harvest, paddocks dried to rusted fawn, hundreds and hundreds of allotments, variegated as a patchwork quilt, speckled with crazy tool sheds, seamed with straight dykes, splashed here and there with the silver-green of cabbages, or the faded motley of a wilted border of July flowers—this was the country that surrounded Marshington. After the ringing splendour of the wind-swept wolds, the stale flatness of the plain seemed doubly depressing.

But Muriel was not depressed. Marshington to her was not a select residential suburb of Kingsport, compensating for its ugliness by its respectability. It was the threshold of life, the gateway to a brimming, lovely world, whence she might start upon a thousand strange adventures. Its raw, red villas were transfigured. Its gardens glowed to meet her. When she could see from the right-hand window the elm-crowned hill of Miller's Rise, her excitement almost choked her.

She leaned back in her seat, half wishing that she need never rise, but Connie darted to the window.

" I say, Mu, hadn't we better pull the bags down ? Look out ! There's your tennis racket. Where's my book box ? My book box, Mu ? Good-bye, Tommie, bye-bye ! See, Muriel, he's ta-ing his little hand at us ! Isn't he an angel ? Oh, there's Father ! Cooee, father, cooee ! We're here ! We're here ! "

VI

IT really mattered. To have a belt that fastened trimly on to one's new serge skirt, a safety-pin that under no circumstances would expose itself to public view, a straw hat that sat jauntily (so long as it was not *too* jaunty) upon one's piled up hair, all these things meant more than just "being tidy."

Being grown up was puzzling. It seemed to make no difference at all in most things, and then to matter frightfully in quite unexpected ways. It meant, for instance, not so much the assumption of new duties as the acceptance of new values.

Was she more stupid than other people, or did every one feel like this at first? She was travelling in a land of which she only imperfectly understood the language. Would she learn gradually, as one learnt French at Heathcroft, or would the new significance of things suddenly flash out at her, like the meaning of a cipher when one has found the key?

"My dear child, you were never thinking of going to the Club with *that* terrible handkerchief? You must have a linen one. Scent? No, I think not for a young girl. It seems a little fast, I think, Beatrice, don't you? And whatever happens, a girl in her first season must not give people the impression that she is fast."

People. People. Until she had grown up, Muriel had been woefully ignorant of how important People were. At Heathcroft, if you were naughty, you offended God. At Marshington, if you were "queer" you offended People. Perhaps the lesser offence was noticed by the lesser deity, and yet the eye of the All-Seeing could hardly have been more observant than the eye of People, who measured worth by the difference between a cotton and a linen handkerchief.

Muriel was going for the first time to the Recreation Club since she had left school. Connie, who, being still a schoolgirl, cared for none of these things, walked beside her in sulky silence. She disliked the Club, because, as a junior member, she could only sit on the Pavilion steps to watch the sedate activities of her elders.

The Club being on the north-west side of Marshington, the Hammonds had about half a mile to walk from Miller's Rise, a half-mile which Mrs. Hammond improved by final injunctions to her daughter.

"The first time *is* so important, dear," she said.

By the time that they had reached the wire-topped gate, Muriel was in a state of frigid and self-conscious terror. In a dream she followed her mother's lilac-coloured linen across the wide grass path to the Pavilion, wondering whether she ought to smile at Mrs. Lane, and whether her hat was straight, and whether that terrible pin was showing yet above her skirt. But at last she was seated safely on the steps with Connie, while Mrs. Hammond was swept away by Mrs. Cartwright for a game of croquet. She sat quite still, waiting for the familiarity of the things she saw to remove the strangeness of her new attitude towards them. At least she could play her old game of Watching People, a game made doubly thrilling by the realization that now she, too, was one of the grown-ups. That thought amused her a little as she listened to Mrs. Marshall Gurney's rich, authoritative voice in conversation with Colonel Cartwright. Absurd that Muriel should now be grown up—like Colonel Cartwright! He was not a real colonel, Mrs. Hammond had once said. He had made lots of money by manufacturing soap. (Was soap more vulgar than sacks? Father made sacks.) But he had taken advantage of the Volunteer Movement to win a bloodless victory over the more exclusive circles of Marshington. Even Mrs. Marshall Gurney, who would hardly otherwise have known the creator of the Cartwright Complexion, loved to punctuate her comments upon life by " Ah, Colonel," and " Oh, Colonel."

She was saying it now.

" Ah, Colonel, if it were merely a question of leaving the Parish."

" Deuced fine girl, though, Mrs. Marshall Gurney, deuced fine girl." The colonel gallantly hid the traces of a Yorkshire accent behind a barrage of military phrases. " We shall miss her at the Club. I must say that I like to see her playing with young Neale. They make a damned fine couple."

" Oh, there's nothing in that, I do assure you, Colonel. Take it from me. He really takes no more notice of Delia than of any of the other girls about here. Except, of course, that she has had rather more practice at tennis than most of the others, and he likes a good game, being such a splendid player. He plays for his college at Oxford, you know. The other day, he told Phyllis——"

"Of course "—Mrs. Parker's gruff masculine voice cut across her pleasant amble—" Godfrey Neale knew the Vaughans long before Mrs. Neale condescended to associate with any of us."

Mrs. Marshall Gurney bridled. Muriel could hear offended dignity in every creak of her basket chair.

"I hardly think so, Mrs. Parker," she said with majesty. "I used to dine at the Weare Grange when Godfrey was quite a little boy. After her trouble Alice Neale turned to me a great deal. Why, Godfrey and Phyllis . . ."

"Godfrey Neale never *looks* at Phyllis M.G.," whispered Connie with scorn. "Old Mrs. M.G. always makes out that they are bosom friends. Doesn't he play beautifully, though ? "

On the court to the right of the Pavilion, a vigorous set was in progress. That tall splendid young man in the perfect flannels, with his shirt just open enough to show his fine brown throat, and the conquering air of the accomplished player in his sure, swift movements, that was Godfrey Neale, really and in the flesh Godfrey Neale, no longer a mythical but heroic figure, whose exploits, riches and tastes were whispered breathlessly at Marshington tea-tables, or described by the more imaginative with the assurance of intimacy. That was Godfrey Neale. And Muriel had actually spoken to him. Once at a dance, years and years ago, a party memorable for bitter shame, Muriel had not only spoken but danced with Godfrey. He had been a witness of her dire calamity. Did he remember ?

"Well, I think it distinctly lacking in a sense of duty, that Delia should go gallivanting off to college just now when her father's getting old," the denunciation from the veranda continued.

"Old ? " snapped Mrs. Parker, who was only forty-five herself. "I was not thinking of his age, but that we should have to get a curate, and I don't know who's going to pay for him. All that I do hope is that, after all this, Delia will

learn a little common politeness. I have rarely met a more
disagreeable young woman than she is now."

" Well, I can't see why we should have to pay for a curate
in order that the vicar's daughter might learn to be a lady,"
said Mrs. Marshall Gurney, quite tartly for her. Usually
her consciousness of her own superiority helped her to regard
with tolerance the failures of other people. But Delia
Vaughan, as the one person in Marshington who refused to
recognize that superiority, had committed the unpardonable
sin. She had done more than that. Mrs. Marshall Gurney
looked across the courts to where Phyllis, charming in her
blue dress, was playing languidly in a ladies' double while
Delia flaunted her intimacy with Godfrey Neale. Her
heavy face hardened. " I can't think where she gets it from.
Her mother was a delightful woman, one of the Meadows of
Keswick, you know, and the dear vicar, even if he is a little
unpractical, is a scholar and a gentleman. I hear that his
last book has been a great success."

Mr. Vaughan wrote books. That was magic in itself for
Muriel. *A Critical Survey of the Relation between Scutage and
the Subsidy*, his latest triumph, did not sound frightfully
thrilling, but it was a manifestation of profound scholarship
which left Marshington mystified but complacent. Marshington liked to feel that its vicar's academic distinction was
in some way a tribute to its own intelligence.

" Jolly good shot ! " cried Connie, as a cannon-ball service
from Godfrey Neale ricochetted along the grass and struck
the step of the Pavilion with a resounding thump. " Muriel,
isn't his service *wonderful* ? "

" Splendid," murmured Muriel absently, straining to
catch further scraps of gossip from the group behind her.
She settled down again just in time to hear Mrs. Parker
remark acidly :

" Delia Vaughan is one of those girls who pride themselves
that, however objectionable they may be to your face, they
are even more offensive behind your back. *She* may call it
being outspoken. I call it sheer ill-breeding."

The set was over. Bobby Mason collected the balls, and

Daisy Parker fluttered round him apologetically. "I'm so sorry that I played so badly."

It always seemed curious to Muriel that Mrs. Parker should have such a fluffy daughter. She supposed that Daisy must have inherited her femininity from her father. Mrs. Parker, with her caustic tongue and masculine garments, looked more like the mother of Delia Vaughan. Muriel shivered with delightful apprehension as the victors strolled towards the steps. Life could never be dull while it contained beings so romantically distinguished as Delia and Godfrey Neale.

She heard Godfrey say, with his charming little stammer, "Thanks awfully, p—partner. That was a splendid game."

Marshington gloried in Godfrey's stammer. In him it appeared as a gracious concession to human weakness, a sign that in spite of Winchester, Oxford, and the Weare Grange, Godfrey was a man of like infirmities to other men.

But not even the stammer impressed Delia Vaughan. That disagreeable young woman dropped idly on to the Pavilion steps quite close to Muriel and sat leaning forward, her racket against her knees.

"Godfrey, is there any tea?" she suggested. "And you need not think that the splendid game was due to *your* good play, my friend. Your first two services were abominable."

Fancy anyone daring to talk to Godfrey Neale like that!

Godfrey handed a tea-cup to Delia.

"Would you like some bread and butter, or shall I g—get you some of those little round buns?"

"Have they sugar on top?" asked Delia.

"Sugar? No, currants, not sugar. There is only one bun with sugar on it, and I want it for myself."

"Then you can't have it. How like a man to think that he has an indisputable right to the best bun. Bring me the sugar one, and—Godfrey, Miss Hammond hasn't had any tea yet. Have you, Miss Hammond?"

"Oh, s—sorry," said Godfrey Neale, and handed to Muriel his other cup.

Never before had Delia appeared to notice the existence of Muriel. Godfrey had never spoken to her since the Party.

And here was Delia attending to her desire for tea, and Godfrey handing her his own cup! The traitor blushes glowed in Muriel's face, and chased themselves across her neck like the shadows of cloud across the tennis courts.

"Oh, I'm all right," she gasped. "Please keep that. It's your cup, isn't it?" She could not bear this unendurable honour.

"You must have that. Godfrey can fetch another. He is growing fat and lazy."

"Connie," desperately blundered Muriel, seeking as usual to cast the responsibility of life's gifts on to someone else, "don't you want this?"

"Godfrey, get two more cups," said Delia.

But Connie unexpectedly replied:

"No thank you, Miss Vaughan, Freddy Mason promised to bring me some."

"Did he?" whispered Muriel, under the sheltering stir of Godfrey's departure back to the Pavilion.

"No, of course he didn't. But do you think I was going to have that Vaughan girl showing off in front of me? You've got no pride, Muriel."

So after Godfrey Neale returned, Muriel, being without pride, drank gratefully the cup of shame, while Connie thirsted proudly by her side.

At that moment, Mrs. Hammond, returning from her croquet, appeared round the corner of the Pavilion with Mrs. Cartwright. She saw Muriel on the steps. She saw Godfrey Neale bending over her with a plate of little cakes. Muriel, looking up, saw the sudden gleam that crossed her face, like winter sunlight on a melting pool.

"Good afternoon, Mr. Neale. Home from Oxford, I suppose? Have you had some good tennis?"

"I thought s—so, Mrs. Hammond, but my partner tells me that I have been playing abominably," smiled Godfrey.

"Muriel, I hope that you haven't been scolding Mr. Neale," Muriel's mother began.

Mrs. Cartwright's eye flashed balefully upon her.

Between them, Muriel was in despair. To say nothing was

to act a lie, to let her mother go on thinking that she had been honoured by Godfrey's partnership. He would think that she was showing off. It was an unendurable position.

Muriel blushed; Godfrey Neale hesitated smilingly; Mrs. Cartwright awaited in triumph the revelation of Mrs. Hammond's error. Delia's clear voice cut the tension of the listeners:

"As a matter of fact, it was I who scolded Godfrey. He and Miss Hammond are just about to take their revenge on me."

"Well, I hope that they are not *too* hard on you," smiled Mrs. Hammond, and passed on to her triumph, while Muriel sat speechless at the unexpected turn of events.

"Look here, Delia, is that a challenge?" asked Godfrey, too polite to show surprise.

"Of course. Directly I have finished my tea. Go and find Dennis Smallwood and tell him that he can play with me. He's asked me about six times to-day, because he wants to practise for the tournament. Of course this is if Miss Hammond has no objection," she added, inclining her head towards the miserable Muriel who sat crumbling her bread and butter, and wishing that she might plunge into her tea-cup and remain engulfed there for ever.

The proximity of the gods is exhilarating, but when they descend from their machines they are apt to be a little overwhelming.

"I—I'm so bad," stammered Muriel. "I've hardly played this year. I shall spoil your game."

"If I had thought that you played well," remarked Delia imperturbably, "do you think that I should have chosen you as a handicap for Godfrey?"

After that, there could be no escape. Godfrey returned, followed by the obliging Dennis. Delia stood up and flung off her jacket.

Muriel felt a little sick. These things simply did not happen. If only she could be a success. If only she could by some miracle play brilliantly. She tried to picture the delight on her mother's face. In a dream she rose, nervously fingering her racket.

"Muriel!" came Connie's hoarse whisper. "Your safety-pin's showing at the back!"

She clutched at her belt. "Excuse me," she murmured.

"Toss for courts, please," commanded Delia, ignoring her.

"Excuse me," she repeated, measuring the distance between the steps and the cloak-room door.

"The sun ought to be fairly well behind the roof," said Delia. "Rough."

"Smooth it is. You'll have to face the sun," cried Godfrey. "Come along, Miss Hammond."

"But——" protested Muriel weakly, but too late. Dennis gathered up the balls and sauntered leisurely with Delia across the court. Muriel was left, her back and the terrible, indecent safety-pin exposed to the full gaze of Social Marshington in the Pavilion. Once, she had a nightmare that while shopping in Middle Street all her clothes fell off. Even that had not been as embarrassing as this.

Godfrey was measuring the net.

"Bit higher, Smallwood. G—good thing that we won the toss, Miss Hammond. The sun's awful."

A good thing that they won the toss! Muriel, hearing a burst of laughter from the Pavilion, felt sure that somebody had seen the pin. She gave a sickly smile.

The other courts were deserted. The whole of Marshington was there on the veranda. The whole of Marshington, finishing its tea, had nothing better to do than to watch the set. Muriel felt fifty eyes boring holes into her humiliated back.

Her mother would see. Her mother would see the pin. And the first time was so important.

She made a despairing effort to recapture her self-possession. At Heathcroft she had been counted as quite a steady player. Well, now she would show Marshington. She would show them that, in spite of the safety-pin, she could at least play tennis. If Godfrey Neale liked girls because they played well, then he should have no cause to dislike her.

"Service!" called Delia.

Muriel steeled herself for effort.

The first ball came driving, clean and straight, across the court. Muriel, dazed but optimistic, put out her racket. The ball sped on unchecked and bounded against the Pavilion steps.

" Fifteen love ! " called Dennis.

" Hard luck," consoled Godfrey.

" I'm *so* sorry," murmured Muriel.

Godfrey returned the second serve to Delia. She flashed it back to him. Really, it wasn't *nice* for a girl to drive so straight and so efficiently. Delia's tall, white figure became to Muriel something malevolent and ruthless.

Godfrey returned the ball again, but Dennis at the net put out his long arm and sent the ball crashing down at Muriel's feet, to rise and soar far above her head, beyond her reach, beyond hope.

" Thirty love," called Dennis.

" My fault. I didn't place it well," said Godfrey.

" I am *so* sorry," pleaded Muriel.

Her time of trial came again. She stood up brave and stiff.

" Play ! " called the vicar's daughter.

Muriel played.

She played with such goodwill that the ball rose up, up into the cloud-flecked sky.

" Forty love," called Dennis, polite but obdurate.

Godfrey Neale, infected perhaps by his partner's impotence, lost the next point.

" Game," announced Dennis. " Neale, look to your laurels."

" Your service, partner." Godfrey smiled his charming smile. " I messed up that last game fearfully."

Had he not seen that it was her fault ? She could have kissed his hand for his forbearance. Negotiating carefully, so as not to expose to him at least the shameful pin, Muriel picked up the balls.

She could not decide whether to hold two or three. Which had she generally done at Heathcroft ? She could remember nothing. They seemed suddenly to have grown large and slippery, heavier than cannon-balls. Surely it must be bowls that she was playing, and not tennis ?

She was losing her nerve. She felt it going, and she could not stop it.

She would not lose her nerve.

She stepped back carefully, three paces from the line.

" Service," she called, in a voice that would not have roused a rabbit.

That, as it happened, was unimportant, for her first ball hit the net, and her second, slow and careful to avoid mistakes, sailed gently into the wrong court.

" Love fifteen," said Godfrey. " Bad luck, partner."

" *So* sorry," repeated Muriel mechanically.

She *would* serve the next one well.

" Play ! " she shouted, and with all her strength she smote.

" Oh ! Oh, Mr. Neale, I *am* so sorry ! " For Muriel's ball, driven at last fair across the court, had hit the unfortunate partner right between his shoulders.

" My fault," he said gallantly. " I got in the way. I stopped a s—splendid service too."

Entirely unnerved, she sent a ball so cautiously that it dropped before it reached the net. Godfrey picked it up and brought it to her.

Crimson-faced now, she was forcing back her tears. He looked down at her, kindly, carelessly, not even noticing her discomfort.

" I say," he said, " I'm awfully glad that you hit me just now. It's a favourite trick of Delia's, but if she sees other people doing it she'll stop, just from perversity. She's a bit like a cyclone when she gets going, isn't she ? "

The humorous twist of his smile, the appeal to her criticism of his friend, the flattery of his attention, soothed Muriel's injured vanity. She giggled. Then with a sudden burst of confidence, she whispered :

" She's like the Day of Judgment, I think. I always remember all my misdoings in her sight. I—I'm terrified of her."

He laughed. " So am I, to tell the honest truth. But she's a ripping sport really, so for goodness' sake don't tell a soul."

They laughed, sharing a secret together, Muriel and Godfrey Neale. With one sentence he had drawn her in to the magic circle of his intimacy. She forgot her double faults and the safety-pin. She began to play to redeem his game against the girl who terrified him.

Her next serve went straight and hard. In her amazement, Delia failed to return it.

"Fifteen thirty," cried Godfrey. "Well done, partner. Do it again."

She did it again, not once nor twice. For the rest of the set, she played with serious care, keeping out of the way for Godfrey's smashing volleys. The air shimmered with dancing gold. Never before shone grass so green. Never were balls so white. Never was the joy of swift movement so exhilarating.

They won the next game and the next. Delia, half amused at the little Hammond child's spirit, was playing badly.

From the Pavilion, Muriel heard Mrs. Waring's voice:

"Your little daughter plays a good game, Mrs. Hammond. You must be pleased to have her at home now."

"Yes, it is delightful. Naturally I missed her dreadfully," answered Muriel's mother.

Someone beyond the net was asking, "Shall we play it out or have sudden death?"

"Sudden death," declared Delia, in the voice of a judge; but Muriel did not care. Neither death, pestilence, nor famine could affright her now.

"Game—and set," said Godfrey Neale. "By Jove, Miss Hammond, we must have some more like that!"

Sunning herself in his smile, she walked back to the Pavilion. Congratulatory smiles met her. For some reason, utterly unguessed by her, she had become a heroine. That Delia's defeat could be sweeter than honey to Marshington never occurred to her. She accepted the glory of the moment as it came.

"I say, Mu"—she had forgotten Connie. She turned upon her now with sudden irritation. But Connie had had no triumph. She was thirsty. She was bored. She thought that Muriel had had enough success—"do you know that your safety-pin's come undone, and you've got your blouse all out behind ? "

Muriel fled to the cloak-room.

VII

THE excitement of Muriel's *début* at the Club was not repeated. She certainly went often enough, and once or twice Godfrey Neale spoke to her. She did not, however, play with him again, but sat for most afternoons on the steps of the Pavilion until asked to join a Ladies' Double with Nancy Cartwright and Sybil Mason and poor Rosie Harpur, who had also just left school, and who could play tennis no better than she danced. Then the tennis season closed, and Connie returned to school, and Muriel learnt how to order joints from the butcher's and stores from the grocer's, and passed cakes at her mother's tea-parties, and helped her with the accounts for the Mother's Union and the G.F.S., and wondered when her real Life was going to begin.

Then came November and the Lord Mayor's dance, and Muriel woke up next morning to remember that she had come out.

It would all have been wonderful, if only her hair had kept tidy. Next morning she sat before her looking-glass and wrestled with aching arms to cure her hair of its irresistible tendency to fall in heavy locks upon her shoulders. It had spoilt everything, the band, the supper, the confused medley of names upon her programme. From her first ball, Muriel brought home only the memory of a scrambling rush to the cloak-room, and of her mother's worried face bending above hers in the long mirror.

She rested her chin on her hands and gazed at her thin, solemn face in the glass, wondering whether she was really very plain, or whether she would improve with time, as Mrs. Cartwright said that Adelaide had done.

She was so much absorbed by these reflections that she did

not at first hear Annie, the housemaid, who knocked and came straight in with the ostentatious familiarity of the old servant.

" Miss Muriel, a telegram for you."

" For me ? " People were not in the habit of sending telegrams to Muriel. She was not that kind of person.

" It's addressed to Muriel Hammond," remarked Annie stolidly. She, too, found something unbecoming in the sending of telegrams to Miss Muriel.

Muriel took the envelope and fingered it. " Where's Mother ? " she asked slowly.

" Mrs. Hammond's in the kitchen."

" Oh."

For a moment, Muriel's training fought with her curiosity. Then her training conquered. She seized her rope of hair, twisted it lightly round her head, and fled downstairs with the unopened envelope.

Mrs. Hammond was alone in the kitchen writing up the menu for the day. She raised her eyebrows at Muriel's flying entrance.

" Well, dear ? Oh, Muriel, what have you been doing to your hair ? "

" Doing it. Oh, Mother, there's a telegram."

" For me, dear ? "

" No. It's for me." She hesitated, still afraid lest her mother should consider the receipt of telegrams by her improper.

To her surprise, Mrs. Hammond took it quite calmly.

" Well, Muriel, who is it from ? "

Muriel opened the envelope and read : " Can you have me week or longer harribels have measles Felix not due England till 24th no money to go Italy Duquesne."

She read it to herself. She read it aloud to her mother. She could not believe her eyes.

" What does it mean ? " asked Mrs. Hammond.

Muriel explained. " It's Clare, Clare Duquesne. You remember, my great friend at Heathcroft, at least she wasn't exactly my friend, but I always wanted her to be. She went to Germany to learn singing."

"Yes, but I don't understand. - Does she want to come here?"

"Well—I—she—I think. It looks as though she had been going to stay with the Harribels, and they had measles."

"But, who is Félix?"

"Félix is her father, Félix Duquesne, you know, the writer; he writes in French, and it's Clare's mother who insists that he shall be called Félix because 'Mother' and 'Father' make her feel so old and when you are on the stage you have to keep young because of the dear public," Muriel explained, feeling that somehow she was not being as clear as she might have wished.

"But, my dear child, you can't expect her to come here on her own invitation like this at a moment's notice. I never heard of such a thing. And uninvited. Really, I don't know what girls are coming to."

"But I did say—I mean I didn't ever think that she'd come, only I did say that I knew we should be pleased to see her. You see——"

Mrs. Hammond frowned. "Now Muriel, this is really too bad of you. Can't you see what a position you put me into? You know how much I want you to have the things that you like, and I should have been glad enough to let you have a school friend to stay at some proper time, but you know that Father doesn't like just anyone, and just now——"

"Well, mother, of course if we can't have her—I mean if it's inconvenient——"

Hope died from Muriel's grey eyes. Four months at home had taught her that argument, when not wicked, was futile. It meant not just difference of opinion, but a way of making things difficult for Mrs. Hammond, who had to see that the house ran smoothly.

"Well, dear, of course you must see how impossible it all is. I don't know anything about this girl. I'm very busy just now, and surely she must have other friends in England? It's a queer name. Is she French or something?"

"Half French, half Irish, I think. I don't think that she has any relatives in England. The nearest that I know of are

the Powells at Eppleford in Donegal." Muriel's voice was
sullen with resignation. She had turned from her mother
and stood, smoothing out the creases from the telegram, while
an enchanting vision of Clare faded into the limbo of impossi-
bilities.

"Powells, at Eppleford ? Surely, where have I heard that ?
Why, is this the girl of whom Mrs. Hancock spoke, Lord
Powell's niece ? "

"Yes. Did she tell you about her ? " sighed Muriel, still
without hope and rather wishing that her mother would close
a painful conversation. She had been good. She had not
pressed Clare's claims. For her mother's sake, no one should
ever know how bitter a disappointment she had swallowed
down, there by the kitchen table.

"But, dear, you never told me that she was a particular friend
of yours. I thought that that Janet somebody or other——"

"Oh, Clare wasn't exactly my friend." These things could
not be explained even to somebody as sweet and beautiful as
Muriel's mother. "She was so lovely and so popular. She
knew all the—all the people I didn't know."

In spite of her resolute stoicism, Muriel gulped. Her
mother looked sharply at her averted face.

"You really want her so much, then ? "

"Oh, mother ! "

"Well, I must talk to your father. It just might be
arranged. But I do wish that you had told me about this
before, dear. You make things so difficult for me. Why
didn't you tell me, dear ? "

"There didn't seem to be anything to tell until now," said
Muriel. "I thought that she had quite forgotten me. She
never answered my letters ; I thought that she hadn't liked
me much."

"Dear, you mustn't be so—so backward. People will take
you at your own valuation, you know, and there is nothing
more objectionable than the pride that apes humility. Now
run away. Have you done the flowers yet ? I thought not.
And for goodness' sake tidy your hair, and tell me when your
father comes in."

3

" Then—then, will you ask him ? "

" Yes, yes, I'll ask him, though I can't say what—— Why, my dear child ! What ? Now don't crush my dress ! "

For Muriel had flung her arms round her mother's waist in an ecstasy of gratitude for her sympathetic understanding.

VIII

BECAUSE he wanted to drive the new chestnut mare, Mr. Hammond chose to go to the station to meet Clare. Muriel could come too if she liked, but the real reason was the mare. If there was one thing that Mr. Hammond prided himself upon more than another, it was his knowledge of horseflesh. The new mare was delicately perfect, from aristocratic shoulder to quivering nostril. A network of soft veins trembled beneath the shining velvet of her neck.

Muriel, terrified lest they should arrive too late, and always nervous in the high dog-cart, watched her father draw the lash of the whip lightly across the mare's back, playing it subtly as an angler plays a fly. He flirted with the mare as another man might have flirted with a pretty girl, chuckling because she was so daintily feminine and capricious. He had forgotten Muriel and Clare.

" Father," she spoke softly, being more than a little afraid of him, " we'll never be there in time." She watched for the curling smoke between the chimneys.

" By Jove, what time did you say that your friend's train arrived ? "

" 3.45."

" Well, now, if I hadn't had to stop to tell Tom Bannister about that order, we might just have done it. Maybe train'll be late."

But the train was not late, as trains never are except when you need them to be punctual. A little stream of Marshington residents had trickled out of the wicket-gate and separated up and down the straggling length of Middle Street before Muriel and her father drew up in the station yard. A shudder of apprehension stirred Muriel, who for one awful moment feared lest Clare should never have arrived, or lest, having arrived, she should have been offended that nobody was there to meet her. How like Father not to bother just because he thought Clare a child !

But when they appeared in the station, there at the end of the platform, surrounded by three suit-cases, a roll of rugs, a side-saddle, a hat box, a long, thin dachshund on a lead, and all the porters, stood Clare. She turned and saw them. She came to meet them. More beautiful and radiant than ever, in a grey travelling cloak, and a little grey toque with a scarlet quill, she hurried forward with outstretched hands to greet them, the dimples flickering in her cheek.

"You are Mr. Hammond, I am sure ? But how good of you to come yourself to meet me ! " Her small *suède* glove slipped into his capacious paw and rested there a moment longer than was necessary, while she smiled up at him, fearless, friendly, the least little bit in the world amused. He was such an enormous father for funny little Muriel Hammond ! Muriel saw her father's big red face, first grave, then surprised, then broadening out into a delighted smile. His blue eyes twinkled.

"Well, now, Miss Duquesne, a nice sort o' welcome we gave you leaving you like this all alone on the platform." He winked gaily at the surrounding porters.

Muriel shrank back, a little hurt. They had greeted one another like old friends, as though she did not count.

Then Clare saw her. "Muriel, my dear ! How perfectly ripping to see you again ! My dear, it is good of you to have me. Behold me, a lone creature lost in London, and the Harribels, with whom I was to stay, all over measles and things."

"Very glad to have you, Miss Duquesne." Mr. Hammond rubbed a stiff hand across his chin, a sure sign, as Muriel knew, that he was pleased. " Now then, what about all this luggage, eh ? "

Clare explained volubly. "Oh, I'm frightfully sorry, but,

you see, I had to bring all my things from Germany because I don't know when I'm going back, and the side-saddle is because Jimmie Powell promised me a mount when I go to Ireland. And Fritz was a most embarrassing gift from a student. I was in such a hurry that I couldn't make up my mind what to do with him, so I brought him all the way through the customs and everything rolled up in the rugs, with my umbrellas. He hated it, and I don't really care for him, and if there's a lost dogs' home here, for goodness' sake let me dispose of him painlessly. Down, my friend, down ! "

" Oh, he's not a bad little tyke," commented Mr. Hammond with the eye of a connoisseur. " But it's all this other stuff I'm thinking about. Look here, Miss Duquesne, can you manage to-night with one of these bag things and have the rest of the caboodle sent up to-morrow ? My man's sick or I'd have him come down for 'em now."

" Of course I'll manage. Only, wait a minute." Clare stood meditating while the youngest porter wrestled valiantly with the dachshund, and the others gazed with tolerant amusement at the eccentricities of this young lady, who at least seemed to be worth a good tip. " Now the point is," continued Clare, looking as though for enlightenment at the youngest porter, " my night things are in that bag, but my yellow dress, which I *must* wear this evening, is in this trunk."

Muriel was about to say, " Oh, don't trouble about that, because we don't change at night, " when she remembered that while Lord Powell's niece was staying at Miller's Rise they were to have late dinner.

" I know," cried Clare. " A sudden inspiration. Can you wait just two minutes ? I'll take the dress from the trunk and put it into the case, and then we'll be all right. Yes, go on holding the dog, please. Muriel, *chérie*, take my gloves. Mr. Hammond, will you be an angel and undo these straps for me ? "

Muriel gasped horror-stricken. Even Clare could surely not take these liberties with impunity. But Mr. Hammond seemed to have forgotten the new mare and to be reconciled to his novel rôle of angel. He knelt upon the platform, breathing heavily as he tugged at straps, unfastened locks, and chuckled to himself while Clare dived into a foam of tissue paper, billowing chiffon and frothing lace.

"There, just hold that a minute." Clare thrust a tray full of gossamer *lingerie* into the arms of the eldest porter, while she herself shook out the cloudy folds of primrose chiffon.

It must have been this that proved too much for the patience of Fritz. A fur-lined slipper fell from the tray, its fluffiness doubtless reminiscent of happy days of rabbiting. With a bound he broke from the hold of the youngest porter. A streak of yellow shot along the platform. The fur-lined slipper vanished, Mr. Hammond dropped the lid of the case, and the dachshund, free at last, forgot the tedium of his late experience.

Clare, regardless of her laden arms, started in pursuit. Muriel followed. Fritz, evading the ticket collector, dived under the bookstall, then out again towards the wicket-gate just as a tall, tweed-clad figure strolled leisurely on to the platform.

"Fritz!" cried Clare. "Catch him, catch him!"

A long arm shot down. A sudden squawk announced the breaking of Teutonic dreams of liberty, and Clare stood, her arms full of tissue paper, a filmy nightdress, a single bedroom slipper, face to face with Godfrey Neale.

Solemnly he held out to her a mangled slipper and an armful of protesting, elongated dachshund.

"I think that these are yours," he said.

For a moment Muriel saw them stand in silence. Then, simultaneously, they broke out into uncontrollable laughter.

IX

"OF course, if it had been your dog, Mu, it would have run into the curate," Connie observed cuttingly.

"But I haven't got a dog," sighed Muriel.

Connie looked at her with pity. Really there were

times when she wondered whether Muriel was quite all
there.

Mumps at Heathcroft had conspired with measles in London
to throw Connie once again into Clare's company. School
had broken up early, and Connie arrived at Miller's Rise two
days after Clare's spectacular descent upon her family. She
failed to appreciate the honour.

"Never in my life did I see any one make so much fuss of
a girl. You're all daft. Mother's as set up as a pouter
pigeon because she's got Lord Powell's niece staying here, and
Mrs. Neale brings Godfrey at last to call—if you can say that
it was a call. I wouldn't stand this eleventh hour patronage
from a duchess, let alone just Mrs. Neale, and every one knows
that she's crazy anyway. And look at Father! The way he
goes on as though he'd never seen a girl before."

"Connie, don't be horrid."

"Horrid yourself. You see if I'm not right. And Mother
can't stand her really, only she won't say anything before she's
had a chance to show her off to the rest of Marshington."

"That isn't true. You're being simply horrid because you
think it's clever, and you're jealous of Clare because Father
takes a lot of notice of her. It's only because she's a visitor.
You're always so unreasonable."

"Wait till she's been in the house a bit longer, and you'll
see who's unreasonable."

Muriel turned away and left Connie to her dark prophecies.
There were times when her younger sister exasperated her by
a shrewd interpretation of their parents' motives which Muriel
rejected as both unpleasant and untrue. Connie had no
business to go about saying nasty things about people, just to
pretend that she knew more about Life than Muriel who was
grown up.

That conversation took place the day before Mrs. Hammond
opened her campaign. She was sitting before the dressing-
table in her room, finishing her morning toilet. She knew
that in her dressing-jacket, with her plump arms bare from
the elbow, she looked girlish and very charming. The silver
in her hair gleamed like moonlight rather than Time's theft

of colour. She rather liked to see it spread softly about her shoulders before she coiled it high upon her head.

From the dressing-room she could hear her husband whistling through his teeth, as a stable boy whistles when he grooms a horse. Through the open door she could see him standing before his shaving-glass, brushing vigorously his wiry thatch of hair.

Mrs. Hammond set down her own brush and called softly : " Arthur ! "

The whistling stopped. Mr. Hammond put down his brushes and began to flex and unflex his arms, then ran his hands down the firm line from his arm-pits to his thighs.

" Hardly an ounce of spare flesh, by gosh," he remarked irrelevantly. " Few chaps o' my age could say the same thing. Have you seen Ted Hobson ? great coarse-looking, over-fed fellow, he's grown. Lifts his elbow a bit too often they say. Nothing like that for——"

" Arthur, you know I think that while Clare is here we ought to give a dinner-party."

" Of course I don't object to a moderate tipple myself——"

A little pucker of thought appeared on Mrs. Hammond's forehead. " I was thinking of just a few people, the Marshall Gurneys perhaps, and Colonel Cartwright, and Mr. Vaughan now that Delia's away. Arthur ! Are you listening ? "

" Yes, yes, my dear. Let 'em all come. Have a dozen dinner-parties for all I care."

" And the Neales, Arthur. I returned her call yesterday, but she was out with those everlasting dogs."

" Knows a good dog, the old lady. Yes, go ahead. Ask the Neales. Ask the Prince of Wales. Ask the whole blooming royal family."

" Arthur, I do wish that you would take this seriously. You know perfectly well that it's as much your duty as mine to do what you can for the girls."

" Oho ! It's the girls, is it ? And what do you expect to get for them out of all this fussification, eh ? " He stood in the doorway now between the two rooms, smiling down at her, his eyes twinkling with amusement. " Are you going to marry Connie off to the vicar ? "

" You needn't pretend to be stupid when you aren't," snapped Mrs. Hammond. When she saw him in a good temper she could sometimes take a holiday from her habitual patience.

She began to gather up her rings, and slip them one after the other on to her white fingers. Here was the diamond half-hoop, her engagement ring. Arthur had been generous but unoriginal. Here was the emerald that he had bought during their honeymoon. Here, the ruby set between two splendid pearls that he had bought her after that affair. She twisted it round on her finger reflectively. Her gentle face hardened. From the dressing-room she could hear her husband jingling pencils, pennies and his watch, as he transferred them from the chest to his pockets. " Does he still keep her photograph in his watch case ? " she wondered. That would be like Arthur, to repent extravagantly, and then to keep one little trace of his misdeed to sigh over.

Mrs. Hammond was not a sentimentalist. She clapped the ruby ring down on top of the emerald and diamond, and smiled faintly without too much bitterness as she heard the faint whirring sound of Arthur winding up his watch. It was his inevitable prelude to descent for breakfast.

" You'll order some more Burgundy, Arthur, won't you ? "

" Better have a few bottles of fizz up while we're about it, hadn't we ? " Mr. Hammond was dressed and disposed to take the world and the dinner-party more seriously. Like many middle-aged men he laid aside maturity with his clothes, and looked like a schoolboy in pyjamas, feeling like one too.

" Not champagne, I think, Arthur. We don't want to be thought ostentatious. Things must be right."

Reluctantly he agreed. Though his taste in parties differed from hers, he had to admit that in these things she was right. Although he chaffed her, he paid this tribute of acknowledgment to the long years of patient sowing of the social ground in Marshington until now at last the Neales were ripe for harvest.

Half amused at the object of her ambition, pleased to allow her to please herself if that did not interfere with his comfort, proud that she was successful in the quest that she had undertaken, Arthur Hammond went downstairs to order some more of the best Burgundy.

X

DINNER was over. It had succeeded so far beyond Mrs. Hammond's wildest dreams. Mrs. Neale had talked dogs and horses with Mr. Hammond, and Clare had been effectively subdued between Colonel Cartwright and the curate. The colonel himself had lent a distinguished air of political interest to the party, proving that these " confounded Radicals will be the death of the country, Mrs. Hammond. All this talk of Home Rule and Insurance and whatnot. What I say is that the people were happy enough before Lloyd George began to give 'em eightpennyworth of conceit of themselves." Mrs. Marshall Gurney, whose efforts to disengage Godfrey Neale's attention from Muriel had been unavailing, had been forced to console herself with the admirable saddle of mutton and the carnations from Kingsport, ninepence each. And the *soufflé* had been a dream, and Connie looked quite nice in her blue dress, and, best of all, something had happened to Muriel to startle her out of her usual dumb nervousness. Godfrey Neale really seemed to be quite taken by her. Why not ? Mrs. Hammond looking down the charmingly appointed table smiled to herself. Why not, indeed, why not ?

Afterwards, when the men reappeared from their cigars and excellent port, there was music in the drawing-room. As he entered, Godfrey Neale looked hurriedly round the room for Clare Duquesne. He was uneasy and puzzled. All through the interminable dinner he had searched across the barrier of flowers for Clare's charming face, but the ninepenny carnations had blocked his view. Once he heard her laugh, full-throated and merry. And all the time Muriel's prim little voice had told him tale after tale of Clare at school, Clare on the Continent, Clare galloping wildly along the sands at Hardrascliffe on a rough hackney, after a mad Saturday outing with a school friend's brother. Godfrey felt somehow that he would not have liked that brother, but he listened to the tales, greedy for more. Muriel, delighted to find in a man such unexpected interest and sympathy, unlocked to him the doors of her mind, and poured forth all the wistful hero-worship hitherto suppressed for fear of ridicule. Godfrey, completely oblivious of her, sunned himself in the wonder of Clare's swift vitality. Only when Muriel had left the past for the future did he check her with abrupt, almost dis-courteous questioning, afflicted suddenly again with his worst kind of stammering. She had faltered then, played with her fork, and looked up at him with wide, wondering eyes. So, for a moment, he had seen, not Clare, but Muriel, facing her as for the first time and noticing her solemn childish face, her mobile mouth, and the questioning trustfulness of her slow, quiet glance.

In a moment she had answered his question, and each lost the sense of the other in the concentration of their thoughts on Clare.

At first, on looking round the drawing-room, he did not see her ; then she became clear to him, withdrawn from the circle round the fireplace, sitting with head erect against a heavy background of dark curtains. The gloom of the unlit window-bay had quenched the glowing crimson of her dress, but its folds of stiff brocade flowed round her like the drapery in a Pre-Renaissance drawing. The dress covered her arms, but left her shoulders bare, so that her clasped hands lay together on her lap like a pale flower, and the faint glimmer of her perfect shoulders moved him to sudden anger against the shadow that robbed him of the purity of their line.

Why did she wear that queer outrageous dress ? Why had she never spoken to him before dinner, but only smiled demurely as she bowed ? What right had she to come straight from Ostend and Naples to Marshington, where the girls were all dull and stiff ? Besides, she was fast. That ridiculous exhibition at the station. That was just the sort of thing that Godfrey hated. And his mother disliked her, though as usual she said nothing, and—well, altogether Godfrey felt that he had good reason to be angry with Clare Duquesne.

He pushed his way through the chairs to the window seat, disregarding Mrs. Hammond's gentle invitation and Phyllis Marshall Gurney's pallid smile. He sat down on the narrow window seat beside her, making himself as uncomfortable as possible out of spite against her. There was a wretched draught.

"Are you going to sing, Miss Duquesne?" he asked.

His usually friendly voice bristled with his grievance.

Clare looked up at him in surprise. "Who told you that I sang?"

"Miss Hammond told me during dinner that you are going to be a professional singer. Are you?"

Clare laughed, still sitting upright with her hands lying on her wine-red dress. He could only see the profile of her face.

"That is as may be. It is not so easy as I had thought to become a great prima donna. They want me to work. I detest working." She shrugged her bare, smooth shoulders. "Life is too short for spending its best years in stuffy German parlours singing scales that no one but an old professor wants to hear." Suddenly she turned upon him her full loveliness. "Why do you ask?"

"I—I——" Godfrey Neale himself was at a loss for words, feeling gauche as any country bumpkin.

"Do you disapprove?" Clare continued cheerfully.

"Yes," he said, unreasoningly rude. "I do. Decidedly. You, singing for the public, for just any ass——"

She opened her dark eyes very wide. "But why not? Not all the public are asses. Besides, my mother does it. She acts."

"Oh, I did—didn't mean that. I mean, it seems somehow such a waste."

"Waste? *Comme vous êtes drôle! Ils sont tous fous, les anglais.*" She laughed again, teasing him, knowing how much he hated for her to speak French, partly because it was a

foreign language, partly because he dreaded more than anything in the world that she should make a fool of him. " Why
a waste ? Is it not better to sing for the many than for the
few ? "

" No, no. It is not." He fumbled indignantly with his
ideas, only knowing that he could not bear the thought of
her, standing on show for any fool to gape at, any ill-bred,
foreign fool, greasy Germans, nincompoop Frenchmen,
Italians—ugh !

" How very English you are, Mr. Neale. That proprietary
instinct. You want everything for yourself, land, ladies, music.
You would like to put up a notice on me like you put up on
your woods. ' Trespassers will be prosecuted.' "

" When did you see my woods ? "

" Hush, I want to hear Mr. Smallwood sing."

Godfrey could not sing. He disliked fellows who chirruped
inanely in drawing-rooms ; but he had to sit there, consoling
himself by watching Clare's intent, uplifted face.

> " O flower of all the world, O flower of all,
>   I see thee in my garden and I dare
> To love thee, and though my deserts be small,
>   Thou art the only flower I would wear."

" O flower of all the world," thought Godfrey, seeing
only Clare's glowing dress, her hands, her perfect arms.

" I dare to love thee," triumphed Dennis Smallwood's
pleasant baritone voice.

Clare Duquesne was going back to Germany, to flirt with
dapper little German officers. A good thing that she was
going. Godfrey knew her type.

" A rotten song, that, isn't it ? " he growled. " Smallwood
plays a decent game of tennis. I wish that he'd stick to it."

" He sings rather well. Ah ! *Mon Dieu !* "

" What is it ? " Godfrey was all solicitude.

" Nothing. Except that our friend Connie is going to sing,
and I—I have heard her before."

Her whisper soothed the young man's ruffled feelings. He

did what all the evening he had been intending not to do. This connection with the Hammond *ménage* had gone far enough. He said :

"Look here, do you ever care to ride, Miss Duquesne ? "

"When I have a mount," she answered.

"When the birds go north again ! " shrilled Connie.

" I wondered if perhaps, I've got rather a jolly little mare, a perfect lady's hack. My mother was going to ride her, but she hasn't been awfully fit, and hasn't been riding much. It would be a perfect charity if you would be good enough to exercise her. If you could come up one afternoon."

Clare smiled demurely. " Well, if Mrs. Hammond does not object, we might all come up one afternoon."

" All ? "

" Well, you can hardly expect me to go alone, surely ? "

He saw that it was not possible, but a new scheme was at work in his mind.

"Look here, I'll get the mater to ask up the Hammond girls one afternoon next week, if you'll sing to us to-night."

Clare frowned. " You see," she confided, " I've received not exactly orders but intimations that I am to keep in the background to-night. I'll sing when I go to tea with your mother."

" You'll sing to-night," said Godfrey. He was determined now that she should do so, not so much because he wanted to hear her, as because he wanted her to do something just because he willed it. " Just wait until Connie has sent those birds north again, and then you shall sing."

She shook her head, but as Connie left the piano, Godfrey rose.

" Mrs. Hammond," he said, " we have had a great stroke of luck. I have persuaded Miss Duquesne to sing."

So Mrs. Hammond had to be delighted, and Clare followed Muriel to the piano, and whispered to her. Muriel nodded once or twice, a frown of responsibility upon her face. She was a good accompanist, and had played for Clare many times at Heathcroft.

Mr. Hammond, leaning back in his chair, winked at Colonel Cartwright. " Now we shall have a treat," he said.

Muriel began to play. Her soft dress faded into the white walls of the room. Her hair was a brooding shadow above her earnest face. But about Clare was nothing pale nor shadowy. Her vivid dress had caught all light and colour from the room, and held them, glowing with barbaric splendour. She stood, not stooping over her music like the Marshington young ladies, but by herself in front of the piano, her head lifted proudly with the triumphant power of undaunted youth.

The accompaniment paused. The last chord hung for a moment poised above the waiting stillness. Across the room Clare looked full into the expectant face of Godfrey Neale.

Then she sang.

She had chosen Mignon's song, and at first she sang plaintively the cry of the lost maiden. But, at the end of the verse, with the sweeping melody of the refrain, she released the full power of her voice.

" Kennst du es wohl ? Dahin ! Dahin !
Möcht' ich mit dir, o mein Geliebter, ziehn."

Mrs. Hammond pulled herself together. She could not understand German. Neither, she was thankful to reflect, could Arthur or the girls ; but of one thing she was certain. No one could have sung with such impassioned appeal a song that was completely proper.

She decided that Clare must sing no more.

Directly the song was over, she rose amid the spontaneous applause thàt for once replaced the conventional thanks of Marshington " musical at homes."

" Thank you so much, Clare, dear. That was very nice. And how clever of you to remember all that German by heart. You must have worked very hard. And now, Arthur, did you say that you were going to carry the colonel and Mr. Neale off to bridge ? Mr. Vaughan, you play, don't you ? "

So Godfrey heard Clare sing no more, but at the end of the

evening, when the company met again to say good-bye, she smiled up at him.

" Well," she said, " and when are we coming to tea ? "

All the way home in his mother's stuffy little brougham, Godfrey forgot Clare and talked about the roof to be repaired on the Thaskholme cottages, and the agent at Mardlehammar ; but as he ran up the shallow steps of the Weare Grange he suddenly saw Clare standing, the delicate contour of her face outlined against the curtain, her provocative smile teasing him.

" Damned pretty little minx," he told himself, determined that he would not be caught so soon. And, as he undressed, the song which he found himself whistling, with a cheerful disregard for time or tune, was not Clare's song, but Dennis Smallwood's.

" O flower of all the world, O flower of all."

XI

DURING the morning, Connie had hoped that it would rain ; but wind and weather never favoured her. She walked mutinously along the muddy road, splashing in and out of puddles in the vain hope that she might thus leave her mark upon Clare's polished boots. How exactly like Clare, to be walking booted and habited along the road to the Weare Grange to ride with Godfrey Neale, while Connie, who adored horses, was only going to tea with his mother.

" And she's mad," reflected Connie bitterly.

" It was nice of him to send for the saddle," remarked Clare. " I thought that I should have to walk there carrying it on my head like the ladies walk in Palestine."

" What ? " said Connie wearily. " Have you been there too ? "

Muriel laughed nervously. It was difficult to keep the peace.

" We've never been allowed to ride since Father's accident," she said. "Years ago he let his favourite horse down on the road from Kepplethorpe market. It was badly hurt, I think, and he had two ribs broken. But he was frightfully angry with it for failing him, so he never said anything to anyone, though he must have been in great pain. He just walked back to the house and got his gun, and went back and shot it. He fainted afterwards, and was brought home and was frightfully ill for ages, and when he got better he sold all his hunters and wouldn't let any of us ride again. But he loves driving."

"Ah, poor Mr. Hammond," murmured Clare, but without much interest, for the road had turned, and to the right the hedge was broken by tall gates of delicately wrought ironwork, as fragile in appearance and as strong in reality as the barrier that enclosed the Neales from Marshington. Beyond the gates, half a mile of straight, shining road led to the grey square house. There was no park, but in the fields between the house and highway fine elms and chestnuts spread their naked boughs above the great Weare cattle, grazing with slow serenity on the vivid grass.

"So this is the Weare Grange," observed Clare. "What a delightful house! But, *Dieu*, how dull to live here all the year round."

But to Muriel the place was magic. She could not believe that real people moved behind those solemn windows. The still winter day, the cold light of the pale sun, the mouldering stonework of the terrace, were all part of a waking dream. A thrush, starting suddenly from a wet bough, shook down the rain-drops on to her face. She woke from her dream. This was the Weare Grange. She and Connie and Clare were going there to tea. This was the amazing adventure which the gods had brought her.

She did hope that Connie would behave.

The bell of the Weare Grange was one of the most powerful defences of that social fortress. It had a round, rusty head, and a long, stringy neck. Muriel put up her hand (and incidentally her new glove) and pulled. There was a harsh screeching sound. The neck extended three good inches from the wall. She let it go. Nothing happened. She pulled again. No faintest tinkle reached her ears.

"Let me try," said Connie.

"No, no, it may have rung "

They waited on the shallow steps, smudged with bird droppings and the multitudinous paw-marks of the dogs. Muriel's courage began to trickle away more rapidly than it had come. No wonder that only the Marshall Gurneys from all Marshington had dared to call upon the Neales. That bell was in itself a social snub.

"You're no good. Let me try," urged Connie. She thrust Muriel aside, pressing her knee against the wall, and tugged at the bell with both hands. A grinding, screeching sound, followed by a far-off tinkle, rewarded her just as a cheerful-faced young manservant appeared in answer to Muriel's second ring.

He took Muriel unprepared.

"Er—er—is Mrs. Neale at home ? "

There was a blurred vision of vast hall, a confusion of shy greetings, the departure of Godfrey and Clare to the stables, and the fortress was entered.

"Once we really get started it will be easier," Muriel told herself.

It was not so. Mrs. Neale had dragged herself away from her kennels and rabbit-hutches at her son's request, but even her devotion to him could not make her genial to the Hammond girls. She disliked the whole affair, and only the knowledge that she could not stop it had brought her to face Muriel and Connie, seated in her great eighteenth-century drawing-room, across the wreckage of her afternoon.

She attacked Muriel first.

"Do you ride too ? " she asked.

"No, I'm afraid I don't."

"I often used to meet your father with the Weare Valley hounds."

Muriel nodded dumbly.

There was a pause.

"Your sister ride ? "

Connie made no answer. She was looking through the long windows, from which she could see Clare and Godfrey cantering side by side along the level green of the wet grass.

Mrs. Neale turned again to Muriel.

" You like dogs ? "

" Not very much."

" Cats ? " flashed Mrs. Neale.

" Fairly, when they're clean."

A withering glance. " Perhaps you like goldfish ? "

" Fairly. Yes. I mean I do rather," confessed the hapless Muriel.

Enchanted castles are apt to conceal an ogress or two. Mrs. Neale felt disposed to let the Weare Grange live up to its reputation. Between her abrupt boredom and Muriel's timidity, the afternoon appeared interminable to Connie. She hated the white and draughty drawing-room. She hated the small gilt clock ticking in the corner. She hated the mixture of ceremony and discomfort, of wealth and squalor that characterized the house shared by Godfrey and his mother. The place seemed to be getting at her, making her feel vulgar and schoolgirlish. The thought of Clare and Godfrey riding together in the winter sunshine maddened her with jealousy.

But it was Muriel who relieved the situation.

After a longer pause than ever, she looked round the room and saw a single photograph on a table near the fire-place.

" Is that Mr. Neale when he was a little boy ? " she asked in desperation.

That was enough for Mrs. Neale. Upon one subject alone could she be trusted to break her habitual silence, and Muriel's ingenuous questioning went direct to her heart. From the drawing-room to the smoking-room, from the smoking-room to the long gallery marched the procession of three, recapitulating pictorially and photographically the stupendous progress of Godfrey Neale from the nursery to Oxford, and from Oxford to the mastership of the Weare Grange and Mardlehammar. Connie, stumbling behind the other two, tripping over dogs and carpentering tools, grew full and more full of passionate resentment. When the riders appeared again by the terrace,

so warm, so happy, so pleased with life and with themselves,
Connie, who was neither warm nor happy, nor pleased, could
bear it no longer.

"Well," snapped Mrs. Neale, with her stiff smile that
seemed to creak from lack of use. "Good ride?"

"Ripping. Golden Girl went like a bird, and Miss
Duquesne is a real sp—sportswoman."

Connie pushed her way past Muriel down the terrace
steps.

"Mr. Neale, can I try?"

"Oh, Connie," began Muriel's shocked voice.

"Do you ride, Miss Hammond? I'm so sorry. I thought
that you didn't. I would have found you a mount," lied
Godfrey.

"I used to ride a lot before Father had his accident and
would not let us any more."

The story was well known in Marshington, where picturesque
incidents were not common. Here was a trouble that Mrs.
Neale could understand.

"If she really wants to, let her have a trot down the drive
while I order tea."

"Connie, you can't. You can't really," protested Muriel.
To have stormed successfully the Neale citadel, to have come
creditably through the ordeal of the drawing-room, and then
for Connie to behave like this, was too bad.

But Connie was determined. The dogged look which
Mrs. Hammond knew well upon her husband's face had
descended upon Connie.

As for Godfrey, he had no desire to ride with a lumpish
schoolgirl after that wonderful afternoon, and yet even he
felt a slight compunction at the way in which he had used the
two Hammond girls. He knew the glacial atmosphere of
his mother's drawing-room.

"But she hasn't a habit or anything." Muriel pleaded.

"That doesn't matter. I have often ridden without,"
laughed Clare. "Here, take my whip."

She held Golden Girl for Godfrey, while he went to tie
his own horse to a ring on the terrace wall. She watched him

loosen Blue Boy's girths and tie one end of the reins round the ring.

" Aren't you going to ride ? " asked Connie.

But even for his conscience' sake Godfrey would not risk the breaking of the yellow mare's knees.

" No, I think I shall walk this time."

Connie stood before the mare. Somehow she seemed to have grown miraculously taller. The saddle upon which her rider must sit was miles up in the air. The chestnut head tossed restlessly. Even Clare's caressing fingers could not quell the baleful frenzy of the rolling eye.

Godfrey returned.

" Now, put your foot on my knee, Miss Hammond, and hold the reins so, and the saddle here. I shall count one, two, three, up. When I say up, you must jump. Don't worry about the stirrup. That comes later."

Connie obeyed the directions. Golden Girl seemed to grow before her like Alice in Wonderland after she had eaten the magic cake. Was it a cake she ate ? Connie could not remember. She could hardly see the sky, or Clare, or Godfrey. A huge yellow mare blotted out heaven and earth.

" One, two, three, UP ! " called Godfrey. " Oh, but you must jump, Miss Hammond."

" So sorry. I wasn't quite ready," lied Connie. " Will you count again ? "

" One, two, three, JUMP ! "

Connie jumped. Unluckily the mare jumped also, and Connie landed back into a puddle sending a shower of water over Godfrey's perfect breeches.

" Oh, Connie, give it up. Don't make a fool of yourself," whispered Muriel. Then she remembered her own school-days, and the rock. " Look how you are splashing poor Mr. Neale."

" That's all right," said Godfrey heroically. After all it was the Hammond girl who was making a fool of herself, not he. " Now then, we'll try again."

Connie jumped. A strong hand seemed to lift her up, up into the cold clear air. She jumped with such a will that she almost seemed to fall on to the other side of the mare, but not quite. There she was, mounted at last, while Godfrey Neale placed her muddy boot in the stirrup, and Clare arranged her short serge skirt.

"Ah, now that is excellent," said Clare. "Hold the reins so, and press your left knee well against the pommel. Sit square and face the horse's head."

"You and your horse's head!" laughed Connie. "You talk as though I'd never been up before."

But for all her defiant gaiety, she felt that indeed she hardly had. Golden Girl was different from the old, lop-lobbing pony. When she thrust down her disquieting head, there seemed to be little enough between Connie and the gravel drive. Still there she was. She looked patronizingly down at the group below, at Mrs. Neale, grimly amused, at Clare laughing back at her, at Muriel, white-faced and anxious.

"I'm ready," she said.

They began to walk sedately down the drive. Now that Golden Girl was actually moving, Connie found it less alarming. Indeed, she told herself, it was good beyond all dreams of goodness. The great house gaped at her from a score of long, blank windows. On the steps stood Clare, now only a spectator in the drama, and by the side of the mare walked Godfrey Neale, Connie's companion for as long as she could keep the mare's head turned away from the house down the long drive.

"You all right?" he asked.

"Rather. Don't bother to hold the reins, please. I'm really quite used to it."

Dubiously he let her go. Just to show her independence, she touched the mare lightly with her whip. It started.

"Steady, steady, old girl. Ride her on the snaffle, Miss Hammond. Her mouth's awfully sensitive. She won't stand the curb."

Curbs and snaffles were all the same to Connie. These slippery, writhing strips of leather slid through her hands as the mare tossed her head. She struggled to arrange them to her satisfaction. In another minute Mr. Neale might say,

" Don't you think that we had better turn ? " and back they
would go to that awful drawing-room and to Clare's easy
triumph.

Connie sat straight, her red, wind-blown head high. The
reins slipped in her left hand, but her right held Clare's riding-
crop. She would show them that even if she could not ride
like Clare she too was a sportswoman.

Again she flicked her whip. The mare broke into an
uneasy trot, shaking Connie up and down in the unfamiliar
saddle.

" Hold hard," called Godfrey, stretching out his hand for
the slack rein.

" It's all right. This is splendid," cried Connie and, with
set teeth, gave the mare another cut.

The mare shuddered. For one moment Connie felt the
earth rise to meet her. Then she was suddenly jolted down
into the saddle. The shaking trot gave place to a rhythmical
rise and fall, the wind brushed past her, touching her wide
bright eyes, her flying hair, and Connie was away at full gallop
down the drive.

" Stop her," cried Clare, running down the terrace steps.
" Stop her, you idiot. The mare's bolting."

" It's all right. The gate will stop her," Godfrey called.
For all his swiftness he could not reach her now.

" It won't. We left it open. Don't you remember ? "

" Oh, damn ! " Connie mattered less to Godfrey than the
mare, but both were serious propositions.

He stopped now. Clare, running, was nearly up to him.
He faced her on the drive. There was nobody else in the
world then but Clare and Godfrey, looking for some solution
of the problem into each other's eyes. Muriel, hurrying
behind Clare, felt this even then.

Without a word, Clare ran back to Blue Boy.

" Quick. You must catch her before she reaches the road,"
she said, tugging at the knotted strap.

" The girth's not fastened," cried Muriel, who knew just
enough to see this.

Godfrey never listened. He was mounted, had turned,

and was off along the drive in pursuit of Connie's flying figure.

The yellow mare was going hard, making for the gate at the south end of the drive. Godfrey, seeing this, swerved suddenly to the right.

"Where's he going ? The gate's not there," cried Muriel, running blindly along the drive. Clare followed, picking her way delicately among the chalky puddles. Then she stopped, watching the stooping figure on the great black horse.

"He's going to take the hedge. And he said that he'd never found a horse to leap it yet ! Bravo, the sportsman !" she breathed. Her eyes shone. A smile of excitement parted her lips. The dimple flickered on her cheek.

Muriel gasped. "To jump ? With his girth unfastened, and only one rein ? " She nearly sobbed. "He'll never do it."

"He will. He will. Did you ever see such riding ? "

Above the blackness of the hedge, against the transparent, water-coloured shimmer of the sky, the great horse and his rider thrust up suddenly a black silhouette. They hung for a moment thus, poised between earth and sky, then disappeared.

"Ah, good," whispered Clare, with a little sigh of pure enjoyment.

"But they'll be killed," moaned Muriel.

"Not they," laughed Clare.

The two girls walked in silence down the drive. By the gate the hoof-marks swerved to one side, cutting deeply into the turf, as though Connie had made one desperate effort to pull up. Then they went on again, along the rough, chalk road.

"They've gone a long way," remarked Clare imperturbably. "Your sister is having a good run for her money."

"Oh, Clare, don't joke. What if they are killed ? "

"Killed ? Nonsense. Why, here they are ! "

Over the brow of the rising ground they came, Godfrey leading both the horses, Connie by his side, limping a little, spattered with mud from head to foot, her hair wild, her cheeks flaming.

"I didn't fall off," she announced jubilantly. "Not until

right at the very end. Oh, it was glorious. I galloped, and
Mr. Neale galloped. We had a race, hadn't we, Mr. Neale ?
Did you see him jump the hedge ? Oh, Muriel, you do look
queer. Your eyes are popping out of your head. Were you
frightened ? I wasn't frightened a bit, although we went at
a terrific rate right down the field."

"I was," laughed Godfrey. "I was in a blue funk."

Clare looked at him. "How high is that fence ? "

"I don't know. N—nothing much." It confronted them
then, laced thick and high with blackthorn, a nasty obstalce
under the best conditions.

"With a loose girth and one rein," half-whispered Clare.
"That was great riding, Mr. Neale."

They walked back to the house together, Connie chattering
all the way. She was upborne upon the wings of triumph.
She had conquered her fear, conquered Muriel's prudishness,
and Clare's attractions, and the indifference of the Weare
Grange. She was happy.

Muriel saw her happiness with a sudden heartache, for she
saw also what Connie did not see.

She saw that this adventure was not even their adventure.
It was Clare's and Godfrey's—Clare's because she had taken
upon herself the command of rescue, Godfrey's because her
whisper of praise had fallen upon him like an accolade. Connie
had been merely a pretext for Godfrey to perform deeds of
daring before Clare. At tea-time, though with remorseful
attention Godfrey handed to Connie cakes and little biscuits
such as she loved, it was Clare to whom, in the intervals of
his duties as a host, he turned and smiled.

XII

THERE was an unwritten rule at Miller's Rise that
one bathed at night, not in the morning. Morning
baths consumed the washing-up water, and even if
they did not they had not been the custom, and so were not

approved. Muriel, who accepted all domestic theories with reverence, frowned anxiously as, on her way to her mother's room, she heard Clare's voice upraised in ablutionary song behind the bathroom door.

Ever since the episode of the ride a week before, Muriel had been worried by her mother's attitude to Clare.

Mrs. Hammond was polishing her nails when Muriel came in. It was their custom to hold a little conference in Mrs. Hammond's room before breakfast if Mr. Hammond had left the house early upon business.

" Well, dear ? You dressed ? Are you tired after last night ? " Mrs. Hammond's nails shone like polished pink glass as she held them up to the light. " Muriel, that wasn't Clare whom I heard just now in the bathroom, was it ? Didn't Annie take her some hot water ? Surely you told her that we——"

" I expect it was because of the dance last night. It was too late to bath when we came in." Recently, Muriel always seemed to be explaining Clare's actions to her mother. It was a duty that she hated.

" I think it unnecessary. Clare is evidently a little selfish, or else inconsiderate. This house is not a hotel."

Wasn't it ? For a moment of bitterness, Muriel wondered whether to Clare it was much more. She crossed to the window, and stood looking out into the rain-soaked garden.

" Muriel," her mother's voice continued from the dressing-table, " do you know how long your friend intends to stay ? "

" Her father comes to England on the 24th." Muriel knew what would follow.

" Oh." There was another pause. Muriel could hear the soft brush, brush of her mother's nail pad. " Well, of course that's all right. We can manage, I suppose, though of course it comes rather hard on me now that I am so busy over Christmas and everything. Still, if Clare likes to take us as she finds us, I dare say that we shall get through. Still I had thought that perhaps she would have been able to—— Oh, and that reminds me, about Saturday night, dear, at the Warings'. There is no need when we go out like that for

Clare to push herself forward in that way. She is only our visitor, after all, and that time Mrs. Waring particularly wanted to hear how Connie's singing had improved. There was no *need* for a stranger to monopolize the whole programme."

" But they kept asking Clare to sing."

" Naturally, they had to say something out of politeness, but nobody meant her to go on and on like that. However, I should not have mentioned even that if it had not been for last night."

Muriel could feel the stiffening of her mother's figure before the looking-glass. She, too, braced herself for battle.

" I—I don't know what you mean, mother."

" Now you know perfectly well what I mean. Clare is a very nice girl in a way, and up till now it has been quite a pleasant visit. I have managed to keep things running smoothly. But I realize that, with her continental upbringing, she has rather different standards from those which we think proper in Marshington. How many dances did she have last night with Godfrey Neale ? "

Then Muriel knew that Clare would have to go. .

" Oh, five or six perhaps. But——"

Between the mist-shrouded valley and the sodden lawn, Muriel could see a vision of Clare and Godfrey as they had danced together, of Clare's laughing face, of her strong young arm pressed firmly against his black coat, of the swing and balance of their turning figures. She caught her breath.

" Well," remarked Mrs. Hammond, " that may be all right for Ostend, but when you consider the position that Godfrey holds in Marshington——"

The dancing figures swayed towards Muriel. So near they came, they almost warmed her with their glowing happiness. She pressed her small, cold hands against the window-sill, and gazed out towards the dripping trees.

" Just come and fasten my dress, dear. No, the bottom hooks first. Clare's very selfish. She wants everything for herself."

Was she ? Was she ? Muriel, fastening hooks and eyes at complicated angles knew that in spite of last night, in spite of everything, she had a fierce desire for Clare to stay. What if she did dance with Godfrey Neale ? Who else could match her for charm and for daring ? Yet, even while Muriel told herself that this was as it should be, she remembered the dragging hours of the Kingsport dance, while she sat by the wall and the couples passed her, the girls' dresses swinging out against her knees. She remembered how she had tried to compose her face into an interested yet indifferent smile above her fan, as though she did this sort of thing because she liked it, not because her mother's valiant efforts to fill her programme were unavailing.

That fear of being left out was horrible.

" If Clare does go," thought Muriel, " that won't make Godfrey look at me."

She went downstairs to order breakfast. " If Clare doesn't go, Godfrey will never look at anyone else." Why care whom Godfrey looked at, whom he knew ? Why did she feel this silent force of her mother's will coming between her and the most glorious friendship that she could ever know ? Who cared if Clare danced every dance with Godfrey Neale—not that she would, because she said that he bored her just a little when he was not riding or dancing or doing something with his body ?

If only all the people whom she loved would care for one another and not make her feel disloyal because she could not share in their distastes, how simple life would be !

As she ran downstairs, Muriel heard her mother meet Clare on the landing.

" Well, Clare, good morning. How are you after last night ? Not tired ? That's right. I'm so glad. *So* nice you looked too ! "

XIII

CLARE went ; the winter dances came, and Muriel's programme still remained half empty. Connie returned to Heathcroft. Aunt Beatrice came to stay and went. Muriel continued to be grown up. Her hair sat more securely on her shoulders now. She grew accustomed to the whiteness of her neck above an evening frock. She paid calls with her mother; she dusted the drawing-room. She went to church assiduously, seeking in the Early Service for an emotional satisfaction that she could find no other way. She bought and read shilling copies of the classics. She began to study Astronomy with the help of three second-hand textbooks and a toy telescope, but here she found herself handicapped by lack of instruments and tuition. She did the Nursing Club accounts for her mother, who was at this time much occupied by charitable works. She took piano lessons with Fräulein Heissler every Wednesday in Kingsport. The days passed quickly enough, and yet something seemed to be lacking. Then, in April, came Clare's letter.

Muriel dear, it may amuse you to hear that I am going to be married. His name is Ferdinando Alvarados. He is a Spaniard, but he lives mostly in South America, where it is gloriously warm and you live on oranges and play the guitar. I am not going to have a career, thank Heaven, but I'm going to try being very rich instead. Félix and Mamma are disappointed but resigned, and Ferdie is the most amusing thing God ever made. I adore him and am very happy. Needless to say, he thinks that I am the loveliest thing in the world, which just shows his good taste. When are you going to get married? How is dear, quaint Marshington? Did I ever write to thank you for the good time that you gave me there? I don't believe I did. Forgive me. I never was brought up properly, as I think that your mother saw. If you ever see Mr. Neale now, tell him that I never met a nicer mount than Golden Girl. My cousin's gees in Ireland were nothing to her.

Yours to eternity,

CLARE.

The letter came the day before the Conservative Club Picnic. Politics in Marshington were of particularly acute

interest that year. Mrs. Marshall Gurney, it is true, held
the presidency of the Club for the third time running, but
when Mrs. Hobson was elected treasurer Mrs. Waring had to
replace Mrs. Parker as the secretary.

"Whatever the men may choose to do," said Mrs. Parker,
justly indignant, "I will not countenance the introduction
of just anyone on our committee. Hobson himself may be a
very decent man and a good Conservative. But we never
have had a publican's wife on the committee, and if I can stop
it we never will. Even if the Duchess of Northumbria goes
in for indiscriminate toleration, in Annabelle Marshall Gurney
that sort of thing is pure affectation. One might as well be
a Radical, like all the Noncomformist clerks in Marshall
Gurney's office."

So Mrs. Parker left the committee, and Mrs. Waring
reigned in her stead. Mrs. Hammond, who had only recently
decided to show an interest in politics (" The new Conservative candidate was such a nice man "), after some mental
struggle resolved not to follow Mrs. Parker into the wilderness,
although she had once been a useful ally, but declared herself
a supporter of Democracy and Mrs. Marshall Gurney.

It was therefore particularly distressing that the day before
the picnic Mr. Hammond should have announced himself
to be unwell, and have retired to bed.

"Oh, well, dear," Mrs. Hammond told Muriel, "you will
just have to go alone."

"Oh, no, Mother. I should hate to do that. Do let me
stay and look after Father, you know that there's nothing
really wants doing. You go instead."

"It's quite impossible." Mrs. Hammond picked up her
husband's supper-tray. "I like to think that you can enjoy
yourself. Go along, dear, and have a good time. I shall
manage."

Muriel knew that her mother had wanted to go. She
knew that, as far as Mr. Hammond was concerned, the maids
could have administered to his wants. But she had slowly
come to realize that the passion which had once led Mrs.
Hammond to commit her single social indiscretion could

still draw her aside from that concentration on her position which had once or twice moved Muriel to vague uneasiness.

She had not wanted to go, and her spring hat had not come yet from Kingsport, and the morning of the picnic had been strained and harassed at home because of Father, and Mother's disappointment, and the rest of it. By the time that she arrived at the yard from whence the picnic was to start in hired waggonettes she was wishing that she never need have come.

There stood Mrs. Marshall Gurney with a bunch of primroses on her sables, and Mrs. Waring, looking elegantly worried as she stooped with her *lorgnette* over a bunch of papers, and Mrs. Hobson, fussing backwards and forwards between the gate and the already laden waggonettes. Everybody looked terribly smart and confident and self absorbed. The space between Muriel and the waggonettes was painfully wide. She wanted to shrink away on to her seat and be forgotten.

" Any room in the last waggonette ? " called Mrs. Marshall Gurney.

" Quite full up," returned Mrs. Hobson, with the metallic crispness of one who may have a Yorkshire accent but knows that she is as good as many of those who haven't.

" Any room in your carriage, Phyllis ? "

But Phyllis Marshall Gurney regretted that she had promised to keep the only seat available in her carriage for somebody else, and blushed deeply as she said it. Muriel was almost ready to retire defeated, when Delia Vaughan called to her from the first carriage. Grateful but embarrassed, Muriel went forward, and climbed in among the knees and new tweed skirts of the élite of Marshington. She counted them surreptitiously, Adelaide Waring and a cousin, Dennis Smallwood, Nancy Cartwright, Bobby Mason and Delia. A man for every girl except herself. Wise by experience, she sighed, thinking of the long day before her. At Heathcroft, if you had no partner, you could at least walk with the last couple in the crocodile. At Marshington it seemed that you could only sit and look forlorn among the sandwiches.

The waggonettes waited.

" Are we never going to start ? " asked Adelaide.

Mrs. Marshall Gurney and her committee were conferring hurriedly.

" Did anybody see Mr. Neale on the way down ? "

Nobody had enjoyed that honour.

" I suppose that he *is* coming ? "

From every waggonette Muriel could feel the tension of anxiety. A Primrose Picnic without Godfrey Neale would be like lamb without mint sauce. Phyllis Marshall Gurney's pretty face grew pale beneath her pink hat.

" Ah, here the conquering hero comes," laughed Nancy, who was still secure in the pose of *enfant terrible.* " It's more effective to be late, isn't it ? "

Godfrey Neale strolled into the yard. His breeches were beautiful, his smile the most disarming, his confidence superb. Phyllis Marshall Gurney gripped more tightly the hand-rail of her waggonette. Delia Vaughan nodded carelessly. Godfrey made his apology to the waiting committee, and moved towards the carriages.

Muriel calculated rapidly. If he joined the waggonette in which she sat he would make the numbers of males and females equal. She held her breath.

Godfrey hailed Miles Buchanan in the last carriage, exchanged a greeting with Phyllis Marshall Gurney in the second, and then climbed up beside Delia Vaughan in the first. The carriages rattled down the village street into a world glittering and green. In every meadow the grass stretched upright blades like thirsty tongues to drink from the dripping trees ; but the clouds had broken and blew about a radiant spring sky like wind-tossed feathers.

" It's going to be fine," observed Adelaide complacently. " I'm glad that I put on my new light tweeds."

" Stunning," commented Dennis, exhibiting his well-shaped leg. " What about my own light tweeds ? "

Everybody seemed to be in high spirits. After all, the drive would not be so bad, thought Muriel. She could watch the grey, flat road unwind like ribbon behind the waggonette. She could see the clay-red furrows of the ploughed land, and she could hear the cry of sea-birds circling behind and around the plough. Some magic lingered in the fresh spring air.

Lunch was pleasant enough too, although she found herself seated on an unsteady log between Mrs. Hobson and Colonel Cartwright, who had motored to the woods. He at least was bent upon enjoyment. As an old campaigner he insisted upon showing every one how to do everything, from lighting a fire with two matches, to opening ginger-beer bottles with a walking-stick.

"Dangerous things, picnics," he declared to Muriel, determined to show her how to be jolly too.

Anxious to learn, she said sedately :

"Why, Colonel ? "

He winked at her. "Ah, the spring, and a young man's fancy, happy hours and woodland bowers, and chaperons asleep under the trees."

"I don't think that that sounds very dangerous," said Muriel politely, and received a light flutter of laughter from the party as a reward for her *naïveté*.

But she was soon to learn where for her the danger lay.

After lunch Adelaide's cousin, Mr. Weathergay, said to Nancy :

"There's a jolly old church, I hear, at Ribbleswaite, that seems the sort of thing one ought to see. Won't you show it to me ? "

And Nancy giggled that churches weren't much in her line, but she wouldn't mind a walk.

Then Miles Buchanan bore off Freda Mason, and her two brothers wrangled for the right to escort Mrs. Farrell, a charming girl, who was staying with the Warings. The company scattered into couples and quartettes. Muriel still sat on her log, playing with a strand of long coarse grass, and hating picnics.

She saw neither the budding woods nor the delicate cream of primroses upon the banks. She saw only the ignominy of her own position, and with averted head she dug her fingers into the soft turf as couple after couple vanished through the trembling curtain of foliage. She was glad that her mother was not there to see her shame, and yet this probably only meant a short respite, because Mrs. Waring was certain to betray, as she had done before, the curious solitude of Mrs. Hammond's daughter.

From the other side of the abandoned meal she could hear Delia's careless voice :

" Well, you can lie and smoke in the sun if you like, Godfrey. The grass is wet, and you are growing fat from idleness, but I don't care. I, the only Socialist among you, am going to celebrate Primrose Day properly and pick primroses. Coming too, Muriel ? "

No wonder that Delia was unpopular, monopolizing Godfrey all through lunch, and then abandoning him to smoke his pipe alone. The sheer wanton waste of it appalled Muriel. She shook her head.

" No, thank you," she said, shivering a little at her courage. To have gone with Delia would have been to put an end to her misery, but it would also have been a confession of defeat.

Delia went, and Muriel was left alone upon her log. Bobby Mason, defeated by his brother in the contest for Mrs. Farrell, was pretending to do something scientific to the fire, and Mrs. Marshall Gurney was directing the repacking of the luncheon baskets. She looked round the clearing, then beckoned Bobby majestically to her side.

" Go and make yourself agreeable to the Hammond girl, for goodness' sake," she commanded. " We want to hold a committee meeting here."

Muriel could feel the young man approaching her. She guessed why he had come. She was half crying with shame and weariness.

" Like to see the jolly old church, Miss Hammond ? "

Dumbly she nodded. They too went.

The young birches curtsied round them. A delicate earthy scent of ferns and leaf mould and wet grass rose to their nostrils. Muriel saw and felt nothing, but she heard Bobby Mason say :

" Been to Burley Woods before, Miss Hammond ? "

" No. Have you ? "

" Er—no."

There was a pause.

" Going to play golf this year, Miss Hammond ? "

" No. I don't think so. Are you ? "

" No—er, in the office you know. Men like myself haven't much time."

" I suppose not."

The silence grew more gloomy.

Muriel rehearsed to herself the coming interview with her mother.

" And what did you do, dear ? "

" Oh, I went for a walk to see an old church with Bobby Mason."

" Oh. That was nice, I expect. That boy's coming on, I think. They say that he's doing very well in his father's office," followed by a swift look at Muriel's face, and a reflection that the Masons were quite successful timber merchants even if the boys were reputed to be a little brainless.

Muriel did so much want to make her mother happy.

The silence oppressed them like a heavy weight. It grew fecund with other silences. They walked through the springing woods.

It was like that all the afternoon.

Then, when they had returned to the clearing and had finished tea, Delia returned. Godfrey Neale had gone to find her and they appeared together. Her eyes shone. Her thin cheeks glowed with colour. An elfish, secretive smile of happiness quivered on her lips, and her hands were full of primroses and great sprays of beech leaves.

" Did you have a good time ? " asked Phyllis Marshall Gurney wistfully.

Delia nodded. She was standing to eat her tea, for the rest had finished. A thick slab of cake replaced the primroses, and she and Godfrey swooped upon the last of the tartlets.

Muriel climbed into the waggonette, and sat still, hating Delia. Somewhere in the woods that day had lurked happiness and beauty and gay liberty. Delia, who cared for no one, who was selfish, had been free to find them. And Godfrey Neale had followed her unsought.

She was talking to him now, softly under cover of the rattling of the wheels, only Muriel with an effort could hear stray fragments of their conversation. Delia was scolding him about some girl.

"My dear Godfrey, you are as tenacious of your rights over a practical stranger as you are over your own tenants. The girl probably forgot you months ago."

The carriage jolted on. Bobby smoked moodily. His duty for the day had been done. Adelaide chatted with her cousin.

Delia was talking again. "You think too much of your unconquerable charm. You won't be fit to speak to until quite three women have refused to marry you."

Godfrey pulled placidly at his pipe. He appeared to enjoy her lecturing, as people do who prefer to have their personality criticized rather than ignored.

Muriel thought that she understood. "They're talking about Clare," she said to herself. "And he doesn't know that she's engaged." She felt glad that she knew something which neither Delia nor Godfrey knew. She was no longer powerless, but armed. She could, if she would, make a difference to the lives of these two Olympians. She, Muriel, could one day say to Godfrey Neale, "Do you know that my friend, Clare Duquesne, is going to be married?" He would take notice of her then.

She still felt proud, though chilled and stiff, as she climbed out of the waggonette, and said good-bye to Mrs. Marshall Gurney.

When Delia Vaughan suggested, "I'm going your way. Shall we walk together?" she answered with indifference, as though she were accustomed to such offers.

"Well, and how do you like living at Marshington?" asked Delia as they left the yard.

"Very much, thank you," she answered primly.

"Good, what do you do with yourself all day?"

"I help my mother. We have been very busy with the Nursing Club lately. And I sew a good deal. And I study music and astronomy."

"Music and astronomy?" The vicar's daughter looked at her in genuine surprise. "How delightfully mediæval that sounds! But why astronomy? You can't study it in Marshington properly, can you? Do you mean it seriously? Are you going to college or somewhere?"

Muriel shook her head. "Oh, no. I could not go away. My mother and father need me at home. I just do a little reading on my own."

Delia looked wonderingly at her small, secret face. "Look here," she began, "you can't go on like that, you know. If you are really keen on a thing, and it's a good thing, you ought to go and do it. It is no use waiting till people tell you that you may go. Asking permission is a coward's way of shifting responsibility on to some one else. Reading at Marshington! It's only a sort of disguise for the futility of life here. I know. I've tried it."

She was warming up to her favourite topic. Her dark eyes glowed above the trailing boughs of beech. Muriel, unaccustomed to exhibitions of strong feeling, looked coldly at her.

"Do you seriously intend to stay here all your life?" asked Delia. "To wash dishes that the next meal will soil, to arrange flowers that will wither in a week, to walk in fear and trembling of what Mrs. Marshall Gurney will say, although you know quite well that she hasn't got the intelligence to say anything worth saying?"

Intelligence? Muriel remembered how once she had suggested to Aunt Beatrice that she would like to go to college, and Aunt Beatrice had replied, "Well, dear, it isn't as if you were as clever as all that, is it?" And reluctantly Muriel, with the memory of the elusive mathematics prize before her, had had to admit that she was not as clever as all that.

"We can't all be clever," she said, without much joy in the thought.

"Clever? who said that we all had to be clever? But we have to have courage. The whole position of woman is what it is to-day, because so many of us have followed the line of least resistance, and have sat down placidly in a little provincial town, waiting to get married. No wonder that the men have thought that this is all that we are good for."

Muriel looked at her with grave distaste. She knew what her mother had to say about the suffragettes.

"Because I happened to be an idealist," remarked Delia, with the solemnity of twenty-two addressing eighteen, "Marshington could never forgive me. It could not forgive me for thinking my education incomplete unless I sought it beyond the councils of Marshington matrons. I happened to think that service of humanity was sometimes more important than respectability. I valued truth more highly than the conventional courtesies of a provincial town, while Marshington spends half its time in sparing other people's feelings in order that it may the more effectually ruin their reputations."

Muriel remembered hearing what Delia had said to Mrs. Cartwright over the Nursing Club accounts. She felt interested but uncomfortable. She had never been to a college debating society, and was unaccustomed to hearing what she called rudeness defended on principle. Also, she distrusted all this talk, feeling that she could be an idealist, too, without making so much fuss about it.

"But of course," continued Delia, "women in Marshington are not expected to have Ideals, only sex."

Muriel knit her brows. Sex conveyed to her merely a synonym for gender, masculine, feminine or neuter. She sought for more familiar ground.

"I certainly am not going to college, because my mother needs me at home. I am not unhappy here. Some of us have to stay at home. I have my duty too," she added stiffly.

Delia looked at her, a queer sidelong glance below her long lashes. Then she laughed a little. "And I am being properly called to order for pursuing my selfish ambitions while you are following the path of virtue?"

They had come to the Vicarage gate, and stood below the budding trees.

"Well, well," smiled Delia, "I hope that you will be happy. I suppose that it's no good arguing. But for goodness' sake stay with your eyes open. Remember, there's only one

thing that counts for a girl in Marshington, and that is sex
success. Turn and twist how you will, it comes to that in
the end. The whole of this sort of life is arranged round that
one thing. Of course it's an important thing, but it's not the
only one. If that's what you are after, stay by all means, and
play the game. But if you can't play it well, or if you really
care for anything else, clear out, and go before it is too late."

She opened the gate of the Vicarage garden, and stood for
a moment looking down at Muriel.

To her surprise Muriel answered her gravely, with a wistful
obstinacy that stiffened her slim, small figure as though for
some great act of courage.

" It's all right to talk, Miss Vaughan, but we all have to do
what we think right, haven't we ? And some of us can't
choose. We have to take life as it comes. I don't see why I
shouldn't be doing just as much my duty here as you where
you are." Then, feeling that she was not being very explicit,
she added, " I hope that you will be very happy at Cambridge."

" Thank you," said Delia with equal gravity. Then quite
suddenly she laughed. " That's the second time you've
snubbed me, Muriel, you strange child. Good-bye. Don't
hate me too much."

She held out her hand, then with a flutter of bright green
leaves she had vanished, lithe as a wood nymph, queer, graceful,
and confusing.

Muriel walked home, thinking of Clare and Godfrey, Delia
and college, and the meaning of sex-success.

When she arrived home, she found her mother coming
from her father's room with an empty tray. The happy,
satisfied expression that her face wore rarely transfigured her.
She looked charming as a girl when she smiled at her daughter
and said : " Well, dear, did you have a good time ? " And
Muriel replied, " Yes, thank you, mother. Bobby Mason
took me to see the old church at Ribbleswaite."

That night she stood before her bedroom window and
pulled back the curtains that Mrs. Hammond liked her to
keep drawn. (" It looks so bad, dear, to see an uncurtained
bedroom window. Even if people can't see anything, they

always think that they can.") There were no stars in the deep sky, but from the darkness of the garden rose the thin and unmistakable breath of the spring. Muriel stood with outstretched arms holding back the curtains.

Down there in the valley lay the wonderful, perilous, grown-up world, holding its carnival of adventure and romance.

She pitied Connie, a child who was still at school.

She pitied Delia, who was, after all, still at college, which was only a kind of glorified school.

She thought of herself, holding the key to Godfrey Neale's happiness or sorrow, she alone, who knew that Clare was going to be married. She was sorry for Godfrey, who, she was sure, had fallen in love with Clare ; but the thought of her power was more exciting to her than pity.

Oh, lovely, rich, full, adventurous life, teeming with experience, glowing with beauty, hurry, hurry, hurry ! Let me come to you and learn your secret, in your strange carnival of love and tears !

The soft wind fanned her cheeks as though it were the breath of life itself. She sank upon her knees, holding out her arms to the heavy darkness of the sky.

Down in the valley, the lights of Marshington winked at her, one by one.

BOOK II

MRS. HAMMOND

JANUARY, 1914—SEPTEMBER, 1915

XIV

AGAINST the car the wind hurled the challenge of a thousand angry spears of rain. With blow after blow they assailed the leather hood, only to break and fall helplessly to the streaming road.

"What a night for a dance," groaned Mrs. Hammond. "If I had known what it was going to be like, I really shouldn't have come, though I hate to disappoint you."

But even if she had known, she must still have come, and not only because she hated to disappoint the girls. For matters at Miller's Rise were growing desperate. Morning after morning Mrs. Hammond had come downstairs to find her daughters confronting her like the outward and visible sign of an inward and spiritual failure, Connie always bored and restless, Muriel becoming yearly more prim and silent. It was 1914 already, and nothing done. Adelaide Waring's husband at York earned £2,000 a year. Nancy Cartwright was now Nancy Buchanan, and even Daisy Parker, as Daisy Weathergay, lived in a little corner house along the Avenue, and kept a nice little maid, and paid calls, and shopped down the village street with one of those painted wicker baskets on her arm.

Of course there was Dr. McKissack. Surely, surely he must mean something. If only one were more certain of Connie. If only that queer, reckless strain in her nature would not make her do unconventional things that men disliked. She was so like Arthur, and yet in a woman, somehow, it did not do to be like Arthur. In the darkness of the car, Mrs. Hammond's face grew weary, thinking of bitter things. Her troubles were not confined to the spinsterhood of her daughters.

The car lurched and jolted round a corner into the mean street that crouched before the Kingsport thoroughfares.

"Muriel, I do wish that you would not tread on my shoe,"

complained Connie. " You know that they're my best ones.
It isn't as if I could get a new pair any day."

" I'm sorry. I didn't see."

" No. You never do see. Mother, why can't we have an
allowance ? I'm sick of this beastly dependence upon Father.
It's all to gratify his vanity. He'll take us in to Kingsport
to buy a rotten hat, like when he bought my velour before
Christmas, and I was simply pining for new furs. It's just
to hear us say thank you, and to feel how generous he is."

" Oh, Connie, I've told you before that I have done my
best. Don't let us start the discussion all over again."

" It's all very well, but if you'd only let me go on that
chicken farm with Hilda there wouldn't have been any need
to discuss it."

" And you wouldn't have been going to a dance to-night
either. You know quite well that you would never have made
it pay. We don't want to start all that again, surely."

They were passing through the main streets now, and
the lamps looked through into the warm stuffiness of the
car.

" At any rate," said Mrs. Hammond, calling up her courage,
" it is going to be a nice dance." She had said that so many
times. " You did say that the doctor was coming, didn't you,
Connie ? "

" He said he might," Connie's manner was off-hand, but in
the darkness her face softened, and her brown eyes glowed
with expectation.

She didn't care twopence for the little Scotch doctor, she
told herself ; but she was sick, sick, sick of Miller's Rise. She
was sick of dressing up her fine young body, which nobody
cared to see. She was sick of living through the long months
of the year all on top of Muriel and her mother, sick of scenes
with her father, because he would neither let her go away nor
give her the allowance that she considered necessary. And she
was sick of her mother's fretful hints and of her father's stupid
chaffing. She was weary of cinema romances, where true
love always triumphed. She was weary of Marshington
reality where her school friends and neighbours smirked at her

above their diamond half-hoops, or simpered at her over piles
of trousseau *lingerie*. At twenty-one she had smiled when
other girls talked about proposals; at twenty-two she had
blushed and answered irritably; at twenty-three she had lied
shamelessly and shrieked her noisy, jolly laugh. At twenty-
four she would have no further need to lie.

She pushed back a curl of springing hair, and tried to imagine
married life with Hugh McKissack. The wind enfolded
the car in the fierce caress of brushing wings, tumultuous as
love, as love, thought Connie. " Love," she whispered to
herself, " Love, love, love," as though by an incantation she
could call it to her.

There was a sentence in *The Romance of Emmeline* by
Sylvia Carlton, that had sung itself into her seeking mind.

" . . . And as he approached her, her heart beat faster.
In all that crowded room they were alone. He only took her
hand, but his eyes caressed her, and youth and spring, sweet
with laughter, clamorous with birdsong, leapt from the loneliness to meet them. Their formal greeting sang like a passionate
poem, and in the shadows of her eyes he saw the amorous
darkness of the perfumed night."

" Hugh McKissack," thought Connie, remembering the
way in which his kind, short-sighted eyes peered through his
glasses. Could men ever make you feel like that ? Godfrey
Neale, Freddy Mason, Captain Lancaster whom they had met
at Broadstairs. She let a procession of " possibles " pass
through her mind. At least if Hugh loved her he would take
her away. " Let now thy servant depart in peace," thought
Connie foolishly, " according to thy word. For my reproach
hath been taken away from me. . . ." She felt strangely
happy and yet urged by a strong desire to cry.

" Muriel, just see if that window is quite shut. There is
such a draught."

" We're just there," said Muriel, peering through the rain-
smeared glass, and wondering if she would be able to catch
Mrs. Cartwright in the cloak-room to ask about the nursing
subscriptions. Muriel's life had centred largely round the
Nursing Club, ever since Mrs. Potter Vallery had taken up the

Fallen Girls' Rescue Work, and Mrs. Hammond had abandoned the Club for her committee.

"Is there an awning up ? I do hope that there is. Where is my bag, girls ? "

The cars crawled forward, spilling their burdens of satin and furs and gleaming shirt fronts on to the damp red felt below the awning. As the Hammonds passed, a girl in a rain-soaked hat trimmed with wilting plumes called from the dingy group watching on the pavement :

"Good evening, Mrs. 'Ammond, 'opes you enjoy yourself ! "

"Who was that girl ? " asked Muriel, slipping off her cloak.

Her mother frowned. " One of the girls who used to be at St. Catherine's. They have no business to come and waste their time watching the people arriving at a dance. We got her into a decent situation too."

Muriel, who liked to see pretty things herself, thought, " Now that is just the sort of thing that I should have thought that those girls would have liked to do." For the streets of Kingsport on a winter evening were curiously devoid of colour, and the procession of pink and mauve and lemon-coloured cloaks gleamed like the lights from a revolving lantern down the pavement.

Connie murmured with a hairpin in her mouth, " What awful cheek." Being unconventional in her own behaviour at times through lack of self-control, she had little patience for other people who had suffered from an aggravation of the same offence. Muriel, whose behaviour was always scrupulously regulated, had more sympathy to spare for the exceptional. All the same, she did not know very much about St. Catherine's. Her mother would never let her go near the Home. It was not nice that unmarried girls should know about these things. Muriel, whose mind was singularly incurious, accepted without question the convention that only substantially married women could safely touch their fallen sisters. Her mother, Muriel heard, was most zealous in their cause, so firm, so sensible, so economical upon the House Committee. It had been her work upon that committee that had brought her to the notice of the Bishop. There was no doubting her ability. Better leave such work to her, thought Muriel; yet, as she clasped a bangle over her white glove in the cloak-room, the girl's eyes haunted her, mocking from the rain. Beyond this room with its cosy fire, beyond the decorous safety of Miller's Rise, lay a world of tears and darkness, of sudden joy and hopeless ruin. Muriel shivered, then followed Connie and her mother from the room. It was, at least, another world.

In the door-way they met Mrs. Waring, still slim and elegant in pale grey satin.

" Ah, I'm so glad that you were able to come," she smiled. "And the girls. How nice; Adelaide has brought a few friends of Sydney's from York. I must introduce them to you. There's an Eric Fennington and Tony Barton, such dear boys and devoted to Adelaide. She's so popular in York, you know. Naughty girl, I tell her that Sydney will be jealous if she always has a trail of young men following her about. And then, what will the unmarried girls do if staid matrons like her monopolize all the men ? "

Mrs. Hammond smiled gently. " Ah, well, you know. There are still just a few men left in Marshington. We are not all as adventurous as Adelaide, going to York. But then, of course, a different generation——" She glanced across the room to the goodly paunch and receding hair of Sydney Rutherford, who was earning £2,000 a year and who looked every penny of it. Then she broke off. " Oh, there is Mrs. Potter Vallery. I promised to keep her in countenance as the only woman here in a last year's dress."

Only since her acquaintance with Mrs. Potter Vallery had Mrs. Hammond dared to say nasty things to the Marshington ladies. The relief, after so many years of restraint, was immense. She crossed the room, leaving Mrs. Cartwright, whom Muriel had just released from contemplation of the Nursing Club, Class A. Subscribers, to keep Mrs. Waring company near the door.

" Poor Rachel Hammond is growing quite thin, isn't she ? "

" Yes," murmured Mrs. Waring into her fan. " Running after Honourables is hard work. And then, of course, they say "—Mrs. Waring dropped her voice—" that Arthur Hammond——" She shrugged her shoulders.

"Well, poor woman! poor woman! I hope it's not true. I dare say that she feels Marshington relaxing." Mrs. Cartwright's good humour led her always to attribute human trouble to the defects of impersonal locality. It saved her from having to blame people. " I'm sure that I haven't been well all this winter. I did think of going to Buxton in the spring, but Mrs. Marshall Gurney says that it didn't do her a scrap of good."

" But I don't think that it was for a change of air so much as a change of scene that Annabelle went to Buxton."

" Scene ? "

" Scene. For Phyllis and for herself. An exclusive view of the Weare Grange becomes a little tiring after a time. I dare say that Mrs. Hammond may try for a change soon, but I rather think that she has the more staying power." Having tried the waiting game herself and abandoned it, Mrs. Waring felt that she had a right to find amusement in a contest that had once engaged almost the whole of Marshington, but which had now, she considered, been reduced to the final round.

Meanwhile, having secured her smile from Mrs. Potter Vallery, Mrs. Hammond reviewed her daughters' programmes. She had grown accustomed to these early arrivals, followed by a determined search for partners, while she shepherded stray young men gently up to her waiting girls. She did it well, and also contrived to achieve a reputation for introducing men to other people's daughters ; this was one of her more clever strokes of statesmanship. To-night she felt that her burden might be easier. For some time things had been working up to a climax. Well, if Connie went before Muriel, what matter ?

" Let me see, Muriel, was it the first waltz or the fifth that you were going to have with Godfrey Neale ? The fifth ? That's right. And Connie, let me see, where was it you said that Dr. McKissack promised to meet us ? "

" He never exactly said," Connie began.

"He's over there, talking to that girl in green. They've just come in," said Muriel.

"I expect that he's waiting for us; I'll go and tell him that we've come." As Mrs. Hammond crossed the room, she was thinking, "Dickie Weathergay proposed to Daisy at the Tennis Dance . . . Hugh McKissack, Dr. McKissack, my son-in-law. A very old Scotch family. I only hope that Connie keeps her hair tidy for once. A doctor. A professional man." But when the tender smile curved her lips as she approached the young man, it was because she had thought for a moment of her husband.

Dr. McKissack turned with a slight flush to face her greeting. Being not entirely shameless, the memory of many Sunday night suppers oppressed him. But he was a Scotchman, and wanted to marry, and had no private means, and cold saddle of mutton had been welcome.

"Ah, Mrs. Hammond, good, good. And how are ye? Glad you were able to come." Seeing her pretty, waiting face, he felt more nervous than was reasonable. But he was a man of courage. Had he not been, he never could have enjoyed his saddle of mutton. "I want to introduce you to my fiancée. I think that you know Miss Hemmingway."

Mrs. Hammond, who did not know the daughter of a retired grocer, bowed. She even continued to smile. "Of course. I am so pleased to meet you at last. Naturally I remember having seen you at dances and things for years, haven't I? But we've never really managed to meet."

She was even able to search out Mrs. Cartwright, and to remark casually:

"Seen the latest couple? That Hemmingway girl and Dr. McKissack? He's just told me that they are engaged."

Mrs. Cartwright nodded comfortably. "Yes, it's been coming on for a long time, I understand. I'm so glad for her sake, poor girl. People haven't been very nice to her."

"Well, I had never come across her before, but, considering who she is, I thought that she seemed quite a nice sort of girl. Most suitable, I think. I know the doctor a little. Used to entertain him when he first came here."

" Yes. I know how good you always are to the boys,"
Mrs. Cartwright said without irony. Because she had a
charitable mind, Mrs. Hammond found her restful ; but when
she had left the shelter of her disarming simplicity, and found
herself surrounded again by Warings, Parkers and their friends,
her courage almost failed her. She had needed it so often
lately. The infamy of it ! The graceless, wicked ingratitude !
All that cold chicken and salmon, and the saddles of mutton.
Besides, she had liked the little man. She had thought that
he liked her. She could have sworn that he liked her. Connie.
Her small, tightly gloved hands locked round her fan. She
felt tired and suddenly old ; but there could be no respite
for her. Already the orchestra was groaning and wailing
before the first dance. The girls must have partners. Connie
must be told without being upset. It was difficult to tell
with Connie. She rather liked to make a scene, like Arthur,
but without his faculty for success. Mrs. Hammond drew
the soft feathers of her fan across her aching forehead, and
went into the ball-room.

Adelaide Rutherford was leading her young men across the
floor. Now if only Connie were sensible and had a fairly full
programme, she might still carry things off. She certainly
looked well to-night, and one of Adelaide's young men from
York, while talking to Gertrude Larkinton, seemed continually
to be watching Connie's gay blue dress. Supposing that
Connie, unconscious of the doctor's perfidy, were keeping
dances for him ? She must be told, and told quickly. Muriel,
who did not mind, would do it best, but Muriel was talking
to Rosie Harpur. That was one of Muriel's irritating habits.
People might begin to think of them together, as poor
Rosie Harpur and poor Muriel Hammond. Failure is so
contagious.

" Muriel, dear, just a moment."

" Yes, Mother ? "

" Is she—do you know whether she has been keeping any
dance for Dr. McKissack ? "

" Several, I think."

" You've got to tell her, now, that he's engaged to that

Hemmingway girl." Her voice quivered fiercely. "It's disgraceful. Disgraceful."

Muriel's mouth twisted into a small, cold smile. "It's not the first time that it's happened. Are you surprised?" Being used to these reverses, she was hardly interested. The little doctor was just one of the many men who had come to their house, and gone. Then she saw that her mother had been surprised. Pity as usual froze her to stiff shyness, though she wanted then to carry Mrs. Hammond away home and kiss her better, for she had looked for a moment as small and defenceless as a hurt child. But Mrs. Hammond was not a hurt child. She braced herself for battle.

"We must tell Connie." She had seen the young man from York leave Gertrude Larkinton to ask Adelaide some question, looking all the time in the direction of Connie's blue dress. If only Connie could have this little piece of flattery to soothe her directly she had been told about the doctor, like a chocolate after the dose, it might just save the situation. Mrs. Hammond hurried to her daughter.

"Connie, you'll never guess." They must take it lightly. "*Such* a piece of news, isn't it, Muriel?"

"Oh, I suppose so. Dr. McKissack and that Hemmingway girl are going to be married," remarked Muriel without enthusiasm.

Adelaide was leading the young man across the room. Connie started and looked up.

"How did you hear?" she asked quickly.

"He told me now. She's here. In the green dress."

They waited for a time that seemed to be years long, while the first notes of "The Pink Lady" summoned couples from their seats. Then Connie's shrill laugh rang out.

"So you've only just heard? You know, he told me days ago."

Adelaide was there with her young man.

"Hullo, Addie, how's the world with you?"

"I am very fit, thanks, and I want to introduce you to Mr. Fennington, or rather, he wants to be introduced to you. He's been pestering me all the evening."

Adelaide smiled indulgently. Out of her plenty she could afford to throw an occasional partner to the Hammond girls.

Mrs. Hammond and Muriel withdrew, well pleased.

" No partner for this one, dear ? Oh, well, that's that. I wonder why she never told us, though ? She'll be all right this evening, I think. That young man meant business. And what about you ? "

" Oh, I'm all right. Don't worry about me."

What need to worry about her, about anyone ? Muriel sat against the wall, her brooding eyes fixed on the kaleidoscope of colour before her. Two years ago, she would have smiled uncomfortably over her fan, pretending to wait for a non-existent partner. But now she was tired of pretence. The world was like that. There were always some people who danced and some who sat by the wall, watching until the candles guttered in their sockets, until the dancers wearied of encircling arms, until the bleak, grey light peered through the curtained window. Muriel was just one of those. That was all.

Connie passed, dancing with the young man from York, her red head high, her eyes bright. Which was Connie, one of the dancers, or one of those who watched ? It was hard to tell about Connie. Nobody might ask her to dance, and yet, and yet, Muriel could not somehow picture Connie sitting by the wall. But to go forward on one's own was against the rules of the game. And never was game more hedged about with rules than this which women played for contentment or despair.

These were silly thoughts. Nobody was asking Muriel to be contented or desperate. She was simply being sentimental because the little Scotch doctor, who was nothing to the Hammonds, had become engaged. Her next partner, Mr. Mullvaney from the Bank of England, had come across the room to claim her.

The dance passed much as other dances. Muriel's partners were scattered but reliable. Connie seemed to be more than usually happy. Everywhere that Mrs. Hammond looked, she seemed to see the bright hair and laughing face of her younger daughter. Then, after supper, the strange thing happened.

Muriel's waltz with Godfrey Neale had come, the waltz

that he unfailingly offered her. Godfrey liked regularity and tradition. They had waltzed sedately, and now sat on a plush-covered sofa in the corridor, silent as usual, for they had little enough to say to one another. Even the excitement of thinking that she really was dancing with Godfrey Neale had left Muriel. He had been too long the goal of Marshington maidenhood.

She wished that the passage were not so draughty, and that she did not feel so dumb.

Suddenly from behind a screen along the passage, rang out a clear, shrill laugh. A resounding kiss shattered the silence more boldly than a cannon shot. There followed the sound of a slap—bare flesh on flesh. A voice called, broken with laughter, " Oh, you naughty boy ! "

Muriel and Godfrey sat up. Such things simply did not happen in Marshington ball-rooms.

Muriel always remembered the stiffening of Godfrey's figure. He hated so emphatically all that sort of thing. And yet, she herself shuddered with fear. For she thought that she had recognized the voice.

In another moment the orchestra would play. The next dance would begin. Probably the couple might emerge from behind the screen. It couldn't have been Connie. She was sometimes rather silly, but she would never do a thing like that. All the same, it was not safe to wait until she was sure.

Muriel never knew whether she ran away because she did not want Godfrey Neale to know, or because she did not want to know herself. She always tried to hide unpleasant truths for as long as possible.

" Isn't there rather a draught here ? " she asked. " Shall we be strolling back ? "

They went, and Muriel thrust misgivings from her mind.

As she undressed that night, her mother came to her.

" I think that Connie's all right now, don't you ? "

The misgivings returned. Had Connie cared ?

" Oh, quite all right, I think, mother."

What business had Muriel with misgivings ? Mrs. Hammond was pitifully tired and needed to be reassured.

" Well, good night, then, dear. We needn't have worried, need we ? Really, I'm very glad that it has turned out like this. He *is* rather a commonplace young man."

" Oh, I never thought that there was anything in it."

The memory of Connie's face before she had laughed returned to Muriel. Yet she could not have cared for him, not Connie, for that little man.

" Well, then, it all went off very nicely."

" Very. Good night."

The door closed. Her mother's soft slippers padded away down the passage, and Muriel went to bed. But through the early morning darkness her thoughts strayed in drowsy confusion, and she saw again the glittering ball-room, and heard that horrible laugh from behind the screen, and saw, though she had forgotten them during the curious evening, the mocking eyes of a girl in the rain-dark street.

XV

IT had all happened so quickly that Muriel found no time to readjust her thoughts to the hurried sequence of events, Delia's engagement, Connie's queerness about it, and the invitation to tea at the Vicarage.

" Go by all means," Connie had said. It was a wet day, and she could not even play golf, and nobody had asked her out, and she was bored. " If you like to be patronized all over about this Twentieth Century Reform League, or whatever it is that Delia runs, go by all means. But don't expect me."

" Didn't Mrs. Cartwright say that he was quite a distinguished man ? " Mrs. Hammond murmured dreamily. It was hard that Delia should not only have defied Marshington, but have defied it with success, moving steadily from college to a secretaryship in London, and from this to the organization of the Twentieth Century Reform League. Mrs. Hammond could not approve of the Reform League, but she had to admit that the list of Vice-Presidents impressed her. And now, here was this Martin Elliott added to Delia's triumphal procession through life. She sighed, aware that she had never thought before of Delia with such toleration. The girl might be unpleasant, but she was not negligible. Perhaps Muriel had been wise to maintain with her that queer, half wistful, half antagonistic friendship.

" His book, *Prosperity and Population,* is supposed to have revolutionized sociology," said Muriel.

" The warden of a slum settlement," Connie sneered. " She's welcome to him. Still, it's surprising really that she's caught anything. She must be over thirty, and that skinny figure of hers and then all those stories about her being a suffragette, and going to prison. It's just the kind of thing that all nice men hate."

So Connie, in spite of Mrs. Hammond's protests, had refused Delia's half-smiling invitation to meet Mr. Elliott at tea at the Vicarage, and Muriel found herself walking down the road alone. She felt strangely excited, because of the absurd though insistent feeling that there existed between her and Delia some tie. It was as though Delia in her London office, looking up from the work which her brilliant, courageous mind directed, might think of Muriel in Marshington, living her drab ineffectual life among tea-parties, and nursing accounts and faded dreams, and might say to herself, " There, but for the grace of God, goes Delia Vaughan." Most successful people, thought Muriel sadly, have a shadow somewhere, a personality sharing their desires, and even part of their ability, but without just the one quality that makes success.

" All the same, I was right," she told herself fiercely. " I had to look after Mother. I had no choice. It was not my fault, but theirs. People don't choose."

She stopped to unfasten the bars of the big Vicarage gate. It had been wet all day, and the garden was musical with the manifold noises of the rain, of the murmuring runnels through the clean washed pebbles of the drive, of the ceaseless rustle of water in the branches. All the spring garden sang with youth and promise. The crocus chalices had overflowed.

Here and there the wind had overturned their brimming cups, showering their burden to the grass below, in a mystical communion of earth and rain.

Muriel stood by the gate, listening and looking. As though this were the last hour that she would look on beauty, she opened her heart eagerly to scent and sound and colour. The deep significance of the spring oppressed her. Beyond the sodden trees, a firelit window glowed like a jewel of warm liquid light. Undoubtedly that was where Delia now sat with her lover.

Muriel had no part in the silent movement of nature's slow regeneration. Delia, who had striven in the artificial world of books and men and jangling rules of government, was now to be akin to wind and water, obedient to an older law than man's. She had won the best from both worlds, because she had been selfish. Wise, fortunate, beloved Delia ! Was there no justice in life's scheme of things ?

Muriel, who had neither success nor love, nor any great emotion, moved forward slowly, a small grey figure beneath the dripping trees.

Delia opened the door for her.

"Did you get wet ? You must be washed away." She was a new creature, thought Muriel, gentler, saner, with an indefinable bloom of happiness that lent to her real charm. "If I had known that you were going to walk, I should have told that idle creature Godfrey Neale to call for you with his car."

"Father does not like us to use our car when it's wet. I did not know that Godfrey Neale was coming." She had not met him since that dance in Kingsport when the girl had laughed. She did not want to meet him now, when she had intended to forget everything except her sympathy with Delia's happiness.

They entered the comfortable, book-lined room, splashed with liquid firelight. The chairs and tables and people seemed to float as in a fiery sea. She could see nothing clearly until Delia followed her with a lamp.

"Father, Martin, Miss Hammond. Muriel, this is Martin. Godfrey Neale you know."

The room seemed to be full of books, tea-cups, and men. Mr. Vaughan smiled blandly through his spectacles. Godfrey rose and bowed beautifully. Then Muriel found herself shaking hands with Martin Elliott.

He was not at all as she had expected him to be, ironic, lean and scholarly. She stared openly at the short, stocky man, dressed like the shabbier kind of farmer, and smiling at her from a broad humorous face. His untidy hair stood up on end, his tie was crooked, giving a curious effect below his unexpectedly pugnacious mouth and chin, so that he always looked as though he had just emerged from a street row, which indeed, more frequently than most people, he had. Altogether the effect of him was so surprising that Muriel forgot her manners.

He bore her scrutiny for a moment. Then he turned to Delia.

" Delia, she doesn't like me. She doesn't like me a bit."

" I'm not surprised. You look like a perfect hooligan. Have you been arguing with Father again ? Muriel, don't mind them. Clear some books off that seat and sit down."

" But I do like him," exploded Muriel, not sitting down, because she found nowhere to sit, except a pile of formidable looking volumes crowned by an ink-pot.

" Delia, you are a shocking hostess," remarked the vicar mildly, handing Muriel his own plate and a half-eaten scone with the well-intentioned vagueness that characterized his dealings with all such mundane objects as tea-things and collar-studs.

" Sorry, Muriel. It's all right, Father." Delia quietly transferred the scone to its rightful owner, cleared a seat for Muriel and passed her a clean plate. " Muriel's used to me. I scandalized her years ago, when I told her that she was wasted in Marshington, and she came prepared for an uncomfortable afternoon."

" My dear, how arrogant of you to say such things to Miss Hammond," reproved the vicar, stirring his tea absently. " That's so like all these strenuous young people who call themselves reformers, isn't it, Neale ? They think all activity except their own a waste of time. They forget that if every one thought as they did, they would be out of work."

"Think, think!" cried Delia, laughing. "We don't expect them to think at all. That would be hoping for too much."

"Delia wants to teach people so many things," continued the vicar calmly. "She is certain that human nature can be rendered perfectible by parliamentary institutions. I am an old man. And I have written three standard textbooks upon parliamentary institutions. And I should hesitate to put into the minds of my parishioners anything but some simple and final expression of wisdom like the Gospels."

"Of course you are right as far as you go, sir," broke in Martin Elliott, obviously resuming some hot but interrupted argument. "My contention was simply that in a district like the Brady Street area in Bethnal Green people cannot understand the Gospels; and in a case like that to sell all that you have and give it to the poor simply is unsound economics. Don't you agree with me, Neale?"

"I'm afraid it's not much in my line." Godfrey was sitting upright in his chair, glowering a little, as he always did if the conversation passed beyond his sphere of interest.

"Muriel is the person to argue with on economics—and on morals," interposed Delia. "Try her, Martin. She has the mind of a mathematician. She ought to have been on the staff of the *Statistician* instead of giving sewing-classes in Marshington."

Martin Elliott crossed to Muriel's side. "How much am I to take seriously from that madwoman? Do you really take sewing-classes? I think that must be rather interesting, because all teaching is rather fun, I think, don't you? If only one's pupils are kind to one; but sewing must be more satisfactory than most things, because you can actually see the work growing under your fingers."

"I know what you mean. But I don't really do much sewing."

"You read then?"

"Not much now. I used to, but the books in the Kingsport

libraries are all so much alike, and one gets out of the way of ordering other things."

She spoke diffidently. It was incredible that a man should really want to talk to her about herself. Men talked about motors, or their own insides, or hunting.

Martin Elliott smiled at her. "Have you found that too ? Don't you think about the books in most circulating libraries that they are nearly all the wrong way round. Short stories with happy endings and long stories with sad ones. Quite wrong."

"Why that ? "

"Ah, surely the short story should end with tragedy, for only sorrow swoops upon you with a sudden blow. But happiness is built up from long years of small delightful things. You can't put them into a short story."

It was true. Muriel looked across at Delia sitting by the tea-table in her red dress. She thought, "This is what he means. Years of sitting by Delia in a firelit room full of books and talking pleasant nonsense. Friends who know what you mean and speak your own language. Rain-washed gardens when the birds call. Work that's fine and hard and reaches somewhere. Marriage, such as theirs will be. Children, perhaps, and laughter that they share. You can't put all those into a short story."

She felt cold and dull, shut out from a world of small delightful things. She made no answer, sitting with her chin on her hand, while the talk flowed round her, talk of books, and socialism, and plays, and people that they knew, and what you ought to take on a walking tour, and whether Sir Rabindranath Tagore should have won the Nobel prize, and school care committees. (They weren't really any use, Mr. Vaughan said.) And all the time she felt herself being drawn to Martin Elliott by surprised delight. She was at home at last, among people who spoke her own language, even though the things of which they spoke were strange. She felt as though after many years she had returned to her own country. But she never spoke.

Then she became aware that her thoughts had slipped away

from the conversation altogether, and that Delia was teasing Godfrey, and that he was protesting, half uncomfortable, half amused, because he could never become really angry with the vicar's daughter.

" Now, look here, D—Delia. That's not true."

An impish spirit had seized upon Delia.

" Oh, yes, it is, isn't it, Muriel ? Godfrey's never yet proposed to any girl because he knows that he'd be accepted, and if he had to marry that would upset his habits. Godfrey dear, you don't realize how much you hate to be upset."

" You know t—that's untrue."

" No, no, no. You're afraid that you won't be able to afford both a wife and hunters, and you prefer the hunters. Martin, Godfrey is one of those people who pretend to culti- vate the earth in order that they may destroy its creatures. He is that odious relic of barbarism, a sporting farmer."

" I—I'm not a farmer," stammered Godfrey.

It was a shame, thought Muriel. Delia had no right to tease him so. How he must hate being chaffed in front of her.

" Then if you aren't a farmer, you are simply a social parasite, and your existence would not be tolerated in any ordinary, sane society. Oh, I don't mean that you aren't very much tolerated to-day, because this society is neither ordinary nor sane. But when Martin and I and the Twentieth Century Reform League have been at work for a score of years or so, say seventy-five . . ."

She rattled on, foolishly, happily, teasing him with the kindest smile in the world on her thin face. But Godfrey was not happy. His sense of humour had become atrophied from want of use. He did not understand Delia's fooling, and to him the incomprehensible was the unpleasant. He passed from boredom to indignation, and yet felt too much his old debt of friendship to show indignation before Delia's lover. He was not going to have the fellow think him jealous.

Muriel watched him and, as she watched, she too grew indignant with Delia. It was unlike the vicar's daughter to go so far, but she had always said that Godfrey needed teasing. All the same, it wasn't fair. She took him at a disadvantage, and he really hated it. Muriel leaned forward, quiet but resourceful.

"Delia," she interposed unexpectedly, "I do wish you'd tell me, for. we hear nothing up here, what do they really think in London about the Irish Question?"

Now Godfrey really did know something about the Irish Question. He had once been asked to stand as the Conservative member for the Leame Valley Division, and although he had rejected the offer, as he always rejected the unknown at this time, yet a faintly political flavour still clung to his mental palate.

He drew a deep breath, like a diver emerging from the sea, then, slowly, with solemnity, he began to contradict Delia's picturesque but unorthodox opinion on the Irish Question.

Not, however, until he was seated again in his small covered car driving back to the Weare Grange did he recover his usual composure. Muriel had been tucked in at his side by Delia, to be dropped at the gates of Miller's Rise. The familiar feel of brakes and wheel, and the smooth running of the little car, reminded Godfrey that there was a sane and ordinary world in which to live. He sighed comfortably.

"I don't think that that fellow Elliott has improved Delia much. She tries to show off a bit, I think."

"Oh, no. It isn't that. She's just happy, and when Delia's happy she talks nonsense."

"All very well for her to be happy at other people's expense," Godfrey grumbled. He was enjoying himself now. The car responded to his touch, and the Hammond girl responded to his mood. The world was all right.

"Oh, I know that she teases. But one doesn't mind, because you know all the time what a splendid person she is. I do hope that Mr. Elliott will make her happy. But I think that he will."

Godfrey liked girls who stuck up for one another. She had her wits about her too, the little mouse of a thing. The Irish Question! He had given Delia as good as she gave about the Irish Question. Delia was a clever woman, but when women got on to politics it just showed. Now Muriel Hammond showed her good sense by keeping quiet when there was a subject which she did not understand. On the whole, he liked quiet girls. Besides, there was another reason why he should feel rather tenderly towards Muriel Hammond.

" You've not been to see us for a long time," he said.

" No. It is a long time," said Muriel dreamily, thinking of Martin Elliott, and what life might be like, if one could meet such men as he. " Not since that time Clare stayed with us, and Connie tried to ride your horse, and it ran away with her."

" No." The car jerked forward under Godfrey's hands. He did remember, ah, how he remembered, the turn of her head, the laughter in her eyes, her clear, triumphant voice. " Yes. I remember, of course. Clare Duquesne." He liked to say her name again. " By Jove, what years ago, and what kids we were ! " He turned the car carefully in to the winding, elm-shadowed drive of Miller's Rise. " Do you ever hear from her now, at all ? "

" No. I haven't heard for years. She married, you know. A Spaniard. They went to live in South America. I have not heard since, but I should think that the life there would suit her. She loved warmth and sunshine and gaiety. He was rich, I believe, and musical too. I don't know much more, but I should think that she would be happy. You somehow can't imagine Clare unhappy."

" No. You can't." He was bringing the car to the circle of gravel before the door. She could not see his face, but something told her that he had been profoundly moved. She became immensely sorry for him and yet glad that he had loved Clare, glad that he had not forgotten. His faithfulness belonged to her romantic dreams of him, when she had been a child, and had worshipped with the rest of Marshington. " If by any chance you should see her again, or be writing," he said very slowly, trying to control his stammer, " you might remember me to her, and say that I—I hope that she's very happy."

The car had stopped before the pillars of the porch. Muriel unwrapped herself from the rugs.

" If I ever am writing, I will," she said. " Thank you for the ride. The car runs beautifully."

" Yes, she's not a bad old perambulator, is she ? Are you keen on cars ? Would you care to come out for a spin in her in better weather ? "

" Thank you. I should like it very much."

It was the first time that a man had asked her to come for a ride in his car. She felt the occasion to be immense.

As they shook hands in the rain, he held her small glove for just the fraction of an inch longer than was necessary. She forgot to ask if he would care to come inside.

" Good-bye, and thank you."

" So long, and we must fix up a day for a run, a fine day." She passed into the house.

" Well, dear," said Mrs. Hammond, " did you have a nice party ? "

" Yes."

" You're back early, aren't you ? Did I hear a car just now ? "

" Yes. Godfrey Neale brought me back."

" Oh." Mrs. Hammond smiled. She was tired, and the day had been difficult for many reasons. Muriel knew this. She felt the passion of admiring pity for her mother, which was always her strongest emotion over any person.

" He has asked me to go for a ride in his new car, some day soon," she remarked indifferently.

Mrs. Hammond threaded the needle that she was holding.

" Well, dear, that will be nice, won't it ? " was all that she said, but as Muriel turned to leave the room she looked at her, and for a moment they waited, smiling a little at each other.

XVI

THE War came to Marshington with the bewildering irrelevance of all great catastrophes. It came also at a most upsetting time for Mrs. Hammond. Really, it was vexatious when everything was just going so nicely. Connie had settled down with quite good grace to the prospect of calling upon Mrs. McKissack, *née* Hemmingway. Two visits to old school friends at Buxton and Harrogate had sufficed to cure her wounded vanity. As for Muriel, of course it was too early to say anything definite, but Mrs. Hammond had confided in poor Beatrice that really, you know, Godfrey Neale was showing her an uncommon amount of attention. Ever since April, or was it March? those motor rides, that party at the Weare Grange, all spoke of possibilities.

"After all, he is really quite young yet, only about thirty. And with his temperament and his social position he would naturally go slowly. That was the mistake that Mrs. Marshall Gurney made. She would hurry him, and he grew frightened. By the way, I hear that she is taking Phyllis to Germany to learn music or something. Very wise, I think."

Aunt Beatrice nodded, approving Mrs. Marshall Gurney's double wisdom. Music was a sovereign remedy for broken hearts, and foreign travel would add distinction to an already pretty and taking girl. Her absence, however, would leave the field clear for Mrs. Hammond, by a process of elimination. Well, that did not show that she was stupid, but only that she knew when she had been fairly beaten. Rachel had been wonderful again, but then Rachel always was. It was impossible to believe that in the end she ever could be beaten.

And then the War came, right into the very middle of the tennis tournament.

Of course, as it happened, the tournament was not going to be quite such an event as usual, for Godfrey Neale had gone camping with the Territorials at Kaling Moor, and Connie had sprained her wrist and could not play. But still it was the Annual Tennis Tournament and that was no small thing.

The day after it had opened was the 3rd of August, and people began to feel uneasy. Just as the Hammonds were preparing for supper, Mr. Hammond rang up from Kingsport to say that he was waiting for the last train to pick up any more news that might be coming through. "Particularly trying of him to-night," said his wife, "because I've got such a nice little duck." After all, every one knew that nothing really would happen. There had been scares before.

The evening was close and, even up at Miller's Rise, oppressive.

"Wouldn't it be rather nice to walk down to the village after supper and see if we could buy a paper ?"

So, after supper, they went.

Aunt Beatrice said that she never had liked Germans, so stuffy, that sleeping with the feather beds on top of them, and then the way they bought all that cooked meat and sausage stuff at shops.

All the way down to the village, she said that she had always known that the Parkers' German governess had been a spy.

The village street was strangely unfamiliar in the half light of the summer evening. Unexpected shadows and whisperings moved and rustled in the quiet air. Little knots of people stood round the open doorways of shops that should have been shut long ago. Noises, from down the road, the horn of a motor-car, the call of children at their play, broke in upon the stillness. With significant reiteration, a dog in a far-off farm-house barked persistently.

"Go into the Ackroyds', Muriel, and see if you can get an evening paper. I want to talk to Mrs. Cartwright. There's that bazaar on the 4th."

The paper shop was small and very crowded. It smelt of paraffin from the swinging lamp above the counter. Muriel watched two great moths flapping with unbelievable clumsiness against its flyblown globe.

She pushed her way to the counter. The proprietor, a meek little man with a fierce black moustache, stood shaking his head nervously. "The ultimatum expires to-night at midnight," he said hoarsely. "That's a very serious thing. A very serious thing." Then he saw Muriel. "Good evening, Miss Hammond."

"Have you any papers left ?"

"I'm sorry, miss, I'm very sorry. I always like to oblige anyone from Miller's Rise. You might get one at the station perhaps."

5

He bobbed with forlorn little curtsies, pulling at his moustache, apologizing for the inconvenience of a European situation for which he, as the agent through which Marshington must see the world, felt a personal responsibility.

" Oh, well." Muriel turned to go.

An old woman in a man's cap, who for some inexplicable reason had planted herself on a chair by the counter, looked up at her.

" War's bloody hell," she remarked mildly. " Ah'm telling you God's truth. Two o' my lads went i' South Africa. Bloody hell. That's what it is."

She rose and hiccoughed unsteadily from the shop, the little crowd making way for her ungainly figure.

Unaccountably stirred by this brief encounter, Muriel left the shop, her mind wounded and yet quickened by the old woman's words. It was as though in her obscenity, she had been a foretaste of something to come, something sinister and violent.

The village street lay wrapped in the grey twilight of a dream. Bloody hell. Bloody hell. She saw the hell of a child's picture book, gleaming with livid flame. The blood smell faintly nauseating, like a butcher's shop on a hot day.

Across the road, Connie and her mother talked to Mrs. Cartwright. " It's all over the village," Mrs. Cartwright was saying. " Mr. Marshall Gurney has telegraphed, and telegraphed, and can't get any answer through. They say that he is nearly mad with anxiety. If the war is declared against us, they're sure to be murdered."

" Nonsense," said Mrs. Hammond. " You don't murder people nowadays, even if there is a war on. The Marshall Gurneys will be all right, though I always did say that it was a mistake to go off abroad like that. It doesn't somehow belong to those kind of people."

Muriel looked at the four of them, and at their eager absorbed faces as they talked about the Marshall Gurneys. Yet somehow she felt as though her mother were not anxious so much as jealous, jealous because it was Mrs. Marshall Gurney and not herself who was enjoying the unique distinction of becoming involved in a European crisis. That Kaiser, whom every one in England was reviling, might turn Mrs. Marshall Gurney's failure into victory.

XVII

MRS. HAMMOND was right.

The ultimatum expired. Great Britain and Germany assumed a state of war; and the Marshall Gurneys, miraculously unmurdered, returned to Marshington in triumph. The news of their escape through Switzerland outrivalled, at hurried and informal tea-parties, the problem of food shortage, the departure of the Territorials to join the camp near Scarborough, and the possibility of a German invasion. It was even rumoured that Phyllis had received a letter from Godfrey Neale congratulating her upon their escape, and that she, with the glamour of adventure like a bloom upon her youth, might yet warm up the tepid interest that her charms had once inspired.

After a spring and summer of reviving hope, Mrs. Hammond found herself facing the autumn of 1914 from much the same position as she had faced it in 1913.

Oh, when one was young and success was one's own to make or lose, then life was easy! But for a wife and mother whose success depended upon other people, then came the heart-breaking years. Of course the War must be over soon, and things would settle down to their normal condition, but meanwhile it was hard to see Mrs. Marshall Gurney becoming President of the Belgian Refugee Committee, while Phyllis, who had nothing like Muriel's ability for handling figures, was made treasurer of the Junior Red Cross Association, and went daily into Kingsport in her becoming uniform.

At the end of November they stood in the gloom of the unlit station, watching the 5th Yorkshire Guards entrain for Aldershot—well, if it was not Aldershot, it was somewhere in the South and so much nearer to the German guns. There was no particular reason why the Hammonds should have gone to see them. They knew no one besides Dickie Weathergay, Daisy's husband, and the station was cold and draughty. Mr. Hammond had stayed in late at the Kingsport Club as usual, but Mrs. Hammond was determinedly patriotic. In spite of discomfort she stood now with her girls among a crowd of curious, laden figures, distorted by their burdens out of all semblance to the human form. It was the world of a dream, when even the corporeal presence of such everyday people as Dr. and Mrs. Parker and Colonel Cartwright became part of a dim and dreamlike darkness. The crowd shuffled and jolted, appearing unexpectedly from the dense shadows into a circle of faint lamplight that flickered intermittently on bayonets and badges.

Mrs. Hammond was suffering from indigestion, the result of fragmentary and scrambled meals. The meals at Miller's Rise had not been hurried because nobody had time to eat them slowly, but because it hardly seemed to be patriotic in those days to sit down comfortably to enjoy them. Mrs. Hammond, dreading the secret murmurings about her husband, dreading the pity which could destroy more effectively than enmity the position which she had won, determined to kill pity by admiration for her patriotism. She stood in the darkness, while passing soldiers lurched into her, and knocked sideways her fur-trimmed toque. This must all be endured as part of the campaign. She felt her courage, born from her supreme passion, riding triumphantly above fatigue and pain.

"It would be nice if there were somewhere to sit down," she murmured, but without complaint. "Is that Daisy over there?"

Muriel, who had been standing all day in the newly instituted Red Cross Depot, shifted her weight from one aching foot to the other, and remarked:

"I'm so sorry. There are no seats," as though it were her fault. She added, "Yes, that's Daisy, in the blue cloak."

Daisy Weathergay stood just within the circle of lamplight. She was not travelling South with her husband because her baby was expected in December, but she had come to the

station to say good-bye to him, and stood beside the 1st class
carriage. Her small, flower-like face was upturned. Her
close-fitting hat shaded her eyes, but the light fell on her soft
little nose, and the sensitive outline of the mouth and chin.

" Isn't she splendid ? " murmured little Miss Dale, who had
burrowed her way to Muriel's side through the crowd like a
small mole. " So brave ! Not a tear ! Like all these
splendid, heroic women, whom one reads about in the papers.
I never knew what it was to be so proud of my country before."

The wind uplifted for a moment Daisy's brave, blue cloak.
She seemed to float, borne high upon a wave of heroism.
Dickie's red, comely face leaned towards her from the carriage
window.

" A symbol of Womanhood," murmured Miss Dale tearfully.

The whistle blew. A feeble, fragmentary cheer rose from
the watchers on the platform as the train moved slowly,
cleaving a line between the moving faces at the windows,
and the crowd that stood below. And still Daisy waited,
her small figure bent sturdily against the wind, looking
at Dickie, while all Marshington looked at her. It was
her moment. Then she was no longer Daisy Weathergay
of the neat little house in the Avenue. She had become a
symbol of womanhood, patient and heroic as the patient
heroism of Nature itself.

" And there's dear Phyllis Marshall Gurney," continued
Miss Dale. " She does look nice in her uniform, doesn't she ?
So splendid of her to have taken on this work in Kingsport,
isn't it ? But of course, after her terrible experiences in
Germany——"

The train swept round the corner into the darkness. The
tension of the watching crowd snapped suddenly. Muriel
became aware of Connie at her side. Connie's eyes were fixed
in front of her. Her breath came in low, gasping sobs. Her
cheeks had flamed from white to crimson, and the hand that
held her handkerchief was quivering.

" Connie," whispered Muriel. " They are only going to
Aldershot."

A sudden suspicion seized her lest Connie's mercurial

affection should have lighted for the moment upon Dickie
Weathergay. But Connie laughed softly.

"Look at the little fool, Daisy! I bet she isn't half enjoying
herself. Knows that she makes a pretty picture and that half
Marshington is watching her. Thinks she's the only girl
interested in this war." Her voice was thick and fierce.

Muriel watched her with wonder. But, then, Connie was
always giving way to unaccountable emotions, and to-night
Muriel also felt weary and sad, because her heart ached where
it had no right to ache, for this was Daisy's war. Daisy
to-night was the symbol of those heroic women who all over
Europe were giving their men to die for an ideal, and
suffering a thousandfold all the possibilities of suffering in
war. Muriel, who could dream at night of unimaginable
horrors, whose thoughts followed to Belgium the fleeting
whispers of atrocity, who heard hammering through her tired
brain the old woman's words, "War's bloody hell," Muriel
had no right nor claim upon this war. She envied those
wives and sisters with that envy of suffering which can burn
most potently of all.

But if Connie was absorbed by finding relief in her emotions,
and Muriel troubled by physical and mental weariness, Mrs.
Hammond was fully alive to the possibilities of the situation.
She, too, as both her daughters in their different ways had
seen it, realized that Muriel and Connie were out of it in
this war. She had seen the admiring group of friends round
Daisy Weathergay, and the becoming uniform of Phyllis
Marshall Gurney, but they summoned her like a call to arms.
She wasted no time on tears nor vague repining. She drew
her fur coat closer round her small, plump figure.

"Poor dears," she sighed appropriately. "Poor dears,
this awful war!" Then, having disposed of her duty as a
patriot, she continued, "Muriel, I've been thinking that since
Aunt Rose has been so ill, and keeps on asking for some of us
to go and see her, you and I might both go for a week to
Scarborough before Christmas. What do you think?"

Muriel did not think anything much. Scarborough or
Marshington was all the same to her, in a world where nothing

ever happened in peace or war to draw her closer to the fullness
of life which other people found and which her youth had
promised. She stumbled along the sodden wood steps over
the railway lines, having even forgotten that Godfrey Neale
with the 1st Yorkshire Rangers was in camp three miles from
Scarborough.

"Oh, I don't mind," she said, with the indifference that so
much disheartened her poor mother; and splashed on, thinking of the cold, flat ham sandwiches and sugarless coffee
awaiting them in the dining-room of Miller's Rise.

XVIII

BECAUSE Aunt Rose was not yet well, breakfast at
199 The Esplanade, Scarborough, was postponed until
nine o'clock. Uncle George, of course, kept to his
usual punctuality of half-past eight. Muriel at half-past
seven that morning could hear him whistling cheerily as he
trotted along to the bathroom.

She lay between linen sheets that felt chill and smooth.
Her hot-water bottle had grown cold as a dead fish. Drowsily
she moved it to the edge of the bed with her feet. She seemed
to have lain like this all night, waiting for the maid to bring
her water, and thinking sleepily of Godfrey Neale.

It had been such a funny evening. She and her mother and
Uncle George had met him at the Princess Royal Hotel, and
had dined together. A queer self-possession alien to her
nature had seized upon Muriel. She remembered looking
at her slim figure in the long glass of the corridor and thinking
that she ought all her life to have worn that vivid cherry
colour instead of blues and greys. It gave her a strange
courage and merriment, so that she had laughed and talked,
conscious of the flame of her bright dress, and feeling like a
princess in a fairy tale suddenly released from her enchantment.

She had seen things about Godfrey too that she had never
seen before. Most clearly she remembered how, when they were

sitting in the lounge after dinner, his lean brown fingers had pressed the charred end of his cigarette into the saucer of his coffee-cup, and she had thought, " He is like that. When he has finished with a thing, he crushes it like that without thinking. He is not cruel, nor ungrateful, only a little stupid and lacking in imagination." She remembered the stories that Marshington told of his flirtations with Gladys Seton, and the Honourable Lucy Leyton, and then Phyllis Marshall Gurney. He had meant nothing. He simply had never given a thought to what they might have dreamed to be his meaning. She had felt old and very wise and disillusioned.

Then the orchestra played, and he had looked up suddenly, twisting his head and frowning and beating time against the arm of his chair. He said to Muriel :

" What is this tune ? I seem to know it ? "

" It's Mignon's song, ' Kennst du das Land.' Have you heard *Mignon* ? "

" No," he said. A shadow of discomfort crossed his face. He struggled to remember something. Muriel, knowing what he sought, remembered the day in spring when he had driven her home from the Vicarage. " No. I can't say I have. Yet I heard that tune . . ."

" At our house," said Muriel. " The first time that you ever came. Had you forgotten ? "

He looked at her then, and seeing that she offered him simple friendliness he said, speaking deliberately :

" No. I have not forgotten. I think, whatever happens, that I shall never forget."

And she had nodded, understanding him. And for the first time she had been aware that some day he might ask her to marry him simply because she would not ask him to forget.

As they walked home, wrapped in furs, along the Esplanade, Mrs. Hammond had murmured happily :

" Well, dear, did Godfrey suggest meeting us again ? "

" Yes, he wants me to go to the Pictures with him on Monday afternoon. We could have tea at the new Pavilion place first."

The wind blew from the darkness against them. It lashed

Muriel's hair against her eyes, and rushed against her, as though it were forcing her back along the road to Godfrey.

Mrs. Hammond seemed to be quite sure now. Muriel lay wondering. Until that night, she had never believed it to be possible, but now she saw that it was almost likely, for nobody else would ask from him so little, and he, she realized it at last, had not been proud but humble, aware how little there was for him to give. She had never liked him so well as now when she knew that he had been true to his idea of Clare. He was conceited. He was sure of himself. He was terribly limited and arrogant and complacent, but he was wistful, too, for something quite beyond his comprehension, and just because of that he might ask Muriel to marry him. There were, of course, other reasons, and to Godfrey they would be important, for nine-tenths of him was just the practical country squire, devoted to his estate and his position. The Hammonds had money. In spite of her father's recklessness, he was himself too able, and Old Dickie Hammond had been too cautious, to allow the business once built up to crumble. With the Hammond money Godfrey could keep hunters. He would not upset Mrs. Neale, who wanted to have a grandson, and who cared little for the smart young women from the county families. Arthur Hammond's daughter would present to her no insurmountable obstacle, because Muriel was also Rachel Bennet's daughter, and the Bennets had once been as good a stock as any in the East Riding. Muriel too, was all Bennet and no Hammond. She was not like Connie, with the coarse strain that gave her vitality hardly curbed by Bennet gentleness.

If he asked her to marry him, she would, of course, accept. It would be a splendid triumph, the end of her long years of waiting and feeling that she was a complete failure. It would be the consummation of her duty to her mother, of her success as a woman. She would be the mistress of the Weare Grange, the mother of its heir. She would be mistress then of Marshington, and of her own rich destiny.

Strange, it seemed to her, that her body lay limp and unresponsive between the cold sheets, that the word marriage conveyed to her, not a picture of Godfrey but of the Weare Grange, that she shrank from the thought of further intimacy with his bodily perfection and his limited mind. He was nice, far nicer than she had thought. There was even that little unexpected strain of the romantic in him. She was sure that she could love him. "I *have* loved him all my life," said Muriel, and lay, waiting to feel the glow of love warming her coldness.

"This is not as it should be," she felt. But nothing ever was as it should be in a world where the best conclusion was a compromise. She turned her face into the pillow and thought of Martin Elliott, and the happiness that glowed about Delia's swift mind. "Well, if Godfrey had been like Martin Elliott," she thought.

Crash!

As though the fury of a thousand thunderbolts had hurled, crashing against the house, the noise shattered the morning and then ceased.

So swiftly the quietness closed in again, it seemed as though the sound were but a jagged rent across the silence, letting into the world for a moment the roaring of the spheres. Yet, though this one blow crashed and then was still, Muriel felt as though such violence must last for ever, and silence became the incredible thing.

She lay quite still, her limbs relaxed in the flat darkness of the bed, her arms lying beside her, heavy with sleep. She did not believe that the sound had really happened. Her thoughts returned to their path. If Godfrey had been a man like Martin Elliott, someone in whom one could seek companion-ship of mind, with whom one could feel as much at home as with one's own thoughts . . .

Crash! Crash! Crash!

It really had happened then.

It was not an illusion. She drew one hand across her fore-head that felt damp and cold.

Of course this was what Uncle George had said would happen. The noise was the noise of guns, big guns firing. This was what the little pamphlets had told them to prepare for. This was the War. Only it had no business to happen so early in the morning before they were properly awake.

Crash! Crash!

Huge sounds, flat and ugly, dropped into the silence of the room. Slowly she turned and sat up in bed. Her curtains were drawn aside, but she could see nothing through her window. The panes looked as though they had been painted grey. Solid and opaque, the fog blotted out the sea.

It seemed absurd that this blinding, shattering immensity of sound should yet convey no impression to the eye.

She lay back in bed, her mind completely calm and rather listless, but she could feel the perspiration from her armpits soaking her nainsook nightgown. That was curious.

"Muriel! Muriel!"

In an interval of silence her mother's voice called to her. The door opened. Mrs. Hammond in her dressing-gown of padded lilac silk stood by the bed.

"Muriel, are you there? Are you all right?"

"Yes. Of course I am all right. What is it?"

She wished that her mother would go away and let her lie there quietly.

"Get up, get up. Come to my room. You mustn't lie there, facing the sea." There was a sharp note of anxiety in her mother's voice.

Facing the sea. Why shouldn't she face the sea? Slowly Muriel thrust her feet out of bed, her toes twitching in the cold air as she felt for her slippers along the carpet.

"Quick, quick, never mind your slippers. Ah!"

Another sound broke about them, sharper than any before, as though the whole world had splintered into fragments round them. Muriel still fumbled below the bed.

"I can't find my slippers," she said stupidly.

"Look!" gasped Mrs. Hammond.

Muriel looked at the window. The shattered edges of the panes still shivered in their wooden frame. On the floor below broken glass lay scattered. The noise had become visible at last.

After that, a series of odd and ridiculous things all happened very quickly. Uncle George appeared in his shirt-sleeves, with one side of his face lathered for shaving.

" I'm going to the Garbutts'. Their car must take Rose. Get her ready."

Mrs. Hammond and Muriel hurried to Aunt Rose's room. Muriel always remembered afterwards kneeling by her aunt's bed and drawing cashmere stockings, two pairs, over those fat legs, where blue veins ran criss-cross below the tight-stretched skin. It seemed to her a fantastic sort of nightmare that could bring her to such close contemplation of her aunt's legs. Then Uncle George returned, and they all bundled Aunt Rose's shawls downstairs into the car, hoping that she was still inside them, for they could see nothing of her.

As the door opened, and Muriel saw the blank wall of fog along the Esplanade, she felt as though she were standing on the world's edge, staring into the din of chaos. All the time the vast noise pounded on above them.

Then they were all running, Uncle George, her mother and herself, down a grey funnel with tall looming sides. They stumbled in a little tripping run as one runs in a dream. Muriel tried to tell herself, " This is an immense adventure. The Germans are landing at Cayton Bay under cover of the fog. Or they are on the foreshore. This noise is a bombardment from battleships to cover the landing, and we are running for our lives to Seamer Valley. This grey funnel is a street leading to Mount Road. I am running for my life and I am not afraid."

The noise crashed above them through the fog, as though a grey curtain of sound had shut out the light. Little knots of people in peculiar attire appeared from the grey mists, and blew like wandering smoke along the alley, only to vanish again into vapour.

" In another moment," Muriel told herself, " we may all be dead." But she could not make herself feel really interested in anything except her stockings, which were sliding to her ankles, and felt most uncomfortable. She would have liked to stop and fasten them, but she felt that it would somehow not be etiquette, to stop to fasten one's stockings in the middle of a race for life. "I was not brought up to adventures," she told herself. "I don't yet know the way to manage them."

Then her mother stopped. "I—I can't—run—any—more," she panted. Her small fat figure in its fur coat had been bouncing along in little hops, like an india-rubber ball. Now she stumbled and clung on to a railing for support. "You—go—on. I'll come."

"Draw a deep breath, Rachel, and count three," said Uncle George solemnly. He performed Sandow's exercises every morning before breakfast and was therefore an athletic authority.

Muriel watched them, while the running figures stumbled past, quiet beneath a canopy of sound.

"You—go—on," Mrs. Hammond repeated.

"Now, Rachel, go steady. Breathe as I count. One, two."

They were not afraid, any of them. They had a strange, courageous dignity, these two comical little people, standing beneath the desolation of deafening clamour and breathing deeply. "Mother," thought Muriel, "is thinking of Father." Uncle George was thinking of Aunt Rose. Muriel was thinking about herself, and the strangeness of it all, and how she was not afraid. For there was something that made each one of them feel stronger than the fear of death.

A woman rushing along the pavement with her perambulator pushed it into Muriel and nearly knocked her over. She sobbed as she ran and the two babies in the perambulator were crying.

"This is real," said Muriel to herself. "This is a really great adventure, and none of us know this minute where we shall be to-morrow and nothing matters like success or failure now, but only courage. This must be why the soldiers sing when they go to the trenches. It's all so beautifully simple." She wanted to die then, when life was simple, rather than face Marshington again and the artificial complications that entangled her life there.

An elation possessed her. She could have sung and shouted. She stumbled down the rough road again, holding her mother's

arm and talking to her foolishly about what they would have
for breakfast when they awoke from this strange dream. She
remembered saying that she would have kippers, although she
knew that she really hated them and rarely ate more than toast
and marmalade. But then she didn't run for her life every
morning before breakfast. She saw Seamer as some goal of
human endeavour, very far away in the distance. It did not
seem to be an ordinary place at all.

Suddenly from their feet, the Mere stretched, flat and life-
less beyond tall reeds, clouded like a looking-glass on which
somebody has breathed. The noise grew louder. Somebody
called, "Turn to your right. Your right. They're firing
straight in front."

And even then, Muriel was not frightened. They wandered
in a vague, irrelevant place among heaps of garbage, and
cabbage stalks, and teapot lids, and torn magazine covers.
Just to their left rose a little hovel, the crazy sort of shelter
that allotment holders erect to hold their tools. She looked
at it, blinking through the mist and noise, and then, suddenly,
it was not there. It just collapsed and sank quietly down in a
little cloud of smoke, hardly denser than the fog. It seemed
appropriate to the absurd nightmare of the whole affair that
a board on a post should grin to them out of the mist, saying,
"Rubbish may be shot here."

"Ha, ha!" laughed Uncle George. "They're shooting
rubbish, and no mistake."

And Mrs. Hammond pushed back her hair feebly with one
free hand and laughed too.

Then they were all leaning over a gate, unable for the
moment to run further. As though for their amusement, a
grotesque and unending procession passed before them on the
road to Seamer. There was a small child, leading a great
collie dog that limped forlornly on three legs; an old man,
leading two pretty young girls with greatcoats above their
nightgowns, who giggled and shivered as they ran. There
were little boys pushing wheelbarrows, and waggons holding
school children, and motor-cars, and bicycles, and ladies in fur
coats and lacy caps. Then a girls' school came trotting, two

and two, in an orderly procession, laughing and chattering as they ran. Then more cars and cycles and donkey carts.

Nothing was quite normal except the girls' school. Every one else was a little fantastic, a little distorted, like people in a dream.

All the time on the other side of the road, the soldiers were passing into Scarborough, some marching, some swinging their legs from the back of motor-lorries, some flashing past on motor-cycles. As they passed, some of them cheered the procession leaving the town and called, "Are we down-hearted ? " And the refugees shouted " No ! " And some cried and sobbed as they ran, and some shouted back and some said nothing, but plodded on silently looking neither to the left nor right.

A cheerful, round-faced man in pyjamas and a woman's flannel dressing-jacket nodded at Uncle George.

"Heard the news ? " he shouted. " They've got into the town. That's why the firing has stopped. Our chaps are giving 'em hell. I'll give 'em half an hour until the fleet comes up."

Everybody talked to everybody else. And Scarborough was said to be in flames, and our men were fighting all along the foreshore, where the little cheap booths stood in summer. While they talked, the mist seemed to break, and the steep hills of Seamer shouldered up from the tattered cloaks of fog.

It was just then that a lorry swung by down the road, and stopped for a moment, blocked by the crowd. The officer in charge stood up to see what had happened, and Muriel saw, standing very tall and clear against the hills of Seamer, her lord and master, Godfrey Neale. He had seen Muriel. Their eyes met, and for a moment they became conscious of nothing but each other. He smiled at her and stooped down from the lorry.

"You are all right ? "

"Quite. We're going to Seamer. We shall be all right."

She thought that he was going to his death, and then the thought came to her that she loved him. Here at last she had found all that she had been seeking. The fullness of life was hers, here on the threshold of death. She knew that it must always be so ; and she lifted her head to meet love, unafraid.

"Good luck to you ! " she called, and smiled to him across the road.

"Good luck ! " he said.

The words came back to her, "Good luck have thou with thine honour. Ride on because of the word of truth of meekness and righteousness, and thy right hand shall teach thee terrible things."

The lorry swept him away along the road.

XIX

IT seemed to Muriel just part of the futility of things in general that there should have been no invasion after all. The supreme adventure had dwindled into an uncomfortable wandering among the smells and indecencies of a refuse dump on the outskirts of Scarborough. There had been no heroism, no glorious simplicity, nothing but shame and querulous fatigue, and a long walk home.

At three o'clock in the afternoon they stood by the remnants of a strange meal of cold roast beef, celery and boiled eggs, discussing ways and means. The afternoon sun glittered on the sea, the cliffs, the metallic smoothness of the Esplanade. It shone through the windows at the back of the house on to the piled up kitchen table, and on to the small black kitten, the one profiteer of the morning's adventure, who, having disposed of all Uncle George's breakfast haddock, slept serenely now among its ruins.

It was the only member of the household who was not feeling very cross and tired.

However, everything had been arranged by Mrs. Hammond. Arthur, to whom she had telephoned, was to come with a car and fetch her and Aunt Rose away to Marshington. Muriel was to stay at Scarborough for the night to finish packing and to look after Uncle George.

That evening Muriel knelt in the littered bedroom before her mother's trunk. Her head ached, but her heart felt still more cold and heavy. She wanted terribly to go away at once somewhere where nobody could ever find her, and cry, and cry, and cry. But there was no time to cry, for her father had arrived with the car, and Mrs. Hammond was wrapping Aunt Rose again into her shawls, while Mr. Hammond walked along the front to see what damage had been done.

Faintly through the house rang an electric bell. The maids had somehow evaporated into the mist. Muriel went downstairs to answer the bell, smoothing her hair mechanically as she went.

On the door-step stood Godfrey Neale, in mud-splashed overalls. His motor-cycle stood out in the road.

" Oh, you are b—back," he said. " I'm on my way to Cayton. I just looked in to see if you were all right."

He came in and shut the door behind him. The hall was almost dark, but Muriel did not lead him into the sitting-room. She could see his tall figure towering above her, but she never moved.

" I saw you this morning," he said.

" Yes."

" What are you going to do ? "

" Mother is taking Aunt Rose back to-night to Marshington. I am staying to pack and to look after Uncle George."

" You don't mind ? You won't be nervous ? "

" No, I shan't mind."

Her hands hung heavily at her sides. The gloom of the hall oppressed her. Her head ached dully. There was something that she wanted to remember, but could not, for her mind was empty of all thought.

" It's quite safe now," he said, as if to reassure her. " Nothing can happen now. A pity our fellows missed them, though, in the fog."

Dully her mind repeated, " Nothing can happen now." She stood there waiting.

But for Godfrey, whose reactions came more slowly, the golden hour had not yet passed. He lingered still beneath

the spell of the morning's high adventure, when Muriel had
smiled up at him out of the mist.

" I'm going away," he said.   " I've got to report to Aldershot to-morrow.   I don't know when I shall see you again."

" Oh, then I expect that this is good-bye."

She felt that she had known this all along, and that it was
good-bye indeed.   Her hour had come and passed her.   She
did not honour love the less, but knew herself to be unworthy
of it.   She stood silently, waiting for him to leave her, though
she felt as though he had left her long ago.   She held out her
hand, but in the darkness she failed to find his.   She touched
his arm instead, with a touch, light as a flower.   He brushed
her hand aside and swept her into his arms.

She lay there, limply, unreasoningly, thinking of nothing
but that the bitterness of parting had passed over her long
ago, like the waters of Mara.   His lips brushed the dark
smoothness of her hair, the pale oval of her upturned face, and
she did not resist.   He had already left her.   This was a
dream.

" Muriel, Muriel ! "   Her mother's voice called from the
landing.   Here was something that belonged to her real life,
that she could understand.   " Muriel, come and help me to
bring your aunt downstairs."

She responded to the claim that she had always known,
broke from him without a word, and ran upstairs.

When she returned, five minutes later, Godfrey had gone.

XX

MURIEL opened the front door wearily and glanced
at the brass tray on the hall table.   Surely it must
come soon, to-day, to-morrow he must write.   He
could not just go off like that into the silence of an unknown
world after what had happened.

There were three letters on the tray for her, one from
Janet Holmes, now nursing in Newcastle, one from the vicar's

wife at Kepplethorpe about the egg collection, one from a Nursing Club member.

Muriel hated the letters, hated the brass tray, hated sullenly and fiercely the weariness of her ankles and her shoulders. She had been standing nearly all day in the Red Cross Depot, lifting bundles that were too heavy for her. She leaned forward with her hands on the cool marble of the hall table, resting for a moment before she climbed the stairs. The smooth blades of an aspidistra plant confronted her. She hated aspidistras too.

From the dining-room came the flat reiteration of her mother's voice, scolding, scolding with gentle but monotonous persistence. Then followed Connie's shrill defiance, and her father's deep-toned boom. They were quarrelling again, always quarrelling. Connie was too bad, always upsetting everybody like this. As though the war in itself were not enough, lying like a heavy weight upon your heart, day and night, numbing your feelings to all but the bitter things.

She could not bear it much longer. She would have to go away. Why should not she become a proper army nurse like Janet ? She liked nursing, that kept her body active and would not let her think. She loved to look after people. It soothed the soreness of her heart. Her daily visits to the Depot, her hours of dusting round carefully disinfected convalescents at the local hospitals were only sops for the unquiet conscience of Marshington. Marshington wanted to feel that it was doing its bit, yet desired the merit without too great discomfort. Muriel was not like that. She had a terror of finding the War over and herself as usual out of it. She saw a triumphal procession marching through the city square of Kingsport, with braying trumpets and flying flags, and herself isolated, sad, standing up a back street because she had no part in the rejoicing. For those who were in it, the War brought suffering, and anxiety and blinding sorrow. But these were glorious. You could make a song of them and sing it through your tears. For those who were not in the War, it was a grinding hunger, an agony of isolation ; and of these things you could not make a song. You felt no pride of loss, no glory of sacrifice.

There were only shameful tears to shed, and the long ache of pain which had no remedy.

Why was her mother so angry now ? Her mother had been splendid. Every one said so. The way in which she had emerged from her terrific experience at Scarborough, shaken but undaunted, to resume her patriotic duties here in Marshington, had been quite admirable. Mrs. Marshall Gurney's escape from Germany paled before her greater heroism. Mrs. Hammond had been rightly elected President of the Local War Services Association.

Why didn't Godfrey write ?

The dining-room door opened, and Connie flounced out, hurling defiance over her shoulder as she came.

" Well, I'm jolly well going, so there ! "

She banged the door.

" Good Lord, Muriel, how you startled me! What on earth are you doing ? "

" I've just come in. I'm going up to change."

" Oh. Then I suppose that you heard."

" No. I didn't hear anything except that you were quarrelling, as usual."

She was not interested. She climbed the stairs wearily, dragging at the handrail, wondering why the last five steps were always so much steeper than the others. Then she told herself that she was only tired, and that she must pull herself together. A hot bath soothed her body and mind. She put out her blue poplin dress on to the bed, and a blue ribbon for her hair. While she was changing, Mrs. Hammond entered the room.

" I suppose that you've seen Connie. Now, isn't it too bad ? "

" I don't know. What is it ? "

It appeared to be a great many things. Mrs. Hammond had gone into Connie's room at midday, and found the bed unmade, and Connie reading a novel. When she had remonstrated, Connie just threw the counterpane above the chaos left by last night's slumber. And when Mrs. Hammond discovered this, and pointed out very seriously what a bad example it set the maids, Connie had said, "That's all we keep maids here for—to set them examples. Why should we keep a dog and bark ourselves ? There's no room for three women in a house. You should have let me go to that chicken farm."

" It's all too bad," sighed her mother. " You don't know how she hurts me." Mrs. Hammond pushed back her tears with a small lacy handkerchief. Connie was her favourite daughter. She had tried to do her best for her. But where Arthur was possible though difficult to manage, Connie was quite beyond her. " Connie's so inconsiderate. I don't know what's happened to her lately. I've done my best. I'm sure that I've done my best for you both. And now she wants to go and work on the land at some horrid place in the North Riding called Thraile."

" Well, why not ? " Muriel clasped her necklace and set straight the things upon her dressing-table. She wished that this domestic wrangle had not come just when she was feeling calmer and more sane.

" Connie ? On a farm ? Well, now, Muriel, you do know her a little. And in any case, her father won't hear of it. The breeches, Muriel. And then, it isn't as if there wasn't plenty to do here. I'm sure that I could do with a little more help."

Muriel was ready to go downstairs. She shivered in the cold room. Her mother still talked.

" If only she would be reasonable. . . . So naughty to her father."

With Mrs. Hammond's complaints still trickling over her, Muriel went down to a supper of fish-pie and apple-tart. It somehow failed to stimulate her. Her father had gone out, as usual. Connie sat glum and injured, eating incredible quantities of fish-pie, to assert her independence.

Muriel lay afterwards in an arm-chair in front of the morning-room fire. There were magazines that Mrs. Hammond had collected for the Hospital, and Muriel loved magazines. She saw photographs of lovely ladies in pearls and white veils, " Working for our brave lads," " Helping with the wounded,"

" Among our hospitals." It had become fashionable for beauty to go meekly dressed, with clasped hands, and the light directed becomingly upon a grave profile.

" I ought to go to bed," she thought, but it was cold upstairs.

The lovely ladies soothed her. She almost forgot to think about Godfrey, and how she had let him go. She almost forgot the deathliness of spirit that her years of failure had left for her, and that had come between her and Godfrey, so that she could not hold him when he came. Indeed, she knew that she had lost him long before he came to her. But until he had kissed her, she had never looked like this into the future, to see how it held nothing more of life for her.

She lay back luxuriously, warming her toes, and letting the friendly heat of the fire steal through her body.

" Signora Clare Alvarados," she read, below a full page photograph of a most lovely lady, " is the daughter of Félix Duquesne, whose delightful comedies have taken by storm the French-speaking public. Signora Alvarados has recently returned to London to take part in the organization of concerts for our brave lads in the hospitals. All society is speaking of her beautiful soprano voice. It will be remembered that her husband was killed about a year ago in a tragic motor accident in Chile."

It was Clare, more radiant than ever, smiling out of the paper at Muriel with the friendliest of all friendly smiles.

XXI

THE concert for the hospital was almost over. Muriel, who had been selling programmes, leant against the radiator and felt its friendly warmth comforting her. Across the row of bobbing heads, she could see Mrs. Neale's gaunt head and her untidy hair. Duty had brought Mrs. Neale to the concert, and duty was keeping her there until the end, but the strained lines about her mouth, and the misery in her long face could hardly be due entirely to Mrs. Purdon's rendering of " Little grey home in the west."

Something had happened to Godfrey. He was still in London, so it could not be the worst thing that happened to men during the war. Muriel hardly thought that it was even a sudden order to the front. She told herself that it was this, but she knew, just as she knew after the bombardment was over, that she had lost Godfrey now a second time.

She wished that the concert was over. She was so tired of everything that happened. Connie, working among the mud and turnips of the sheep-fold at Thraile, was immensely to be envied. How like her to win her domestic battles, when Muriel always lost hers! Since Connie had gone, Muriel was more securely tied to Miller's Rise than ever.

Against the other radiators, and by the two curtained doorways, the other girl programme-sellers talked, as they waited, to officers from the Wearminster camp. It was the same everywhere. At the Pictures, on motor-cycles, at the garrison sports, here at the concert ; everywhere life was regulated upon the partner system. Since their visit to Scarborough, Mrs. Hammond had taken fewer pains to provide Muriel with a man to save her face, because she too was expecting Godfrey Neale to write. She did not know what had happened in the hall at 199 The Esplanade. She did not know that Muriel had made herself cheap and then just let him go.

A scattered fusillade of clapping followed the stately exodus of Mrs. Purdon from the platform. One far more vigorous heralded the entrance of Queenie Saunders, a florist's daughter from Kingsport. Queenie was an L.R.A.M. and really she played the piano quite well, thought Muriel. Also her silk-clad ankles below her short skirt were pronounced fetching by Captain Galtry.

" Fetching. I should call her very fetching," he remarked to Mrs. Waring with the air of a connoisseur.

" Fetching ? " echoed that lady archly. " What does she fetch ? "

Muriel turned away. That precisely was what she wanted

to know more than anything else in the world. She lost the end of the concert in a bitter reverie.

Mrs. Neale stood beside her.

" Ah, good evening, Muriel."

" Good evening."

They made way for the crowd brushing past, and Muriel was conscious then that Mrs. Neale approved of her.

" It's a long time since I saw you."

"Yes." She would speak naturally. "The last time was when Godfrey brought me over to tea, when we met out walking."

" Yes." Mrs. Neale now was silent.

Muriel thought, " I believe that she would have been glad if he had wanted to marry me." She felt grateful to Godfrey's mother.

" Have you had any news of Godfrey lately ? " she asked, feeling that it was perhaps the bravest thing that she had ever done.

" Yes. I suppose that you would call it news."

Muriel knew then what was coming. She knew too that she herself must say it.

" Is he engaged to Clare yet ? "

Mrs. Neale turned upon her. " You knew ? "

".Clare was my friend," said Muriel.

" She wrote to you ? "

Muriel shook her head.

" I have not heard from her since she wrote to tell me of her engagement to Signor Alvarados."

" Then how did you know ? Godfrey wrote ? " Mrs. Neale's dark eyes flashed an accusation at her, as though she said, " You little fool, why couldn't you hold him ? You had your chance, and you would have been inoffensive. If he had married you, he would still have been mine. You could never have stolen him from me, and now he has gone. You little fool."

" I knew that he was in love with her. I knew that she had returned to England. He loved her from the time that he first met her. And he has been accustomed to get what he wants."

"That was a boy and girl affair. And, then, she's so unsuitable. A girl like that would never settle down to the country. She'll paint the drawing-room yellow with black stripes and fill the house with Italian tenors and try to be Bohemian. Godfrey would hate it."

"Godfrey wanted to marry her. She—she'll find him a change from the men whom she has met lately." The thought came to her, "Who is Godfrey, that here we all are with our lives centred in his?" She thought of him as she knew him to be, a little stupid, kindly and sure of himself. Only in loving Clare had he ever been brushed by the wings of divinity, and Clare was the one person whom he could encounter who valued her own personality before she thought of his. "When it comes to it, Clare will be more selfish than Godfrey," she thought, and yet knew that for his sake she was glad that they had met again. For herself, she only knew that life had conquered her. She could not look into Mrs. Neale's sad, ugly face.

"I'm sorry," she said, shuffling her foot along the floor. "Men do as they like. That's where they're different. We just wait to see what they will do. It's not our fault. Things happen to us, or they don't. We stretch out our hands and grasp nothing."

Godfrey's mother turned on her again.

"Stuff and nonsense. A clever woman can do as she likes. I was eight years older than Godfrey's father, and I have never been a beauty, but I married him and I bore him a son, and I've kept Godfrey's confidence till now. I let him do as he pleases, because I want my son to be his own master. I did as I pleased when I was young. He must face his fences and take his tosses himself. He's been his own master since his father was killed, but he is that because I please that he shall be."

"Some people never do as they please. They are bound by a sort of burden that they call duty."

"Duty? I've no patience with this pother about duty. I suppose that some people would say that it's my duty to keep Godfrey from making a fool of himself now. I shan't. Life's too short. I've no patience with this talk about souls."

Nobody, reflected Muriel, had been talking about souls, but Mrs. Neale was like that, frequently breaking through the barrier of speech and alluding to the hidden thought that lay beyond. That was why Marshington privately thought her a little mad.

"My Sealyham bitch pupped in the drawing-room on Tuesday afternoon. I've lost my parlourmaid in consequence."

"Really? Oh, aren't maids impossible these days?" broke in the soft voice of Mrs. Hammond. She had drifted gently up to Mrs. Neale, after having just given Mrs. Waring to understand that the present mistress of the Weare Grange was talking to her successor.

Her mother would have to know about Godfrey, thought Muriel. This was going to be the part that hurt her most of all. She remembered the incident of Connie and Dr. McKissack. Better use the same treatment here, and have it over quickly.

"Mother," she said brightly, "have you heard Mrs. Neale's splendid news? Godfrey's engaged to Clare, Clare Alvarados, Clare Duquesne, you know. They met again in London."

Only for the flicker of an eyelid, did Mrs. Hammond hesitate.

"Really?" she said. "How splendid, dear! I am glad, Mrs. Neale; such a nice, bright girl. Do you know, I always had a feeling that something like that might happen there. I've always had a warm place in my heart for Clare."

She did it so well that Muriel herself hardly knew how much was true. Perhaps more than she thought, for her mother had already seen a way to transform her defeat to victory. As Muriel bent over the treasurer's table five minutes later, counting the money from the programmes, she heard her mother say to Mrs. Marshall Gurney:

"Yes, you know, she was Muriel's great friend. We are so delighted. Right from the first. . . . I take quite a credit to myself for the match . . . Lord Powell's niece, you know, so suitable. And so nice for Muriel if she comes to live at the Weare Grange."

XXII

" THE strain of this terrible time," remarked Mrs. Hammond, " is almost too much. We must have a little recreation sometimes to take our mind off —all the horrors." Her small hand fluttered vaguely, brushing aside the horrors like a swarm of flies.

On the table before her the cards made bright little flower-beds on a green baize lawn. She touched their shining smoothness delicately, reassuring herself that her room was all right, and her guests, and the tall vases filled with daffodils and expensive branches of white lilac. Empires might crash and gay youth march to dark destruction, but the ace of trumps was still the ace of trumps, and Mrs. Hammond had taken her place in Marshington.

"Hearts," announced Mrs. Parker. "Connie home on leave, I see."

"Two diamonds. Yes. She's home for ten days. So nice to have her back," murmured Mrs. Hammond, hoping that Mrs. Parker had not seen the vision of Connie in her breeches. "The girls have gone to Kingsport to the Pictures."

"She looks well."

"Yes. The country life suits her splendidly. She always was fond of animals and things. Oh, what a *nasty* hand you have given me, Mrs. Cartwright! I'd never have let you be dummy if I'd known. Of course the work is hard, but so many girls are working so hard now. The Setons of Edenthorpe, both Gladys and Hilda, you know, are helping on the stud farm at Darlidd."

The Setons, thought Mrs. Hammond, gave a flavour of respectability to Connie's doubtful profession. Again, since Connie had gone, she had been forced to build a victory on the foundations of defeat. It was lonely, tiring work, though the bright room helped a little, and the flowering chintzes, and the sight of Mrs. Parker's sensible face across the table. But all the time, at the back of her mind, a memory haunted her

of Mrs. Neale's gaunt face, and of Muriel saying, " Have you
heard the news ? "

" So nice," she murmured above her cards, " to know that
at last Connie has quite found her vocation."

She smiled gently, as she gathered up the odd trick with the
gesture of innocent surprise that explained why Marshington
never realized that Mrs. Hammond always won her games.

Mrs. Parker raised her bushy eyebrows.

" Vocation ? Girls have no business with vocations. Their
vocation is to get married, as I told Daisy when she wanted
to study art. Art ! Have you seen the great child lately ? "

Mrs. Cartwright made the appropriate observations upon
the charm of Mrs. Parker's grandchild, and then asked her
hostess, " You mentioned the Seton girls just now. Wasn't
it Gladys that Godfrey Neale used to flirt with so ? "

" Gladys ? Well, people talked of course, but we knew that
there was nothing in it. All the time since he met her at our
house when she was almost a schoolgirl he has been in love
with Clare Duquesne. He and Muriel are such good friends,
you know. He used to confide everything in her."

If only Muriel would give her a little help ! The girl had
been so secretive and queer lately. Mrs. Hammond knew
that she used to adore her. But she had been so silly, always
so cold and stand-offish even with Godfrey. She never gave
him half a chance.

" No trumps," she declared vigorously, and settled down to
enjoy a sporting hand.

But she was to be allowed no peace.

" Have you met Lady Grainger yet ? " asked Mrs. Parker.

" Er—no, not yet. Dummy's lead, I think."

" Of course they are bound to be rather exclusive. People
in their position. I naturally had to call, because my husband
is to be her doctor. Lady Grainger is quite charming."

Mrs. Hammond rearranged her cards, stately queens, complacent kings, cherubic knaves. The hearts were chubby and
gracious, but pointed too, like herself, the diamonds slim and
elegant, like Mrs. Waring. If only people could be arranged as
easily as cards ! Here was a shy spade queen, and here the

king of hearts, magnificently stiff and spectacular. Put them together, Muriel and Godfrey. Here was Connie, a jolly little diamond queen. One could couple her with this club knave, and so be spared from the menace of any failure there. And Arthur, he was this diamond king, blandly helpless, staring at her face upwards from the cloth. She could lead off with him, seeing that she held the ace in her own hand (she would always do that, she thought) and then gather him, safely, safely, into the pile of tricks before her. There need be no more nights of waiting, no heart-breaking humiliation when she held her head high before Marshington, knowing that Arthur down at the Kingsport Arms was making love to the fat barmaid. Of course he was drunk. He had once told her that no husband of hers would make love to another woman while in his sober senses. But since he had taken to playing billiards with that Ted Hobson, there were too many occasions upon which his sober senses forsook him. Ah, if only she could gather him safely in among the decent people. If only, for instance, a man like Colonel Grainger, horsy, genial, yet to be trusted, so they said, would take him up ! Arthur responded so to his environment.

"I have done my best. I have done my best," she told herself. But she knew that there were new heights to scale. Besides, now, the stakes were doubled. She felt that Arthur's future depended upon her success with the Graingers. If the new Commandant at Kepplethorpe Camp opened the doors of his Mess to Arthur, then Mrs. Hammond might sleep at nights again. Besides, in spite of everything, she loved him.

She marked her score in firm old-fashioned figures, beautifully formed. It was from her that Muriel had inherited her pretty writing. Her jewelled fingers hovered above the tablet. She knew what she must do. As though she had hitherto been too much absorbed in the game to mention it, she said, " I haven't called on Lady Grainger yet, but Mrs. Neale has promised to take me up with her one day."

As she shuffled the cards, the rings on her white fingers twinkled above the green baize table, but though she drew

satisfaction from her lovely, polished nails, she sighed a
little.

XXIII

MEANWHILE Muriel and Connie sat luxuriously on
the two-shilling red plush seats at the Palace Picture
Theatre in Kingsport. Muriel had paid for the
tickets and for the blue paper bag of chocolates on Connie's
knee. This was to be Connie's evening out, because Thraile
was a remote place, dull and far away from cinemas or railway
stations. Even if you have found your vocation, reflected
Muriel, it must be queer to live eight miles from a railway
station.

That was a rhyme. Station, vocation. " Dear Connie has
found her vocation, eight miles from a railway station."
" Dear Muriel has found her vocation in no particular occupa-
tion." So nice, you know. That was the kind of thing that
Mrs. Hammond was always saying.

Well, perhaps it was true, regarding Connie at any rate.
Somehow the calves and sheep-folds described in her uncom-
municative letters had smoothed the lines of discontent from
her full lips, had deepened the glow of her rich hair, and lit
in her eyes a light of happiness. Connie talked so much that
she never explained anything, but all day long her jolly laugh
filled the house. When she was silent, Muriel could hear its
echo. Yet it was difficult to believe, although Mrs. Hammond
said that it was so, although her common sense told her that it
must be so, that these changes were only due to sheep and calves.

The film which Connie had chosen to see was called, " The
World Heart of Woman, a Story of Deep Human Interest, of
the Triumph of the Mating Instinct. For Adults Only."
According to the Cinema authorities there was only one thing
in which adults took any interest. But Muriel found that
this bored her rather terribly.

She turned from the triumph of the " Mating Instinct "
on the screen to its manifestation among the audience. She

could watch that little girl nestling cosily against the soldier's tunic just in front of her. She could watch the couple on her right, while they groped for each other's hands before the warm darkness shut them in together. She watched the couple on the screen, grimacing through a thousand flickering emotions, until they faded into each other's arms and out of the picture, to the long drawn wail of violins from the Ladies' Orchestra. Why did everything always conspire to mock and hurt her? To show her how she sat alone, shut out from the complete and happy world?

The man on the screen wore his hat like Godfrey's, a little to one side; but he lacked Godfrey's solemnly unconscious realization of his own importance. There was a moment during the picture when he stooped above the heroine and brushed with his lips her hair, her forehead, her upturned face. The heroine appeared to respond in the correct and satisfactory manner. Why could some women do these things, and others simply throw away their chances? Muriel hated this competent cinema heroine.

"I wish that they'd put on Charlie Chaplin, or some one really funny," she said crossly. "I'm so sick of all this sentiment."

She disliked the couple in front of her so much that she wanted to hurt them. Their smug, self-satisfied faces munched chocolates so stupidly. The girl lifted her lashes just as Clare lifted hers, heavily as though they were weighted.

"I adore Angela Tharrap, don't you?" mumbled Connie, her mouth full of chocolate cream. "I saw her once at the camp cinema at Hurlescar. They get some jolly good films there. This was called 'Midnight Passion,' and was simply great."

"I thought that she was much too fat for the part and was rather vulgar," said Muriel.

"Oh, Mu, she's ripping. And the fellows at Hurlescar all go crazy over her. Have another choc? You're so terrified of anything with a bit of go in it. You ought to let yourself go a bit more. Be jollier. I wish that you could meet Poppy Saddler, one of the girls at Thraile. Now she *is* a

sharp little customer, vulgar as you make 'em, but clever.
By Jove, she can beat Violet Lorraine on her own ground any
day. We have some ripping sing-songs after work."

Muriel did not reflect that the life at Thraile sounded less
desolate than they had all imagined. She was thinking, " Let
myself go ? " and feeling again the gloom of the passage closing
round her, and the numbness of her will as she lay in Godfrey's
arms, and the shock as her mother's voice dropped into the
emptiness of her mind. She had broken away because she
always had run when her mother called ; but Godfrey would
never understand.

The thought that she too had known romance came to her
from the scented darkness of the cinema. For the first time
she felt pride in the episode at Scarborough. She began to
hug the thought that, if they all knew what had happened to
her then, they would feel greater interest in her. " I am like
Mariana in the Moated Grange. I am like Elaine the Lily
Maid of Astolot. I loved him, and he left me. He would
have loved me if Clare had not come." She told herself that
Clare had wooed him away ; Clare, La Belle Dame sans Merci,
the enchantress who had cast a spell upon his heart long, long
ago, so that when she called him he must go to her, though
it were half across the world. And he had followed, lured by
her strange wild beauty, and she would lead him through perils
and dark places, hungry and thirsty for her presence. But
now and then in the hot evenings, he would remember a grey
northern town, and the crashing tumult of those nightmare
guns, and the face of a girl who smiled at him below the
lifting fog. Surely he would remember her as a cool, gracious
presence. Perhaps, even, long afterwards, when Clare had
wearied of him and left him sad and old and disillusioned, he
would return to where Muriel awaited him, faithful and
tender still across the years.

The Ladies' Orchestra played slowly, the long notes dropping
one after the other into the close atmosphere.

> " The winter has gone and the spring is here,
> The spring is here."

They played Solveig's song, and Muriel followed to herself the wistful words, building a charmingly sentimental dream out of her relationship to Godfrey.

When the Pictures were over, she walked with Connie to the station.

" Jolly good ? " said Connie.

" Not bad at all. I liked the funny one at the end," replied Muriel, still in her softened mood.

But they missed the 9.45 train, and had to wait for the 10.20, and Muriel, as she walked up and down the platform, began to remember that all this was nonsense, that Godfrey Neale had never thought about her any more than he thought of Phyllis Marshall Gurney or Gladys Seton, that every man kissed a girl these days before he went off to the front, and that she really had not even loved him, and never would be loved, and that the world was a grey place where nothing ever happened.

The station seemed to be perfectly enormous and nearly empty, except for some porters playing about with milk cans that they clashed together like giant cymbals. The London train slid silently along the platform, its doors falling open and the passengers tumbling untidily out on to the platform.

" Why," said Connie, " isn't that Delia ? "

Turning, Muriel found her hurrying along the platform, a suit-case in her hand.

" Good evening, is the 10.20 still running ? Good. I did not want to spend a night in the hotel. Hullo, Connie. You having a holiday ? How goes the land work ? " As usual, Delia went straight to her point.

" Great, thanks ; I'm chief shepherd, head cook and bottle washer to the pet lambs." Incredible good humour ! Muriel, accustomed to Connie's sulky antagonism to the vicar's daughter watched them with amazement. Connie continued, " And how are you getting on ? Got leave ? "

" Yes, ten days. I've come home to be married." Delia's fine lips twisted comically. " A fearful indiscretion, but Martin bought a special licence, and Father insisted on doing the thing himself. We had not intended to ask the blessing of the Church upon the union of two sceptics, but it appears that Father hardly thinks a registry office legal."

The solemn round face of the illuminated clock stared down at them. Muriel expected Connie to say something nasty, but she disappointed her. With a shock, Muriel realized that she was disappointed, that she would have taken satisfaction in her sister's sarcasms, though she herself felt incapable of showing the unaccountable resentment that she felt against Delia's drooping slenderness, and the ironic delicacy of her pale face.

"'The Triumph of the Mating Instinct,'" whispered a horrid little voice in Muriel's mind. "She's just like all of them, fearfully proud of herself."

Connie merely said :

"Oh, how exciting. Which day ? When are you expecting Mr. Elliott ? Shall we be allowed to the wedding ? What are you going to wear ? "

It was all very curious, and not a bit like Connie.

As they jolted back to Marshington in the hot, stuffy train, Muriel looked at Connie and Delia sitting opposite her, side by side. And on Delia's thin brown face, and on Connie's plump jolly one, brooded the same expression of serene expectancy.

It was very curious indeed.

XXIV

MURIEL could not forget that expression upon Delia's face. It haunted her throughout a restless, interminable night. It rose with her next morning and stared at her across the breakfast table. All the way down to the hospital she repeated, "Martin Elliott's coming home to-morrow to marry Delia." Somehow she felt that if it had been anybody else but Delia she would not have cared.

At the hospital she was cross and intolerable. She snubbed poor Rosie Harpur, who gushed to her about the beauty of

Delia's face now that she was happy. When she stood behind the screen, dusting the mantelpiece in the hall outside the nurse's room, she heard their voices as they drank their eleven o'clock cup of tea.

" My dear, don't speak to Hammond unless you want your head snapped off."

" What's come over her these days ? She used to be so meek and mild and now she's like a hedgehog—all claws where she isn't prickly." That was Nina Farrell, whom Muriel had liked.

" Sour grapes, I should think. Sick that her little friend, Delia, has got off at last, and they say that Connie's clicked with a young farmer up in the North Riding. Muriel's just getting to be a thorough-going cross old maid "

" Oh, no, she's not," protested Rosie Harpur, in her thick, rather foolish voice. " She's all right. She told me this morning that she does not want to get married, she doesn't approve of it or something. She's frightfully clever really, full of ideas and things."

Muriel flicked her duster above charts and inkpots, and then fled. She knew now what they thought of her, a thorough-going old maid, mean and spiteful. She saw herself with the eyes of those young girls beyond the door. She contrasted their gay, ruthless youth with her bitter maturity. She saw the ten wasted years that lay behind her, and her barren future. She saw herself, grown sour with disappointment, grudging to Delia her happiness, to Connie her liberty, fretting herself over tasks that others might have performed as well, and having to learn generosity from women whom she despised, like Rosie Harpur.

She did not go to the Nurses' Room for her tea. She loitered instead about the wards and passages. The hospital was as usual over-staffed, and there was little enough to do. She walked the mile and a half home, hating herself with a fierce and bitter hatred.

Yet where had she gone wrong ? What had she done ? All her life she had tried to do the right thing. It was not her fault that things had gone wrong. She had wanted to be clever, but had sacrificed her intellect to her mother's need.

She had meant to be like Delia and had grown like Rosie Harpur, because her duty had lain at home. She could have made Godfrey propose to her, but her fatal diffidence betrayed her. She could not stir herself to effort for her own sake. She had let him go.

And Delia was to be married to-morrow.

She endured the evening, though at supper she was curt and silent, hardly speaking to Connie, who had returned in high spirits from playing tennis with the Masons. Deliberately she seemed to wound herself by her resentment, forcing her lips to ungraciousness and her eyes to cold distaste, because she was conscious of having behaved badly, yet felt too weary of spirit to make amends.

Later, when Connie settled down to play rag-time, she could bear it no longer. She took her hat and walked out by herself along the road to Wearminster. She did not care in which direction the road lay, so long as she could walk away from herself and her own wretchedness. Her feet were tired, and her back ached, but the more her physical weariness oppressed her, the more she forced herself to go forward.

A dull sea of mist covered the valley, and the road stretched before her into a grey twilight.

Martin Elliott was coming back to Marshington to-morrow. On Friday he would marry Delia. Nobody would ever want to marry Muriel, and Godfrey was engaged to Clare.

She thrust her head forward, and walked into the mist, blind with pain. She never saw Delia until she was right upon her. They stood on a slight rise of the ground, where the tattered foam of mist curled round the hedge, like waves of a soundless sea, then fell away into the low lying fields. Delia had been walking towards Marshington, and the two women met face to face.

Afterwards Muriel remembered that, clear beyond the haze, three bright stars shone above the sycamore tree. She looked at the stars, because she could not bear to see Delia's face.

"What has happened?" asked Muriel, with a small hushed gesture.

Delia's voice came out of the mist, flat and dead :

" Martin was killed yesterday. Knocked down by a motor-lorry in Amiens station. Just the sort of idiotic thing that he would let happen to him."

A light breeze crept up the valley and shook the branches of the sycamore tree. It lifted a lock of dark hair and blew it against Delia's eyes. Delia never stirred nor spoke. She and Muriel stood quite still, with the knowledge of this thing between them.

" If he had been killed in action," Muriel said at last.

" He had no business to go and die now," stormed Delia. " He hated the war. He hated its barbarous futility and cheap sentiment. He only wanted to finish his great book. There were a thousand things for him to do. He had a great desire to live."

" You must finish the things for him."

" Don't be a fool. It was his work. He wanted to do it. If he had been a cripple, he could have borne it. If he had been blinded, he would have triumphed over it. There was no handicap that he could not have conquered. But now, now, he has no chance to fight."

She struck her hands together, in her urgency of pain. Then abruptly she said, " Good night," and swung off down the road. Her tall, bare-headed figure was engulfed in the soft grey distance.

Muriel did not go on, and would not follow her. She sat down on a heap of broken flints beside the road, feeling as though a storm had swept past her, with the force of Delia's angry grief.

Her lips moved, " Poor Delia, poor Delia," but there was no pity in her heart. She thought of Martin Elliott as she had seen him that afternoon at the Vicarage. She remembered his words, " Only sorrow comes upon us with a sudden blow, but happiness is built from long years of small pleasant things. You can't put that into a short story."

Where was Delia going, raging with her grief and anger through the mist ? What should she do ? She would walk away into the night with her sorrow, but she would return to face what life might bring her. And she would find that there were still amusing and exciting things, interesting friends, companionable talk, a little fame perhaps, and the consciousness of good work done. She would not forget, but her busy mind would have no time to linger with grief, and when she remembered it would not be with bitterness. She would still keep her love letters to read over, and her fresh unspoilt memories of happy hours. She had been lifted above envy or reproach. Sorrow such as hers would give her pride to bear it, and everybody would honour her dignity of loss. The dead, reflected Muriel, at least are always loyal.

" But I—but I," she moaned, " have been cheated even of my memories. There is no past hour on which I can think with pride. Delia thinks herself sad because she was once loved. But I would give all that I possess to share her tears if I could have her memories. I—I am hungry for her pain."

Then like a storm her tears swept down upon her.

XXV

THE spring passed ; the summer came, and in September Mrs. Hammond gave her dinner-party. It was no formal party, and therein lay the proof of that lady's genius.

The Graingers had been satiated with Marshington hospitality. Their simple souls had quailed before champagne suppers with the Marshall Gurneys, and exclusive little dinners with Mrs. Waring. But these Hammonds seemed to be natural, homely people. Where other ladies talked of the County and politics and the vulgarity of their neighbours, Mrs. Hammond gossiped gently about servants and the price of butter. She seemed generous too, and spoke kindly of the queer, absent-minded vicar, attributing much of his parochial deficiencies to the shock of that terrible tragedy in the spring when his would-be son-in-law was killed. The old man had cared so much more than his daughter. So Lady Grainger came to think of Mrs. Hammond as a nice woman.

Meanwhile, Miller's Rise had been thrown open to the young officers of the camp. Sunday after Sunday they came to play on the tennis-courts, to strum rag-time on the drawing-room piano, and to consume quantities of cigarettes. Two pleasant but foreseen results rewarded Mrs. Hammond. The first was that Mr. Hammond became interested in the young men, and liked to talk aeroplanes with Bobby Collins, and machine guns with Captain Lowcroft, and horses with young Staines. The boys found him to be a jolly good sort, and missed him when he was not there. All of which was excellent for him.

Secondly, the fame of Miller's Rise reached the ears of Colonel and Lady Grainger, and since they took a real interest in their subalterns, and since the tone of Marshington society had distressed. them, they became immensely grateful to the Hammonds. So it happened that one evening in September Colonel Grainger met Mrs. Hammond at Kingsport Station, and stopped to thank her for her kindness to the boys.

" I wish that Maude and I were young enough to be included in your invitation," he added wistfully.

" Well, if you promise not to spoil their fun, as a great favour, I'll give you a pass ! " laughed Mrs. Hammond. " As a great favour."

The only thing that spoiled it was that Mrs. Marshall Gurney could not hear.

On this Thursday evening, the colonel and his wife had joined the party. Till now, it had been uproariously success- ful. The colonel sat pulling at his moustache and smiling quietly,. and Lady Grainger's kind little round face beamed all over with pleasure, and Mr. Hammond was on his very best behaviour. He had told her only his most presentable stories, and treated her with the exaggerated gallantry that he sometimes thought fit to show to his wife's friends, and which Lady Grainger found to be " so quaint and old-fashioned and nice."

As for the boys, they needed no entertainment. They were. eating dessert now, and Bobby Collins with an intent, serious face, bent over the orange skin that he was carving.

" What is it, Mr. Collins ? " asked Muriel. She rather liked these boys, who treated her like a pleasant kind of aunt, and whom even Mrs. Hammond never regarded in the light of anything more intimate than a stepping-stone to the Graingers.

" Pig," replied Bobby comprehensively.

" I beg your pardon ? " Young Smithson raised his head from Muriel's other side. " Kindly repeat that word."

" Pig," repeated Bobby obligingly, and continued to play with his knife.

" Do I understand," shouted Smithson in mock wrath, " that this epithet is intended as an insult to that charming lady ? "

" Understand what you like. Aha ! I've done it," cried Bobby in triumph.

Smithson rose with dignity and bowed to his hostess. " Pardon me, Mrs. Hammond," he declared with dignity. " But words have just now been said in this room which no gentleman could pass. An insult has been offered to your charming daughter. Ahem ! Mr. Collins, in the name of Miss Hammond, I demand satisfaction."

The table was in an uproar. Muriel, blushing but amused, looked along a line of laughing faces to her mother.

" A duel, a duel ! " shouted Captain Lowcroft. " Pistols for two and coffee for one on the Hangman's Heath in the morning."

Bobby Collins, very round and solemn, arose and faced Smithson across Muriel's dark head.

" A plague upon your mornings, sir. I will fight now, with oranges, upon the lawn. And it shall be to the death."

" Outside with you then, for goodness' sake," cried Mrs. Hammond. " Remember my china ! "

They trooped outside together.

The September night was warm and still. A great harvest moon hung low above the elm trees. The windows, carefully curtained by order of the government, left the house mute and dark, but white moonlight lay along the level lawn, and moonlight touched the laughing, running figures.

There was madness in the air. Even Muriel, as she stood

on the steps with Lady Grainger and her mother, felt the excitement, and laughed with them. She watched the figures on the lawn, moving out of the black shadows of the elm trees into the white field of moonlight. She watched young Staines and Captain Lowcroft separate the antagonists, measure sedately the paces between them, and supply them with their ammunition. Quick words of command rang out. A handkerchief fluttered down, silver-white in the moonlight. The fruit flew, the oranges glittering like golden metal.

" Your oranges," murmured Lady Grainger. " They are very naughty boys."

" Not at all," sighed Mrs. Hammond. " This is so good for them, a little innocent fooling. The oranges will be all the sweeter." She waved a pathetic little hand. " You see, I had no son to give."

" You have at least a very nice daughter."

" Two. My baby, Connie, is working on the land."

There came a burst of shouting from the combatants on the lawn.

" A hit ! A hit ! A palpable hit. (Whatever that means. I seem to have heard it somewhere.) Miss Hammond, your insulter is wounded."

With a groan Bobby Collins flung himself upon the lawn.

" Come and render first aid."

Muriel ran down.

Always afterwards she remembered kneeling there with her delicate dress carefully tucked up, binding a silk scarf round an imaginary wound in Bobby's shoulder. She remembered the sticky feeling of his tunic where an over-ripe orange had burst, and the sound of mad-cap laughter and those gay young voices. Then something made her look up, and beyond the drive, in the shadow of the elm trees, she saw a figure moving. Somebody was walking slowly and furtively, stealing from the darkness of one tree to another, a figure bowed and drooping, as though in pain or weariness. Almost it seemed to be familiar. Muriel thought of Delia, who had walked off through the mists four months ago ; but it was not tall enough for Delia.

6 *

" It'll be somebody coming to see one of the maids," she told herself, and rose to her feet, for Bobby Collins was being lifted from the ground by three of his friends, and the procession moved towards the house.

Mrs. Hammond opened the front door to receive them. A flood of golden light poured out on to the steps, the drive, the disordered returning figures. Colonel Grainger bore a dish piled high with yellow oranges. Bobby was carried shoulder high by the laughing boys.

" The children. The absurd children," laughed Mrs. Hammond. " Come in. The Zeppelins will catch us if we leave our lights showing, and Arthur is a special constable."

As she watched the colonel tossing oranges to her husband, her face was happier than Muriel had known it for many years.

" Are they all in ? Shut the door," said Mrs. Hammond. Muriel turned to obey.

Out in the garden the watcher from the shadows had crossed the lawn. Somebody stood in the moonlight on the edge of the drive. The face was hidden, but again a curious familiarity in the attitude stopped the beating of Muriel's heart for a moment.

" I'm seeing things," she told herself. " That can't be Connie, for she's at Thraile. Somebody has come from the road to see whatever we were doing. We are being mad enough to bring anyone in."

She drew the heavy curtains across the hall door.

They flocked into the drawing-room for music, such music as had become part of the Miller's Rise programme. Mrs. Hammond and Lady Grainger sat in the big armchairs, and Colonel Grainger and Mr. Hammond looked as though they had smoked cigars together all their lives.

The boys grouped themselves around and on the piano at which Muriel sat, accompanying indefatigably.

" Prithee pretty maiden, will you marry me ? " sang Bobby Collins, still bandaged and orange-smeared.

" Hey, but he's doleful, willow, willow, waly," shouted the chorus cheerfully.

Annie came into the drawing-room, her face stiff with

importance, and crossed to Mrs. Hammond. Muriel saw her mother leave the room.

" The coffee's overboiled again," she thought, and yet for some reason, she felt stupidly uneasy. She could not put out of her head the thought of that watching figure on the lawn.

Mrs. Hammond did not return. The singers laid aside Gilbert and Sullivan, and took up the Globe Song Book.

" There is a tavern in the town, in the town,
    And there my true love sits him down, sits him down,
    And takes his cask of wine across his knee
    And never, never thinks of me, thinks of me ! "

" We want a drummer," declared Bobby.

" The gong. Where's the gong ? Miss Hammond, may we get the gong ? We can't live without a drum."

" Of course you can have it. Mr. Collins, go and fetch it from the hall."

Bobby went, leaving the door ajar. They watched for their drummer, Colonel Grainger and Mr. Hammond in high good humour, humming the refrain,

" Fare thee well for I must leave thee,"

From the hall came a sharp exclamation and the sound of a scuffle.

Then Bobby questioned sharply and a voice, Connie's voice unmistakably, was raised in protest.

They all turned towards the door.

Then Bobby returned. In one hand he carried the large brass gong and its padded stick ; the other hand was firmly grasped round Connie's wrist.

" See what I've found," he cried triumphantly. " Not only a drum, but a drummer ! Allow me, ladies and gentlemen, to introduce to you Miss Constance Hammond, youngest daughter of our respected host and hostess, just this moment returned on unexpected leave from her strenuous duties upon a farm in the North Riding, where she has been carrying on the splendid work of feeding our nation in its hour of peril."

They rose, they shouted, they went forward to drag Connie, blushing and protesting, into the room.

" Three cheers for Miss Constance Hammond ! Hurrah ! Hurrah ! Hurrah ! Three cheers for the land girls in khaki ! Cheers for the girls who grow the spuds to beat the U Boats ! "

The room rang with their cheering. Colonel Grainger stepped forward and introduced himself, shaking both Connie's red, trembling hands, and telling her how good her mother had been to his boys. Muriel, mystified, profoundly stirred by some strange premonition, stood silent while Connie shook hands with the colonel and kissed her father. Then she asked :

" Have you seen Mother ? "

" Yes," said Connie, and no more, for Bobby made all the necessary explanations with delighted volubility.

" She was sneaking away upstairs because she didn't want to see us before she'd made herself look beautiful. She came from Market Burton on the 9.50 unexpectedly to give her family a surprise. *I* think that it was to see how they behaved while she was away. Aha, Miss Hammond, but now we've caught you, we'll keep you. You are conscripted as our drummer."

Muriel, from the piano, said :

" Connie, this is nice. How long have you ? "

Then for the first time she saw Connie clearly through a crowd of chaffing, chattering boys. Connie's cheeks were flushed. She held her wild head high and recklessly, but her eyes were fierce with the desperation of a trapped animal.

" I don't know for certain," she said, in her high, shrill voice. " It depends on how you treat me." Then quickly she turned to the men. " What were you singing ? Come on. Don't stop. Where's my drum ? " She sprang on to the back of the sofa, and Bobby held the gong before her. " Go on. Play up, Muriel ! "

With a sense of impending doom, totally unreasonable, Muriel struck the keys with stiff, frightened fingers. The voices shouted again, madly joyous, punctuated by Connie's crashings on the gong.

"He left me for a damsel dark, damsel dark,
    And every night they used to spark, used to spark,
    And now my love, without a thought of me
    Takes that dark damsel on his knee, on his knee."

Crash-crash-crash, went the gong. The room rocked to the stamp of feet and the roar of voices, while high above them, from where she stood on the sofa end, smashing at the swinging gong, shrilled Connie's wild, mad gaiety.

So Mrs. Hammond, returning to the drawing-room, found them and stood spellbound, like a frozen figure in the doorway. Lady Grainger saw her and smiled, beckoning. Muriel, between the gusts of laughter, heard their voices.

"They kept you a long time," murmured Lady Grainger. "I hope that it was nothing bothering. You—you'll excuse me saying so, you look a little tired. I hope that our rowdy boys are not too much for you."

"Oh, no. Not at all. I like it."

"I'll hang my harp on a weeping willow tree,
    And may the world go well with thee, well with thee."

chanted the chorus.

"Chorus again," called Connie. "I'm bandmaster to-night."

"Fare thee well for I must leave thee,
    Do not let the parting grieve thee . . ."

As the refrain died down to the reverberations of the gong, Muriel heard Lady Grainger say:

"If only more girls were brought up like yours, with such a healthy, homely influence, an atmosphere, I'm sure that you'll understand me, dear Mrs. Hammond. It does help the boys so."

Then her mother answered in that soft hurrying voice that was so much her own:

" It's very kind of you to say so. I don't know, I'm sure. Of course I've always tried to—to give them a high ideal of —of home life and—and so on."

She faltered, and Muriel, looking over her shoulder, saw her mouth set to a despairing smile, and her tongue pass over her dry lips.

" I—we try to, you know," repeated Mrs. Hammond, as though she were saying a lesson.

Connie, from the sofa head, turned round and looked at her mother. Muriel felt the tension in the room to be unendurable. Somehow they were torturing that gentle little lady on the sofa. The evening became abominable to her. The laughter, the rollicking songs broke round her like a nightmare sea. Her hands slid from the keyboard and she clenched them on her knee.

" Oh, come along, Muriel," called Connie. " Are you tired ? Then let me come."

Muriel was pushed aside from the stool, and Connie swung herself into her place. Connie's red, work-soiled fingers rattled over the keyboard.

" What shall we have now ? " Her jangling discords changed to the clashing refrain of an old song.

> " I went down south to see my Sal,
>   Singing Polly Wolly Doodle all the day."

The party was jollier than ever.

At last they began to go. There was a scramble for coats and scarves and leather gauntlets. Then the lamps of the motor-cycles would not light. Captain Lowcroft's little car refused to start. The colonel stood on the door-step and smiled down on them benignly.

" I can't tell you how grateful we are, Mrs. Hammond. This is just the sort of thing to keep the boys out of mischief, what ? Your husband has promised to come and look over our horses one day. I hope that we shall see you both up at the Mess one of these days."

The boys shouted. Somebody began to sing, " For He's a

jolly good fellow." Muriel went back to the drawing-room. Her mother still stood on the steps. Mr. Hammond had gone to lock up the garage.

Connie stood in her tweed coat and skirt still by the fire-place, kicking a smouldering log with her mud-splashed boot. Her face was turned aside from Muriel, but her whole figure drooped with weariness.

" Connie, has something happened ? "

" You'd better ask Mother," replied Connie's muffled voice.

Muriel looked round at the desolation of the disordered room, the cigarette ash spilled upon the carpet, the scattered sheets of music, the cushions overturned. Outside she could hear the hum of the motor, the call of last farewells, and her mother's answering " So glad that you were able to come."

Connie lifted her head to listen, and Muriel saw then that she had been crying.

" Oh, Connie," she began.

Mrs. Hammond came into the room and shut the door behind her.

Connie stood looking at her. " A top-hole evening, Mother, was it ? So glad that they were able to come."

Then the storm broke.

" Connie, in Heaven's name, what induced you to come in ? "

" Come in ? I didn't come in. Do you think that I wanted to come and entertain your jolly friends ? I was going upstairs when that young idiot found me. Then I had to come. But at least I played up. You must own that. I saved your party for you."

" Oh, yes. You played up." Mrs. Hammond came forward and sat down, crouching over the dying fire, a tired old woman.

" Well," demanded Connie, " now that I am here, what are you going to do with me ? "

" We must tell your father," said Mrs. Hammond. " We shall have to tell your father." She spoke as though in this telling lay some unendurable agony. Her voice was bitter with defeat. " Yes," she repeated softly. " We must tell him."

" Oh, tell as many people as you like. Tell Muriel. Tell

her now. She'll have to know some time. I'd lie willingly, only I can't. I can't think of a good enough story. You've always been so much better at that sort of thing than the rest of us."

Mrs. Hammond did not speak, but sat, crouching forward, sliding a pearl and ruby ring up and down her finger.

"Why don't you tell her ? " jeered Connie. " You do so hate doing anything disagreeable, don't you ? Very well, then I will. Muriel, you may be interested to hear that I have left Thraile because I have been dismissed. And I have been dismissed because I am going to have a baby, and the baby's father is Mr. Ben Todd, and I do not happen to be Mrs. Todd. And the worthy Ben's respectable parents seem to object to my staying in the house. Well ? . . . Don't LOOK AT ME LIKE THAT ! " Her voice rose to a scream.

Muriel felt her way to a chair and sat down.

"Well ? " persisted Connie. " Well ? "

"Oh, Connie, I'm awfully sorry. I——"

"Are you ? Do you hear that, Mother ? Muriel's awfully sorry. It's more than Mother is. Mother's awfully angry, because I let Bobby Collins drag me in to the party, which I couldn't help. And she's angry because I'm going to make this family not respectable, but she isn't sorry."

"That's not true, Connie," came the stifled voice from the sofa.

"She's always brought us up to have such high ideals, you see," Connie continued, in her high, hard tone, ignoring her mother's protest. "She liked us to have a good influence over the young men, so that Lady Grainger would be awfully grateful to her, didn't you, Mother ? And you wouldn't let us work or go away, or have any other interests, because you were afraid of our spoiling a chance of a good marriage. And if we didn't get partners at dances we were beastly failures. And if our friends attracted more attention than we did they were sent away. And it was all because of our healthy homely influence, wasn't it, Mother ? And now that one of us has taken the only means she saw to fulfil your wishes and get married, *and* it hasn't come off, you're very angry, aren't you, but you aren't sorry, and if I'd been successful, you wouldn't have been angry, would you, Mother ? "

As though Connie would strike her, Mrs. Hammond held up her hand against her face. Her small figure rocked backwards and forwards on the sofa in comfortless distress.

" If I'd been like Muriel," cried Connie, " I'd have sat at home perhaps and waited for things to happen. But I wasn't like that. I wasn't made to spend my life sewing for the G.F.S. If you wanted your daughters to be perfect ladies, why did you marry Father ? You knew what he was like ! "

" Connie ! Be quiet. You shan't speak like that. Oh, what shall I do ? The shame, the shame ! Connie. Don't take it like this. I didn't know . . . I couldn't . . ."

As though it had been broken, the delicate mask of prettiness fell from her. Uncaring for the crushed silk of her new grey dinner frock, she flung herself forward among the cushions of the sofa, utterly defeated.

Muriel sat as though frozen, helplessly watching.

The front door shut with a clang. There was the sound of a key being turned. A bolt was shot. Mr. Hammond's voice hummed cheerfully :

" And now my love without a thought of me
Takes that dark damsel on his knee."

" There he is," choked Connie. Hysteria was sweeping down upon her. She began to laugh, very softly.

" I can't, I can't," said Mrs. Hammond.

The door opened.

" Hullo, hullo, hullo, not to bed yet ? Why, hullo, what's wrong ? "

The room was perfectly quiet. Through the open window from the moonlit garden came the dreary call of an owl. Far off in the valley a train whistled, leaving Marshington station.

The four in the room stayed quite still.

" Now then, Connie," asked Mr. Hammond, grown suddenly serious, " what's the meaning of all this ? "

BOOK III

CONNIE

September, 1915—February, 1916

XXVI

THOUGH there was no wind that evening to disturb them, the chintz curtains falling before the morning-room window would not hang quite together. A moth with heavy, powdered wings flopped through the open space and blundered blindly round the flaming gas-jet.

Muriel rose and drew the curtains for the third time. The garden outside lay quietly waiting, black shadows outstretched prostrate before the moonlit elms. No sound of horse hoofs trotting up the road greeted her straining ears. Only the soft thump of the moth's wings on the ceiling, and the rustle of her mother's sleeve as she flicked faster and faster at her tatting broke the perfect stillness.

Would he never come ? The 7.40 had arrived, whistling up the valley. The 8.15 had come and gone. There was still the 9.50.

Muriel returned to her book and glanced mechanically down the page. Why didn't he wire ? He had no imagination of what they must be feeling.

She read, "Of late years, I say, an abundant shower of curates has fallen upon the North of England, but in eighteen hundred eleven-twelve that affluent rain had not descended : there was no Pastoral Aid, no Additional Curates Society to stretch out a helping hand to worn-out old rectors and incumbents, and give them the wherewithal to pay a vigorous young colleague from Oxford or Cambridge."

Muriel was not interested in curates. She let *Shirley* fall unheeded on her lap, and sat again listening for the sound of her father's horse along the road or of Connie's footsteps in the bedroom overhead.

The clock ticked stupidly, marking minutes, half-hours, hours ; but at Miller's Rise endless years had passed since Mr. Hammond drove away that morning to catch the 10.20 train to Market Burton, and so on to Thraile. Centuries

had passed while Mrs. Hammond sat with her tatting, staring
into the painted glass fire-screen, and Muriel picked up books
and embroidery and the nursing accounts and laid them aside
again, and Connie up in her room, with red eyes and swollen,
distorted face, passed from defiance to despair, and from
despair to bitter comfortless surrender.

The telephone bell suddenly pealed into the silence.

Muriel rose, but Mrs. Hammond waved her aside.

" No, no, I must go. We don't know what—what——"

She rustled from the room, and Muriel heard her quick
light step in the hall and the click of the receiver as she lifted
it. Upstairs a door opened and footsteps crossed the landing
hurriedly. Connie too was listening.

" No, no—Yes. This is Rachel Hammond speaking. Mrs.
Waring ? Oh, good evening, Mrs. Waring. No, no. I'm
so sorry. Not to-night. Yes. That's quite true. Connie
came home last night for a short leave. What ? No—no.
Well "—only Connie and Muriel could detect the strain in
that familiar flutter of laughter—" perhaps we *may* have some
news for you soon, but I'm saying nothing now. Good
night."

The whirring jar of the bell as she rang off snapped the
tension of the house.

Muriel returned to her seat as Mrs. Hammond re-entered
the room. Her quivering lips were almost as white as her
drawn cheeks. She groped her way unsteadily to a chair.
After a minute she said :

" That was Mrs. Waring. She wanted us to go and play
bridge."

It seemed to Muriel incredible that people like Mrs. Waring
and Mrs. Daunt should still be living in Marshington, playing
bridge, chattering at the War Depot, and discussing the
length of autumn skirts. For Miller's Rise that life had
ended centuries ago, cut off by the startling anguish of Connie's
wild confession. The echo of that storm still seemed to ring
in Muriel's ears. Its violence had bruised and hurt her.
She had been deafened by the raging of her father's voice,
by Connie's shrill defiance and gusty tears. She could not

bear to enter the drawing-room now lest she should see again
her father standing by the fireplace, his great neck red and
swollen with anger, his voice hurling at Connie those questions,
unbearably coarse and brutal to Muriel's shrinking mind.
She wanted to shut out for ever the remembrance of Connie's
flaming, tear-stained face, and of her mother's terrible weeping
as she lay crushed and broken, beaten out of her delicate
composure into an abandonment that had tortured Muriel by
its blind surrender to astonished pain.

And then slowly, from the terror and confusion, her mother's
courage had risen above her agony. Muriel, watching her
now as she sat fidgeting with the black tatting spindle, could
feel again the effort of that re-assertion, until in the grey
dreary hours of early morning, Mrs. Hammond had risen above
her circumstances, quietly dominated the three of them, and
had sent her husband off to Thraile to do the one thing left
to save the Hammonds.

If Mr. Hammond could persuade young Todd to marry
Connie immediately, this month, if Connie could be bundled
away again to the isolated uplands of Thraile, then the tennis
club need never know; then Lady Grainger would still smile
graciously upon the Hammonds; then the Bennet relations,
and the flouted malice of the Marshington Chapel folk need
never jeer at Rachel Bennet, who against reason, against
prudence, almost against decency, had married Old Dick
Hammond's son.

Why wouldn't he come? Why wouldn't he come? Had
the trap broken down? Had he missed the connection at
Hardrascliffe? Supposing—supposing he had failed? Supposing? You never knew with Father. He had assurance
and courage and cleverness, but still, still—

A door clicked again. Both sat up stiffly, listening. Steps
descended the stairs. The door opened, and Connie entered
the room.

"I can't stand it. That room upstairs gives me the horrors.
I can't stand being alone."

She sank into her father's big arm-chair, exhausted by the
strain of the last twenty-four hours. Muriel looked at her,

thinking that this passion-torn creature was a stranger, queer and terrible, belonging only to the nightmare year since last night when that dark figure had crept along the drive. Her sister Connie had been gay and reckless, had loved flamboyant colours, and the harsh merriment of rag-time tunes. Muriel remembered her at Kingsport dances, flushed and exultant, with blue ribbon in her bright wild hair.

" I won't do it." Connie's voice, flat and dead, came from between the hands covering her bowed face. " I won't do it. I hate him. I hate Ben Todd." She lifted her head with sudden fierce energy. " Mother, let me go away. By myself. I'll manage. I'll do anything. I'll work my fingers to the bone. I'll never come near here again. Let Father give me some money. I can't go through with it."

Mrs. Hammond's trembling fingers set down the foolish white cotton, the little looped edge of her work.

" Connie," she said quietly, " you know that's impossible. We—your father and I—are doing the best, the only thing we can for you. You must help us, we——"

" But if he can't——" In an urgency of appeal Connie lifted her eyes. " You don't know Mrs. Todd. She'll lie and lie. They'll say—they'll say I encouraged him. He—Ben— does what she says. He's always done what she's said."

Mrs. Hammond opened her eyes and stared unseeing across the room to her elder daughter. Then she spoke softly, almost as though entranced :

" He can't fail. He can't fail."

" Yes, but I can ! " cried Connie, springing to her feet. " I won't go back there. You don't know what you're sending me to. You don't know. The Todds were awful, awful. You should have heard them when—when they thought—— You don't know what it's like up there. The lot of them. They'll be all against me. They're proud. They're terrible. There's no bitterness like theirs'll be to me. If you send me there, I'll never, never have another moment's happiness. They'll watch and they'll watch. They'll suspect everything I do or say. Oh, they're hard, and that fearful old cripple —sitting in a corner, watching, watching——   You'll send me to that, just to save your skins, just to save your snobbish, rotten little ideas you'll send me to—to——"

Muriel couldn't bear it. She couldn't bear again the clash and jangle of that terrible violence. " Connie ! " she cried. " Connie, don't, it isn't true. It's for your sake—it—they—— You mustn't say things like that."

Wide-eyed with astonishment Connie faced her, amazed that Muriel could so assert her personality.

Then she laughed. " You're backing them up too, are you ? Of course. Your mother's little darling always ! But I'll get round Father. I'll make him understand."

" Connie dear, you must see that for your own sake, and for the sake of the child, there's no other way. What would you do ? You could not earn your own living alone, much less burdened like that."

" Who's to blame for that ? "

" And then—the scandal. Your name . . ."

" I'll run away," sobbed Connie, for the twentieth time. But even then the shrewd common sense that underlay her recklessness realized the hopelessness of her position. Without support from her parents or from Ben, she could not face the world. Beyond her hysteria she foresaw defeat, yet could not yet acknowledge it. The desire to find an outlet for her emotion was too strong.

" I'll never face it," she repeated softly. Then, " Why doesn't he come ? "

Far off a train whistled, entering the station.

" That will be the 9.50," said Mrs. Hammond.

Muriel realized then that she did not want her father to come and tell them. Her mind was chaotic with emotion. She only knew that she could not bear to face a repetition of last night's scene. Something whispered in her mind, " Father and Connie enjoy letting themselves go." If she could have brought herself to desert her mother, she would have left the room.

A motor-car hummed up the road. A motor-bicycle throbbed noisily. Then a horse came trotting, clop-clop, clop-clop.

Connie jumped up. "I can't—I can't," she gasped.

Mrs. Hammond rose, and with sudden tenderness went forward. Connie was, after all, her child. She laid gentle hands on Connie's arm that grasped the mantelpiece, but the girl pushed her roughly aside.

"Don't touch me. I don't want you!"

Clop-clop. Clop-clop. The horse-hoofs rang clear and hard on the dry road. With a swish of dead leaves and scattering of pebbles, the cart turned smartly on to the gravel of the drive. A lantern light moved beyond the slats of the venetian blind down the side window. The groom's voice spoke. Mr. Hammond answered.

They heard his footsteps pass the window. They heard him in the hall.

Connie stood quite still as her father came into the room and stopped, facing her. She did not look up.

"Well," he said heavily, "I've fixed things up. Wedding's on 21st, Connie."

"No, it's not. I'm not going through with it." She spoke sullenly, bending towards the fireless grate.

"Ay, but ye will. Young Todd's a fool, but he seemed to be rarely set up to have you. The missus says she'll treat you well. They weren't the sort o' folk I'd thought on, Connie. I can't rightly size the whole business up, for they're decentish people."

"Decent? The old man's a fiend."

"Nay, nay, lass. Thou's not behaved so well thysen' that thou canst pick and choose. It's not the old man you'll be marrying. I cannot rightly see how it all came about."

Muriel looked at him. On his face was no longer the dark fury of resentment, but a rough tenderness, born of compunction and bewilderment. In his voice lay a new note of pity, almost, it seemed, of understanding. To Muriel this was the strangest thing in those strange days; but to Connie looking up from her clasped hands, it shone like a light through her darkness of rebellion.

"Oh, Dad, you'll help me," she cried, and stumbled forward, blindly sobbing, into the clumsy shelter of his arms.

XXVII

"TUM! Tum! Ter-um, tum, tum, tum!"
It was all over, then. The smooth bluish page scrawled over with signatures had completed the deed performed with greater solemnity in church. That was the wedding march of course, and soon they would process back down the aisle, following Connie's white fox fur and the tall shambling figure of the young man. All Marshington would watch them pass, and Muriel could imagine the things that would be said afterwards round luncheon tables all over the village.

"What do you think of the new bridegroom, Mrs. Daunt?"

"Hem, not much. A decent young man I dare say. Probably good enough for Connie Hammond." They would not be merciful, for they had been cheated out of their champagne reception. "Should ha' thought Hammond would ha' done things better," Colonel Cartwright would complain, and ladies who had hoped for an opportunity for new clothes would sniff surreptitiously over the announcement in the *Kingsport Chronicle*: "Owing to the severe illness of the bridegroom's father, no reception will be held, but all friends will be welcome at the church."

It had been a little weak, that, but if Mr. Todd Senior had not been conveniently indisposed what other excuse could have kept the Todd family away from Marshington? True, he was no more ill to-day than he had been for the past ten years or more, but nobody at Holy Trinity Church was likely to know the High Farm, Thraile, except the bridegroom, who would keep his own counsel. And the Todd family, as a visit of Mrs. Hammond to the High Farm had revealed, was quite impossible.

That visit had almost shaken Mrs. Hammond's confidence, almost, not quite. After it she had plunged with even greater thoroughness into the preparations for the wedding. "She must have cared," thought Muriel to whom the whole business appeared intolerable. She had not thought that anything

Connie might do could have touched herself so closely.   Yet, if Mrs. Hammond cared, she continued to hide her feelings with superhuman self-control.   Of course it would have been almost impossible to preserve in private that attitude of shamed reproach while in public she posed as the proud mother, but Muriel was deeply shocked in some obscure pride of soul when Mrs. Hammond adopted almost at once her public pose for domestic purposes, and began to order clothes and household linen with the wholehearted interest that she usually devoted to such things.

Only Mr. Hammond ever seemed to doubt the wisdom of her policy, but he too followed where she led him with uneasy meekness, clumsily trying to comfort her with lace scarves brought from London, and an almost pathetic consideration of her wishes that drew them closer together than ever before since their days of love-making by the one passion that could steady his uncertain nature, or make her forget for a moment her quiet calculations.

Her mother and father were all right.   They had each other.   Connie was all right.   She was going to be married. She had new clothes, presents and attention, all of which, her first rebellion overcome, she accepted with complacent satisfaction, as though they were her due.   Night after night, Muriel had thought of it, feeling that sometimes she had been mistaken, that Connie's behaviour had not been disgraceful, outraging all her sense of delicacy and reserve.   Perhaps to Connie it had been a swift romance, the madness of moonlight on the darkened moor, the sudden call of youth and brave adventure, then fleeting fear and hot rebellion to be assuaged by final victory.   Sometimes Muriel had tossed on her bed, feeling the fury of her outraged virtue ; sometimes she found in her own loneliness the greater shame.

And now it was all over.

The vestry was hot and stuffy.   Muriel wished that they need not all wait so long.   Why did the bridegroom hesitate so while signing his name, Benjamin Durdletree Todd, in weak slanting copper-plate across the page ?   Constance Rachel Adeline.   Muriel had almost forgotten that all this was Connie's name, sprawled in her dashing black signature almost into the columns for Spinster, Age and Parish.

Mrs. Hammond rustled forward in her lilac silk. " Muriel dear, won't you sign too ? "

So Muriel's small, symmetrical signature went below, and the little crowd rocked and stirred about the vestry table.

" Well, is that all ? " laughed Connie.

" Quite all, Mrs. Todd," smiled Mr. Vaughan. " Please let me offer you every happiness."

But his thin queer face looked troubled as he shook Connie's hand, and he glanced at the tall sheepish young man with an expression of veiled bewilderment.

Muriel put down the pen, wondering why the pens in vestries and offices always disguise one's signature so effectively.

And then she caught sight of the bridegroom again and began another wonder. That is Connie's husband. That is my brother-in-law. They are married. They will share the same house, the same room. She will see him always, at breakfast, at dinner, when they get up in the morning. His relations are my relations. Connie is going to live at his father's house. Connie, Connie, who used to play in the day nursery at weddings, with a lace curtain over her head.

The bride did not wear a veil now, for this quiet war-wedding was far more chic. Dorothy Daunt and Peggy Mason, who had secured their young officers, assisted by six bridesmaids and a military escort were made to feel hopelessly ostentatious by the aristocratic restraint of the Hammond wedding. So Connie hid her bright hair beneath a large, white hat, and her white coat frock of soft silky material spoke the last word in decorous elegance. Her eyes shone with excitement, and she held her head high with reckless pride.

" She's almost beautiful," thought Muriel, and was dazed by the wonder of it all. For two days before, Connie had broken down again, and declared that whatever happened she could not go through with it. Mr. Hammond had said gruffly, " Look here, Rachel, had we better chuck it ? I'll do something for the kid." But Mrs. Hammond had persisted, declaring that it was too late to withdraw now, when the wedding had been arranged, and every one would know. Then finally Connie herself had saved the situation, by crying out that since they'd pushed her into it she supposed that she'd go on. But if they knew what Thraile would be like, they hadn't the feelings of a toad, and for God's sake they weren't to fuss her any more, for she was fed up with it all.

But, after that, she had recovered her spirits. Even during the awful hour before the car arrived, she had not faltered in her attention given to gloves and hat and white *suède* shoes. And now she looked as though she had just gained her heart's desire in the rather pale, dark young man who kept looking sheepishly askance at his newly acquired father-in-law, as upon one who had bought, at the price of paying off the Todds' long-standing debts, the honesty of his erring daughter.

They stood waiting for something, the bride, the bridegroom, the Hammonds, the best man—a vaguely non-committal cousin of the Todds selected after much diligent searching by Mrs. Hammond, and imposed upon the now thoroughly intimidated Ben without compunction—Aunt Rose, Aunt Beatrice and half a dozen Bennet relatives.

"Well, Ben," smiled Mrs. Hammond tremulously, "aren't you going to do your duty ? "

He blushed. He hesitated. Then he turned and kissed Connie with clumsy awkwardness that knocked her hat aside. While she straightened it, he kissed Mrs. Hammond, and came in her turn to Muriel. It was as he bent above her, very lanky and tall and smelling of the earth and leather and warm black clothes, that suddenly she doubted.

Had they been right to force Connie into this ? What had they done ? This terrible young man ! But even then it was Connie again who reassured her.

"Come on, Ben. Stop kissing Muriel. You know she isn't used to it. Pull up your socks, old man. We've got to face them ! " She seized his arm and started almost at a run down the long aisle. They followed her, Mr. and Mrs. Hammond, Muriel and the strange young man, the trail of relatives behind.

Tum, tum, terum—tum, tum—tum ! triumphed the organ.

A sea of bobbing faces greeted the procession, pallid in the dimness of the church. The scent from Muriel's bouquet of pink carnations choked her. The organ shook and quivered in its ecstasy. She saw Connie's white dress gleam before her. She felt a curious sensation of unreality, as though her mind were quite detached from her body, and she were looking down upon Muriel Hammond's saxe blue dress, upon her flower-crowned hat, and the rocking sea of the congregation. Suppose that this had been her own wedding—hers and Godfrey's ? The young man at her side grew taller ; his pleasantly mediocre profile hardened and straightened into Godfrey's features as she had last seen them, the straight fine nose, the splendid sweep of his dark eyebrows, the curve of his too-handsome, rather obstinate mouth, his firm chin uptilted against the dark pillar of the aisle.

People were shaking hands at the church door, crowds and crowds of them. Connie, laughing and blushing, was thanking them for their good wishes so volubly that nobody noticed the bridegroom's silence. Even if he had spoken, so many quite eligible young men in Marshington talked with York-shire accents that nobody would notice how common Ben's voice sounded. Here was Lady Grainger smiling down at them, and Lady Grainger's kind, guileless face, and her pleasant voice saying, " Well, Mrs. Todd, when I first made your acquaintance so short a time ago, I hardly thought that to-day I should come to your wedding." Mrs. Hammond replied laughingly, " Wasn't she a sight that night ? Coming into the drawing-room all muddy ! I was ashamed of her."

Really, thought Muriel, is Mother just being wonderful, or does she really feel quite happy ? But she knew that Mrs. Marshall Gurney's presence luring Lady Grainger's little speech had helped Mrs. Hammond over a difficult place.

Little Miss Dale, being as usual unable to make her presence felt at the centre of interest, pushed her way to Muriel's side.

" A charming wedding," she said tearfully. Nobody knew whether Miss Dale always wept at weddings out of sympathy for the bride or sorrow for her single state. But she always went, and she always wept. " I love a wedding," she con-

tinued, " And *how* sweet Connie looks ! and positively everybody here. The Graingers of course, and I am sure that
Mrs. Neale would have been if it had not been for her sad news."

" Her news ? What news ? "

" Oh, well." Miss Dale hesitated, darting quick, bird-like
glances at Muriel and the bride. " I wish that I hadn't
mentioned it—at a wedding. We must think of bright things.
Happy the bride that the sun shines on, and of all such good
things. The sun *is* shining. Dear Connie. A nice young
man, I expect. Younger than she is, surely ? But I thought
that you would be sure to have heard."

" No. We've been rather absorbed by our own affairs for
the last few weeks, I am afraid." Then, with sharpening
anxiety, " Not about—her son ? " She could not say his name.

" Poor Godfrey. Yes, poor Godfrey. We only heard last
night over the telephone. Mrs. Marshall Gurney rang up
about the nursing fund, and then . . ."

The crowd moved forward. In another minute Miss Dale
might be swept away and Muriel would not know. She
stretched out her hand and caught at the little woman's sleeve.

" You said—you were saying—Mrs. Neale had heard . . ."
Her heart cried, " Tell me, tell me," yet she did not want to
know.

" Poor Godfrey—— She had a telegram from the War
Office—— Reported wounded and prisoner of war. Of
course reports are not always true. As I said to my sister
Maud . . . you know, she was *so* sorry that she could not
come to-day," and Miss Dale proceeded to describe all that
Muriel had known for weeks past about her sister Maud's sciatica.

But Muriel did not hear. She was picking at the silver
paper round her pink carnations while she fought for self-
control. She saw all sorts of irrelevant, meaningless things,
her father's broad, black back, the frightened pertness of the
bow in Miss Dale's hat, Mrs. Marshall Gurney's flowing
scarves and veils. Part of her mind recalled the stale Marshington joke that Mrs. Marshall Gurney wore as many veils as a
widow because she had forgotten her husband's existence long
ago. The other part remembered as though she herself had

seen them, the horrors that she dreamed of at the front. She
saw again pictures drawn by the too graphic pencil of a war-
artist. She saw the wooden face of an old woman in a lamp-lit
shop, who said, "War's bloody hell, ah'm telling you, bloody
hell." She saw Godfrey's splendid body torn and broken, his
handsome face distorted out of its complacency, his smiling
eyes looking straight into despair.

She supposed that she must have followed her sister out
into the sunlit churchyard, where fallen chestnut leaves spread
a carpet of mottled gold and green before the bride. She
supposed that people must have thrown confetti at her, for
afterwards she shook it from her hat and it lay on her bedroom
carpet like the fallen petals of pink and white may. She must
have sat through the long luncheon party, and have helped
Connie into her brown travelling dress, and have talked to
Uncle George and Aunt Rose, and the long-legged cousin,
Adeline, from Market Burton, who would stay until the
evening train.

Only when she had helped to tidy the abandoned luncheon
table, and helped Annie to pack in their tissue paper the rose
bowls and silver inkstands destined incongruously for the High
Farm, Thraile, horror and desolation overcame her. Perhaps
the act of packing away Connie's presents reminded her of
that evening at Scarborough when she had packed her mother's
trunk, and Godfrey found her. Perhaps, all the time since
Miss Dale spoke to her, her imagination had been feeding
upon horrors. But suddenly she put down the painted blotter
that she was holding, and fled from the room. The house was
full of borrowed maids, and aunts and stray acquaintances.
She rushed to the only sure retreat and locked the bathroom
door behind her. Flinging herself down beside the towel rail,
she stifled her sobs in the rough softness of her father's bath
towels.

"Oh, Godfrey, Godfrey!" she moaned. "Oh, poor
Godfrey. He mustn't be hurt. He mustn't." Her own
body writhed as with acute physical pain. She could feel the
agony of his wounds. They tore her without mercy.

The light of motor lamps in the yard shone through the

uncurtained window on to her small, shaking body and the bowed darkness of her head. Her lips moved.

"Oh, God, don't take him out of the world, don't let him die. Even if he has to marry Clare. Make him come back. Come back to me, some day." She remembered one dreadful night, soon after Martin Elliott's death, when she had wished Godfrey dead too, in a storm of jealous bitterness. She felt herself a murderess.

"Don't let him die. Don't let him die!" Her hands tore at the thick towels. Her imagination, beyond all control, tortured her with his pain. She had heard tales of prison camps. . . .

"Muriel, Muriel," called her mother's voice. "Where are you, dear ? Come and help me to forward these telegrams to Connie."

With her hand to her mouth, choking the little sobs that broke from time to time, she stared round the room like a trapped creature. The wan light from the yard gleamed on the enamel bath, the metal rails, the polished taps.

"Muriel ! Muriel ! "

The house claimed her. She was bound to its routine as to a wheel. It would not stop, wherever Godfrey lay, his broken body nursed by alien hands.

"Come along, dear."

Slowly, as in a dream, she rose and turned the key.

XXVIII

THE wind shrieked through the cutting and dashed itself against the crawling train. Up and up the steep curve of the gradient panted the blunt-nosed engine. Pushing forward slowly, it flung two streamers of fiery smoke out for the swooping hurricane to snatch and tear to ribbons. From the carriage window Muriel could see blank walls of grey rank grass, scarred by rough boulders and disfigured here and there by the blackened skeletons of burnt-out gorse.

Once or twice a wheeling sea-bird with strong, outstretched wings swept across the sky, and twice since Aunby Station the embankment had dipped, revealing the huge desolation of the moor beyond. Only once she had seen through a gash in the hill-side the dark tumbling water of the wintry sea, whirled into patches of white foam and driven ruthlessly against the broken cliff.

She consulted again the map on the other side of the railway carriage, flanked by pictures of Whitby Abbey and Scarshaven shore. She could trace there the railway straggling up the coast past Scarshaven, Aunby and Flying-fall, before it branched inland again to Follerwick. Only one more station separated her from Connie. It was surprising how little Muriel had thought about her for the past four months. The news of Godfrey's disaster had wiped her sister as completely from her mind as a sponge erases writing from a slate, and even the later information that the disaster was less terrible than she had feared had not so much recalled the Thraile family to Muriel as it had recalled Muriel to Marshington. Mrs. Neale had heard of Godfrey. His wound was a slight one, and the worst consequence of his prison life seemed to be an exasperating but tolerably safe boredom which at least might save his life until the end of the war. That was a vast relief. It had enabled Muriel to face with greater equanimity the post-girl's rap at the door, and the soft flutter of letters into their wire cage; but at the time when Muriel heard it she was racked by another anxiety that engrossed her mind and body. Mrs. Hammond had caught influenza. She began with it one morning early in November and continued to have it badly for about six weeks. " She has got thoroughly run down—seems to have been worrying. You ought to take care of her, you know," said Dr. Parker; and Muriel, who considered that she had done nothing else for the past twelve years, thought this a little hard. Nor was Mrs. Hammond easy to nurse. When Muriel brought her Benger's food, she wanted Bovril, and when Muriel brought her Bovril, then she didn't think that she really could eat anything just then. For three weeks Muriel nursed her night and day, sleeping in her father's dressing-room, or rather lying there in drowsy apprehension waiting for her mother's call.

And now she was better, and Christmas was over, and Muriel was being carried in the train to Thraile. Connie had responded to her offer without enthusiasm, she thought ; but Connie's letters never were particularly indicative of her feelings. Her handwriting did not adapt itself to lucid analysis. Yet a secret apprehension drew Muriel from Marshington into this bleak country where everything was just a little sinister, and therefore where anything might happen.

The rain rattled now against the window. It flooded out the landscape, leaving for Muriel's eyes only a blurred line of horizon and for her ears the howling of the wind. Sound rather than sight gave to Muriel her first impression of the Follerwick moors.

The train came to a standstill with a grinding scream of brakes. Muriel pulled her suit-case from the rack, buttoned her fur collar more tightly, and wrestled with the door. The wind caught it from her and almost hurled her out on to the platform. She staggered out into the driving rain. For a moment she stood bewildered, facing a short stretch of wooden platform, a deserted shelter, and the grim pile of the moors beyond, hill after hill shouldering up into a melting sky.

The wind flung itself upon her like a fury and almost tore her suit-case from her hand.

Then, just when she was beginning to wonder whether this could possibly be a station, Connie bore down upon her ; Connie wrapped in a great man's mackintosh, her dripping arms outstretched, her cheeks wet and her eyes shining through the rain.

" Oh, here you are ! Good old Mu ! By Jove, it's good to see you ! "

She enfolded Muriel with a damp but unequivocal embrace.

" Oh, Connie," shouted Muriel reproachfully ; she had to shout because of the wind and the rain. " You shouldn't have come. This awful day ! "

Connie laughed, and Muriel was glad of her laugh. It

seemed to loosen the tight feeling of doubt and fear that ever since her father's illness had bound her chest uncomfortably.

"This? Oh, this is nothing! My dear, we didn't know what weather was at Marshington. That your bag? Come on."

On the road outside the station stood a high-wheeled, springless vehicle known, possibly on account of its cumbrous heaviness, as a "light cart." A red-nosed youth in oilskins held the reins of a very old, yellowish horse that stood dejectedly, its tail between its lean legs, and its back hunched against the blinding storm.

They climbed into the cart and Muriel wondered how ever Connie could endure the constant jolting as the wheels jarred over stones, jerked in and out of ruts, and set the cart rocking like a ship on a rough sea. Wind and rain prevented any attempt at conversation. Muriel, sitting sideways behind the driver, could see Connie's profile, her eyes, swollen with wind or tears, the sullen misery of her mouth. She turned away, sorely troubled, but there was nothing else to look at. Grey curtains of rain shut down the travellers. They seemed to be isolated from all life or colour. Marshington and the warm comfort of their mother's drawing-room was in a far-off world. It seemed impossible that the journey would end at another house, where there would be fires and tea and dry clothes to wear.

The thick black waterproof rug across Muriel's knees grew heavy with rain. She found that she had been sitting with her hands in a pool of water. Timidly she shook it off her knee, and watched it run away through the cracks in the bottom of the cart.

They had been driving for years and years, while Muriel's courage fluctuated between fear of the unknown and gladness that a change had come at last into the monotony of life. Slowly the second feeling conquered the first. This was Thraile. Connie was here and unhappy. Something had to be done and if possible done by Muriel. She lifted her chin obstinately, determined that no fear should shake her purpose, though what she had to do or how to do it were equally unknown to her. Her imagination already raised her to

unfounded ecstasies, and through the rain her eyes shone as
in her mind she sang Bunyan's hymn :

> " Hobgoblin nor foul fiend
>   Shall daunt his spirit . . .
> There's no discouragement
> Shall make him once relent
> If he do but consent
>   To be a pilgrim."

The driver unfastened a gate and led the cart along a rough
field road bordered on one side by a broken wall of piled grey
stones.   At the top of a steep incline another wall enclosed
a narrow strip of mud, and tangled, stunted bushes known as
the garden.   Beyond it, facing westward across the moors,
stood the High Farm.   Stark bare to all winds that blew were
its grey walls.   Five narrow windows above and four below
stared blankly at the winding road, like eyes without eyebrows.
A few farm buildings huddled to the south and crept behind
the shelter of the hill, but the house stood square to the wild
wind and the wild sky and the waiting menace of the moor.
" Is—is this Thraile ? "   Muriel faltered.
Connie smiled at her, a queer light smile of pride, of fear,
of challenge.
" Yes, this is Thraile all right.   The High Farm—Muriel.
Muriel—the High Farm.   Now you are properly introduced.
And very nice too, I *don't* think ! "
The wind caught her laugh and snatched it away, as it had
caught the smoke of the ascending engine.

XXIX

MRS. TODD drew her pie from the oven and sniffed
it appreciatively.   Its billowing crust was slowly
ripening to the rich gold of maturity.   Its savoury
smell satisfied her.   She replaced it, shut the oven door with

meticulous care and rose stiffly to her feet, her corsets creaking as she moved. She began to grumble aloud cheerfully :

" All I can say is—if Miss Muriel can't eat a bit of good pie like that, she can go without. Good meat houses there is, and bad 'uns there is, and no one can say that Meggie Todd's near wi' her lads, nor lasses neither, though I'm fair sick o' these Hammonds. What wi' Mr. Hammond trampin' round like a mad elephant an' Mrs. H. mewing round like a sick cat, you might ha' thought Ben had murdered their lass instead o' marrying her."

She clapped a dish of bacon on to the long table and whisked her oven cloth on to a nail beside the stove, for she did nothing without enormous vigour.

" A fat lot o' use it is, me havin' Connie front ways if she's not going to give a hand wi' t'work, but s'always gadding round after her fine relations. Ah suppose William 'ud tell me that the wife's kin are a scourge sent from God for t'original sin o' t'husband," and she tossed the head that had once been the pertest in Follerwick. But she was not William, nor did she really dislike Connie as much as her words implied ; but she found in these monologues of indictment an outlet for the accumulated irritation of reproaches born without resentment. She contemplated the clean white cloth on the table, straightened a couple of dishes on the dresser, then flew towards the yard door and the coal-house, murmuring as a parting message to the kitchen, " I'm sure the Lord made relations-in-law to square up for them as can't get married."

She had, indeed, good reason to see in relations-in-law a doubtful blessing. As Meggie Megson, the bright-eyed daughter of a Follerwick publican, she had been wooed with greater enthusiasm than discretion by William Todd of Thraile. A hasty marriage ensured the legitimate birth of her eldest son, Matthew, but did not quiet the uneasy conscience of her lover. For a year of bitter recrimination alternating with reckless passion, he had lived with her as her husband, but before her second son, Benjamin was born, the Lord took vengeance upon the wickedness of William. A false step while manœuvring the thrashing-machine robbed the wild young

Todd of his left leg, and so much injured his spine that he lay now always on a couch in the front parlour, contemplating the inexorable justice of God and the unending pageant of the sky from the west window. William Todd did not so much find religion as religion found him, the sunless, menacing religion of a tramping preacher, part Calvinist, part Wesleyan ; a religion wherein strange anomalies of predestination strove with a Pauline emphasis upon justification by faith, without which, in spite of the admonition of St. James, works were dead. Meggie accepted her husband's religion as she had accepted his love. Finding herself regarded as an enticement sent from the devil, she listened with patience to the out-pourings of St. James, " Let no man say when he is tempted, I am tempted of God . . . but each man is tempted, when he is drawn away by his own lust and enticed. Then the Lust, when it hath conceived, beareth sin, and the sin, when it is full grown, bringeth forth death." But she endured with less tranquillity the continual assurance that from her sons, Matthew and Benjamin, such sin and death should come. Since, however, things were as they were, she proceeded to her cooking, scrubbing, baking and nursing with undiminished vigour, comforted, perhaps, by the thought that if her husband despised her only less than he despised his children at least he could not do without her.

William's mother unfortunately also tended to regard her son's accident as something in the nature of divine retribution, not for compromising a publican's daughter, but for marrying her ; and when it became known that Ben, the weakling, the awkward boy whom every one conspired to brand as " want-ing," had got Connie, the land-girl, into trouble, then the fierce scene of personal remorse, impotent bitterness and denunciation had been visited, not so much upon Connie, as upon Mrs. Meggie, since she was clearly the root of all evil at the High Farm. Yet, after Connie had returned to the High Farm as Ben's wife, it was Mrs. Meggie who continued to make her new life bearable. To tell the truth, Mrs. Meggie was secretly glad that Ben had married under any circum-stances. Between the grim couple of invalids in the front parlour and the boisterous conviviality of farm workers in the kitchen, she had been unconsciously numbed with loneliness, and the prospect of a daughter-in-law pleased her gregarious temperament. Then too, she was glad that Ben, whom his father and brother despised for lack of virility, should have been the first to marry after all.

As she bustled from the stone-paved yard this evening, and called up the long passage, her heart, though she hardly knew it, was softened to the thought of her Ben's little child.

"Polly, Alice, Gert, come on some of you. Give me a hand wi' t'table, now."

From the draughty darkness came a gust of song and laughter.

> "Who, who, who, who, who were you with last night ?
> 'Twasn't your sister, 'twasn't your ma !
> Ah, ah, ah, ah, a—ah, ah ! ah ! "

The voices rose to a shrill crescendo, accompanied by the screeching gasps of Bob Wither's concertina, and the tramp of nailed boots on the floor.

Mrs. Todd opened the door of the back room, releasing a flood of lamplight and tumultuous clamour.

"Come on, you lazy good-for-nowts. Put down yon thing, for goodness' sake, Bob. Alice, where's Gert ? Feeding pigs this time o' day ? What, how often did I tell you that ye'll never make a farmer by gettin' up to feed stock ower' nights ? Be off now, some on ye, to see if light cart's come yet. Hurry and get gone, then you'll get back."

They scattered under her genial despotism.

"I'll help, Ma. Where's forks ? "

The kitchen rang to the clatter of pots, of tongues and the shouted refrain of their song, "Who were you with last night ? "

Thus Muriel, who had clambered down stiffly from the dog-cart, and dragged her suit-case along the unlighted corridor, came suddenly upon a scene of firelit tumult and huge gaiety. Connie pushed open the kitchen door and marched in. The noise stopped. Every one looked at the new-comers.

"Well I never! If you're not here already and no one ever heard you! Connie, did Sam go to loose out for you? So this is Muriel? My, aren't you wet! You're not as big as your sister, are you? Take after your mother likely. Here, Mat, where are your manners? Dolly, Alice!"

"Pleased to meet you," said Dolly pertly.

Alice set a saucer cheese-cake on the table, nodded at Muriel, and took from her pocket a bundle of crochet that never left her. Some women take to crochet as others do to cigarettes. Alice, flicking at hers with unsteady fingers, was hiding herself from any possible embarrassment. Her thin face bent above her work.

"Where's Ben?" asked Connie abruptly.

"Didn't he come to help you down? There now! Well, he must be up in fold yard. You'd better go and get your wet things off. Go on. Take her up, Connie. Polly go and help carry Muriel's bag. Connie, get a dry pair o' stockings on for Heaven's sake. We can't have you catching cold, at all events." This with an uncontrollable wink at Muriel.

"When did Ben go out?" asked Connie stubbornly, ignoring her mother-in-law's injunctions.

"I don't know. When did he go, Mat?"

"Half an hour. He went to help Sam." Alice the land girl raised her face for a minute from her crochet to give her information, then thrust it down again. It was a thin, freckled face, with long fair lashes and a sharp up-tilted chin. Muriel found herself standing and facing Alice, while the rain dripped from her coat on to the white scoured floor.

"Go along with you now, messing up my floor!" cried Mrs. Todd, and shooed them vigorously from the kitchen.

"Well," remarked Connie, as they stood together at last in the large square room to which she had brought Muriel. "And what do you think of it all?"

Muriel looked round the bare walls, papered with a grotesquely botanical pattern and texts on strips of cardboard. The wind blew the texts backwards and forwards against the wall. It drove the lace window-curtains out into the room, and sent the carpet rippling in long waves across the floor. Through the window she could see nothing but a veil of twilight rain.

"How can I say what I think of it till I've seen some more?" she temporized, pulling off her wet coat and pushing the hair out of her eyes. "It's all frightfully different from what I expected. The front of the house is so grim, and yet, when you come to the back and see all those jolly people—— They seem to enjoy life, Connie. And then Mrs. Todd. She may be a bit of a Tartar, but I like her eyes. And then, there's Ben's father, and old Mrs. Todd, aren't there?"

Connie laughed bitterly, "Oh yes. There's my respected father-in-law *and* old Mrs. Todd. I wonder if you'll like *her* eyes?"

"Why not? Oh, Connie, you ought to take your wet things off. Now, at once."

"I'm all right." Connie pulled off her oilskin and felt the sleeve of her woollen coat below. "I'm quite dry." But she sat down on the bed and began to unlace her boots.

"Why shouldn't I like old Mrs. Todd's eyes?" persisted Muriel.

"Oh, she gets on my nerves. She sits in her chair in that awful little room and looks and looks and looks. She looks right through you, Muriel. She sees just everything. All the things you ever thought or did or—anything.

"They say she's got the 'sight'—you know, second sight. I think she's just uncanny. And she's so frightfully old, you know. Not like a person at all—like a tree, all twisted. And then she's always nibbling things, little bits of biscuit and soft sweets and things. Like a mouse. And then her bright eyes. Ugh!"

"But then, do you see her much?"

"No, thanks! I keep out of her way. But she sees me. She never misses anything. Oh, dear me, no! and she knows all about—all about Ben and me. It's awful, Mu. Sometimes I think I'll have to kill her or run away or something."

"How do you mean? She knows all about Ben and you?

Every one here does, don't they ? " said Muriel slowly. She
had understood from Mr. and Mrs. Hammond that the Todds
had accepted Connie's position as regrettable but without
alternative.

" Oh, yes, in a way they know. The girls don't exactly,
but they suspect. Mu, it's awful. We used to have such jolly
times, singing in the back room and going off to concerts at
Follerwick camp, and all that. Now it's awful. I'm out of
it all. They hardly talk to me, and we all used to laugh at
Ben, and they don't know what to make of it. And old Mrs.
Todd hates me, and the old man's mad. He's got religious
mania or something and he's quite potty. Mrs. Meggie's all
right, but nobody cares much what she says except Ben, and
he's still more scared of his father." Connie's bootlaces
dropped from her hands and she sat forward, huddled on the
edge of the bed, staring at her sister.

" I don't see that they have any right to hate you," cried
Muriel hotly. " After all—it was their precious son—
who——"

Connie's blue, miserable eyes darted a quick glance at her
sister's face, then dropped again to her boots.

" Oh, yes, I know, but you could hardly expect them to
remember that."

She kicked off her boots and sat with her feet in their black
woollen stockings swinging from the bed.

" Every one hates me," she said miserably. " Mr. Todd
thinks I'm a judgment from hell fire or something, because
he was a bit wild when he was young. And Alice—well, to
tell the truth, I think that Alice was in love with Ben and
she'll get her knife into me whenever she can. She's as jealous
as anything. And Mrs. Todd's a bit queer because she's so
fond of Ben and is afraid I shan't make him happy. She
knows I'm going to get him away from this place too as soon
as the war's over and we can get a farm. Oh, it's no picnic
I can tell you."

Muriel was apparently engaged upon fastening the front of
her velveteen dress. Really she was thinking about Connie.
" I mustn't be sentimental. Connie evidently pities herself

quite enough. She's not really displeased because Alice is jealous. And Mrs. Todd is kind, I'm sure. Mother said I hadn't to let her harrow my feelings. Connie always did make the most of her own sufferings." She fastened a press hook below the brown fur edging of her dress and asked quite casually :

" But Ben, of course he stands up for you ? "

" Oh, Ben would be all right. But he's frightened of his father, and Alice worries him, and it's rotten living on here in this house. You never get away from them all for a minute, and tea's the worst. They all sit there round that big table and they eat and eat. And I've got to sit there and feel that they're looking at me and thinking things, an' nudging each other if I've got a headache. And then they all go giggling and carrying on in the back room and I've got to sit about with Mrs. Meggie. And I can't go into the farm because it's such hard work, and it's such beastly weather. And you never see anyone. Oh, I'm so bored and bored and bored ! "

" It'll be better when the baby's come. You'll have lots to do then."

" I don't know. Sometimes I just get scared. I wish I was going home to have it. It's awful here. Ben gets fed up with me because I'm not so jolly as I used to be. He doesn't say anything, but I know. Why didn't he come and meet us to-night, I'd like to know ? Oh, they just treat me here as if I was dirt. They think it's an honour for me to have married into their beastly family. The Todds ! who live in the kitchen, and Mrs. Meggie was a barmaid, and—well, look at this room ! You see what they're like."

" I don't. I haven't seen them all yet. I haven't even seen Mr. Todd."

" Oh, he's mad. He's gone quite potty. He reads the Bible all day and talks like a lunatic. Ben says he's not so frightfully poor really. They've done badly since his accident and all that, but he's got a lot of land. There's a little farm over at Fallowdale that's let out to tenants. If he'd let Ben and me go there——"

She leant forward, biting her nails, a singularly unattractive figure in her sagging skirt and the old crimson jersey that she had worn at Marshington. Muriel deliberately went to her case and drew out a clean handkerchief from her lavender-scented satchet. Part of her mind was conscious of a satisfactory contrast between her own trim orderliness and Connie's abandoned self-commiseration. Part of her thoughts were dazed with a sad wonder. Was this the ennobling power of suffering and tragedy, this nauseating muddle of petty resentment and self-pity ? Wasn't it really rather a waste of time and energy to try to help people as impossible as Connie ?

She stood with her face towards the window, a pucker of thought between her brows.

Suddenly from the bed came a little cry. " Oh, Mu, Mu ! I am so awfully glad you've come. I know you'll help me. You will help me, won't you ? I've been so beastly miserable ! "

Muriel capitulated.

Her position in this household might be most unpleasant, and Connie might not be an easy person, but at least she had appealed to Muriel. Somebody wanted her. Somebody needed her.

She returned to the bed and opened her arms wide. Tear-stained but comforted, Connie tumbled in. They sat there until Mrs. Todd called up the stairs :

" Come along, girls. Tea's ready."

" Oh, Connie," cried Muriel, " and I've never let you tidy ! "

" Oh, Lord, and there's such a song and dance if we're late. For goodness' sake go down and say I'm coming."

Go down ? All alone ! into that formidable crowd of quite strange people ? Muriel hesitated. Then the courage of her new resolve returned to her.

" Oh, well, I suppose I shall have to do harder things than this if I'm really going to help Connie," she reflected.

With her head high and her eyes shining she felt her way down the uneven stairs.

The battle of Thraile had begun.

XXX

IT was not going to be easy, but then Muriel was not quite sure that she wanted ease. She found herself at last comforted by a situation that demanded from her action, prompt action. That was what she found so terribly difficult, the action on her own initiative. Thraile was alarmingly different from Marshington, where nearly all judgments could be obtained ready-made from social conventions or from Mrs. Hammond. At Thraile nobody seemed to care what she did except Connie, and Connie as a councillor was worse than useless, for between moods of sullen silence, boisterous humour and hysterical despair she had lost even her very moderate supply of common sense.

For a fortnight Murial stayed on at Thraile, watching and talking and thinking, thinking, thinking. She had tramped over the dark moor before the house ; she had wandered down the farm that fell away behind it, acre after acre of drab stubble and harsh grass land, to the swirling waters of the Fallow. But whether she trod the sheep-tracks girdled with frost, or sat in the stuffy parlour listening to the endless tale of Connie's woe, the same conviction urged her.

She would have to speak to William Todd.

Last night she had written to her mother :

You see, the position here for Connie really is intolerable. Mr. Todd, the cripple, really rules this house. He loves Matthew ; but because he considers him to have been " born in sin " he doesn't think it right to love him, and makes up for it by hating Ben, who has always been rather weak and sickly. Or else he just pretends to hate him, and really loves them both. I cannot say, for he is a queer man. Every one is terrified of him, though the girls think that he's quite mad. Anyway the point is that Ben and Connie are unhappy here and ought to get away. The farm girls suspect things and make jokes about Connie. Mr. Todd and Matthew both bully Ben. Ben and Connie are never alone together for a minute except at night. They are getting frightfully self-conscious and always under a sort of restraint which must be bad for them. Mr. Todd has a little farm at Fallowdale, quite a nice little house, which he was going to give to the first son that married. Now he says that Ben can't be trusted away from him at Thraile. I am sure that if Ben and Connie could get away together, they would be happy. Ben really seems to be very fond of her. I am going to speak to Mr. Todd myself, but, if he won't listen, I do wish that you or Father could do something. And couldn't we take Connie into a nursing home for when the baby comes ? It's not that they are unkind to her here, and they make her as comfortable as they can, and she need do no housework unless she likes. It's only that they ought not to be here with all these people.

I am so sorry about your cold and father's indigestion, and I quite understand how busy you are about the luncheon party. I would come home and help you with it, but I really don't feel that I can leave here just yet, please, if you can do without me. If Mrs. Cartwright worries you about the Jumble Sale again, do tell her that Mr. Vaughan specially told me that we could not have the Parish Room until February 14th because of the Red Cross Exhibition. It is very nice of you to say you miss me, and you do understand why I'm staying on, don't you ?

Please give my love to Father.

Your loving daughter,
MURIEL.

P.S.—Can't you get Aunt Beatrice for the luncheon ?

She simply could not help writing her letter. It was the nearest approach that she could make to asking for the advice that she so sorely needed. It brought her into touch with homely and familiar things before she plunged irrevocably into the deep waters of her own decision.

She had sat wrapped up in her thick grey cloth coat in the bare chilliness of her bedroom, reading and re-reading the neat, small handwriting that always looked as though it might be going to say something interesting and that never did. She

felt about it as soldiers feel about letters written on the eve
of an advance. From a strange place she stretched out her
hands to grasp, perhaps for the last time, at the safety of the
known world.

But she had not posted the letter. Re-read in the cold
light of early morning criticism, she had decided that it
promised more than her feeble courage might perform. A
scrupulous mental honesty had made her recognize her weakness long ago. "I am going to speak to Mr. Todd," she
wrote, but nobody should read the words till she had spoken.

All the same, the last letter from Mrs. Hammond, one of a
resigned but plaintive series, had to be answered. That was
just as well, for it set a limit at last to Muriel's procrastination.
The postman came to Thraile at six o'clock, leaving the letters
and taking away with him any written by the household. If
Muriel could only end that awful interview before six, she still
might post her letter to her mother.

On paper it had seemed so simple ; but then on paper and
to Mrs. Hammond it would have been impossible to do justice
to the atmosphere of Thraile. Those were two terrible
people, sitting in the small front parlour ; the old lady mumb-
ling and rustling from the arm-chair by the fire, whose bright
unseeing eyes could yet see everything ; the cripple lying
stretched before the window, his fiery spirit slowly burning
through his mutilated body, until it seemed that it must
quite consume all that was mortal and regain the liberty it
proudly craved.

It was all very well pretending that she did not mind. For
nearly an hour that afternoon, Muriel had walked along the
steep moor road with Connie, listening to the angry emphasis
of her reiterated words. To comfort her, Muriel had said,
" All right, I'll speak to him." She did not add that for nights
now she had dreamed of the approaching interview, had seen
herself standing in the bright stuffiness of that over-heated
room, confronting the fierce relentlessness of those piercing
eyes, feeling her own gentleness driven away in blind surrender
out into the whirling darkness of the passage. And supposing
that she made things worse ? Supposing that he resented her

interference ? That he himself had been thinking of sending Ben to Fallowdale, but perversely changed his mind at Muriel's blundering suggestion ?

Standing in the corridor she pressed her thin hands against her face. As though she could feel through the door the repulsion of his violence, she shrank against the wall. His fierce tongue probed her softness; his strength had outraged her submission; his independence, exaggerated almost to insanity, bruised and bewildered her well-tutored mind. "He's mad. He's mad," she thought. "Better not go at all than break down in the middle."

From inside the parlour the cuckoo-clock piped suddenly five hollow notes. "Five o'clock. If I mean to post that letter I must go in now—now."

She went forward and tapped at the door.

She had been in before several times with Mrs. Todd, but always had retreated as soon as courtesy made possible. Never before had she been in alone.

The room now seemed to float in liquid firelight. Upborne upon the flickering flood she could see here a jar of delicate gilt and ivory beneath a fiery glass bubble; there the corner of a polished picture-frame; a wool worked footstool, the basket of sewing that Mrs. Meggie had left on the table. Slowly the quivering movement steadied before her eyes, and from the dancing shadows the solid bulk of old Mrs. Todd's chair rose like an island, and there by the window she saw William Todd.

He lay as usual gazing out across the moor, his hawk-like profile outlined against the melting silver of the wintry sun that flowed between dark banks of hill and sky. All the Todds had sharp features and noses hooked almost to a deformity, but sickness had emaciated a naturally lean face, until William Todd was terrible enough to see.

Muriel closed the door very quietly, and went across to the couch in the window. Even when she stood beside him, he did not seem to see her, but lay as still as the furniture or the dark moor. The room was silent. Only the light flames rustled like the restless wings of a bird imprisoned in the hearth and the old woman nibbled and mumbled in her sleep. Far, far away from Marshington was this firelit parlour. Muriel spoke timidly.

" Please, Mr. Todd, can I speak to you a minute ? "

" Evidently. You see that. Ah cannot get away."

A certain broadening of the vowels betrayed William Todd's county, but he spoke with a readiness unusual among the tongue-tied farmers of the Riding, and possessed a command of language won from long reading of the Bible, dog-eared theological tracts, and a surprising quantity of the more easily acquired English classics.

" I wanted to talk to you about Connie," Muriel continued. " You know that when—when she had—to—to——"

" To marry my son to save her own name from the disgrace that justly followed her own action. Well ? "

This was not a promising beginning, but at least it seemed to Muriel, that, considering his own record, he was being a little unfair.

" Well," she said, more hotly than she had intended. " I don't see myself that it was such an awful thing to do. After all, many people don't even marry."

" Because the many have sinned, does that excuse the guilt of one ? I think not."

This was dangerous ground. Muriel shifted her position. It was too late now for retreat. She spoke hastily.

" I didn't come to talk to you about whether Connie sinned or not. I don't pretend to judge such things. What I do feel is that somebody ought to tell you that living on here is being frightfully bad for them. They're never really alone together for a minute. Every one whom they see and every one where they go reminds them of what they once did. People laugh and sneer—and—oh, it's terrible. You can't see it of course, or you'd have known, I'm sure, how impossible it is."

" Please go on. This is no doubt very interesting."

" It isn't interesting, Mr. Todd, really. It's horrible. Oh, do let them go away. Please let them go. You've got a farm at Fallowdale, haven't you ? "

No answer came to her from the shadows. Fearfully she continued :

"Well, why don't you let Ben farm it ? Let them go off and live together, make a fresh start all on their own. I'm sure they could be happy. Connie loves farming, and they'd have the baby. Oh, I know you'd find they'd be far happier. Just those two, where they could forget what a bad start they'd made. It's cruel, it's just cruel to make that one mistake an ever-living shame to them because other people smile and sneer and insinuate, people who are probably every bit as bad but just more careful. How can they be happy like this ? "

She stopped, amazed by her own temerity. Beyond the moor the last silver gleam of sunlight lay like an outstretched sword between the dark embrace of hill and sky. William Todd lay watching it for a long time before he moved. Then he said slowly :

"You seem to set great store by happiness."

She was surprised. Eagerly she tried to see his face through the growing shadows as she said :

"I do, I do. Surely it's the right of people to be happy ! "

"Really ? To think o' that now ! Are you happy ? "

"I ? " Three months ago she had told herself that she was the most miserable of frustrated women, but to a stranger she would have laughed nervously and answered, "I'm all right." Somehow at Thraile and to this madman, one spoke the truth if possible. She answered thoughtfully. "I'm not sure. No, I don't think I'm happy. I've never really had any of the things I wanted most. I've never done anything I meant to do. I'm a failure, I suppose. Nobody needs me . . ."

"Well ? " He cut short the flow of self-revelation, so alien to Muriel's usual habit. "And do you think that I am happy ? or Meggie, my wife ? or my mother there ? Do you think that God Himself is happy ? What then do you expect for your sister and my son, eh ? "

She could answer this, but her speech came stumblingly.

"But if we see any way to make people happy. . . . They have a right to all possible happiness. Now if Ben and Connie

could go to your farm at Fallowdale, they might forget—
everything, and just be—happy."

"You think that they have a right now to be happy, having
sinned. I tell you, young woman, that I too sinned when I
was young, and walked wildly before the Lord after the lusts
o' my own flesh. And I too thought to cover the wickedness
o' my ways from the sight o' men by asking the Lord's blessing
on a union made in hell. But the Lord is righteous and in
Him is no shadow of turning. He laid upon me the blessing
of this judgment. I had desired with the desire of the flesh
for my own lusts, and with the desire of the world for my
ambitions. The Lord took away from me the means of all
fulfilment. He laid His hand upon me, and I lie here while
others reap what I have sown. I lie here while my own sons
bring forth the fruits of destruction. The Lord is just. He
gave, and He hath taken away. Blessed be His name."

"I know you've suffered," she cried softly, " but, because
you are unhappy, do you think that you have the right to make
them suffer? After all, it's a tremendous responsibility to
undertake the Lord's judgments without His wisdom. I
thought that you were keeping Fallowdale from Ben because
you couldn't afford to let him have a separate farm, or
because you were afraid he couldn't manage it; but if it's
just because you think he ought to suffer as you suffered. . . ."

"Did I speak o' suffering for myself? You seem to have a
queer notion of the ways o' things. Do you think that I
could make your sister happy if I wanted to, or Ben the godly
man I would ha' had him be? From their own hearts and
deeds comes their own misery."

"Yes, but really, Mr. Todd," persisted Muriel desperately.
"Really and truly living here makes it all worse. It's estrang-
ing them."

"Their shame estranges them."

"It's making Connie bitter. She's getting to despise Ben
because the girls laugh at him."

"That is part of their punishment."

"It's not. It's not. Why should they be punished?
And why should you do it?" She drew a deep breath and

felt as though all winter's storms passed over her as she said,
" It's like a sort of pride to you. You think that because the
Lord punished you in a special way you sinned some great,
particular sin. I don't believe that it was a great sin and
probably your accident was nothing but an accident, and you've
been brooding and brooding until you think that you had a
dispensation of providence specially made for you, so now you
are going to make one for somebody else. I hate your religion
or whatever you call it if it gives you the right to make other
people miserable ! " She broke off, suddenly appalled at her
own arrogance. This was what people did if they spoke out
of character. They always went too far. Oh, it was this
queer, terrible place that made every one behave unlike themselves ! If Connie had never come to Thraile, nothing would
ever have happened, she was certain.

She stood in the dark room, waiting for him to destroy her.
She had to wait for a long time.

The clock ticked. The fire rustled. From the old woman's
chair broke little snatching sounds of difficult breath. Her
asthma was troubling her in her sleep.

At last Muriel heard the slow voice of William Todd.
Again his gentleness amazed her.

" I rec'lect when I was a lad that I thought I knew pretty
well everything worth knowing. My father went t'chapel
and my mother went to church, and I'd have naught to do
with either. So you hate my religion, eh ? Now, I wonder
if ye know at all what my religion is ? Mebbe ye think ah've
just got a kind o' spite against my son and your sister and ah
justify it by the cloak of righteous disapproval, eh ? That
ah've just lain here fashing myself over my own soul and forgetting the right sense o' the great wisdom o' the children of
this world. Is that it ? "

She did not answer because she could not. She had said
more than enough. Her mind was a dry husk, empty, blown
before the wind of his strange spirit.

" Ye'd better sit down. Ah've had to listen to you say
your piece. Now mebbe ye'll listen to me for a bit. You
took it upon yourself to hate my religion. Ah misdoubt if

you know what you're talking about." He paused, as though
he sought a difficult word. "There is only one thing that
matters, and that is the vision of the spirit. Men are poor
things at best, but there's one power that dignifies them,
and that's the sight o' something greater than this world.
Folk nowadays are apt to call it truth or Science or whatnot.
I call that glory God. We are born in sin and reared in
wantonness, and there are those of us to whom no light is
shown. We worship false gods most of our time. Our bodies
and our pride and the opinion of our fellow men ; but to the
Elect there comes a day when they see, though through a
glass darkly, the shadow o' that light."

"Well ? " murmured Muriel.

"The Lord has said, 'Thou shalt have none other god
but me,' but we can only worship what we know, and to all
men the light is not vouchsafed, so that they worship false
gods thinking them to be the true. Ah'm telling you, though
ye'll forget it, and mebbe ye'll never understand, that the
most precious gift to man is just this vision of his God. And
once he has seen, then he must never rest. I remember when
I was farmin' how always the moors were pressing on these
lands. They never sleep, if we do. Ye may build your walls
high, an' weed and dig, but slowly by night creep up the gorse
an' heather, an' who's to say 'an enemy hath done this ' ?
'Tis the same wi' vision. Once ye have seen, there's never
sittin' down and waiting for the Lord to come to you again.
All foolishness an' rioting, all chambering an' wantonness
comes in between a man and his own sight. Purity is a matter
o' the spirit you may say, and what is a man's body that he be
so mindful of it ? In the body we live, and from the body we
die, and a man can give his body mastery over his immortal
soul ; but the things o' the body come like wind and weather
between a man and his clear spirit. For it is hard enough
for any man to see the light, and harder yet to keep it burning
clear. And if your light be darkness, then is man robbed of
God. The last betrayal and the ultimate unworthiness is the
defilement of the vision."

He paused, it seemed to be for a long time. Then he said :

" I cannot let it be as though my son had never sinned. Wouldn't it be far easier for me to say, ' It doesn't matter. It was a little thing ' ? To say as you say, ' Well, he married her,' as if it made amends to God to hide your own wrong from the eyes o' men ? I let him marry her, because it did no good to keep them from each other, and he would. But if my own son will use his own body as an instrument of pleasure, and thinks that as long as he gives his name to the child he does no ill, I'll not be still. If all this happiness you prate of were but the gratification o' their lusts ah'd say no more. But till he's shamed to his soul at what he's done, ah will not let him go."

"Oh, but he is ashamed!" she cried, striking her hands together with the force of her sudden sight. "They are ashamed, but of the wrong thing. They're ashamed not because they did wrong, but because they were found out. They must go away from this place to forget that. Please let them go. You'll see. Talk to Connie if you like. She does not understand you. Only let them go. If not——"

" Well ? "

" I'll have—I'll have—I'll make my father come again and force them from you."

The man on the couch laughed at her. "Do ye think your father could do ought about it ? While I mean Ben to stay here, here he'll stay. He married Connie because ah gave him leave. The boy's no man yet, and he's been living in sin. It must be as the Lord wills, I only wait upon His guidance."

His voice became suddenly flat with weariness.

" Go now and ask my wife to come to me."

She felt her way to the door and knew that she was defeated. She had done nothing, less than nothing. What could she do against the fires that consumed that fierce, relentless cripple ? He puzzled her. He puzzled her. Her father had found him shrewd and grasping, well able to strike a good bargain. Her mother had found him strange but interesting, a self-educated man of unusual refinement for his environment. And she—surely he was sincere ? He *felt* sincere. Yet, what was one to do for Connie ?

She groped her way towards the kitchen door that thrust a bar of light across the blackness of the passage.

The postman leant against the table, a slab of saucer-custard in his hand, a mug of tea beside him. She remembered now her letter to her mother. What use was there to send it ? They would never understand. She delivered her message to Mrs. Todd, and received in return a letter addressed to

" Miss Constance Hammond,
Miller's Rise,
Marshington,"

readdressed to The High Farm, Thraile. The envelope was crushed and dirty, and bore the foreign service stamp. She carried it to the room where Connie lay upon her bed, reading a novel.

" Letters ? " she asked sleepily.

" One—forwarded from Marshington. That's all." Muriel retreated to her own room, sick and weary with defeat. She had done nothing, nothing. She had helped neither Connie nor herself. She felt that she hated William Todd.

XXXI

CONNIE did not come downstairs at tea-time.

" She'll be tidying herself after lying down," said Muriel.

" She'll be crying over a letter from an old sweetheart," laughed Dolly.

Matthew winked at his brother. " There, Ben, lad, off ye go and see what's up wi' your wife. You'll have t'keep an eye on her letters now. Connie always was one for the lads. No followers ! "

" Shame on you, Mat. Give over now," soothed Mrs. Meggie, pouring out the tea from a great brown pot. " You'll be bringing home a wife yourself one of these days, and then you'll laugh with the other side of your face. Well, Muriel, since you're the greatest stranger, bacon, cake or ham ? "

Muriel gazed at the characteristic profusion. She was thinking of William Todd and the terrifying strangeness of the front parlour.

"Ham, please—a very little," she said.

"Muriel's lost her appetite because she hasn't had a letter too," jeered Dolly.

Alice said nothing. She lifted her heavy-lidded eyes to Ben's red face and sat watching him. Ben bent his head above his cup, drinking great gulps of tea.

"I found an old ewe on her back i' forty acre," he remarked to change the subject.

"Not one o' the cross-breds ?" asked Mat with interest.

"Or was it our old friend Agatha ?" interposed Gertie.

"Agatha ? Who was Agatha ?" asked Muriel. Her head ached and she wondered why Connie did not come downstairs, but she knew that tea-time at Thraile was a convivial meal and that "moping" was against the rules.

Dolly explained to her with avidity. "Last spring at Follerwick Camp an old bird called Agatha Anderson brought a concert affair down to give improving music to the fellows. You never saw such an old geezer ! She had sort of woolly white curls round a long solemn face, just like a sheep. Well, one night Connie was coming back from Follerwick and right halfway across the moors she heard a sheep bleating, for all the world just like old Agatha. It had got strayed and hurt its leg, and was sort of huddled on a bank like the old platform. So she got up and brought it along with her and we called it Agatha."

"Brought it home ? All by herself ? Wasn't it heavy ?" asked Muriel without interest. Surely Connie had had time now to do her hair. Wasn't she feeling well ? Muriel knew how much she hated those Thraile meals. Perhaps at the last moment she had taken fright.

Polly was giggling. "By herself ? I ask you ? Our Con walk home from Follerwick by herself ? Not 'arf ! Ben, you were with her, weren't you, when she found Agatha ?"

"No, I wasn't," said Ben stiffly.

"Oh, well then—it was one of the other fellows. Bill or Tubby or——"

"Wasn't it Eric Fennington ? " asked Alice very quietly. She picked up her cup and drank, her light eyes never leaving Ben's flushed face.

Eric Fennington ? To Muriel the name was not quite unfamiliar. " Who was Eric Fennington ? " she asked, but without much interest, because she felt as though the powers of darkness were behind her locked away in the front parlour, and she was afraid.

" Eric Fennington," explained Dolly volubly, " was one of the lads all right. You bet he was ! He was one of the officers at Follerwick Camp, two pips up, and a great flame of Connie's. I thought you'd know him. She said she met him at Kingsport, knew him well at home. My word, he was a knut ! D'you remember when he hired a car and took us to the Movies at Scarshaven, Alice ? And that time he put the alarm clock in the Major's box and it went off during the third act of ' Romance ' with an awful row—just when that curate was beginning to carry on ! "

" Old Eric's married, isn't he ? asked Matthew heavily.

" Married or engaged or something. It was you who saw that bit in the paper, wasn't it, Alice ? Anyway he's in Mespot."

" Just as well, Ben, eh ? " laughed Matthew. Ben rose, his mouth still full of pie. " Where you going, lad ? "

" Up t'see why Connie don't come down," interposed Mrs. Meggie. " That's a good fellow."

Muriel watched him shamble from the room, an uncouth figure, part boy, part man. This overgrown weakling whom Connie had married, how had he done it ? What had induced Connie to—to—Muriel wondered for the hundredth time how it had come about. Had she been sorry for him ? Surely he cared for her. There was in his manner a hint of wistfulness, of manhood undeveloped. Had the craving for self-assertion forced him to madness, aping the passion of a man without a man's self-mastery ? Connie had said that he had over-mastered her. It was difficult, watching him now retreat before his family's rough humour, to imagine him mastering anyone, even himself.

He did not return soon. Muriel sat through the long meal uneasily. What was happening upstairs ? Had William Todd, as a result of her interview, sent for Connie, and was he convicting her again of sin ? Poor Connie ! Finally, when tea was cleared, Muriel climbed to Connie's room. The staircase was dark. Only a glimmer of starlight from the narrow window guided her. She paused outside her sister's door and called. No answer came. She opened the door. No light came from the room. She was about to go downstairs again, when the shadow by the bedside quivered suddenly. She stared into the darkness.

"Connie !" she said softly. "Connie, what are you doing there ? Where's Ben ?"

"Is that you, Muriel ?" The voice made her start violently. "It's not Connie. It's me—Ben. Come in and shut t'door."

"Ben ! What's the matter ? Where's Connie ?" A shrill little quiver of fear crept to her voice. "Why are you sitting in the dark ?"

"Aw—come in and shut the door," he repeated. His voice terrified her. It was as though a dead man spoke. "Connie isn't here. She's gone."

"Gone ? Gone where ? I don't understand."

"She's gone to do herself in."

"Ben, what do you mean ?" Oh, if only there was a light ! The darkness pressed in suddenly upon her face and choked her.

"She's gone to do 'erself in. And I don't care. I wouldn't ha' stopped her anyway. She'd gone before I came upstairs. I expect she's gone down to the Fallow. She once said she would."

"Do you mean," said Muriel quietly, "that you think she's gone to—to kill herself ? Oh, but what nonsense, Ben. Why should she ? What nonsense ! How dare you talk such wicked nonsense !" She stretched out her hand for the brass bed-post and stood there clinging to its solid comfort. "It's nonsense, nonsense. Connie—kill herself ? Now—when I've just made things——"

"It's not nonsense," Ben said heavily. "I'll show you a letter."

"Letter? Letter? Did Connie write a—— Oh, for goodness' sake get a light and don't talk in riddles."

The bed creaked. Somewhere from the darkness moved a blacker darkness yet. She heard Ben's laboured breathing.

"Oh, be quick! Be quick!"

If they stood in the dark another minute she would scream.

Ben stumbled across the room. She heard him fumbling on the mantelpiece. Something fell against the fender with a light, splintering crash.

"I can't find matches," growled Ben.

"Oh, you idiot!" It was incredible that two people in such dire consternation should be tortured because they couldn't find the matches. It made her terribly angry, with a cold fury that she had not known before.

Ben was cursing softly in the darkness.

"I'll go and get some——" said Muriel.

She stumbled frantically along the passage. From the room shared by the land-girls came a flood of light, flowing out across the passage. Alice was sitting beside the lamp, darning a stocking.

Muriel looked at her with wonder. People were still darning stockings then? What a funny way Alice's hair grew back from her ears, with little silvery tufts along her neck. You could see them in the lamplight quite distinctly. What had she come for? Oh, the matches.

"Please, Alice, have you any matches?"

Alice looked up. "My! What a start you gave me! Matches? No. I had to borrow Mrs. Todd's! Why don't you get Connie's? She bags all my matches."

On then to her own room she must go. Hours, interminable hours stretched between her and the horrible nightmare of Ben's voice. Her own matches lay on the candlestick by her bed where she had left them. She lit the candle with shaking fingers, then ran again down the long corridor. The draught plucked at her candle flame; it fluttered ruddily within the pink screen of her hand.

She came back to Connie's room.

" Ben !   Ben !   Where are you ? "

She set the candle down by the disordered bed.   The little flame shook itself, quivered and then stood gallantly upright, showing the flower-decked walls, the coarse white counterpane, all heaped and crumpled, and Ben's white face—blank and passive, staring at her from beside the mantelpiece.

" Where's that letter ? " asked Muriel.

As though in a trance he came forward and handed her a sheet of flimsy paper, pencil written.   She glanced at it.

" This isn't from Connie !   What do you mean ?   Where's Connie ?   What have you done with her ? "

" Read yon," said Ben.

After one glance at his set face, she read :

Dear old girl,
There ain't no flies round Christmas time in Blighty, but there's jolly well nothing else in this old hole.   It's as hot as —well any place we specially used to think of as being hot. I say, Kiddo, who's been having you on that I'm engaged ? Your stately letter—written by the way some time in August —has been chasing me across the desert sands and under the deodar and all the rest of it until it knocked the portals of my heart (Good that ?   What ?) about—well may be—two months ago.   Who sprung that yarn on to you about Cissie Bradfield ?   It's old Ernest, my brother, she collared.   They were married last July.   I can't think how you made the mistake because Alice knows Cissie and knew all about it.   If you'd asked her she could have told you.   We have the same initials of course.   Honest, Kiddo, I'm no hand at letter writing and time dashes by here, but you're barking up the wrong tree this time.   You must know that you are the only girl in the world as far as I am concerned.   Rumour hath it that in another two months we may get leave and then what about another room at Scarshaven Hotel and you " on a visit to your friends at Buxton," eh ?   I'm not the marrying sort you know, but sometimes I think that when this war's over, I'd like to settle down.   How would the idea of being

Mrs. E. F. seem to you, old girl ? Not much in your line,
what ?

Anyway don't forget me,

Yours to a cinder,

ERIC.

She read twice through this strange production, straining
her eyes to decipher the crude, boyish writing. Then she
looked at Ben. " I don't understand, what does it mean ? "
she said.

" Don't you ? Don't you ? Ay, but you do. You
Hammonds, you're all alike, you, you——"

She gazed at him with open-eyed amazement. The boy
whom she had thought of as a poor thing became instead a
sneering raging fury. Completely beyond self-control, he
turned upon her.

" You and your snivelling mother, coming down and weeping
piety and her daughter's honour ; and your bullying rip of a
father, damn him ! I bet you're all the same. You know
jolly well what this all means. ' What about another room at
the Scarshaven Hotel,' eh ? And then she comes whining and
sobbing to me and saying I must marry her because I've ruined
her life ! She and her honour. How do I know how many
more Erics she's fooled on with ? Blast her ! Curse
her ! "

His weak face was distorted by rage. The candlelight
danced on the red rims of his swollen eyes and on his trembling
hand upraised as if he would strike Muriel.

She still sat on the edge of the bed, quite quietly. Her
mind refused to register any thought but the name of her
sister, Connie, Connie, repeated again and again without
significance.

Ben dropped his hand. " She taunted me. She said I was
no man. She pretended that she knew nowt o' this sort o'
thing. She told me that she'd carried on with other fellows,
just a bit, just playing like. And there was I, cursing myself
because I'd done it. Calling myself a black sinner when I
had no call to marry her, not even a farm o' my own yet, and

all the time she was just laughing at me, fooling me. And I've been feeling myself under a heavy burden o' sin, with my guilt an' hers upon me, an' not daring to go round to chapel, and feeling the hand o' the Lord upraised against me. She led me on. She led me on. Let her drown now. Let her drown. I reckon she'll not swim long i' Fallow, and her burden o' guilt will weigh her down."

Muriel stared at him. " Ben. You've lost your head. It mayn't mean all that. She's your wife."

" She betrayed me. She betrayed me." He dropped his face into his hands and sat with quivering shoulders on the bed by Muriel's side. " She's shamed me. And I meant to prove myself a man." He began to sob, bitter grinding sobs that tore him with grief for his shamed manhood. " Ah never had a wife. Ah never had one. She fooled me. Ah've been fooled all my life. Ah've been fooled by God an' fooled by her. There's no faith left."

" Ben. Pull yourself together. You've got no right to accuse her till you know. When did she go ? Are you sure she left the house ? Which way would she take ? "

He raised his haggard face and jeered at her. " Go an' find her. You're scared o' the dark, aren't you ? Go an' find her corpse knocking about i' Fallow like an old sow drowned last Martinmas. Go on. Get out o' way." His voice rose to the shrill note of hysteria. " Get out o' here ! This is my room. What are you doing in my room—you——"

He called her a name that she had never heard before. She turned to run, and saw him towering above her, fantastic in the candlelight. As she ran, she heard his voice behind her, calling, " Run, Muriel ! Run ! It's nice and cold in t'river."

The echo of his laughter drove her down the passage.

Outside the kitchen door she paused. The firelight, the call of cheerful voices beckoned her. From the back room came the shouted chorus of a song.

" If you were the only girl in the world
And I were the only boy."

The desire to tell some one, to find a sane and comforting adviser in this world gone mad, urged her almost irresistibly. She would go and tell Mrs. Todd. She would tell Mat. They would help her to look for Connie.

> " Nothing else would matter in this world to-day,
> We would go on loving in the same old way."

She laid her hand upon the latch of the door.

If she told, they would all follow her. They would all know what had happened to Connie. They would all know what Connie had done.

She had to tell. She could not bear alone this dreadful burden of responsibility.

If she went now either she would find Connie, reason with her and bring her back, or else it would be too late for any one to help Connie, too late for any army of lanterns, swinging down the hill, to pierce those dark waters of the Fallow.

> " There would be such wonderful things to do
> I would say such wonderful things to you ! "

A chair shrieked against the paved floor. Somebody was going to leave the room. If she told now, it would be a betrayal. She must go alone.

With a little choking cry she turned and fled.

The bolts were stiff and heavy, but when she had dragged them aside the wind tore at the door and hurled it open. The frail strength of her shoulder could not push it back. She let it swing.

Along the flagged yard, down the two steps and into the strip of narrow garden Muriel ran. Oh, but she must hurry, hurry, hurry, or it would be too late. The garden path was steep and slippery. A thaw had set in, and the ground under her thin shoes was wet and yielding. Once she leapt aside as a white cat darted out at her from the potatoes. Once her serge skirt caught on a stunted gooseberry bush.

Out through the wicket gate and on to the field road ran

Muriel. The first field was a grass pasture ; she remembered that. It led straight down, with the bottom gate a little to the right. If only she had stopped to find a lantern ! It was quite dark now. The stars were veiled by tattered shreds of cloud. She could not see the road before her feet, but only feel the short, uneven turf, and the steady sloping of the long hill. If she faced down hill she would find the way.

The high heel of her shoe caught in a rut, and she fell headlong, her cheek against the chill, wet turf. Even as she lay there for a second, dazed and breathless, something moved from the shadows at her side, and with a little shriek of horror she remembered that in this field wandered the cows and horses.

She sprang up, never heeding the pain of her wrenched ankle or the mud clinging to her skirt. Every breeze that touched her hot cheeks was now the fiery breath of bulls ; every clump of furze the dark form of a furious stallion. Blindly sobbing she ran, while the strong wind seized her and blew her kindly down the shadowed hill.

Almost before she hoped for it she found the wall. But the gate ? The gate. Standing to regain her bearings, she heard the dull thud of feet tramping behind her down the hill.

The wind whistling on her neck came like the breath from a bull's nostrils. Clutching at the rough stones, bruising her knees and her thin elbows, she scrambled up the wall.

By this time she did not know whether she was running to save her own life or her sister's. The black arms of the trees swept over her, their wild heads tossing, tangling the vagrant stars. Their branches creaked ; their twisted fingers snatched at her, caught at her hair and scratched her face, only to swing back again with mocking lightness. The trees terrified her. At any minute they must come down upon her. She heard the sharp splintering of the wood ; the rush of branches like a mighty sea ; the vast arms that embraced her, dragging her down, down as they fell faster, faster and the great weight overwhelmed her.

There she would lie crushed and bleeding on the hill-side,

and Connie would lie deep below the swirling waters of the Fallow.

She dared not risk the trees. She scurried towards the centre of the field, stumbling blindly among the turnips. Twice she struck her foot against them, falling and recovering herself.

Her breath came now in painful sobs. Across her chest lay a sharp bar of iron that hurt her as she breathed. The wind through her silk blouse whipped her shoulders.

Oh, she would never find her way. Why hadn't she brought a lantern ? Why hadn't she told the others ? What madness sent her alone, running wildly down these dreadful fields ? And when she reached the river, if Connie were not there, what could she do !

A rope, stretched straight across her way, nearly flung her down again. Panting, she felt along it. A rough net—a net. Her mind, unaccustomed to the ways of farming, refused to register its use. She forced it down with both her hands and stepped across it.

As she paused, it seemed as though again she heard those footsteps following ; but perhaps they only were the beats of her own heart. She started forward.

A worse nightmare than ever laid hold upon her. She was surrounded by a moving horror. Soft formless things pushed up against her knees, her waist. Each way she stumbled, they bore down upon her. The starlight showed her just a dim, pale sea heaving waist-high all round her, before the wild clouds swept across the one patch of clear sky and left her blind with panic and the dark.

She could bear no more. Perils of darkness, perils of tempest, perils of bulls and wild living things she had withstood. Even the peril of Ben's frenzied face and uplifted hand had not appalled her. But this heaving horror engulfed her. She must fall.

She put out one hand and touched rough, soft wool ; a familiar cry rang out beside her, " Baa-a-ah ! " another followed. Echo followed echo across the sheepfold. She turned and pushed her way out from among the clustering flock, regaining the assurance of the road. The trees might swoop above her. Her feet might slip beneath her, but the road was sure. On and on she ran, though now she knew no longer the object of her running. Through one gate, then another, then another, and the woods closed down upon her. The path grew steeper. A light rain blew in her face like wave-flung spray. She did not notice it. The bushes caught at her. The branches tore her hair. Then, suddenly, quite close beside her, she heard the rushing of the river.

She remembered why she had come, and stood quite still to listen.

" Connie ! " she shouted. " Connie ! Connie ! Connie ! "

Parallel with the river ran a narrow path. It wound up Fallowdale for several miles until it crossed the Pilgrim's Bridge at Barwood. Up this path Muriel ran, the tangled woods on her left hand, the river on her right. Without a gleam the water swirled beside her, now dashing angrily against the stones, now sliding deep and dark between the banks.

" Connie ! Connie ! Connie ! " called Muriel. The wind snatched at her futile little voice. The river drowned it. The high trees mocked her, clashing their long arms together.

" Connie ! Connie ! " she sobbed. The pain in her bruised ankle throbbed unceasingly. Her hands were torn. Her knees hurt. She felt forlorn and utterly defeated.

" Connie ! Connie ! "

Along the path before her, something moved.

" Connie ! "

The figure stopped. It hesitated, then started forward. A twig snapped in the darkness. Then, though the river ran silently here the noise of it rose like a flood, thundering in her ears.

" Connie, darling ! Stop ! I want to tell you something."

She dared not run too quickly. A false step, and she might feel those ice-cold waters close above her head. If she delayed, though, she might hear the splash of Connie's final plunge.

" Oh, Connie, please don't go so fast. I can't keep up. Please stop."

In the dark, Connie turned to face her.

" Muriel—what do you want ? Why have you come ? "
With a sudden sharp anguish, " Have you got my letter ? "

" Your letter ? Your letter ? No. Ben's got your letter."

" Ben ? Of course he has ! Of course. Oh, isn't that like
you, Muriel ! You come down here to me, but you let Ben
have the letter ! I might have known. Here I've been telling
myself that perhaps you'd find it and not say anything and
just come down here, and now—I might have known ! "

" But Ben found it first. What could I do ? "

" Of course he did. He would. Oh, now for Heaven's
sake go home. I'm sick of you. Can't you leave me alone
just for a minute ? What do you want ? Why did you follow
me ? Go back. Go back, I tell you."

" No, no. I can't leave you here. You mustn't—you—
you'll make yourself ill."

" Ill ? Shall I ? "

Muriel dared not move. If she advanced one step she feared
lest Connie, mad with recklessness, should plunge into that
dreadful river. And if Connie did jump in, what could she
do ? Connie was heavy. The river was so deep, and Muriel
could not swim. She became dazed with panic.

" Connie, dear. Connie, come home. It's terrible for you
out here in the dark. Come back with me. It's all right.
I won't leave you."

" If you come a step nearer," cried Connie's furious voice,
" I shall jump straight into the river. So there ! "

Suddenly the absurdity of the situation struck Muriel.
Here she was. Here was Connie. If Connie chose to drown
herself, Muriel was completely powerless to stop her, because
she was so small and Connie so much stronger.

At the realization of her impotence, Muriel's self-control
gave way. She flung up her head and laughed, peal after peal
of helpless laughter.

It was the last sound that Connie had expected.

" What's the matter ? Are you mad ? That's right then,
laugh away ! I suppose that you think it's funny that I should
have made a mess of my whole life. I can be in hell if I like,
and all that you can do is to stand there and laugh. I suppose

that you read Eric's letter and saw that he—that he would
have married me—Eric. Eric."

Muriel stopped laughing and came forward, laying her small
hand on her sister's arm. Connie seemed to be unaware that
anyone was touching her.

" Oh, it's damned funny, isn't it ? I wonder that I don't
laugh myself. You never thought at Marshington that your
respected sister was anyone's mistress, did you ? Only once,
I tell you. I thought that he would marry me. I'd heard
they would. I was fed up, and at least it was worth trying.
It was that little fiend Alice who ruined me. Of course she
liked him, but she kidded us that it was Ben she cared about.
Ben. Ben ! Come to think about it, we might ha' known
that she was fooling us. Who'd care for Ben, with his great
gawky body, Ben the big soft idiot ! I ask you ! That's my
husband, Muriel. Good joke, isn't it ? I swore to love,
honour and obey that thing, because Alice told me Eric had
married Cissie Bradfield and showed me a newspaper cutting,
and I was green enough to believe her. Oh, she was clever.
My God, she was clever. I'd just been home on leave, you
know, that time we met Delia on Kingsport Station. I was
happy then. I thought he cared. Then I came back here
and Alice told me—showed me the cutting. He was just
going to Mespot too. I wrote. He never answered." She
stopped, choking.

" Never mind that now, Connie, dear," Muriel said timidly.
" Come back with me. You'll get so wet."

Connie shook off her hand and went on speaking. It was
as though, having decided to tell the truth at last, she could
not stop.

" If I'd been cheap with one, I'd be cheap with all. There'd
be no end to my cheapness. If Eric had had me and didn't
want me, then Ben, who wanted me, should have me. Oh,
I was wild, I didn't care. I didn't care what happened.
Muriel, you don't know. You'd never been like that, stuck
there in Marshington, longing to get away, every one round
you getting married. It wasn't as if I hadn't tried other
things. I wanted to chicken farm ; I wanted to go away

and do just anything. But Mother wouldn't let me. It was just men, men, men, and make a good match."

She shivered violently. The rain was now sweeping in great gusts along the valley. It splashed from the bare branches on to their heads. Slowly they began to walk along the path.

"Well—I didn't make a good match. Look at Godfrey Neale. When I was a kid I used to think him wonderful. Then Hugh McKissack. Mother made me think I liked him and that he would marry me. Look how he fooled us both. Then Eric came——"

Connie's voice mingled with the rushing of the river and the rustling rain among the trees. She lifted her head and spoke into the darkness, taking no heed of Muriel.

"He wasn't much of a fellow perhaps, in lots of ways, but he was a jolly sight better than lots of the men we used to meet. And I wanted so much to be married. He said his father wouldn't let him marry till he'd become a proper chartered accountant. He was still articled or something when I met him that night at the Kingsport dance. Hugh McKissack had just turned me down. Oh, I was desperate. I flirted with him. He said I was a sport. We—we got on. Oh, you won't understand. When I went to stay with Betty Taylor at York, I met him again. I went there so that I could meet him. Chase him? Who'd taught me to chase men? Of course I did. Don't all women? Hadn't mother? Then he said I didn't care for him. I wasn't going to show him at first, so he said 'Prove it.' I—you don't know. I thought he'd slip away just like the rest of them. I said I'd prove it. We went away to Scarshaven together for three days, before I went to Buxton to the Marshalls. You thought I was there, and nobody found out. I thought he'd marry me. If anything went wrong, he said he'd see me through. There was a time, just once, on Scarshaven station when he came to meet me, I thought I couldn't do it. Then he smiled. Oh, you—you—you don't know what it's like to love a man! I couldn't turn him down."

She stopped and clung to Muriel, who could only hold her

tightly, murmuring silly words of comfort, neither shocked nor grieved, but gently pitiful. "Poor Connie. Oh, poor Connie!"

"Then the war came. He was sent up to Follerwick. I stuck it at home for a bit. I tried once to get through to see him, but I couldn't arrange it easily. I saw that if I stayed at home I never should get away without being found out. Then he told me about Thraile. The Todds were advertising for land-girls. I'd always liked outdoor things, and I was mad to come. You know the row we had at home. Then Mother heard that the Setons were doing land-work. How I blessed those girls. So she gave me her blessing too and off I went. Oh, but I was happy. You don't know. I'd never been happy like that before. He was at Follerwick and I at Thraile. We used to go for concerts and things, and I'd meet him and go off for long walks on the moors. We didn't do anything that you'd call bad. Somehow when it was so easy, we did not want to in the same way. We were like kids. We'd race up and down hill hand in hand. He'd come and sit sometimes on the old sheep trough when I was cleaning turnips and we'd talk. It was all as easy as the beasts and flowers and things. I dun'no. We were just great pals. We didn't talk of marriage or anything. That didn't matter. Then I came on leave." Her voice hardened. "When I got back that Alice told me he'd had to go off suddenly to Aldershot. He didn't write—or, if he did, she got hold of the letters. Possibly he didn't write. He wasn't the pen-scratching kind. Then the news of his wedding came, and the newspaper cutting.

"Oh, I think I went mad. I do really. You see—I'd been fooled so often. I wanted to hurt every one, myself most of all. And Ben was always hanging round. I hadn't noticed him while Eric was there. But after—after I heard about Cissie I used to tease Ben, just to spite him and myself. I said he wasn't a man. I—Oh, I led him on. He was such a great, green, religious baby, terrified of his father. Then I made him—do it."

Her hands clutched at her sister's arm. Her dragging step

moved onward, and her toneless voice talked on and on, taking a bitter satisfaction in the telling.

" When I found out that I was going to have a baby, I was scared. I told you that they turned me out. They didn't. I ran away. Father found that out after he came down to Thraile that day. Really, he was awfully decent to me. He seemed to understand. But at first the Todds were awful. That terrible old man. Only Ben was decent. I believe he was fond of me. Funny, wasn't it ? He thought he'd sinned black sin for me, and made me sin, and he must make it up to me. And then, while I was waiting for the wedding, that was a queer time. I used to pretend that it was Eric I was going to marry. Honest I did. I quite enjoyed it. Even when we got here, married, it might not have been so bad. Do you know," she said reflectively, " I believe that if I'd never known Eric I'd have been content with Ben. He's a dud of course, but he'd do anything for me. It's nice to have someone who'd sell their souls for you, until they think they've sold it. That was just it. Old William Todd would never let Ben alone. He was always on at him. If we could have gone away together. . . . Well, I used to think we would go and get a farm and settle down. I like children too. Then—to-day." It was Connie's turn to laugh now.

" I say, if there's a God, mustn't he have a jolly time laughing over the things that come too late ? Here's a priceless joke now—me married to Ben, and a kid coming, and Eric ready to marry me when he comes home. Ben's child ! Ben's child ! And it might have been Eric's ! " The laughter turned again to choking sobs. Breaking suddenly from Muriel's arms, Connie collapsed on the bank and crouched there, crying softly.

" I meant to kill myself. I knew I might funk it though. I always do. I put that letter where Ben would see it and know what had happened. So I could never go back to him. I thought I'd settle it for good and all. And I'd hurt Ben too. He'd been so stupid. The more beastly I was to him, the more patient he was with me. Rather like you, Muriel. Oh, you patient people ! I bet you're responsible for half the suicides that happen. He was so proud to think I'd marry him too! He—me!"

Muriel knelt beside her on the wet stones. "Get up, Connie. You'll be ill. Get up. It's so wet."

That was all she could say, silly futile things.

"Ill? Oh, Muriel, you are a fool. Don't you see, I can't go back? I can't go anywhere. Oh, my God, I haven't got the pluck to kill myself, and there's nowhere in the world for me to live! You're a beauty, you are. You always turn up when it's too late to help. What shall I do? I don't want to die."

"We'll go away together. Listen. Listen. I'll make Father let us have some money. He's fond of you. If Ben turns you out, he'll pay. I can get work now in war-time too. We'll both go away. We'll—Oh, what's that?"

A light, swinging between the trees, gleamed suddenly round the angle of the rocks. A yellow splash of lantern light moved along the path. Through the rain came the sound of running footsteps.

"Who's that? Who's that?"

Her voice was sharp with fear.

"Is that Muriel?"

Connie's hand gripped her like a vice. Connie screamed in sudden terror.

"Muriel, it's Ben. Don't let him hurt me! Don't!"

Muriel stood up. "Ben, what do you want?"

The lantern swayed and stopped. In that moment Muriel thought that Ben had come to kill his wife.

"Is Connie there?"

"Yes." Connie's voice was calm now.

"Ben, you shan't hurt her," cried Muriel.

"I shan't hurt her." She could hear that he too was now calm. The voice that spoke from the darkness was a man's voice. "Connie, I want to ask you something."

"Well?" Still she was defiant. "What do you want?"

"When did you last see—yon—yon fellow?"

"Eric Fennington?"

"Ay."

" In the summer. Before I went on leave, but——"

" I thowt so. You fooled me properly, didn't you ? "

" But——" Connie rose slowly to her feet. She stood now facing her husband. He raised the lantern and flashed it full upon her. " Ben," she said.

" Have ye anything to say ? Ye laughed an' mocked at me. Ye treated me like a boy without pride, or honour. Then, when yon fellow let ye down, you found that I was man enough to give his child my name." He spoke now without bitterness. His steady, even voice was strange to them. They stood before him, afraid of his new dignity. Then Connie said :

" Ben, that's not true."

" Eh ? "

" I—I saw Eric in the summer, but it was—in March when we—when we went together. The only time, I swear."

" And when is the child coming ? "

" April."

" Is yon true, Muriel ? "

" Yes."

" How many lovers did yer have before this—officer fellow ? "

" Eric, only Eric."

" Is yon true, Muriel ? "

" Yes, Ben, I am sure of it."

They waited, while in the darkness Ben received back his lost honour. When he spoke again it was with a shy confidence.

" Oh, well, I reckon ye'd better come home out o' t'wet, Connie. I wanted ye to kill yourself at first, and then I thought mebbe I'd better let you speak for yourself first. But if yon's false, what you've told me——"

" It's not."

He sighed wearily. " Oh, well, best come home, Connie."

" Do—do the others know ? "

" Nay. An' they won't. This is our affair. T'letter's in my pocket. I'll burn it an' fake some tale. Coom on, Connie. I——" He had forgotten Muriel. They were alone together in a world new made.

" I want my child," said Ben.

They turned ; he put his hand on her arm, and they went up the path together.

Muriel stood alone beside the river ; then she too moved forward, following the lantern's light.

XXXII

THE situation having been lifted again out of Muriel's hands, she did not for some time contest the way in which it was being handled. For the space of one evening, Ben seemed to have attained to manhood. So much the better for Ben. So much the better for Connie. So much the worse perhaps for Muriel, who was again left with no one in life having great need of her. Directly Connie was better, Muriel meant to go home. For Connie, not unnaturally, was ill. The evening's escapade had resulted in a severe chill, caught, she explained, because while going for a walk to cure her headache, she had fallen and wrenched her ankle, and lain in the rain until Ben and Muriel found her.

Well, she would soon be better. It never occurred to Muriel to protest against the standard of Thraile nursing. She followed Mrs. Todd about the chill, dark bedroom, acquiescing in suggested remedies. After all, what else could one do in someone else's house ? It was nobody's fault that the fire in Connie's bedroom smoked, or that Dr. Merryweather was old-fashioned. Besides, she herself had a sore throat, and a bruised knee, and a weary battered spirit. Events must take their course. The whole household being incalculable and detached from sane life as she knew it, Muriel could not bring herself to think it real at all. She brushed her own torn skirt and Connie's, and carried trays upstairs for Mrs. Todd, who, with three invalids and the large family to manage, still remained imperturbably cheerful. Then, somehow, quite without Muriel realizing their importance, several things happened very quickly ; the doctor's second visit ; Ben

driving off into the rain to Follerwick; her mother's arrival
by the evening train.

Muriel stood in the room once shared by Alice, Gert and
Polly, fingering silver jars upon the roughly stained dressing-
table, and wondering how her mother always contrived to
carry an atmosphere of Marshington drawing-rooms into the
most incongruous surroundings.

" I can't understand it. I can't understand it," repeated
Mrs. Hammond, methodically unwrapping her slippers from
her linen shoe bags. " You say that she went out in the
rain . . ."

" It wasn't raining when she *went* out," explained Muriel
for the second time. " It began to rain later—after she had
fallen."

" I can't help thinking, dear, that there was some grave
irresponsibility. Knowing how careless she is, you never
ought to have let her go out alone. It never should have
happened—and then—since, Muriel, why didn't you see that
a second opinion was called in ? "

" We didn't think that she was so ill—Dr. Merryweather——"

" Oh, Dr. Merryweather ! A North Riding country
practitioner—really, Muriel. But of course, dear, you never
had any initiative, had you ? Well, it may be all right now."

With gentle efficiency, Mrs. Hammond took control of the
situation. Never had her conduct been more completely
admirable. She had found her younger daughter seriously
ill with pneumonia, her elder daughter in a strange condition
of nervous paralysis, an impossibly inconvenient house, and a
family complicated by the most uncomfortable relationships.
Almost at once she made her influence felt. Muriel found
herself shrinking into the shadows. She never remembered
afterwards how she passed her time in that house grown hushed
with concentrated anxiety. Once she remembered meeting
Ben upon the landing. His face was drawn and grey. She
remembered his long feet in their drab worsted stockings and
the silly appeal in his light grey-blue eyes.

" Muriel," he had said in a hoarse whisper, " she ain't
going to die, is she ? "

" No, of course she isn't," Muriel answered irritably. How could she die, now that everything had just been put right ? Of course she wasn't going to die !

He twisted the smooth knob at the top of the staircase. " She mustn't die," he whispered again. " I couldn't stand that, I tell you I couldn't." He cast a sidelong glance down stairs towards the passage where the door of the front parlour stood open. " Father says that it'll be the judgment of God upon our wickedness if she does die."

" What does he know about it ? She won't die."

" I can't bear it," he repeated, his mouth agape, his eyes that nature had intended to be meek and kind staring ahead with a sad, unnatural concentration. " I couldn't abide to think of her dying in her sin."

" You don't think that at all. She's not in sin—any more than I am. You're talking nonsense. She's going to get well. And in April your baby will be born. And Mr. Todd will let you both go off to Fallowdale." She nodded at him reassuringly, as one nods to a child, and then went upon her quiet, mouse-like duties.

Three more days passed. A nurse had come from Hardras-cliffe. Mrs. Hammond sat up half the night, and Muriel the other half. Mrs. Hammond wore a white apron over her pretty dresses. Her cool fingers had been denuded of their rings, but their little pink nails shone like jewels. The farm girls all had lost their heads and hearts to her. They wondered how on earth a dowdy little thing like Muriel, and a big jolly girl like Connie, could have had such a duck of a mother. Mrs. Todd treated her with cheerful and unimpressionable independence. Muriel followed her submissively, like a scolded child, knowing herself to be in disgrace, and yet never hearing a word of the reproach that she knew her mother felt.

Connie, she found inarticulate and pathetic, only occasionally cross and difficult. Most of the time she seemed to be uncannily obedient.

Once in the early morning, when Muriel was so sleepy that she had to hold her head right forward, so that it would not fall back against her chair, Connie's queer, grating whisper roused her.

" Mu——"

" Yes."

" It would be a queer thing if I was to die after all—wouldn't it ? "

" Don't be silly. You aren't going to die."

" I don't want to. I want to have the baby. I'd like to have a house of my own, and a little Ford car, so that Ben and I could run in to Hardrascliffe for week-ends."

" Of course you will."

" Don't let me die, Mu."

" There's no question of your dying."

But she did not get better quickly. One night her temperature raced up, and she began to talk dangerous nonsense about Eric, while Muriel endeavoured to keep her mother from the room, and Mrs. Hammond, with heroic fortitude, stayed in and quietly controlled the situation. Then there was a miserable early morning when the oxygen cylinders did not arrive from Hardrascliffe ; and, when the light crept through the curtains, Muriel stood in dry-eyed wonder while Ben buried his head in Connie's counterpane and wept loudly with an illogical wholeheartedness.

It was most terrible to see men cry. Muriel wondered whether her father would cry when he came. Anything might happen in a world where Connie had been allowed to die. A sense of baffled impotence seized Muriel. Connie had been preserved so miraculously through two crises—God could not really have let her die.

She wandered round the silent house, very weary but yet more bored, wishing that she could even join the nurse's secret ministration up in Connie's bedroom, rather than have this desolating feeling of no purpose. Then Mrs. Todd, with practical kindness, set her to wash up breakfast plates, with a significant nod to Gertie—" Muriel is going to be taken bad next if we don't look out." And afterwards Mrs. Hammond, with a dignity of self-control that astonished every one but Muriel, called her upstairs and gave her letters to write, and began to discuss details of the funeral.

Mr. Hammond was in London. He could not reach Thraile

until Tuesday morning, even by travelling all night. Mrs. Hammond therefore had to make her own arrangements—the funeral to be at Follerwick, the letters to all relations, the notices to the Yorkshire papers.

"Have you been to see Mr. Todd, since——? " asked Mrs. Hammond, delicately pressing down the flap of an envelope.

" No, Mother, why ? "

" Well, dear. I do think that one of us ought to go to him. Just to show that we—that, well, I do think that we ought. And I don't feel——" Bravely she pushed aside her tears with a small handkerchief.

Muriel walked slowly down the stairs. The little parlour was flooded with afternoon sunlight. Through the uncurtained window, Muriel could see the moors frozen to hard, black beauty, cold as stone beneath the cold, clear light.

William Todd was lying by the window. Ben, a forlorn and uncouth figure in his ill-fitting black clothes, sat on the chair beside him, his large red hands upon his knee.

Muriel came into the room quietly and shut the door. She wished that she knew what was the right thing to say.

" I am very sorry, Mr. Todd," she said at last, feeling that somehow it was what he should have said to her.

" You are sorry. Your sister is dead. My son tells me that she did not die unrepentant. I am glad. It is a fearful thing to fall into the hands of the living God. When men shall say Peace, and all things are safe, then shall sudden destruction come upon them, as sorrow came upon a woman travailing with child, and they shall not escape."

" No," answered Muriel, " I suppose not." But she thought all this to be irrelevant. She felt sorry for Ben, who sat there with bent, dumb bewilderment, but she did not know what to say. She wanted to tell him that she was sorry that the baby for whose sake he had forgiven Connie had never been born. She only said : " Ben has been splendid, Mr. Todd, all through her illness. I am sure that you will understand far more than I—— Do be—please be—nice to him."

The cripple's bright eyes seemed to pierce her brain.

" Shall not the Lord deal justly with his own ? You tried to save your sister from the punishment of man ; but a greater than man had judged before you. But, thank God, her death has not been quite unfruitful. My son, my son has even seen the error of his ways."

William Todd turned his face to the young man. A queer twisted tenderness broke for a minute the clear lines of his face. Then it hardened again. His son sat without movement, his eyes upon the carpet.

" Ay. That's so," he murmured dully.

The old lady by the fire nodded and smiled at Muriel, nibbling a pink sweet. She was happy because she had outlived her grandson's wife.

Ben followed Muriel from the room.

" How much does your father know ? " asked Muriel.

" Nay. I don't know. He's said nowt but what he knew before. But he is right. The destruction of the transgressors and of the sinners shall be together, and they that forsake the Lord shall be consumed. It was for the ungodliness o' my soul, he says, the Lord took my wife and my child."

He raised his head with a smile of ghastly pride, as though consoled by the Lord's impressive punishment of his offence.

" Ben ! " cried Muriel, no longer sorry. " You don't really think like that. You can't think like that." Connie and miserable sinners simply could not live together in the same thought. Connie was a person, intensely alive, wilful and foolish, made for enjoyment and companionship. She was not an instrument of God sent for the punishment of any man's misdeeds.

Ben stared at her foolishly. Then without a word he passed her by and stumbled up the stairs.

Next morning Mr. Hammond came. He saw Muriel in the hall.

" Where's Rachel ? " he asked.

" Upstairs, Father. I'll show you."

He followed her, stepping softly up the winding stair. Mrs. Hammond stood in the doorway. On her face was an expression of relief, anxiety, tenderness. Now that he had come, she wanted nothing more.

Muriel watched her father enfold her mother in his great arms. She, the imperturbable, the gently adamant, gave herself up to his rough mastery, and found rest there. Neither of them noticed Muriel.

"There, there, little woman," he said softly, stroking her bowed silver head with his large hand. "It's all right. It's all right. Poor Connie. You did your best. You did everything, little woman, I know. You've been wonderful."

She let him treat her like a child. Before him alone she lost her perfect self-command. Muriel saw this with the jealous perception of the onlooker. "They don't want me," she told herself, and went downstairs.

On the morning of the funeral came the wreaths, piles and piles of them, colder than the snow now white along the moorland. Their sickly smell filled the stone house. "It is the smell of death," thought Muriel.

The land-girls stole about, red-eyed, admiring, with *crêpe* bands round the arms of their tunics.

Dolly lifted a card.

"Oh, come and look at this," she whispered to Gert. "With deepest sympathy from Colonel and Lady Grainger."

Mrs. Hammond, black-veiled and pathetic, entered the hall. They all fell back respectfully. She leaned above the lilies, touching their waxen trumpets with a gentle finger. She also lifted the card.

"Oh, Muriel, how kind of them!" she cried softly. "How very, very kind."

But Muriel went away and cried bitterly because Connie was dead, and now she had not even a sister left who needed her.

BOOK IV

DELIA

March, 1919—January, 1920

XXXIII

THE meeting of the House Committee for St. Catherine's Home was over when Muriel entered the room. Down the dining-room table of Miller's Rise were scattered notebooks, sheets of blotting-paper, and occasional inkpots. Mrs. Hammond, in her black and white dress, talked with animation to the Honble. Mrs. Potter Vallery. When Muriel saw this, she smiled a little. Nobody noticed the smile but Mr. Vaughan, and it made him feel vaguely uneasy.

He had not been to Miller's Rise for a long time, not indeed since the spring of 1916, when he had called to offer his sympathy after Connie's death. Miller's Rise was not very near to the Vicarage, and he hated calls, and though Mrs. Hammond was charming up to a point—rather a low point perhaps—the vicar never felt quite happy in her old-rose drawing-room. He sat now a little apart from the assembled ladies, hoping very much that Mrs. Cartwright, or Miss Rymer, the Matron of St. Simeon's, would not consider it their duty to approach him sociably. He found that Marshington committees depressed him because nobody was quite whole-hearted over anything. Even when the House Committee laid a request for new clothes-horses before the General Committee, everybody seemed to weigh the question in the balance against Mrs. Potter Vallery's approval or Mrs. Cartwright's possible discomfiture. Hedging from self-interest to sentimental altruism, weighing a hundred side-issues against the case presented, they gave their opinions from policy rather than conviction. This distressed the vicar. But he had decided long ago that these committees were very good for the ladies, and did little harm to the Rescue Work, and that God frequently pours the waters of His mercy from imperfect vessels. So, with one eye on the clock, the vicar had taken the chair at this " extraordinary " but quite usual meeting, wondering how soon he could escape to his peaceful library and " The

Personnel of the Estate of Clergy during the Lancastrian Experiment." Whenever particularly bored by the limitations of his parishioners, he fled to the study of the limitations of his countrymen in former centuries and found it consoling.

"You're always thinking about the identity of the pseudo-Walsingham or whether the Confirmatio Cartarum was a propagandist forgery," scolded Delia, " while all the time souls are being snatched away by the devil under your very nose."

" My dear," he would assure her mildly, " if I did not sometimes remove my attention from the short-comings of my neighbours, the first soul to be so snatched would be my own. Nothing leads so promptly to damnation as the critical contemplation of other people's souls." And yet it seemed that here before him was a soul in evident need of some form of salvation. The vicar felt unhappy.

Muriel Hammond had no business to be cynical. Now, Muriel Hammond, Muriel Hammond. What had happened to the child ?

The vicar cast back his thoughts. " I ought to keep card-index biographies of my parishioners," he told himself. He could remember so little about her. A small, very shy school-girl, a quiet little thing at tennis parties, and—hadn't she once been secretary of the Nursing Association ? Surely those beautifully symmetrical figures still decorating the books were hers. And then—till about a year ago, she had been a regular communicant. The vicar was stirred by a recollection of that small virginal face upraised in an austere rapture of devotion. Her great shining eyes had looked beyond him, as though they gazed on holy mysteries.

The eyes that now stared coldly at Mrs. Hammond could certainly see no holy mysteries. It was doubtful whether they saw even the common kindnesses and uncertain altruisms that lit occasionally the drawing-rooms of even Darkest Marshington —another phrase of Delia's. The vicar studied more closely the neat, indifferent figure. Muriel's clothes were prettily chosen but negligently worn. Mrs. Hammond, perhaps, had been responsible for the choice. Muriel's manner combined the boredom of distaste with the confusion of timidity. The vicar watched her moving from chair to chair, picking up conversations, hovering on the edge of confidences, turning away again before contact was established. He watched her shepherding the committee ladies into the drawing-room for tea, hearing her half-apologetic invitations, her laugh abruptly breaking off, her sentences deferentially curtailed. Her indifference shattered his serene detachment. No girl of her age ought to look like that. He screwed up his mild short-sighted eyes, seeing her for the first time not only as a personality but as a problem.

What had been happening to the girl? Her sister had died; but mortality was a usual experience, and the vicar had seen no sign of affection deeper than the unexcited tolerance common to most sisters in the relationship between Muriel and Connie. A love affair? He had heard of none, and Muriel seemed to lack that particular intensity which made of love a devastating experience to women like—well, Delia. She had not even been away doing war-work, where the realism of more harsh experience might have cut her off from her old interests.

The dining-room had emptied.

Muriel turned from the door and saw the vicar.

" Aren't you coming into tea, Mr. Vaughan ? "

He smiled his shy conciliatory smile. " Has Mrs. Cartwright gone into the drawing-room ? "

" Yes, I think so."

" Muriel—I appeal to you. I want some tea, I would like one of your mother's scones. Are there scones ? Good. But to get them I must face Mrs. Cartwright, and Mrs. Cartwright wants to tell me for the seventh time this afternoon that it was false economy to refuse to pay Sister Lilian's railway fare to Hardrascliffe. Now won't you take pity on me ? Mayn't I be spoiled for once and have my tea in here ? "

" Oh, yes, I should think so," said Muriel in the tone of one but faintly interested in the eccentricities of an old clergyman.

As she left the room, Mr. Vaughan frowned and accused himself with quite unusual acrimony for having been led aside by the raptures of constitutional research from the more pressing spiritual needs of his parishioners.

" Only," he explained to himself, rather as though he were arguing with Delia, " they probably know so much better than I do the things belonging to their peace." At the thought of the limitations of his wisdom he groaned wearily and bowed his head forward into his hands with a half humorous despair.

Muriel re-entered the dining-room with a tray and tea. He noticed that she had taken the trouble to arrange a small tray daintily with a white cloth and a little teapot and a covered dish of toasted scones. Usually he ate his meals with impatience at the inconvenient necessity, but this afternoon he had set himself to observe.

" Won't you bring a cup too ? Have you had your tea ? "

" I—no, really. I shall have mine afterwards in the drawing-room."

" Do have it with me now. There's heaps of tea here. I feel greedy drinking all alone."

When she left the room to fetch her cup he sadly recognized her complete indifference, coupled with her recognition of him as a privileged person. Vividly aware of his unworthiness for privilege, he awaited her return.

She came in and sat down by the long table to pour out his tea. Her movements were gentle but hesitating. She held the china cup, the teapot, the sugar-tongs lightly but never firmly.

" Sugar ? "

" Please—four lumps."

" Cream ? "

" Please. A lot."

She did not smile and humour him as other girls would smile. Gravely she dropped four lumps and poured him a generous portion of cream. He frowned as he stirred the over sweetened tea, and only then remembered that he really hated sugar.

" Muriel, you don't belong to the St. Catherine's Committee ? "

" No, Mr. Vaughan. Will you have a scone ? "

"Thank you. Work among girls—you don't find it interesting ? "

"Oh, quite. I hadn't particularly thought about it. I don't suppose that I should be much good."

"Well, it was not so much the girls that I was thinking of. The House Committee needs somebody to help with the accounts. I remember your excellent work with the Nursing Association. Mrs. Cartwright is a conscientious lady but no mathematician. It would be of immense service both to us and to the home if you would sometimes help her with the books."

"I'll ask Mother. I dare say I could."

He smiled at her. "I am sure that Mrs. Hammond could not mind. It depends upon what you would like. I don't want to urge more work upon you if your time is full."

She shrugged her thin shoulders. "I don't do anything much. I'll ask Mother——"

A hat-stand would have been more responsive.

He changed the conversation.

"Have you noticed much change in Marshington since the war ended ? "

"Change ? Here ? No, I don't think so. People are still washing dishes to be dirtied at the next meal, and sitting at the same stools to add up other people's accounts, and giving tea parties to be envied by other men's wives."

"That's rather a pessimistic view of it, isn't it ? "

"Is it ? Yes, perhaps it is. I'm very silly I know." She laughed nervously. "Of course it's not as bad as that. But sometimes—one wonders—you know, I don't know how the war could have made a difference. It was only a grocery shortage here, and an influx of officers and the arrival of the Graingers."

"Ah, the Graingers. She was a nice woman. A friend of your mother's, I think."

Again that fleeting, unpleasant smile crossed Muriel's face. "Was she ? " she said. "Oh, I suppose so."

"You know, you're a little hard on Marshington in war-time," he continued. "Did you never think of Mrs. Pinden

carrying on her husband's business, of Dickie Weathergay, of
Bobby Mason, of the women who sent their children to
school, kept their homes together and spent their spare time
doing all that they could at the depot and hospital although
the postman's arrival was an hourly torment and the sight of
every telegraph boy turned them sick ? It may have been
all rather small and petty, but it was a multiplication of that
spirit that formed the bulwark of civilization."

" Oh, yes, of course," acquiesced Muriel, but her face
seemed to ask " Is civilization then worth saving ? "

" My daughter Delia, you know, was working in the Women's
Army at the end of the war. She said that it was a revelation
to her—the possibility for development among trivial-minded,
half-grown, half-educated girls—a pity that it should have
been left to war-time."

" Yes, wasn't it ? "

The vicar could not face it. Conversation with Muriel was
like conversation with a gramophone. There was something
almost indecent in her apathy. She could not even uphold
her own opinions.

" I am unhappy about Delia," he continued, experimenting.
" She is working herself to death, living in one of these terrible
clubs, and enjoying a diet almost exclusively composed of
boiled eggs and fish kedgeree, as far as I can discover. She
is very thin."

" She never was fat, was she ? But I dare say that she will
look after herself all right. She was always very capable."

" Since Martin Elliott's death," remarked the vicar meditatively, " she seems to have been capable of almost anything
but sanity about her personal surroundings."

A gleam of the faintest interest awoke in Muriel's eyes.

" Poor Delia. Of course. It was terribly bad luck. But
then, she has her work. Women who have their work have
an immense thing, even if they are unfortunate in the people
whom they love. It is when you have nothing, neither work
nor love, nor even sorrow, that life becomes rather intolerable."
She laughed again. " That does sound a dismal picture,
doesn't it ? "

He looked at her sharply. " Delia saw Godfrey Neale in London—he had just come back."

Muriel's tea-cup clattered softly in her saucer. The vicar almost started at his discovery. At last he had probed her terrible indifference. But even while he was congratulating himself, the light had died and Muriel's chill, equable little voice continued :

" I am very glad to hear that he has come back safely. Mrs. Neale worried terribly, and I am sure that Clare must be glad."

" Senora Alvarados was your friend I think ? "

" A school-friend, yes."

The door opened and Mrs. Hammond entered.

" Oh, there you are, you two culprits ! Really, Mr. Vaughan, I can't have you stealing my daughter like this, you know ! Muriel, dear, there are thousands of empty cups in the drawing-room. My wrist aches. Do come and relieve me. Mr. Vaughan, Mrs. Cartwright is asking——"

" Oh, I know, I know," pleaded the vicar. " She has asked several times. Mrs. Hammond, don't you think that it would be a good idea if Muriel came to help us with the accounts for the House Committee ? You know how difficult we people who have not mathematical minds all find them."

Mrs. Hammond raised her pretty eyebrows. " On the House Committee of St. Catherine's ? Muriel ? Well—really—I hadn't thought of it. Hardly the kind of work—I mean—not for a young girl—in contact with the sort of home like—well, really, what do you think yourself, Mr. Vaughan ? "

" I think that the checking of bills for dust-pans and stair-rods can hardly be contaminating, even if they are to be used by reformed prostitutes," remarked the vicar dryly.

" Oh, well—it isn't quite that, you know. It's the idea of it. No other unmarried girl is on St. Catherine's Committee. It doesn't somehow seem to me quite the thing. Of course, if Muriel wants to very much—I never stand in her way over anything—girls do as they like nowadays, don't they ? But I have always tried to keep her away from all that *sort* of thing as much as possible."

The vicar was uncertain afterwards whether he had really seen that expression cross Muriel's face then—that scornful yet submissive aversion, which lacked spirit even to be violent. He answered bravely :

" I think that Muriel is almost old enough to judge for herself."

" I'm not really keen, if Mother doesn't want me to," said Muriel.

And yet, in the following silence, the vicar could feel the clash and tension of their personalities as clearly as though swords had crossed. In the St. Catherine's incident lay some secret significance for Muriel and her mother. Behind Muriel's untranquil quiet lay a suppressed resentment, and somewhere, but Heaven knew where, lay the solution of her problem.

The vicar sighed, shook hands and walked unhappily homeward to write a long and troubled letter to his daughter.

XXXIV

MURIEL had been to tea with Daisy Weathergay. She had nursed the Weathergay babies (there were now two) and looked at Weathergay photographs, and endured the reiterated recital of the heroism of Captain Dickie Weathergay in the Great War. She had been made to understand, if indeed she had not already understood, that the War only really affected the lives of those women married or engaged to soldiers at the Front ; and the recollection that she was of those who had no right to feel anxiety or relief brought sharply home to her the thought of Godfrey at the Weare Grange.

" They say she's never been up there to stay since he came home," Daisy remarked with the confident knowledge of the already married. " Of course I was always sure that it would never come to anything and I still don't believe he'll marry her. A foreigner——"

" She's not," protested Muriel.

"Oh, well, she's half French or something, isn't she? Anyway, I'm sure she'd never do for Godfrey. Now poor Phyllis—— Really, it is terrible, isn't it? Ever since he came home, she's looking so ill and pale, though I do think that she's a little fool to wear her héart on her sleeve like that——"

A pleasurable pride lifted for a moment the depression of Muriel's mood. She at least evidently did not share in the folly of Phyllis Marshall Gurney, yet as she said good-bye at the garden gate of Daisy's little villa her depression returned to her again. It accompanied her on the walk homeward, blinding her to the clear tracery of budding trees across the sky, to the silver serenity of the spring evening. She thought, "Connie's baby would have been three years old now. They might at least have left me the satisfaction of being an aunt." She thought, "What on earth shall I do when I get home? Read? All books are the same—about beautiful girls who get married or married women who fall in love with their husbands. In books things always happen to people. Why doesn't somebody write a book about someone to whom nothing ever happens—like me?"

She thought, "If only I'd done what Mr. Vaughan suggested about St. Catherine's Home, I'd have the accounts to do this evening. Mother says that Mrs. Cartwright's got the tradesman's bills into an awful mess. But it's not the sort of thing that young girls do. Oh, no! Men hate to think of girls being mixed up in that sort of thing! O God, O God, what am I going to do! How much does Mother know about Eric? How long can I bear living in the same house as those two, knowing what I know, guessing what they know, and hearing them lie and lie and lie?

"I must be sensible. What could Mother do about Connie but pretend that she knows nothing? Did she know about Eric, though, before she made Connie marry Ben? There was something between them. How much did she guess? Oh, what is the use of going all over this again? I must think about something else. If I don't think about something else I shall go mad. What's the good, what's the good?

What else is there to think about ? The tennis club opening ?
The Nursing Association, the Marshington people ? What
shall I do—having nothing to think about, and nobody's going
to marry me, and I'm here always, always ? How many years ?
Three since I left Thraile ? Then I shall probably live
another fifty."

She tried as always, to reason herself back into sanity.
" Even if I can't love Mother any more as I used to ; even
if I know that she's calculating and hard and insincere, at
least Father needs me. He has come to like me a little more
—to know me." But Muriel knew this to be at least uncertain.

When she opened the door of Miller's Rise, she felt the
atmosphere of the house close in upon her. She heard through
the morning-room door her father's voice, " But, look here,
Rachel, for the Lord's sake ! " And her mother's, gently complaining, " Oh, of course, Arthur, I know. You always thought
of the girls before you thought of me. You always preferred
to have Muriel do things for you——"

" Oh, by gad, this is too bad ! Muriel's a good lass enough,
but you know it's nothing to do with that. A husband's and
wife's income are clumped together for taxation, and I'm
damned if I'll let this rotten Government fleece me right and
left. Muriel will get it anyway when we're gone, she might
as well have a bit now—I'll tie up the capital so that no rascal
can marry her for her money——"

" Oh, I don't think that you need fear that she'll *marry*,
and it's all very well putting it down to the income tax, but
you know as well as I do——"

Muriel put down her umbrella with a clatter on the hall
table. She went into the sitting-room to find her father
standing in flushed exasperation near the mantelpiece, her
mother sewing with indignant concentration at the table, and
Aunt Beatrice, ignored as completely as the carpet, crocheting
doilies in the window.

Lately Mr. and Mrs. Hammond had argued much more
frequently. Again it had been the Thraile incident that
seemed to mark the turning point in their relations. Mrs.
Hammond was blaming her husband for his bequest to

Connie of the ungovernable temperament which had nearly brought ruin on the Hammond family. She was sore at her one failure, terrified now of another. Muriel could read in her increasing plaintiveness the anxiety that racked her, lest her elder daughter also should defeat her ends. And this continual strain was telling upon Mr. Hammond. He had married Rachel Bennet largely because she was pretty, clever and a lady. She brought things off. Arthur Hammond loved people who brought things off. He liked to pay dearly for good stuff, but he expected it to be good. Muriel remembered his advice, applied equally to horses and workmen, and, she supposed, to his wife, " Go for the best i' the market, pay top price, and let 'em rip." He had gone for the best on the market. He had given Rachel a free hand, till now she had always brought things off, but just recently she had begun to doubt her own capacity to triumph, not so much over circumstance as over other people's limitations. Connie had jarred her self-confidence, Muriel was wearing it fine, and Arthur Hammond was becoming bored.

Without taking off her hat, Muriel sat down by the table, wondering whether they would tell her about the argument. Whatever it was, it evidently concerned her closely.

" Muriel, dear, I wish that you would not sit about in your coat and skirt. You know how it spoils it to sit about in it indoors."

" Oh, all right, Mother." She rose to go.

" Here, M.," her father called her back, " I've got some papers I want you to sign after supper. Come to my desk in the dining-room."

Muriel guessed what these were. She saw her mother's eyes, hurt and angry, looking across the table to her. She went slowly from the room and closed the door.

She had not been in her own bedroom more than five minutes, and was slowly taking off her silk shirt blouse, when her aunt tapped at the door and came in.

" Oh, you're changing ? "

" Yes," remarked Muriel, lifting a grey velveteen dress from her wardrobe. " What is it, Auntie ? "

"Oh, I don't know, dear. Nothing in particular. Did you hear anything interesting in the village ? "

"Nothing. Does one ever hear anything interesting in Marshington ? What was the trouble downstairs, Auntie ? "

"Trouble, dear ? What trouble do you mean ? "

Muriel picked up her dress and pushed it over her head. When she emerged from her temporary eclipse she said " Father and Mother."

"Oh—er—nothing, dear."

Muriel fastened an amethyst brooch carefully into her dress. She was thinking, " I really can't stand this feeling of secret exasperation in the house. I can't stand not talking to someone." Aloud she asked :

"Auntie, have you noticed—Father and Mother seem to get on each other's nerves now, like they never used to do ? "

"Oh—I shouldn't say that, you know, Muriel."

"Oh, Auntie, you must have noticed it. What was it now about the income tax ? "

"Oh, well, your father wants to invest some money in your name, to save super tax—just as a business investment, you know, and your mother——"

"Thinks that she ought to have it ? "

"Well, yes, dear. But you know that wouldn't do. As your father pointed out, it doesn't act somehow if the wife has it."

"Mother doesn't like Father—doing things for me, does she ? " Muriel reflected. " Perhaps you've noticed. She doesn't like my doing things for him either."

"Well, dear," Aunt Beatrice sat down in Muriel's arm-chair, eager to clear away doubts and difficulties, her eyes shining with excellent intentions, " you see, your father and mother have always been so very *much* to one another. Far more than most husbands and wives. Your mother gave up a great deal for your father—my family weren't at all pleased at a Bennet marrying a Hammond. We held a very good position in Market Burton, you know. And your mother has been wonderful, she has never looked back once. But naturally

she expects—wants—would like to have the—the first place
in your father's consideration."

"Of course," murmured Muriel," and she is inclined to
fear anything that might come between them ? "

"Oh, yes, dear. Naturally. Though of course this
money——"

"Of course—this money. That's hardly the point, I
know. Just a trifle, which of course she will come to see in its
true proportion. The real thing is that she does not like the
idea of anyone else getting the attention which she naturally
expects from Father."

She began to arrange the little silver-topped boxes and
hairpin tidies and pincushions upon her dressing-table with
light, careful movements, while her mind worked feverishly.

"Father admires Mother immensely, doesn't he ? More
than most husbands about here admire their wives ? "

"Yes, yes. I always said so. He thinks her wonderful.
You know dear, of course, when you were younger I should
not like to have said anything ; but you must see some things
for yourself now—your mother's influence has been wonderful
over your father. She—she's always so—splendid," Aunt
Beatrice returned to the word for lack of better definition.

Muriel, however, supplied the deficiency. "Yes, she
always carries things off, doesn't she ? It would be terrible
if for once she did not carry things off. That's the quality
he most admires in her. I'm afraid," she continued dreamily,
"that that's why he's been less—less *certain* of her lately,
aren't you ? Because he isn't certain whether she's going to
carry things off——"

"I don't quite see, dear—well, what ? "

"Me, for instance," murmured Muriel. "It would be a
terrible thing if after all she never got me off, wouldn't it ?
Especially after Connie's death. You know, it was a pity that
I hadn't any brothers. Boys can go and get married on their
own. But when women like you and I, Auntie, are left unmarried, it is rather a trial for our parents, isn't it ? "

"Oh, but, dear, of *course* you will marry one day. It's
early to talk——"

" Is it ?   Do you think I shall ? "   Muriel turned from the dressing-table and looked at her aunt. " I'm nearly thirty. Nobody has ever proposed to me yet.   Do you think that it's likely ? "

" Why, of course, dear. Heaps and heaps of girls marry *long* after they are thirty."

" Of course—there's a hope, isn't there, that one's life may not be utterly wasted—even at the eleventh hour—one might—marry ? "

Even Aunt Beatrice could not bear everything. She rose from her chair and crossed to the window, a timid, inefficient, untidy little figure, with weak wistful eyes and a stubbornly submissive mouth ; but there was a quiver of animation in her voice that Muriel had never heard before.

" I hope very sincerely, dear, I always have hoped that you would marry, both for your own sake and for your mother's. I am very fond of your mother.   I was bitterly sorry about her terrible trouble with dear Connie, though I dare say that no one but another mother could know quite what it felt like to lose her child and grandchild together, so to speak.   I should like for her sake to see you married.   It would repay her for many troubles she has known."

Aunt Beatrice looked from Muriel's room to the darkening plain beyond the garden.   Her gentle voice grew sharp with unconscious bitterness.

" But even more for your own sake, dear.   You will marry, I am sure.   Marriage is the—the crown and joy of woman's life—what we were born for—to have a husband and children, and a little home of your own.   Of course there are some of us to whom the Lord has not pleased to give this.   I'm sure I'm not complaining.   There may be many compensations, and of course He knows best.   But—it's all right while you're young, Muriel, and there's always a chance—and when my dear mother was alive and I had someone to look after I am sure no girl could have been happier.   It's when you grow older and the people who needed you are dead.   And you haven't a home nor anyone who really wants you—and you hate to stay too long in a house in case someone else should want to come—and of course it's quite right. Somebody had to look after Mother. Everybody can't marry. I'm not complaining. I'm sure they're very kind to me, but I sometimes pray that the good Lord won't make me wait here very long—that I can die before every one gets tired of me, and of having me staying round——"

The room was growing dark. Shadows grey and desolate stole from the long curtains. Only in the small, dim woman's voice lay the intensity of realization that has passed despair.

" I used to pray every night that I should never come to a time when nobody wanted me. There's no real need for me in this house. Rachel's only kind to have me here when there's room. Oh, Muriel, my dear, if ever a good man offers you the chance of a home, of children, of some reason for living, don't throw it away, don't, don't."

" I don't suppose that there is any prospect of my doing so," said Muriel. Part of her wanted to go and put her arms round her aunt and be gentle to her. The other part was fighting a grim battle to defer her vision of something that she wanted not to see.

It fought during the whole evening, during supper, during her signature of unintelligible papers at her father's desk, when he told her gruffly that she would now have an income of £350 a year minus income tax, which would return to her in some mysterious way after negotiations. " I could understand this myself if he would once explain," she thought. But he did not explain, and she had to return to the gas-lit drawing-room to face her mother's drawn mouth, her aunt's timid efforts to keep out of the way, and the aftermath of her father's temper.

There was nothing to do.

She sat down at the piano and began to play drearily. Her father rose, looked at her, and a few moments later left the room. They heard his car humming away down the drive.

Mrs. Hammond glanced up at Aunt Beatrice, then she continued to sew without further comment.

The silence grew unbearable.

" I suppose—er—Arthur's gone to the club, Rachel ? "

"I suppose so. Muriel, pass me my other scissors, please."
Not a word was said about the money.

As soon as she could escape decently, Muriel kissed her aunt and mother, and went upstairs to bed.

The moon had risen. It threw light panels of grey across the dark floor of her room. Muriel left her blind undrawn, and went to stand where that afternoon her aunt had stood, gazing towards the twinkling lights of Kingsport.

Of course she had known for weeks that this was coming, but she had tried to shut her eyes against the truth. She could not stay at Miller's Rise.

Ever since Connie's death she should have known this. Her mother had failed with Connie, yet she had met bitter failure with such outstanding social strategy that it had become transformed to something like a triumph. But it had opened her eyes to the knowledge that with Muriel she might fail without hope of safety. You can hide the unhappiness of a marriage, but no one can hide in a provincial town the glaring failure of no marriage whatsoever, and every one in Marshington knew that poor Muriel Hammond had not had so much as an affair.

No, it was quite certain; she would never marry now. Better to face the fact and deal with it unflinchingly. What then? Could she stay there at Miller's Rise to "help her mother" indefinitely? She knew that her mother had never wanted help. Always the hope had been that she would marry. To this end alone had she been trained and cared for; and now she sat, meal after meal, between her mother and her father. She knew that they found her presence secretly humiliating. She was spoiling the best thing in the lives of both of them.

"I ought to go," thought Muriel. "But where? How?" What in the whole world was there left for her to do? She had abandoned all hope of a career to help her mother, and her mother did not need her, and she was unmarried. "Nobody wants me—I'm like Aunt Beatrice, living in fear of an unloved old age. I must have some reason for living. I must, I must. I can't bear to live without. I just can't bear it. Oh, what am I going to do with myself?"

From the calm valley the mist-veiled fields gleamed silver
like still water. The unanswering moon sailed on across the
sky.

She began to walk now up and down the room. She could
not bear herself. She wanted to fling off her body. She
wanted to become wildly hysterical, to sob and scream with a
pain of despair that was physical as well as mental.

"What have I done to bring this on myself?" she asked,
she to whom this terrible burden of negation proved a torture.
"I always tried to do the best that I could see."

The best that she could see. She pressed her hands against
her head. Some fugitive echo of memory lay in the words,
sight, sight. "The last betrayal and the ultimate unworthiness is the defilement of the vision." That mad fanatic at
Thraile, that warped religious maniac, what right had he, with
his crude theories of self-mortification and God's vengeance,
to come before her now with his dark prophecies of vision?
Sight? What sight? Had she not always done the best
that she had seen?

"We can only worship what we see." All very well to
talk. She pressed her hands against her eyes and in the
darkness she tried to read again the visions she had seen.

She saw the God of her early school-days, a benign and
patriarchal creation of her own emotions, bidding her be
submissive and content, and smiling on her with approbation
that curiously resembled Mrs. Hancock's.

She saw Clare; and immediately her desires altered. To
be good meant to be gay, to be loved, to be beautiful, to dance
through life right up to Godfrey's arms.

She shivered. That vision had soon died. Beauty and gay
success in love could not be hers. What vision then? She
saw her mother, the passionate devotee of the great god of
People. She saw herself accepting now new standards. The
thing that mattered in Marshington was neither service nor
love but marriage, marriage respectable and unequivocal,
marriage financially sound, eugenically advisable, and socially
correct. She had sought it. Oh, no doubt she had sought it
but never found, for though Godfrey Neale had kissed her he

had not unnaturally forgotten. In the emotional reaction after a crisis of fear, she had found the only sign of the satisfaction that she had sought as love.

Then she had gone to Thraile. She saw more clearly now the reeling nightmare of those days, when she had lost all touch with sane reality. At Hardrascliffe and at Marshington she could deal with a given crisis according to known rules, but at Thraile she had been swept right off her feet, having no standard of her own to hold by. She had wanted to help Connie and had followed a policy of blind opportunism, blundering from one notion to another. Connie in trouble must be married. Connie, when married, must have life made tolerable. This she had seen, and, seeing thus, had acted. But never once had Muriel Hammond, Muriel who sought before all things excellence of conduct, never once had she thought clearly about what it all meant. She had never once lifted her head higher than Connie's, but had left to Mr. Todd the task of trying to make clear what her sister and Ben had done. But when you faced it frankly, you saw that it all came to this. At Marshington the only thing that mattered was marriage. Connie, who knew this, who was wild and reckless but who at least was brave, had ruined her life and Ben's, had saddened Eric's, and had brought her family to bitter shame. Muriel, with no less intention but less courage, had sat at home and waited and grown bitter. And now she was still waiting and her youth was passing by.

And yet, and yet, it had not been her own way to want this only. A respectable marriage had not always been the one goal of her life. She had dreamed dreams. She had seen visions, but her visions had faded before the opinion of others ; she had lacked the courage of her dreams. And now there was left to her nothing but Marshington. She could not even go away. It had trapped her in the end, for she had shut her eyes to anything beyond its streets, and was a prisoner now to her own blindness.

"The only thing that Marshington cares about is sex-success." Delia Vaughan had said that. Muriel did not believe her. It was true enough, quite true.

Her hands dropped from her face. She looked as she had looked thirteen years ago across the moonlit fields to the dark city.

Well, Delia had been proved right at last. What next ?

XXXV

"M Y dear," remarked the vicar, far more gravely than he was accustomed to remark upon things in this curious, interesting, troublesome, but not grave world, " you are killing yourself."

Delia lit another cigarette with trembling fingers and swung herself on to the library table.

" Nothing of the sort," she replied brusquely. " Merely a little run down by an unvaried diet of quarrelling, press campaigns, acrimonious public meetings and stale fish. I don't know whether the indigestion has been due to the debates or the fish. I suspect the former. Most of my co-habitants at Morrison House seem to survive the fish with imperturbable appetites. My dearest Father, do not at your eleventh hour begin to play the heavy parent with me. Always hitherto I've admired your dignified self-restraint about my eccentricities a good deal more than I have considered it advisable to state—and now—well, really, just because I happen to have had two or three bilious attacks ! "

The vicar removed his glasses slowly, leaned back in his chair, and looked up at his daughter. " It seems to me a little uncharacteristic of you, my dear, who have always been almost arrogantly neglectful of your bodily needs, to throw up your work in the middle of what I take to be a monumental campaign of militant good intentions, and to come down for a fortnight into the country because you have had three bilious attacks."

Delia removed her cigarette from her smiling lips and blew out a squadron of smoke rings that floated in beautiful order along the firelit air.

"Oh, well," she said, swinging her legs. They were painfully thin legs, thought the vicar, judging from what he
could see of them. Owing to his daughter's attitude he could
see a considerable extent. "I suppose that I might as well
tell you—I've not been particularly well for some time. I
don't know what it is. I suppose that I have been overdoing
things a little."

"Sixteen hours a day?" queried the vicar mildly. "Meetings in Hyde Park, heart-to-heart talks with bishops, members
of parliament, and prostitutes—really quite alarming articles
in the Press, my dear, and all this office work. Your Twentieth
Century Reform League sounds so terribly—strenuous."

"The twentieth century *is* strenuous. To tell the truth,
there are so many men and women doing nothing with their
leisure that those who have any sort of responsibility towards
society are nearly bound to overwork. However, Dr.
Boden——"

"You went to a doctor then?"

"She's a friend of mine. She works at the crèche and
shelter home we run in Plaistow. She said that I ought to
live somewhere—not in a club—where they'd keep meals and
things for me. I ought to diet or something—you know, on
unstale fish and eggs and things. But you know, Father, it's
all absurd. How can I afford a house and servants—or to live
in one of these communal palaces where everything is just so?
She suggested that I should take unto myself a friend and
share a flat with her—someone of a meek and domestic dis-
position—not herself. She's married and has four children.
But now, father, can you honestly imagine me living peacefully with another woman, installed à *deux* in—say Aberdeen
Mansions? Why, the poor creature would have a fearful
time."

"She would. The worst of being a reformer is that you
can't stop—even at your friend's characters, can you?"

Delia rose and pressed out the ashes from her cigarette
against the hearth rail.

"I haven't any friends—of that sort," she said slowly.
"You can't when you're really working hard. I have heaps of

colleagues, but "—she shrugged her shoulders—" you know, since Martin was killed I do find it so awfully hard to keep my temper with other people. They infuriate me simply for not being he—because they dare to go on living, being so much less worthy of life, when he is dead. Of course it's entirely my own fault, and in my sane moments I realize how impossible I am to live with. But, however hard I work for some sort of vague idea of a regenerated society, I always seem to be fighting people instead of loving them." She laughed, pushing back her smooth black hair with her tobacco-stained fingers. " I am like one of St. Paul's unfortunates, who give my body to be burnt, not having charity. So I suppose my sacrifice is worth nothing."

. There was a little catch in her voice. Her face in the firelight was almost fantastically wan, the face of a fighter prematurely old.

" Really," protested the vicar, " you terrible idealists give more trouble to law-abiding, peaceful people like myself than all the sinners God ever put into the world to leaven the lump of good intentions. Which reminds me—I've got one coming to tea."

" Good heavens ! Who ? Which ? Idealist or sinner ? "

" I don't quite know. A problem anyway. I do wish that you young women would let me alone."

" A young woman ? Oh, father dear, *don't* you think I've had enough young women ? I wanted the cloistered solitude of male society for a little."

" It's Muriel Hammond. You remember her ? "

" Oh, yes. Well, it might have been worse."

" I'm worried about her, Delia."

" Hum. I gathered from your letter that you were. Light gone out or something ? "

The vicar nodded, his finger-tips pressed together.

" Yes, I suppose that is it—her light has gone out. Why, Delia ? You know that I cannot provide myself as you can in a moment with biographical information to come to the aid of my psychology. What is wrong with her ? "

" Wrong environment, intellectual idealist of limited

capacity, not too much will-power, immense credulity and ridiculous desire to live up to other people's ideas of her, stuck in Marshington. Of course she was bound to find out some time."

" Find out what ? "

" That this is the last place on earth for a woman whose mind runs upon other lines than the smooth road to matrimony, and whose personality isn't usually attractive. I'm glad she's come to her senses at last."

" She hasn't."

" She's not going to marry Mr. Robert Mason, is she ? "

" Not that I know of. But I believe that she'd marry the dustman if he asked her."

" Good Lord. Bad as that ? Poor child. Well, what are we to do. Take her and shake her ? "

" I don't know. I leave her to you, my dear. As I have always said, I disapprove entirely of your sweeping condemnation of provincial towns. Your views on matrimony are appalling, especially as——"

" As I was inconsistent over Martin ? But, Father dear, haven't I explained to you a million times that it isn't marriage I object to—only marriage as an end of life in itself, as the ultimate goal of the female soul's development——"

The door opened.

Mrs. Raikes, the vicar's housekeeper, looked in.

" Miss 'Ammond, sir."

They rose to welcome Muriel.

She came forward with characteristic timidity and shook hands with Delia and her father.

" I hope you're better ? " she inquired of Delia.

" Better ? I'm all right. Never been ill."

" You look very tired," remarked Muriel.

They gave her tea, the vicar absent-mindedly poking the fire with his boot. Now that he had handed over the problem of Muriel to Delia, he felt that he had done his duty, and might return to the congenial contemplation of mediæval taxes.

When tea was over he murmured some vague excuse about preparing a sermon and vanished hurriedly.

" Doesn't Mr. Vaughan want to prepare his sermons here ? " asked Muriel.

" Not he. He hasn't gone to prepare a sermon either. If we went into the garden we should probably find him wandering up and down among the daffodils swearing softly over Pollard's *Evolution of Parliament*, which he calls a brilliant book, but most wrong-headed. Isn't it extraordinary that historians always seem quite pleased to find each other brilliant, but simply can't admit that they are anything but wrong-headed ? "

" Do they ? I don't know any historians. They don't live in Marshington—except your father, and of course we don't see much of him. I'm not surprised. We really aren't a very exciting lot of people." Again she laughed self-deprecatingly. " You know, you are very lucky, being so clever and going to Newnham like that. It must be frightfully nice——"

Delia lit another cigarette thoughtfully. " Smoke ? No ? You don't, do you ? " Muriel shook her head. " You don't mind if I do, do you ? I've got into rather a bad habit of doing it too much lately. You know, I've often wondered why you didn't go to college."

" I—oh, I—well, really as a matter of fact I did once think that I should like to. But I wasn't particularly clever you know."

" The last thing that one requires to make good use of a college education is brilliance. You want intelligence and industry and a sound constitution. The brilliant people can manage without it."

" Oh—well, it wasn't only that." Muriel leaned forward with her small hands stretched towards the fire.

" She doesn't look more than eighteen now," thought Delia. " What a solemn little child she is."

" You see Mother wasn't frightfully keen on it," explained Muriel sedately.

" Did you ask ? "

" No, not exactly. I sounded Aunt Beatrice, who always knows these things. She said that they would be awfully disappointed if I wanted to leave them, and it did not seem worth while to me to make a fuss and to upset every one because I overestimated my own ability."

" Usefulness seems to me a question of intention rather than ability," remarked Delia. " Don't you think that this self-deprecation of yours was a little like cowardice ? You hated an upset, and so you decided that you lacked ability."

She glanced sideways at Muriel, who still looked primly meek, facing the liquid flames.

" I wanted to help Mother too," said Muriel, seeking justice.

" Hum. And you thought that by helping your mother you would escape the responsibility of having to help yourself, didn't you ? It was the difficult choice you couldn't face, not your own inefficiency."

Would Muriel take offence ? Delia, well used to the outrage of her companions, watched the sensitive curve of Muriel's mouth tighten. Would she be too poor-spirited to make defence ? Or too ungenerous to accept criticism ?

For some time she did not speak. Delia was half afraid lest at the outset she should have wounded her too deeply, have frightened her away from any possibility of contact. She began to abuse herself as a tactless fool before Muriel's quiet little voice began again reflectively :

" I think that you are probably right. I was a coward. I've always been afraid. Desperately afraid—but not of unpleasantness exactly. I was afraid quite genuinely of hurting other people, of my own limitations, of the crash and jar of temperament. I—you won't laugh at me, will you ?—wanted frightfully to be good. I did not realize what life was like, that nobody has a chance. It's all very well saying that I should have done this or that. Things happen against our will. Always being driven and we follow—voices." Her own voice gained intensity. Bright patches of carmine flared into her pale cheeks. " They promise us all sorts of things," she said, " happiness, success, adventure—don't you know ? Of course you don't, you're clever. But we listen, we think that we are moving on towards some strange, rich carnival, and follow, follow, follow. Then suddenly we find ourselves left alone in a dull crowded street with no one caring and our lives unneeded, and all the fine things that we meant to do, like toys that a child has laid aside."

" My dear "—Delia's voice was softer now—" you are very, very wrong. You speak as though we had no choice in the matter."

" We haven't," said Muriel stubbornly. " Oh, you're clever and all that," her manner seemed to say, " but you can't deceive me now a second time."

" You are quite wrong," Delia answered slowly. " It's all very well to talk about life this and life that. You can't wriggle out of responsibility by a metaphor. Your life is your own, Muriel, nobody can take it from you. You may choose to look after your mother ; you may choose to pursue a so-called career, or you may choose to marry. You may choose right and you may choose wrong. But the thing that matters is to take your life into your own hands and live it, accepting responsibility for failure or success. The really fatal thing is to let other people make your choices for you, and then to blame them if your schemes should fail and they despise you for the failure. What did you mean to do in Marshington ? "

" I hardly know. All sorts of silly things—I put fine names on to all the conventional ways for killing the time between a girl's school-days and her marriage." Again Muriel laughed. " Oh, I've been a fine fool, fine. You know what you once said to me—' The only thing that counts at Marshington is sex-success.' I didn't know then what you meant, and I hated your criticisms of the sort of life my people lived. I thought them so disloyal."

" I know. Loyalty plays the devil with people until they see that it's first true demand is honesty."

" If only I'd been like you," continued Muriel. " It's all very well for you to talk about choices and things, you know. You've really had everything. The best of both worlds——" She looked up unexpectedly. " Do you know that there was a time when I could have killed you—just for jealousy ? "

" Really ? When ? " asked Delia with interest.

" Just after Martin Elliott was killed. You'd had the best

of everything. Love to remember and work to do. Oh, I know you think you've suffered. Every one says 'Poor Delia!' I could have killed them. There you were with nothing to reproach yourself for, with no bitterness of shame, but a mind full of sweet memories. Why, you don't know what it is—the awfulness of a life where nothing ever happens; the shame of only feeling half a woman because no man has loved you; the bitterness of watching other girls complete their womanhood. And I didn't so much want marriage. I wanted to feel that I had not lived unloved, that there was nothing in my nature that cut me off from other women, made me different—Oh, I know that this sounds very primitive. We are primitive perhaps in Marshington. But what do I know of the world outside this village? I'm nearly thirty. People tell me that I look like a child. I feel like a child—beside you, for instance. But I do know this. That if ever I had a child and it was born a girl and not beautiful, I believe I'd strangle it rather than think that it should suffer as I've suffered!"

"Why—Muriel!"

"Oh, yes. Perhaps you're shocked. I know." The fire died from her voice. She dropped her head on to her small, clasped hands. Very wearily she spoke, "Oh, well. I suppose it does me good to say what I think, just once. Anyway what does it matter? I'm twenty-nine and to all useful intents and purposes my life is as much over as though I were ninety. I'm stuck here, I shan't marry. I don't know what else to do. You say that I've never made a choice—through cowardice. I dare say that you're right. But it's too late to begin now."

"Things are never too late, only more difficult."

"You would say that, now, wouldn't you? I'm sure that you're a splendid lecturer, Delia. You must be able to tell people an awful lot of good home-truths. You get so much practice, don't you?"

Delia smiled ruefully. She rose and crossed to the tea-tray and poured herself out a cup of quite cold tea, allowing Muriel to talk on.

" Do you know," said Muriel with mild surprise, " I never could stand up on a public platform, but I do believe that if I could I should be able to tell your audiences things you never could ? "

" Of course. I'm sure of it."

" You know," she paused, as though she were thinking of some quite new thing, " you don't know half the time what you are talking about."

Up shot Delia's eyebrows. " I might have expected this," she told herself gleefully. " I might have known that when Muriel really did begin to talk we should hear some surprising things." Aloud she said, " Go on."

" You rail against faults like mental slackness, and sloppiness and being content with other people's standards. But you don't know what they mean. You're clear-sighted. I don't believe that's nearly so much a merit as a gift. How can you know what blindness is when you can see ? But I know what it's like. I know what fear and stupidity and muddle-headed-ness can feel like. Because I did not recognize them till it was too late does not take away from me now the right to see them in other people—But I can't. What's the good here ? Only—I wish—I wish that if you see anyone else in the same sort of muddle as I was in—ten years ago—you'd—you'd really make it clear to them."

" I blame myself—I blame myself," said Delia. " I should have made things clear."

"Oh, no. You mustn't think that. Why, you were the one person who ever lifted a hand to undeceive me. It was my fault. I was too arrogantly sure of my own righteousness to listen. I was too much set on living up to other people's expectations of me. You—you always——" She swallowed heavily, but went on. " Do you know, you've always meant a lot to me—I think—I think I used to sort of idealize you— as the person I might have been if I had not been such a fool."

" Me, Muriel ? "

" Yes—er—it was impertinent, wasn't it ? " Again she laughed, and rising hurriedly began to draw her gloves on, blushing and shy. " Good-bye, it has been most awfully

good of you to talk to me like this. I—I shan't forget it.
Please will you say good-bye to Mr. Vaughan for me ? "

Delia turned from the tea-tray.

" Where are you going ? "

" Going ? Back—home—to Miller's Rise," said Muriel
with surprise.

" Oh, no, you're not," commanded Delia. " Sit down a
minute."

" But I'm keeping you—I——"

" No, I'm going to keep you. Please sit down."

Meekly, Muriel sat down and waited. She had to wait for
a long time. Delia folded a derelict slice of brown bread and
butter and began to cut it into neat, rectangular disks upon her
plate. When she did speak, her question was quite unexpected.

" Have you a great deal of patience, Muriel ? "

" Patience ? Me ? I—I haven't much idea."

" No—no. N—o." Delia's fingers tapped at the round
brass tea-tray. " No, you wouldn't know. Really it seems
incredible that—however—you're keen on accounts and
things, aren't you ? "

" Yes—I—suppose I am. I'm not much——"

" Good at them, though ? Of course not. Nobody is
without a proper training. However, if I remember the
Nursing Association you have quite a genius for method. Do
you like house-keeping ? "

" That depends. At home it's such a routine now. I
often used to think it would be lovely to have a little house all
of one's own—only again the necessity of sharing it with a
husband was an obstacle."

" I see."

" But I must really go. You'll be getting tired of talking
about me——"

" Oh, no, I shan't. For Heaven's sake sit down and do
be a bit more interested in yourself. You'll have to hear a
lot of home-truths before I've finished with you. By the way,
I'm ill."

" Ill ? Oh, I was afraid——"

" Not very ill. But I shall be, unless I change my way of

living. I ought to move into a flat, where I can have special
meals and a more or less selected diet. I have enough money
for the diet, but not for a whole servant to cook it, nor a whole
flat to keep her in, and I certainly haven't time to cook my meals
myself. What would you suggest ? "

" Why ? I should suggest that you should get some one to
share a flat and do the housekeeping."

" Yes, of course. That would seem to be the obvious thing
if it were not for one difficulty. I am an impossible person
to live with. Look at me. I live largely on platforms and in
publicity, which is always uncomfortable for one's friends. I
suffer abominably from indigestion and consequently my
friends suffer from my temper. I insult bishops and civil
servants from platforms for the good of their souls. I'm
running one of the most provocative and militant societies in
England. I'm pursued by anonymous letters, threatened
libel actions, and clergymen with outraged susceptibilities—
and I mind it all damnably. I'm not a scrap heroic. I quail
before every adverse criticism ; I'm hag-ridden at night by
memories of things that I might have done, and haunted all
day by a sense of furious impotence. I'm never in the same
mood for two minutes running, and all my moods are irritating.
Worst of all, when my own affairs go wrong, I always blame
the first person who happens to be near, and, try as I will, I
can't reform myself. You see, I have no right to ask anyone
to live with me."

Muriel was silent for a long time. Then she said :

" You may be partly right, but I think you exaggerate.
The girl who came to live with you might be happier in some
circumstances, but those might be beyond her power, and at
least she'd have the satisfaction of knowing that she was
living with someone who needed her. If you are unpleasant
to your immediate neighbours sometimes," recollections of
early chapters in Delia's career lit the ghost of a smile in
Muriel's eyes, " at least you try to be of some use to the world
at large. One may be alarmed by you, but one can't despise
you. It's living with people whom you suspect are using you
for ends that you yourself despise that kills you. It's having

nothing to do, not having too much, which is intolerable. I should go ahead and ask anyone whom you can think of. Let them refuse if they will. But do see that you get a good cook."

" Muriel," laughed Delia, " do you know that you are quite a lamb ? "

Muriel stared at her as though she had gone mad.

" It's all right," Delia reassured her. " I'm not going to tax your charity."

" How ? What do you mean ? "

" By asking you to come and share my flat and work during the day in the office of the Twentieth Century Reform League."

Into Muriel's face the quick light leapt and died.

" No, no, of course not. I'm much too stupid. But I hope you'll find someone nice."

" You—you can't *want* to come—if I did ask you ? "

" You mustn't ask me. I'd get on your nerves."

" But you can't *want* to come ? " repeated Delia incredulously.

" More than anything I can think of at the moment," said Muriel.

" But you can't think what it's like. It's quite impossible."

Muriel stood looking at her. Then suddenly she sat down at the table facing Delia.

" I want to get away from Marshington," she said. " I've wanted to for months—for years I think. I didn't know how—I'm no good at acting for myself. I thought that there was nowhere else for me to go. I thought that the only means of escape for me was marriage. But if you want me, if you'll help me," her urgent, hurrying voice was not unlike her mother's now, but there was in it a note of appeal that puzzled Delia, " If you'll only help me to get away. You said that I never made a choice. I didn't only because it seemed to be no use. It's no good choosing a thing that you can't do. But if you'll give me work, show me some way of being useful——"

" But supposing you get tired of it ? Or supposing I do ? Supposing that you get on my nerves ? I shall not scruple to let you know, and there's even the conceivable possibility that

I might not live very long. They say I must be careful.
I can't be. I shall be impossible to live with and possibly
worst of all from your point of view, you may find yourself
totally unsuited for the kind of life."

" Well, I could always go again."

" And come back here ? Muriel, would you ? I'm
terrified of taking you out of the one environment you know
into one equally impossible for you, and leaving you neither
fish nor flesh nor good red herring."

" But I don't know this environment and it doesn't know
me. I'm living like—like a person that I'm not. Oh, you
don't know it all, I can't explain, I never can, but I've seen
things that happen out of this environment. I've seen
cruelties and ruin and wretchedness that even you don't dream
about, and if you don't help me to get away, I've got nobody,
I've been—nearly mad sometimes—just trapped, feeling
there's no escape from Marshington—Please, Delia, oh, I do
so—need you."

Delia took out her handkerchief, rolled it into a ball, opened
it out and looked at Muriel.

" You need my need for you more than you need me, I
suppose really," she said. " Well—we must think it over,
but I warn you you'll be exchanging the evils that you know
for an infinitely worse evil that you don't know——"

" I don't care——"

The door opened and the vicar wandered in.

" Delia, Delia, have you seen my glasses ? "

" Oh, Father, come in, do. We want you," said Delia
quickly. " I'm in such a mess."

XXXVI

MRS. HAMMOND'S elder daughter left Marshington with far less ceremony than had attended
Connie's departure. When it actually came to
the point of telling her mother that she was going to London,

Muriel was astounded at the ease with which she gained permission. Mrs. Hammond of course, would not find it at all pleasant living alone without her only daughter. Aunt Beatrice might be persuaded to stay, but nobody would consider that quite the same thing. And then, what would people *say*? People, who saw that Muriel was leaving her mother, and with Delia Vaughan of all people, and for the Twentieth Century Reform League of all terribly " modern " and uncomfortable organizations.

" Naturally, you would not be expected to consider me, dear, I suppose," Mrs. Hammond had said, " but when you think what the Reform League is and how immensely people criticize it—I've heard that the new branch started in Kingsport has already upset the vicar of St. Simeon's, because several of the girls from his Bible-class have joined the club and are talking about politics and their votes and things—so very unwise, when most of them ought to go into service. The crèches and things may be a good thing, but I do think . . ."

Nevertheless, she had let Muriel go, publishing over the bridge table the news of her conversion to modernity.

" What I think," she had informed Mrs. Marshall Gurney, with a delicacy in refraining from comparisons that could not fail to point more strikingly at Phyllis, " is that it's so very *wrong* of mothers, in these days, to stand between their daughters and progress. The girls nowadays are doing such splendid work. Of course it needs a certain amount of brains, but Muriel always was so excellent with figures. I understand that Lady Ballimore-Fenton—the President of the League, you know—is a simply charming woman. Muriel will find it most interesting."

Muriel found it interesting, but the interest hardly surprised her so much as the difficulty, and this Delia had in no way exaggerated.

Muriel arrived at King's Cross with her ham sandwiches still untasted, her mind confused, and a terrified determination to be successful. She had half hoped that she would find Delia waiting for her at the station, and a flat waiting for her ready warmed and furnished in some convenient part of London. She found instead a gloomy, indifferent terminus, a rattling taxi, and the comfortless austerity of Morrison House, the interior of which reminded her more nearly of the Kingsport Baths than anywhere else. The small guest-room into which she was shown by a slatternly maid had been christened " The Morgue " and lived up to its name.

She heard that Delia was ill in bed, and went along the passage to her room. She found her propped up by pillows dictating letters to an obviously intimidated but competent secretary.

" Oh, Muriel—wait a minute. Yes, yes, Miss Beach ? Where were we ? ' The demonstration proposed to take place on July 15th in the Kingsway Hall will be postponed in order that an answer from the Home Secretary may first be received. As the deputation has been fixed for July 30th, we hope to hold the Kingsway Hall meeting on August 1st, which will just avoid Bank Holiday. I hope that the altered date will not affect your kind promise to speak for us—Yours truly . . .' That's all, I think. Well, Muriel ? Arrived ? Found a flat for us yet ? I've got an internal chill or something and can't get up, as you see."

Muriel, who had caught the early train, forgotten to eat her lunch, and found her own way to Morrison House with much fear but with considerable self-congratulation, felt that this was a cold reception.

" You'll have to do it yourself," continued Delia. " Get a furnished one. I'll give you the addresses of some agents in Bloomsbury. Miss Beach, have you a directory there ? You might go round this afternoon, Muriel. The sooner the better."

But, after Miss Beach had left the room, she had turned to Muriel with her rare swift smile.

" My dear child, you are in for a dreadful time. I've got my hands full of work. I'm feeling perfectly rotten—which means bad tempered and you'll have to do everything yourself. Can you face it ? "

" Do you want me ? "

Delia glanced comically round the room. A cup half full of boiled milk that stood on a pile of papers on the dressing-table had grown cold; the washstand paraphernalia had been swept aside to make room for a typewriter; ink pads, stamps, directories and ledgers strewed the chairs and floor; and in the middle of the litter Delia lay on the disordered bed with a coat buttoned over her blue striped pyjamas.

"Now, doesn't it rather look as though I wanted you?" she said.

That was enough for Muriel.

House agents scared her, but furniture shops offered her unalloyed delight. Her instincts of economy refused to allow her to take a furnished flat. She braved motor-buses and tubes, she faced landladies, caretakers and decorators. When Delia, nearly convalescent but still shockingly unfit for work, departed northwards on a speaking tour, Muriel worked almost day and night to prepare a home for them both. She spent part of her own dress allowance on blue curtains and hand-painted lamp-shades and the most luxurious of soft arm-chairs for Delia's weary body. Here at last Delia, who had missed the softer things of life, should find a home.

On the afternoon of her expected return, Muriel could hardly keep still. Twenty times she went to the window, twenty times she looked back with satisfaction on the restful charm of the sitting-room. Roses in rough blue vases; dark bookshelves ranged against the plain buff walls, space, space everywhere and a complete absence of irritating decoration—surely the room meant the materialization of her dreams?

"She must like it, she must like it," she told herself, and for the first time in her life was confident that she had done well.

The electric bell pierced the silence with deafening shrill-ness. She ran to the door. Delia's figure stood in the passage. Delia, tall, dynamic, ruthless, swept in.

"Muriel, oh, thank goodness you're here! What did you do with Hansard for May 21st last year? That wretched Cutherlick man has threatened to denounce me for misstate-ments in my Lincoln speech. We shall have a libel action

some time. I've got to fly down to South Cross by the 5.40
if I can catch it to answer him to-night at this meeting."

"What meeting ? What speech ? Oh, Delia, you can't ;
you're worn out. You must——"

But Delia brushed past her into the lovely little room.
She never saw the blue vases nor the lamp-shade nor the
cushions. She was down on her knees flinging books from
the shelves on to the beautiful new carpet.

"Where in the name of fortune did you put the Hansards ?
I'll never catch that train. Why couldn't you put the things
where I'd find them ? Have you a kettle boiling ? Can't I
have some tea before I go ? "

But, when Delia had found the Hansards and the notes of
her Lincoln speech and had telephoned to Lady Ballimore-
Fenton, no time was left to drink the tea that Muriel had
prepared. She rushed away to catch her train, leaving the
overturned dispatch case on the floor, the bookshelves in a
chaos and her bedroom littered with the disorder of her
haste.

It was then that Muriel realized the disadvantages of trying
to please people possessed by an idea. For nearly two hours
alone in the flat, she forced back a desire to run away—could
she face this continual possibility of Delia's displeasure ?
Could she continue to please somebody who never acknowledged
her efforts ?

"I'm being just as unselfish as she is," Muriel told herself
indignantly. "This is my flat as much as hers. I've spent
far more money on it. I've had all the trouble of making it
nice. She ought just to have *said*—it doesn't take a minute
to say ' how pretty.' "

But Muriel's resentment passed when Delia, almost blind
with fatigue, stumbled into the flat just after midnight.

"It's all right," she said, and that was all. But she allowed
Muriel to take her hot tweed coat, to pull the hair-pins out of
her heavy hair, to bring her soup in a blue and yellow bowl,
and a fish *soufflé* made as only Rachel Hammond's daughter
could have made it. For half an hour she accepted passively.
She ate, drank, and allowed Muriel to prop the cushions

behind her in the new arm-chair and put the bowl of yellow roses on the table by her elbow and light her cigarette. Then she lay back, smiled, and looked round the room.

"Well, Muriel," she said, "I always knew that you had discrimination, but this amounts to genius. One day your husband will be grateful to me for giving you a little training in the wifely habit."

"But I'm not going to marry," protested Muriel.

Delia flicked the ash off her cigarette. "You must learn never to argue with tired people," she said sternly, then smiled and fell fast asleep there in the big arm-chair without even waiting to be taken to her pretty bedroom.

After Delia's return, Muriel's life in London fell into its new routine. She spent her mornings in the office of the Twentieth Century Reform League, entering figures in big ledgers and reviving her acquaintance with double entry and other mysterious systems. She found that her old love of figures returned to her. Method was pure joy. She reduced to order the chaos of the office slowly and peacefully, taking each day a new section at which to work.

She organized the little household in 53a Maple Street, keeping a stern eye on the " daily help," the housekeeping books and Delia's appetite. She filled her days entirely with small trifles, seeing at first no farther than her ledgers and Delia's hollow cheeks, which surely began to fill out a little under her vigorous treatment of stout and milk and new-laid eggs. Yet somehow she did not feel completely safe. Such obvious things as there were to do she did and did quite competently, but always she felt that one day some problem would present itself or some crisis arise and that she would be lost again.

Delia seemed to be both pleased and fattened by her ministrations, but that did not make her entirely contented with Muriel's companionship. One night she came in irritated and disturbed. A newspaper article had questioned her sincerity. She pretended to ignore such criticisms, and could not. They rankled while she laughed at them. She stalked up and down the flat, hurt and sore, and uncertain what to do.

" I'm awfully sorry. I wish I could *do* something," sighed
Muriel helplessly for the fifth time.

" Do. Do ? Oh, you never do anything except the
things I tell you. You're always wringing your hands
and looking sorry, but I always have to think of the things
to *do*."

This statement Muriel felt to be true rather than kind, but
she accepted it with chastened fortitude.

Between alternating doubt and happiness, Muriel worked
throughout the summer and the autumn. There were weeks
when she was oppressed by fear and wretchedness. Her life
counted for so little. She was not really helping Delia much.
Each week brought tenderly reproachful letters from her
mother. They stirred Muriel to vague disquiet. All this
sort of work was well enough—this Reform League, for
instance. No doubt it was a good thing that a great society
run by women should try to draw all classes into social service,
by clubs and settlements in every town where mill girls might
meet with daughters of barristers or squires to discuss crèches
and canteens and recreation rooms, or to carry out political
propaganda for the purposes of forcing through social legisla-
tion. Still, was it quite the thing for which she had been
born, or was she only trying to cover the shame of her retreat ?
Delia would talk for hours of this dream of service ; of an
army without distinction of class or age moving forward
towards the betterment of England. " Political knowledge,
education in citizenship, co-operation, sympathy, no one class
needs these things," she used to say. " We shall never see
any improvement while the rich and the well-educated think
that they can help the poor exclusively. The rich and educated
need the experience of the poor. The poor need contact
with culture and with leisure. We all need the organization
of our capacity for citizenship. The realization of the cor-
porate Will." Muriel sat and listened, thinking hard. Sometimes her own life seemed to her a very little thing, of bitterness
born from brooding over folly, of petty disappointments
magnified to tragedy, of imagination run riot. " But Connie ? "
she would say. " You can't argue away Connie's ruined

life. Even if I have simply been foolish and mistaken, what was it that forced Connie to seek escape in such wild recklessness ? There must be other people like her ; what can we do ? "

She was beginning to find a new foundation for her thoughts. Her concentration upon the intensely personal problem vanished.

She used to talk to Delia, in her soft, serious voice, feeling her way towards her new ideas.

" I can't help thinking that Lady Ballimore-Fenton rather *likes* a fight for the sake of a fight," she reflected. " Surely it doesn't do any good to pretend that all the people who don't quite agree with her are scoundrels. She knows it isn't true."

And Delia would smile and shrug her shoulders. " I believe that you think that we're a poor lot, Muriel."

" I don't. I'm awfully happy here. Only it does some-times seem very difficult for people to be really interested in questions like housing or illegitimacy and to keep their sense of proportion. So often things are wrong just because nobody quite knows how to put them right. And gentleness *is* a great power and a great beauty."

Delia smiled her twisted smile. " You put all your platform pearls into your private conversation, Muriel. I wonder ? I wonder how much you really care for all this. After all, you are right in one sense. We are all rather apt to lose our sense of proportion. But, because we deal with people in their social capacity, it doesn't mean that we disregard their private selves. We are all of us partly workers for some movement and partly men and women. It's a queer thing, this sex business. You go along quite happily disregarding it for years, then suddenly something comes along that rouses the sleeping thing—and away we go, over the windmills." She caught her breath.

" Martin ? " whispered Muriel.

" I suppose so. We've all got a—Martin. That was physical as well as mental suffering. That was why it was so damnable. My mind misses him still—will always, I suppose.

My body—well, thank God, who made a singularly imperfect world in order that men might work off their superfluous energies in order to straighten it ! "

" But, Delia," cried Muriel, " you don't only do this work in order to forget—as a sort of *faute de mieux* ? "

" No, no." Delia sat down in the arm-chair, her chin on her hand. " No. Two-thirds of me are wholly engrossed in it, and those two-thirds are of the more enduring part of me. You too. You won't always be content to stay with me. You've got the domestic instinct too, which I haven't. And you're not really absorbed heart and mind in the work. It interests you now—but—I wonder. One day some one will call to you, and back you'll go to Marshington."

" No. Not to Marshington. Never. Besides, nobody will call."

" Won't they ? Won't they ? You can't get out of it like that. Wait a little."

Muriel waited.

XXXVII

MURIEL sat by the fire at 53a Maple Street knitting a jumper for Delia. The flames glowed on the silk between her fingers, until the sheen of it gleamed like molten copper. The supper table was laid for two. Blue and yellow pottery, a vase filled with tawny chrysanthemums, and Muriel's workbag of bright-coloured silk hanging from the chair, gave to the room an intimate charm.

Muriel herself was pleasant enough to look upon. Her thin cheeks still were pale, her features insignificant ; but instead of diffidence and dissatisfaction her face now wore a look of quiet waiting, of humour nun-like and demure, of a composure that would quicken to keen sympathy. Her parted hair was brushed sedately from her small, serious face ; her blue dress of soft woollen stuff was finished daintily by collars and cuffs of finest cream material, the firelight sparkled on the coquettish buckles of her really pretty grey *suède* shoes. Muriel Hammond of Miller's Rise had vanished ; Miss Hammond of 53a Maple Street was a very different person.

When the bell rang sharply, she put aside her knitting, glanced round the room, and went to the front door. Callers were always coming to the flat at all hours. At first they had come intent upon finding Miss Vaughan and laying their troubles before the redoubtable champion of social reform. Latterly many had been quite content to find Miss Hammond, no longer a nonentity, but a grave little lieutenant, who listened to their protests or pleadings or denunciations with serious attention, and upon whose undemonstrative considera- tion they relied. Muriel did not know this. She still held herself to be very stupid, and dreaded committing the final error of judgment which should cut her off from Delia's tolerance for ever. Even now as she went to the door, she was reckoning rapidly the many people who might even at this hour be coming to lay their recriminations or requests before the organizing secretary of the Reform League.

She opened the door and looked into the gloom of the passage.

" G—good evening," remarked a voice, incredibly familiar, yet unexpected. " Is Miss Vaughan in ? "

She opened the door wider and the light from the electric lamp fell upon Godfrey Neale's tall figure. He was staring past her to the sitting-room, not recognizing to whom he spoke.

Godfrey. Godfrey. For a moment Muriel was dumb. A thousand doubts and fears and memories rushed to her mind. An emotion that she hardly recognized clutched at her throat. Tenderness, consternation and regret all smote her. She shrank back into the shadows of the little hall.

She could not face him. Godfrey, who had been wounded and a prisoner ; Godfrey, who must have suffered agonies unthinkable ; Godfrey, for whom she had endured such suffering—it was impossible that she should speak to him unmoved. She was caught in a trap, whence she could not escape. She forced herself to answer :

" Miss Vaughan is out."

He recognized her voice. "Muriel Hammond? By all that's wonderful? W—what are you doing here?"

If only his voice had not faltered with that familiar heart-rending little stammer. If only his face, smiling down upon her, had not recalled the moment when he smiled down from the motor-lorry, riding towards the peril of a bombarded city; if only the lean hand that he thrust forward had not reminded her of his hand outstretched in congratulation after the tennis set, when she had made her *début* at the Recreation Club; if he had been quite different, she might have borne it. But his familiarity stunned her. His nearness raised a thousand instincts and emotions that she had thought to be long dead and decently interred.

She gave him her cold hand quietly.

"Won't you ask me to come in?" he asked. "Or shall I be in the way?"

Without a word she went before him into the sitting-room, and stood, dumb and unnerved, beside the supper table. His quick glance seemed to take in everything, each charming detail of the long, low room, the firelight leaping on the plain blue carpet, the piano, the books, the flower-decked table.

"You were just g—going to have your dinner?" he asked.

He seemed to be taller than ever, and his brown face was thin. Those were the only differences. His nose still hooked very slightly over the small winged moustache. The brows over his kind, honest eyes were still dark and smooth and level. He still had the same regal aspect of bearing himself as though the whole world knew that he was Godfrey Neale of the Weare Grange, confident, dominating and victorious. No, that was wrong. The victory had somehow failed him. Something had subtly changed his self-confidence, his air of conquest, and with the loss of confidence some slight charm failed.

"I had thought that Delia would catch the 5 train. That means that she would have been home for supper. But she must have missed it by now," she said in a low voice.

"When will she be back?"

"I'm afraid not until late now—about eleven. It means

that she will stay for dinner at the place in Sussex where she's speaking."

"Are—are you staying here, then ? "

"I live here. Didn't you know ? "

He shook his head. "Stupid of me. I hadn't realized. I've not seen Delia for ages. Only once since I left Germany, and then she was in such a hurry I hardly grasped anything but her new address. I never thought that she would be out."

It was like him to forget that people had other interests beside those concerning him.

"I'm sorry she's out. Won't you sit down ? "

She prayed that he might go. She dared not trust her composure for much longer. She looked blindly round the room for help. If only he would go ! His nearness hurt and bruised her. If only Delia were here, so that she were not left alone, trapped in the flat, bound to her task of hospitality by her recollection of his friendship for the vicar's daughter.

"Thanks, very much," said Godfrey. "If I may really—a —look here—are you doing anything to-night ? "

"I ? No—not exactly." She spoke before she thought.

"Then won't you come out and have some dinner with me ? I'm up in town alone, missed the 5.30 train for Kingsport. It's rotten spending the evening alone at an hotel. You'd be doing a work of Christian charity to come."

"I suppose Clare's out of town," thought Muriel. She said : "I really don't think that I'd better leave the flat. Delia might still come." Her hospitable instincts overcame her panic. "Won't you—won't you stay and have supper here with me ? "

She had not meant to say it. She did not want it. Even as she spoke she felt the whole of her personality rising in revolt, seeking to drive him from her. But he could not be so cruel as to accept. He would not force her thus to sit alone with him, in the unavoidable intimacy of that room.

He put down his hat with a sigh of relief.

"By Jove, are you sure that you can do with me ? It's awfully g—good of you. I do so loathe a beastly evening alone in London."

"He takes it for granted that we've got plenty of food," thought Muriel. "He takes it for granted that I shall be pleased to see him, to wait on him, to give him supper. Oh, how dare he come here ? How dare he ? How dare he ? " Aloud she said : "Yes, do sit down. Take a cigarette. There are some in that little carved box on the mantelpiece. You don't mind if I go and get the supper ready, do you ? "

He stooped to light a paper spill from the fire. "Sure I can't help ? Sure I'm no trouble ? "

"None, thank you," she said, and left the room.

Out in the kitchen, she did not begin to cook the fish that lay prepared with breadcrumbs and butter on the table. She crouched down upon the single chair, her face hidden in her hands, her body shaking. She felt herself to be outraged and assaulted. The agitation which he aroused in her violated her sense of decency. It was an outrage, a torture that she could be made to suffer by his presence. Did he think of her as a person ? Did he remember that one kiss at Scarborough ? The memory of his enfolding arms tormented her like the shirt of Nessus. Sham kiss, sham love, sham pitiful adventure, stirred by the recollection of sham peril—nothing more. Was this the emotion that had driven Connie to the river when she saw Eric's letter, knowing what she had done with Ben ? Was this the revolt that had burnt and shamed her ? What did she feel for Eric, love or hate ? Violence of repulsion, or of love ? Was this the love that she had always so idealized ? No, no, a thousand times no.

"What shall I do ? What shall I do ? " moaned Muriel.

The evening stretched before her in her imagination, a time of interminable misery. While Clare and her mother had been with her, she had been able to face Godfrey in Marshington ; but to sit opposite him, alone and quite defenceless, while every word that he said, every line of his face lacerated her quivering nerves, how could she bear it ?

She sat very quietly, only from time to time shivering a little, her thoughts beating back and back against the same stark problem. "How shall I face him ? "

Then she rose, and as though spellbound began to move

about the kitchen. She lit the gas stove, set the pan of soup on to boil, and began to fry the fish, not knowing what she did. On the table a newspaper had been spread to shield the scrubbed, white wood from grease. Mechanically she read : " At the reception given by Lady Marion Motley, several people of note were to be discovered among the crowd of guests thronging the historic stairway." What did she care for guests or stairway ?

" L—look here, are you sure that I can't help ? " said his voice from the doorway. " I'm an awful genius at cooking really."

She shook her head, not trusting herself for a moment to speak. Then she answered :

" I shan't be a moment. Go in and sit down. Don't be impatient."

She carried in the little bowls of soup.

" There's only cider, and lemonade ; would you like lemonade ? "

" Cider, please. You know, this is enormously good of you."

He smiled at her across the table.

" Not at all," she answered primly.

She felt as though the soup must choke her, and glancing towards Godfrey she saw that he too seemed to find it difficult to swallow. His lean brown fingers crumbled the bread upon his plate.

When she rose to bring in the fish, both of them had left their soup half finished. Conversation seemed to be difficult, but silence was quite unendurable. She lifted her eyes from her plate at last.

" Are you staying for long in town ? "

" Only to-night. I'm going back to-morrow, thank the Lord. It's a filthy place, isn't it ? What on earth makes you girls choose to live here, I don't know."

" Our work's here," remarked Delia-instructed Muriel. " Whatever its disadvantages, it is infinitely preferable to Marshington."

" Don't you like M—Marshington ? " he asked simply.

"I loathed it with all my heart and all my soul and all my spirit," declared Muriel fiercely.

He stared at her in amazement that so guileless a creature should show such emphatic disapproval of something that he had always taken quite for granted until two hours ago. To her profound surprise he asked:

"I say, is there really something about M—Marshington that makes girls hate it?"

She blushed to the white parting between her smooth, brown wings of hair.

"Yes," she gasped softly, pleating the tablecloth between her fingers. "But I couldn't possibly explain to you."

"By Jove, I wish you would!"

".But it doesn't concern you," she said more softly. Neither of them took any notice of the meal before them. They faced each other like antagonists.

"It concerns me damned well," he muttered.

"You'd better ask Clare, then. She might tell you."

"Thank you—I don't need to ask Clare's opinions."

"No. I suppose not. I suppose that you wouldn't mind much either what she thought: opinions of women don't usually matter much to people like you."

He looked at her, his face drawn to an expression of pained surprise.

"I say—you know—don't be too hard on a fellow. I d—did jolly well care."

"Did?"

"Yes, did. She can go to the devil now for all I care."

"Really——" said Muriel, then most unnecessarily she added: "Have you—have you quarrelled?"

"No. We've not quarrelled. We just—I just—— Oh, damn it all. We've just come to an end of it, that's all."

"I'm sorry." It was all that Muriel could trust herself to say.

He rose abruptly from the table, went to the fireplace and leant against it. "Oh, it's all right. You'd have to know some time. Every one will know soon enough. I should have known. It was the b—beastly place. She said that she

couldn't stand living at the Weare Grange—wanted to drag
me up to town. Good Lord! One would have thought a
kid of two would have known I couldn't stick leaving the old
place. 'Tisn't as if there was only oneself to consider anyhow
—let alone hunting and shooting and all that, I've got to look
after the estate."

" Of course," said Muriel softly.

An extraordinary thing was happening to her. The pain
of agitation slowly faded. She found herself growing calm,
and detached, and full of sympathy.

" I might have known that she could never stick it," he
continued, hardly noticing her, " all that being engaged to
me when I was in Germany and all that—it wasn't so difficult.
But I suppose that being engaged to a fellow is one thing
and marrying him another. I might have known." Fiercely
he turned upon Muriel. " I suppose you knew ? "

" What ? "

"That she—she'd never st—stick living at the Weare Grange.
You were her friend."

Muriel shook her head. " I did not think," she said.

Indeed, she realized now how little she had thought of
Clare and Godfrey. Never once had the question of their
real happiness entered her mind, so much engrossed had she
been with the thoughts of her own misery. It had been
herself, not Godfrey, who had filled her dreams. The
recognition of her own past egoism shocked her.

" You might have thought. You might have told me," he
continued. " There I've been thinking, for years, that I was
going to marry her. And all the time it really was impossible.
She couldn't stand that life—wasn't fit for it. Spoiled by
all this singing and publicity and having her photograph in
the papers—wanted to fill the house with damned foreigners
and Jews and things."

He was hurt and angry, wounded in his self-assurance,
wounded even more deeply in the one thing that he had cared
about more than he had cared for Clare.

" Wouldn't see it either. Wouldn't see my point of view.
Didn't see why I shouldn't shut up the Grange and come to

live in London, or Paris or some filthy hole. Good Lord, as
if I hadn't had enough of dirty foreigners. Wasn't three years
in Germany enough in all conscience ? But no, she'd have
her own way. She——"

He lit a cigarette with trembling fingers. Muriel sat
quietly, at the table, watching him.

" I told her that I wanted to marry a wife, not a p—prima-
donna," he stormed. " I wanted someone who'd be a
companion, who'd take an interest in my work. A man in
my position wants some one to be his—his hostess, and look
after his home and all that sort of thing. By Jove, she d—doesn't
know what she's missed, though."

He turned to the fire, speaking gruffly and shamefacedly,
amazed at the affront to his fine self-esteem, and too much
of a child still to avoid seeking sympathy.

" I'd have been jolly d—decent to her. There aren't many
men who'd have been as patient all these last months, though,
standing meekly aside while she filled her flat with dirty little
Jewish swine and mugs and pacifists. I—good Lord, I wonder
how I stood it ? " His voice dropped. It's wistfulness wrung
Muriel's heart. " She used to be a jolly little kid, though."

He lowered himself into Delia's big arm-chair, and sat
smoking fiercely. Without a word Muriel cleared the supper
that they both had been unable to eat, and brought in coffee.
He took it, thanking her but hardly noticing who she was.
She realized that he had to talk things out, to run to somebody with his sad story. For indeed the thing that had
happened hurt him deeply. He lied when he said that all he
had sought in Clare had been a wife. Muriel knew that he
lied, but because it was a lie she could have loved him. For
Clare had been far more to him than a woman, beautiful,
radiant, of rich vitality. She had been his ideal of all women,
the star remote and bright which he could worship, the
beauty that lay beyond all lovely things. Thus, though he
had not known it, though now, perhaps thought Muriel, he
would never know it, he had loved her ever since as a wild,
pretty child she had smiled herself straight into his heart.
But Godfrey was not the man to cast off everything for an

ideal. He stood, and Muriel knew it, rooted and grounded in tradition. "He has roots," she thought and compared him with her father. Where Mr. Hammond was reckless, Godfrey was cautious. Where one was volatile, having no standards but his transient desires, no traditions but those of his creation, the other's life was only the chapter in a story, a long and not ignoble tale of Neales, stretching far back into the dim but dominating past. Mr. Hammond, standing alone, master of his own wealth and his desires, would woo or discard where he would. But Godfrey was far more than just himself. He was an embodiment of a legend, not all of his own making. He belonged to the Weare Grange far more than it belonged to him. So, when the inevitable conflict came between Clare and his home, there had never been cause for half a minute's hesitation. But the knowledge that such a choice had been inevitable, that his dream and the prestige of his position had not sufficed to hold her, had been very bitter. It was this that had robbed him of his air of conquest. His years in Germany had never touched him, for he carried the environment of the Weare Grange with him. That he could never lose. What he had lost was that fine and fugitive ideal, that sense of beauty born from something more universal than his own position, more sacred than the traditions which had formed his conduct. He, the man of property, of dignified assured possession, had been pursued by the passing urgency of that idealism which makes men poets and visionaries. The dream had left him now, and he would never see again the light that once had glorified his youth.

And Muriel, who realized this, for the first time considered him rather than herself. She saw that, with his dream, the legend of his strong, all-conquering charm lay broken. He had lost something that neither she nor anyone else could give him, and she was sorry, sorry, sorry—for him, not for herself.

She let him talk and smoke and fall into long silences, sitting moodily beside her fire. At intervals the cuckoo clock upon the wall called softly, clear small woodland notes. Her knitting needles clicked convulsively. At last he said :

" I suppose that I cared for her really less than I thought."
But this was disloyalty, and Muriel would not have it.

" No, no. You loved her truly. It was she who was not
—quite what you thought you loved."

" I've been a damned fool," he muttered.

" You haven't. You must not think like that. Your love
was fine, not foolish. You must not get bitter about yourself ;
don't spoil it. Don't think of her or of yourself as small.
Think of her still as noble and beautiful. You were right to
love her. You were." Her small voice grew urgent. Her
grave, earnest eyes implored him. " Think of her as the
loveliest thing that you knew, and of yourself as fine in loving
her."

" She was a ripping kid—that time she came to Marshington."

" I know. I thought that too. I loved her at school as
though she were something wonderful. She was like that."

" By Jove, she was," he said.

Though she knew him to be inarticulate, Muriel could
imagine how the dancing flames again turned for him the rich
silk of Clare's dress to the colour of very old dark wine. She
could think of him seeing Clare's head uplifted proudly, and
her white arms lying along the gracious flow and rhythm of
her gown ; she could feel his response to the gallant challenge
of her youth.

" She's selfish—heartless as hell," half whispered Godfrey.
" I was a fool."

" She's not. That's wrong and wicked." Forgetting herself, she slipped on to the hearth-rug and knelt there facing
him, her eyes glowing, her small figure pregnant with the
desire to save for him his dreams. " She's not selfish, nor
were you a fool. She had an artist's temperament, swift and
changeable. One should have seen—one should have seen.
She did not understand you. She could not see what the
Weare Grange meant for you. Look at her life—the publicity,
the applause, the sunlight. She fed on the love and praise
of people. It was her right. How could she come and bury
herself in the country ? How could she understand ? "

He looked down at her eloquent face and her great shining eyes.

"Don't you see?" she implored him. "Don't you see you weren't a fool? It was inevitable that you should love her, seeing how beautiful she was. But it would have been wrong to try to make her your wife. You can't help yourself, any more than she can help being what she's like. Your wife must be quiet and controlled, understanding the ways of country life and the requirements of a house like the Weare Grange, valuing it as you value it, honouring its traditions. Over that at least, there must be no misunderstanding between you—and don't you see, however much Clare had wanted to, she couldn't understand!"

He looked at her, and slowly realization dawned upon his mind, clearer than resentment or self pity. "By Jove, you're right," he said. "She couldn't understand."

They did not speak again for some time. She, suddenly grown self-conscious, took advantage of her unconventional position to poke the fire, and then retreated to her chair.

At last he rose.

"It's after ten. I really m—must go. I say, you've been a brick, Muriel. I'll never forget it. I'm awfully glad that you were in. I believe that you understand me better than anyone—even than Delia. She's a decent sort but a bit—lacking in imagination if you know what I mean! You've been more decent than I can say."

"I haven't. I've been glad to be here." Her low voice never faltered. "You see, I loved—Clare. I should have hated it if you'd gone away—bitter—— It was all unfortunate—but—don't—don't be sorry that it happened, will you?"

She had risen now, and they stood facing one another, he, tall and weary, she, small and stiff with the battle for his dreams.

He thought, then slowly came to a conclusion.

"No. I'm not sorry that it happened." With the simplicity that she liked most of all in him, he held out his hand. "Thank you," he said, and at that moment was conscious neither of his magnificence nor of his wrongs.

She smiled up at him bravely.

" You've been a brick," he continued. " I felt that I had to tell someone. It's not the sort of thing, though, that you can talk over with another fellow quite, and I can't tell the mater much. She hates to think I've been upset."

Again his niceness and his simplicity moved her. She only shook her head.

" I'm glad you came."

They shook hands, and he left her. She heard his heavy footsteps down the stairs. For a long time he seemed to walk away from her, then, very far off, the street door slammed.

She went back to the fire and sat down on the hearth-rug. The room was full of his remembered presence, the scent of tobacco smoke, the crumpled cushion in his chair, the cigarette ash that he had spilled on to the hearth.

She leaned against the chair where he had sat, and so lay very quietly, gazing into the fire with eyes that did not see.

When Delia came in, nearly an hour later, she found Muriel asleep, her eyelids red with crying, her head down on the big arm-chair, and a little smile, childlike and tender, tilting the corners of her mouth.

BOOK V

MURIEL

August, 1920

XXXVIII

MARSHINGTON was triumphant. The garden fête for the British Legion to be held in the park of the Weare Grange meant far more than a local entertainment. It meant the final abandonment of six years' gloom and difficulty. The war and all the inconvenience of war-time was past. The months following the armistice, months of intoxicating rapture, disorganization, irritating delays, and disillusionment, had gone. August, 1920, marked a turning in the ways.

Indeed, its triumph was not merely negative. It marked the promise of good things to come as well as the forgotten dream of dark things past. Marshington boomed. The new motor-bus service in and out of Kingsport, the projected town hall, the recently opened golf course, were signs of prosperity not lightly to be dismissed. There were, of course, disadvantages. Trade was bad, but undoubtedly it would improve. Unemployment was disquieting, but always this happened after any war. The British Legion, linking up village with village and class with class in memory of a glorious army, was not this a noble thing? And surely the symbolism of this fête to-day, Godfrey Neale opening the ceremony, Major Godfrey Neale, once prisoner of war, now squire of Weare and Marshington and lord of the Mardlehammar property, stooping to comradeship with the men who had once fought with him—surely this was a hopeful sign! And he looked so charming too! No wonder Phyllis Marshall Gurney, pretty and soft and pale in her rose-coloured crêpe de Chine, looked wistfully up at him as before the opening he talked with his mother on the smooth, grass terrace. No wonder that little Miss Dale, radiant in sprigged muslin (pre-war but renovated) should whisper buoyantly to Mr. Potts, the curate, " Isn't he like the Prince of Wales ? "

And then the day, too, after that terrible July with its

incessant rain, the day was perfect. Little feathery clouds floated along the sky. The spacious lawns of the Weare Grange lay green as emeralds. The stonework on the terraces foamed over with crimson ramblers. The flagged paths lay like white ribbons between herbaceous borders flaming with phlox and sunflowers and campanula. The beeches spread above a company as gay and flowerlike as the crowded borders. Mrs. Marshall Gurney in lilac charmeuse, Mrs. Cartwright in a saxe blue foulard, Mrs. Parker, manly and imposing in a black suit with a white pin stripe, and her flowerlike daughter —how on earth had Daisy Weathergay happened?—delicate as a fairy in pale blue, darting in constant pursuit of a small, charming child, all white frills and pink ribbons, who strayed like a wind-blown flower from laughing group to group on the wide lawn.

Every one, positively every one, was there. The Avenue, in ready-made crêpe de Chine, and ditto suits; the village, in cotton voile and muslin and reachmedowns; the Houses, resplendent in charmeuse and foulard and, even occasionally, in morning coats.

But, of all the people there, the happiest, the most radiant, was probably Mrs. Hammond. She sat below the terrace against a background of gay flowers. Her dress of grey georgette, delicately and demurely coquettish, made her seem more than ever a small and dove-like nun, except for the bright cerise sunshade that had somehow found its way into her little hand. Not far from her stood her husband, hands in pockets, great head thrown back, talking to Colonel Grainger. The Graingers had come over for the ceremony and were staying at the Weare Grange. But they had promised to dine that evening with the Hammonds, and it was at Colonel Grainger's jokes that Arthur Hammond's laugh rang out. But even that had not filled quite the brimming cup of Rachel Hammond's triumph. There, under the trees beside the shallow steps, stood Muriel, her daughter, talking to Godfrey Neale. Every one saw them, and every one could not fail to recognize the significance of their conversation.

Three nights ago, Muriel had come home for her summer

holidays. Immediately, Mrs. Hammond's quick, motherly
eye had seen the change in her. Quiet she was still and
always would be, but her quietness no longer expressed discomfort but composure. Her manner had changed. She
was more sure of herself. She expressed her opinions with an
assurance that amazed her mother. And people seemed to
be interested in her. The Honble. Mrs. Potter Vallery had
seen her photograph twice in the papers. Mrs. Hobson, the
vulgar, detestable Mrs. Hobson, on tour on a woman's political
delegacy (her fare paid out of Marshington funds, so like her
to get a nice trip for nothing!) had actually seen Muriel on
the platform during an important conference. She did not
speak of course, but sat, taking notes or something, and had
been seen afterwards speaking to Lady Cooper and Lady
Ballimore-Fenton. Then, look at the way she dressed now!
That charming mauve frock had amazed Mrs. Hammond, and
the deeper mauve hat, charming, charming, and the bunch
of violets tucked into her waist. Why, she was quite delightful! Everybody noticed it. Tears had come uncomfortably
near Mrs. Hammond's eyes as one lady after another had
murmured: "So nice to see dear Muriel again. So well
she's looking! And that charming frock! How nice to be
able to buy one's clothes in town—or does she go to Paris?"
Even Mrs. Harpur's aggrieved: "I suppose that Muriel won't
have time to come and see us now? She's much too grand,"
had been nectar and ambrosia to Muriel's mother.

And then, but nobody except Mrs. Hammond knew this,
had come the glorious realization of Godfrey Neale; quite
by chance she learned that he had taken to Muriel his trouble
over Clare's broken engagement. "By mutual agreement"
it was understood, that most unnatural union had been
dissolved. "Of course, we really knew all the time," Mrs.
Hammond had announced. "Muriel, being such a friend of
Clare's—a boy and girl affair—quite, quite unsuitable." But
she did no more than smile significantly when people said:
"Muriel saw quite a lot of him in London, didn't she?"
"Of Godfrey?—oh well, of course—— Now, Mrs. Thorrald,
I can't have you thinking things—really nothing in it." But

she knew that her tell-tale blush left little doubts in Mrs. Thorrald's mind.

For herself, what need had she to doubt? Indeed, looking back over the past thirty years, how could it have been otherwise? One by one, other women had given way—except Mrs. Marshall Gurney, and her resistance was quite unintentional. By a process of elimination Godfrey and Muriel had been left together. The affair with Clare had of course been inevitable. Godfrey had to sow his devotional wild oats; but with Clare vanished, no other obstacle could stand between them.

Rachel Hammond was justified at last. At least she had paid heavily. Nobody, nobody would know the price. Her marriage to Arthur had been her one act of spontaneous folly. Every other step of the way had been calculated. Well, it had been worth it. The first few fearful years, when she had braved the outraged feelings of the Noncomformist friends of her husband's family; the careful tact of years of social climbing as one by one the houses of the respected and unquestioned had capitulated; the choice of the girls' school; her battle to keep them both at home; the fears, by day and night, lest one single venture should miscarry; the episode of Connie.

Her small kid gloves clenched round the slender stem of her sunshade. Her face, looking downward to the sunlit flags, became grey and haggard.

At last she knew that she had acted wisely on the terrible night when Connie told her about Eric, when Connie had implored that she might not marry Ben, that she might take her child and live alone with it, anywhere rather than tie herself to the man who was not Eric, do anything rather than become Ben's wife with that deception; then Mrs. Hammond had faltered. Could she go on, could she defend her reputation, and that of Muriel and of her husband, at the price of Connie? But Connie's scruples had been madness. To tell Ben would almost certainly have stopped the marriage. To allow her daughter to bear the child of a rough farmer and to face her shame would have been folly, absurd and fruitless.

She had been right in her superior wisdom ; right, although
that deadening stupor of blind acquiescence had descended
upon Connie ; right, although when she sat by Connie's bedside and guessed, though she had never dared even to hint
at her fears, that Connie's death had been avoidable ; right,
although even now at night terrors will assail her, and she
would remember the passion of entreaty in her daughter's
face.

But she had been right, for not one shadow of misgiving
had touched Marshington, and now, in the awakening interest
of Godfrey Neale, she would reap her reward.

Her old fears fell from her. As the sunlight poured upon
her arms, her shoulders, her uplifted face, so a great peace
descended on her soul. Triumphantly she rose, and moved
across the lower terrace to the couple below the trees.

Muriel greeted her with the new assurance that so well
became her.

" Mother, Godfrey says that he and Mrs. Neale want us to
go up to dinner to-morrow night. We haven't anything on,
have we ? "

Mrs. Hammond smiled. " Well, really, won't you be tired
of us ? "

And she was sure, quite sure, that Godfrey smiled down at
Muriel as he said :

" No, r—rather not."

" You've got a lovely day for your fête ? "

" Yes, splendid."

" Are you nervous about the opening ? "

" Beastly." He laughed. And then to Muriel he said :
" You swear that you won't tease me if I break down or
something ? "

" Of course I won't. I'd never dare to do it myself. I'm
sure you'll do it well."

" Look here "—with a sudden inspiration—" do come on
to the top terrace and back me up." With a concession to
decorum, he added, " Both of you."

Mrs. Hammond's eyes flashed. For a moment she hesitated.
Here, unequivocal and public, would lie the announcement of

her triumph. Godfrey, of course, did not think what he was
asking. He was too lordly to see how significant his actions
were to Marshington. If anything should happen, if at the
last moment her plans should all miscalculate—— A cold
terror seized her. The rose-pink frock of Phyllis Marshall
Gurney floated towards them down the terrace. No, no, it
was impossible, for here was Muriel and here Godfrey. To
refuse now might offend him. She had been bold before.

"Well, if you like," she said, and, lordly as he, never hinted
that she could have no right there.

So when the opening ceremony was announced, Marshington
saw assembled on the terrace, together with officials of the
British Legion and the Graingers and the Neales, the small
but conquering figures of the Hammond ladies, mother and
daughter, applauding Godfrey Neale.

Like wild-fire the rumour ran round Marshington that
Godfrey Neale at last had come to his senses, and that a
Marshington girl would become lady of the Weare Grange.
Even Mrs. Neale's gaunt, sallow face bent above Muriel with
a gracious smile as she said : " Nice of you to come and back
the boy up. He's a bit nervous about speaking."

" It g—gives me very great pleasure," said Godfrey Neale,
standing upon the rose-covered terrace, his face turned above
the throng below him towards Marshington, " to be here
again, among my own people. I shan't say much. I'm no
great hand at speaking, and anyway the place to speak is hardly
mine on this occasion. It was the fellows who fought all
through the war, and not us who just sat and ate our heads
off with the B—Boches "; laughter and applause and cries of
" No, no ! " " Good old Neale " interrupted him. " I
mean——" he stammered, he lost the place in his carefully
thought-out speech, prepared for him partly, it must be
confessed, by Miss Hammond of the Twentieth Century
Reform League. Then his own charming smile broke out.
He looked down at the people. " Here, I can't talk, we're
all friends together, this fête's open. Let's get on with it."

They clapped, they cheered, but always through their
cheering they seemed to look beyond Godfrey to Muriel, as

though they included her also in their approval. And Mrs·
Marshall Gurney, with dignified resignation, clapped her white
gloves, and Phyllis, rising gallantly above spite and jealousy,
looked straight up into his dear, forbidden face, and clapped
him too. And Godfrey, who liked Phyllis Marshall Gurney,
and thought her a pretty kid, and wondered why on earth she'd
never married, and liked the way that her chin uplifted when
she smiled, looked back at her, and their eyes met, and she
faced with courage the happiness that she might have
known.

The crowd scattered. There were coco-nut shies in the
park, and tea on the top terrace, and stalls in the rose garden,
and a bran-tub and fortune-telling and a concert. The
British Legion band blared suddenly into brave music, and the
group on the upper terrace prepared itself to be gracious to
less-favoured groups. Finally Mrs. Hammond found herself
drinking tea beside Lady Grainger, while Muriel handed
cakes to Mrs. Neale.

" How well she fits in to this charming atmosphere," reflected
her proud mother. " That little air of quiet dignity—Mrs.
Neale of the Weare Grange. ' Mr. and Mrs. Arthur Hammond request the pleasure of Mrs. and Miss Marshall Gurney's
company at the marriage of their daughter, Muriel, with Mr.
Godfrey Reginald Mardle Neale at Holy Trinity Church,
Marshington, and afterwards at Miller's Rise.' " They would
have a real reception this time.

XXXIX

GODFREY and Muriel walked below the heavy elm
trees. This part of the garden was deserted, but
from far off, through the enshrouding greenery, came
vagrant echoes of tunes played by the band. So thick was the
cool, deep gloom of the great trees, that only here and there a
golden point of sunlight fell on the shadowed path, and lay
quivering as the dark leaves stirred.

They did not speak. A rabbit scuttled across the drive, bobbing suddenly below the tangled bramble sprays. Above in the elms a dove cooed sleepily, with all the warmth of drowsy summer in its call. The path was smooth, with small rounded pebbles sunk into the moss, and on each side the deep, dark grasses tangled round tall spears of willow herb, of sombre undergrowth, of hedges foaming cream with old man's beard.

At a turn of the avenue they came to a space where the trees to their right were cut away.

"I want you to see this," said Godfrey.

Beyond the low hedge, beyond two fields of the wide grass-land where Connie had once ridden, stretched the long terraces of the Weare Grange. The house itself crowned them, grey and beautiful, looking down upon the coloured throng of people in the garden. Blue, white and pink, like shifting, wind-blown petals, the dresses of Marshington girls moved on the green. Clearer along the breeze came fitful gusts of music. Hidden by half a mile of winding avenue, the two looked back together on it now.

"It's singularly beautiful," said Muriel quietly.

"You t—think so? I'm glad. You don't think it's all rot?"

"What is rot?"

"Liking the old place and all that."

She shook her head. "Of course I don't. Who could? I think that it is a beautiful place. You're a lucky man in many ways, Godfrey. You have power and privilege and a tremendous influence." She looked as though she would have said more, then stopped and just stood, gazing towards the house.

"I suppose I have," he said. "I don't know that I'd thought about it quite like that. It gets into your blood though, doesn't it? By Jove, you know—the shooting down here is worth living for. Now do you see those bullocks there, in the far pasture? They're Jerseys—I'm breeding them as an experiment. M—Maddock, my agent, says they're the best of anything he's seen of the sort."

"Does he?"

" And you know, we're starting the Witchgate hounds again this autumn ? I've been fixing it up with young Seton and Colonel Macallister. Seton'll be Master I think—in place of his brother. Rotten luck young Seton being killed. No son either. Do you know, Muriel, there were times during the war when I used to get the idea that I might never come back to it, and I used to lie awake at night and sweat with fear ? "

" I do believe it."

" It gets you, you know. It gets you. There's not an acre that I don't know in Weare or Mardlehammar. Jolly good lot of tenants too. Have you ever met Willis of Ringpool Farm ? —that's on the Mardlehammar land. Fine chap Willis, and brainy, too. You'd like him."

Again they were silent, watching the little Jersey cows in the far pasture, golden, like browsing flowers under the warm sunlight.

" You know," he went on, " you were right that evening in London. By Jove, you were. Clare could never have understood this. You've got to have a wife that understands. I was pretty well knocked down then, but I'm glad now."

He paused as though thinking this over.

" I'm glad it happened," he repeated solemnly, " the whole thing I mean. I wouldn't want not to have known her— except for one thing."

" What's that ? " asked Muriel.

She turned to look at him, and below the broad brim of her charming hat her face was grave and sweet.

" Look here, Muriel, if I wanted a girl to marry me, would she mind that I had given Clare something—something I'll never have to give again ? "

" Most girls wouldn't," Muriel said solemnly. " Very few women marry the man whom they first loved. Very few men marry the girl who first attracted them. When they do, those marriages don't seem to be the happiest."

He sighed with a great relief. " You really think so ? "

" Yes."

Again they paused. So quietly they stood that a squirrel

rattled nimbly down the tree beside them and flashed across the path. Then Godfrey spoke again, stammering badly, but smiling down at Muriel :

"Muriel, with everything that I didn't give to Clare, I love you. Will you marry me ? "

She did not speak.

"I know," he went on, "that you know all about me. I've told you about Clare. But I shan't love her again. Anyway she's going to marry that fellow from Austria. That's all quite over. And I believe that all the time, if I hadn't been a fool, I should have wanted you. You understand me better than anyone, and I don't believe that you're the kind of girl who'd want a fellow so much to love her that way— you're too sensible."

Still she did not speak, but smoothed with her soft fingers a broad leaf of the climbing hop plant that spread twisting green tendrils across the hedge before them.

"Don't hurry," he said magnanimously, "take your time and think it over. I'd be good to you. I swear I'd be good to you—little Muriel."

His voice was assured, but it was very kind. His clear blue eyes were honest. More handsome than ever was his lean brown face bent above her.

"I don't think that you dislike me—somehow. Couldn't you find it possible to care ? "

She lifted her candid eyes to his. "Once I thought that I loved you very much, Godfrey. When I was a little girl, before I ever went to school, I once danced with you at a party. I was very shy, and rather left out of things, and you only were kind to me. I think I fell in love with you then. You seemed to me the true ideal of manhood."

"Did I ? " His blue eyes softened tenderly.

"And afterwards, when I lived in Marshington, we played together at the tennis club the very first time I played."

"Did we really ? "

She nodded. "That was Delia's doing. She wasn't thinking about you or me, but only about getting her own

back on some other people. You were the king, the wonderful
one. I hardly dared to play with you. I was a funny child
in those days. I thought a lot of queer mistaken things. I
made a sort of hero of you, Godfrey."

" You silly child," he said, but she could see how much his
pride was loving it.

" I came home from school meaning to do such a lot of
things. Every one was wonderful. The world was full,
brimming with adventure. I meant to be so good."

He nodded. " I'll swear you did."

He would have caught at her small ungloved hands, but she
put them behind her back and stood looking up at him, like a
child saying its lesson.

" My head was full of dreams about love and service. I
wanted to be wise and unselfish and to serve God. I gave up
the idea of going to college or anywhere to train for working
in the world outside, because I thought that Mother needed
me."

He nodded, a little puzzled that she should consider this
long preamble necessary ; but liking her more and more for her
solemnity. It seemed to him very sweet that she should tell
him all her girlish hopes.

" I threw myself into the life of Marshington, meaning to
give to it and to get from it only the best. I wanted to give
it all of me, my intelligence, and my love, and my desire to
serve. I began to go to parties and picnics and the tennis
club. But, do you know, the things here weren't quite what
I had expected ? People did not seem to want me frightfully ;
I wasn't pretty—I was rather shy. I didn't understand the
teasing and the jokes and the way that the other girls behaved.
People began to avoid me. I remember a picnic once, when
I walked for all the afternoon with Bobby Mason, because
I was so terrified of being left behind "—she swallowed hard,
but went on steadily—" without a man to walk with. I had
not been at home for more than a year when I found that only
one thing mattered here in Marshington for a girl, and that
was to get married."

He was frowning a little now. Those things perhaps were

true, but somehow he did not like his future wife to say them. She, however, continued to disregard his feelings.

"It took me about six years to discover that I was not the sort of girl whom men wanted to marry. Other girls found partners at dances easily. I sat against the wall, shivering lest every one should see that I was a wallflower, feeling terribly ashamed because to fail in this way was to fail everywhere. I used to think of life as a dance, where the girls had to wait for men to ask them, and if nobody came—they still must wait, smiling and hoping and pretending not to mind. One by one the things that I cared for fell away. Music, mathematics, beautiful things to look at—none of these mattered. They were only quite irrelevant details, because at Marshington there was only one thing that mattered and I had not got it."

He was about to protest, but she silenced him :

"No, no. It's no use saying that it wasn't so. Try to cast your mind back. Can't you remember ' poor Muriel Hammond '—she and Rosie Harpur—the ' heavy ' people at the dances whom the nicer men would try to be polite to ? Why, you used to be kind to me yourself. You always came and asked me for a waltz when we went to the same dance. I used to stand and watch your programme pencil breathlessly. Would you give me one dance, or two ? You never thought that it mattered as much as that, did you, Godfrey ? "

He shook his head.

"It mattered everything. Or rather I thought it did. Do you remember the day of the bombardment of Scarborough ? And after the bombardment, in my aunt's house ? "

Her face was flooded now with glowing colour, but she spoke on, in her small even voice :

"You kissed me. Perhaps you had forgotten. These things pass easily, don't they ? When a man kisses a plain girl. It was kind of you. I expect that you thought I should be pleased and flattered." She paused. "I was pleased."

He made a gesture of protest.

Far away down the park a little burst of cheering rose into

the silence and died down. They were beginning the sports that were to be the final entertainment of the fête.

"I was pleased," said Muriel. "I thought of nothing else by day or night. You had kissed me. You, who were the ideal, the prince, of all that Marshington thought splendid. I thought at first, daringly, that it might mean that you could come to care for me, to marry me, to take away from me the reproach of failure. I knew about Clare of course, but I thought her married, and that you had decided that she was quite impossible. I used to grow sick, waiting for the posts. I would lie awake half the night, thinking that a letter might come in the morning. And half the day I would have a pain here, in my side, with the feeling that a letter might come by the afternoon's post. You never wrote. I heard that Clare had come to England. Then, one night at a concert, your mother told me that you were engaged."

"I didn't know," he cried, really remorseful.

"Of course you did not know. I remember that. But, oh, I knew. I don't know what became of me. I think that I fell into a sort of stupor, thinking of all that I had thrown away to follow this, and in the end to fail."

Her voice died away. The aching pain of those past days had left her, but it was not easy to recall them now.

"There's something else," she almost whispered. "Something that I can't tell you much about because it's not my story. I was made to see—the Marshington way—carried to its logical conclusion. Girls do not always wait to be asked. Instinct, you see, is on the side of the tradition. In every woman there must be so much nature—of her womanhood. Take from her all other outlet for vitality; strip her of her other interests, and in some cases the instinct, reinforced by social influence, breaks down her control. I had to stand by helpless and watch—somebody else—come to complete ruin. And just because I had believed what people once had told me, because I had accepted Marshington standards without question, I found myself quite powerless to help. Indeed, I even made things worse, far worse. I think that I went almost mad then. My mind had a kind of shock—— You see, there was nothing left. Even mother—belonged to the things that had failed me. Nothing had happened. People, knowing my life, would have said that I had never known great sorrow. There was just nothing.

" If it hadn't been for Delia, I should have died—not with my body, but my mind. She could not give me back the things that I had lost. She took me away instead. She let me see, not that the thing that I had sought was not worth seeking, but simply that there were other things in life. To fail just in this one thing was not failure. A perfect marriage is a splendid thing, but that does not mean that the second best thing is an imperfect marriage."

" I know," he said. " I know. Look here, I'm sorry, Muriel. I'd no idea what a rotten time you'd had. But now, forget it. We'll make our marriage perfect."

" Dear Godfrey," said Muriel, " if you'd asked me to marry you any time during the past twelve years until last winter, I would have married you, without hesitation. And we should both have made a great mistake."

" No, no," he said, " not we."

" Oh, yes, we should. That time you came to me in London —I'd never seen you before—only a sort of legend of my dreams. You're a dear, Godfrey. I like you immensely. And you'll make some wife very happy yet—but not me——"

" But why on earth ? "

" Because—of—every reason. It's too late."

" Do you care for someone else ? " he asked sharply.

" No. Not that way. Please, I want you to understand." She smiled suddenly. " This isn't a devastating experience, you know. You like me, but not more than you could like lots of women."

" That's not true."

" Oh, yes, it is. You'd like to marry what you think is me—what I was, but that's not what I am. I'm only sparing you the pain of discovering too late that I'm an uncomfortable person to have married. To begin with, Godfrey dear, I can't stand Marshington. The Weare Grange is a heavenly place, and Delia tells me that there are prospects of regeneration

for Marshington. She believes that the Twentieth Century
Reform League is going to remedy its faults. I don't know.
It may do. But not for me. It's cost me too much. I'm
too near the shadow of its influence. I should slip back
to it."

" But why——— ? "

"Why shouldn't it ? Because I'm—myself, that's all.
I found that out in London. I've actually got tastes and
inclinations and a personality. And they're all things that
you would disapprove of immensely. Oh, yes, you would.
You want a good wife, Godfrey, someone who'd be the hostess
of shooting-parties, who'd listen to your hunting stories, and
who'd be interested in your tenants. You'd want somebody
who would be satisfied by your possessions and by your prestige,
and whose goal in life would be to make you comfortable.
Clare wouldn't have done that. In one way, it's a pity you
didn't marry her. You'd have been miserable, and she'd have
broken away, but it might have been better for you. As it
is—it's too late, Godfrey. Some day perhaps, I may marry,
but it won't be you. I once was in love with you, but I don't
love you. Your interests are not my interests—we haven't a
taste in common.

" I'm going back to London. I'll go to-morrow. I'm
learning there a lot of things and it hasn't done with me yet.
Delia mayn't want me always. Probably she's going to
America soon anyway. It isn't that. I've got an idea—I
don't know how to express it—that I think I've always had in
my head somewhere. An idea of service—not just vague and
sentimental, but translated into quite practical things. Maybe
I'll do nothing with it, but I do know this, that if I married
you I'd have to give up every new thing that has made me a
person."

" You wouldn't."

" Oh, yes, I would. Can't you just picture us, Godfrey ?
You, the typical country squire. I, the epitome of all
Marshington virtues."

He frowned at her. He was a little sad, a little hurt, a little
disappointed. She knew that he was not heart-broken.

" I can't be a good wife until I've learnt to be a person,"
said Muriel, " and perhaps in the end I'll never be a wife at
all. That's very possible. But it doesn't matter. The thing
that matters is to take your life into your hands and live it,
following the highest vision as you see it. If I married you,
I'd simply be following the expedient promptings of my
mother and my upbringing. Do you see ? "

" I don't see. It's all that London nonsense. It's Delia.
It's——"

" No it isn't. It's Muriel—at last. You see, when she's
really there, you don't much like her. Godfrey dear, how
could we live together ? We'd quarrel from the first."

" You said that you might marry—one day——"

" Who knows ? But it won't be you. Why, you'll be
married long before."

A little breeze blew along the avenue. Muriel shivered.

" I think we'd better go. I've talked too long. There's
nothing else to say. Don't be more angry with me than you
can help. We've both been honest with each other."

" Yes—— We've been honest."

He liked that. She felt his eyes straying again towards the
open vista, to the fields where now long shadows stretched
across the gilded grass, to the crowded terraces, to the grey
house. He would find comfort there for whatever soreness
she had left with him.

" I'll go," she said. " And—very good luck to you,
Godfrey."

Shyly she held out her hand.

He frowned. For a moment his wounded pride withheld
him, but she looked so very small and powerless before his
height, his strength, and his position. His smile came suddenly
and he took her hand.

" By Jove," he said, " I'm only just beginning to realize
what I've missed."

He stood, holding her small hand, under the arching elms.

" You won't remember long. And, when you do, you'll be
glad that I did not marry you."

He shook his head. She broke from him and walked quickly

away along the drive. Chequered sunlight and shadow fell on her small, upright figure. She moved steadily forward, not looking back at him. As he watched her go, an expression of tenderness, compassion and regret crossed his face. He sighed a little. Perhaps she was right. A wife with ideas? How queer women were! It always seemed as though he, who knew himself to be sought after, only wanted what he could never gain. He felt older and a little weary. Certainly it would be good to go where he was wanted, to have his vanity soothed by a simple, loving woman who would accept him as he was.

Queer little thing, Muriel. If he had known what she was like, would he have spoken? After all, perhaps it had been an escape.

With a sigh he turned again towards the house. Far away, on the high terrace, fluttered the rose-pink dress of Phyllis Marshall Gurney.

THE END

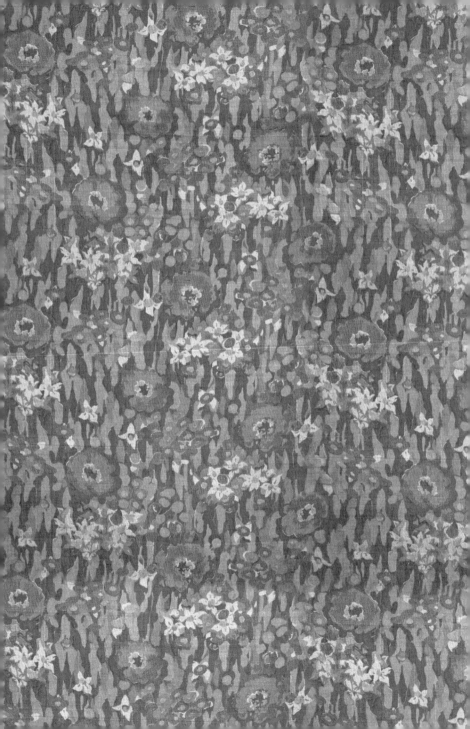